Gretel (Gretel Book One)

Christopher Coleman

CHAPTER ONE

She'd never gotten used to the taste. Even with the life and strength that teemed in every molecule, the russet fluid always went down heavy and crude. Like swallowing a fistful of thin mud that had been lifted from the bottom of a river.

There was a time in the early years of her life—this second life—when she was forced to mix the liquid with soup or tea, or to stir it into the batter of the sweet confections and pies that even today she took pleasure in baking. She had experimented relentlessly with temperatures and combinations—using ingredients she wouldn't have otherwise fed to a cockroach—hoping to create a formula that, if not tasty, was at least palatable enough to override the involuntary rejection by her mouth and throat.

But she'd had little success, and soon began believing the more she tampered with and diluted the delicate recipe, the more the regenerative effects were diminished. Her nails and hair didn't seem to grow quite as quickly, and her teeth, though they were restored, felt as if they had just a bit less length and severity.

Of course, it was plausible she was entirely wrong about the effects of the tampering, and she accepted the possibility that her observations were paranoid inventions of an overprotective mind. But she also wasn't taking any chances, and over time she had trained herself to drink the mixture straight. After all, it took mere seconds for the solution to make it over her taste buds and down to her belly. After that, it was ecstasy.

The mixture usually began its rolling boil within seconds of reaching the acid that lined her stomach, before shooting into her blood stream and picking up the platelets in perfect stride. From there the journey through the body took less than a minute, administering almost instant relief to pains both bitter and dormant alike. There was a sense of rejuvenation in the bones and ligaments that went beyond simply where they joined. It was cellular.

The feeling in those first few moments was literally indescribable. On the rare occasions she had tried to explain it aloud, she always found there was simply no adequate experience with which to compare it. The benchmark didn't exist. Sex—usually the standard by which all great feelings were measured—didn't come close. Though it had been decades since she'd had a man, and in her lifetime had little experience with them generally, she knew even with the greatest lover in history, sex was a laughable comparison. As was the feeling elicited by any other potion, and potions she knew. What she lacked in bedroom prowess, she made up for in a long resume of chemical experiences.

But the physical feeling, as glorious as it was, was inconsequential. A minor side effect of the greatest treasure the Old World had ever produced, and one that she had captured and preserved in the Northlands for centuries. Whether she alone was in possession of the knowledge she couldn't be sure; it certainly wasn't impossible that another had been given the precious gift to which she had clung so tightly for the last three hundred years. But if she did share it with another, she would likely never know; her isolation had become almost absolute. The Age of Transmission had transformed her existence from that of a private villager—having few social connections other than in passing and commercial exchanges—to one of complete withdrawal. There were no neighbors to speak of, and any mail or necessary supplies were delivered to the receiving station she had built for herself just over a half-mile from the cabin.

The woman picked up the large, stone container and swirled the liquid into a clockwise vortex, careful not to lose any of it over the top—though caution was mostly unnecessary, since what remained of the potable would have fit easily into a jigger.

This sip was different, however, and her careful attention was not without cause. This swig was the last of her batch. It was the final priceless ounce. She knew in her core it wasn't really enough for full revitalization; it would replenish for another year if she limited her energy, even two if she did nothing but sleep. After that she would decline quickly. And since the elixir didn't spare her from the necessary provisions of all human beings—food, heat, and so on—languidness and hibernation were no more a possibility for her than they were for the woman she was in her old life. In fact, she would need to exert more energy than most people, since she was not surrounded by the accommodations of a modern world. She would need to farm and gather, and even hunt if the harvest didn't last through winter, as well as keep an ample supply of kindling and wood. And she wasn't the youngest maiden in the court when she began the regimen—certainly past sixty years as she recalled—so though the potion sustained her and kept her strong, what was done was done: the contaminations of time did not reverse.

The woman raised the stone cup, which was little more than a small bowl, careful not to breathe the rancid aroma. As it reached her lips, the woman hesitated. This was it, she thought, this last drink would drain her supply, leaving her cabin empty of the fluid she'd come to worship over the many decades.

She willed a pragmatic moment into her addicted mind. Maybe she could hold out for a few months longer. Just a few, until she identified the source of her next supply. There really wasn't the urgency to drink today, she still felt strong and capable. Why, just this morning she had restocked the wood pile after several hours of brisk chopping. And besides, it had only been fourteen months since her last dose. Certainly she had gone without for much longer.

All of that was true. But the reality was that the effects had diminished over the years, and she needed larger doses now than in the past. As it was, her last drink had been meager, having been divided in half to leave today's swallow. No, she needed it today, all of it, and if it was enough to sustain her until the end of summer, she would be lucky. The woman figured by June she would need to be blending.

She pinched her nose and drank slowly, relaxing the pharyngeal nerve at the back of her throat to prevent gagging. The sickening warmth lingered on her soft palate, and then descended the length of her windpipe. The woman could feel the pulp of her victims organs catch and then release in her esophagus, and she lamented that, although she'd always spent days pestling, she had never been able to thin out the concoction completely. This part had always been the hardest—in the early days often inducing violent spasms of choking and expectoration. What she had coughed up over the years! The amount could have sustained her for another generation.

But those reactions had subsided long ago; aside from the taste, she had mostly gotten used to the process. Like the gypsy sword swallowers she had seen as a girl, so nonchalantly on the backs of their wagons immersing those giant blades, inconceivably, down into their bellies and back up again, before packing up and quietly moving on to the next village, she had learned to ingest the pungent broth with little effort.

But there was still the taste. She could never get used to the taste.

She placed the ceramic cup on the edge of the cast iron stove and gently walked to the lone wooden chair that occupied her kitchen. She sat wide-eyed and rigid on the edge of the seat, anticipating the impending experience of which she never tired. Then the slight hint of a bubble began in her abdomen, and a smile formed on the ancient woman's face.

***

When she awoke it was just before dawn, and she could hear the first whistling of the woodcocks as they began to pester the sun. Spring had arrived weeks ago, but the chill of the morning stung the back of her neck and prompted an exaggerated shiver. She reached instinctively for covering, and instead created finger tracks in the thick dust of the wooden floor. She grasped her hand again in a slight panic and was now quickly awake.

This wasn't the first time she had gone black—it had happened several times over the years—but those incidences had occurred mostly in the beginning, and never lasted this long, apparently, judging by the position of the sun, almost a full day. She was weaker than she thought, and the truth, which she had numbed her mind to, was that the mixture was old and diminished. Perhaps even toxic. She thought back to when the batch was originally concocted but couldn't recall. Forty years perhaps? Certainly well past the period for which she could reasonably expect it to remain fully viable. What if it had become inert and didn't deliver the effects this time? That seemed unlikely, since the immediate burn and thrill in her abdomen was just as magnificent as ever, but the unusual side effect of unconsciousness suggested a serious problem.

She tried to stand and was prostrated to the floor by a stab of lightning to her back. In disbelief, the old woman tried again, this time using the seat of the chair as a crutch. She was able to rise to her knees before the pain delivered another bolt. A scream attempted to escape her mouth but was immediately intercepted by phlegm and sickness. She laid her forehead on the chair and took deep, panicked breaths. It hadn't worked! This couldn't be happening! She lifted her head and glanced frantically around the room searching for the empty stone cup, hoping beyond reason that whatever trace amounts remained at the bottom of the urn would somehow be enough to release the magic. Maybe one last drop was all she needed.

She spotted the cup. It had rolled to the door of the cabin, the rim edging against the jamb as if waiting to be let out. She got down on all fours and crawled slowly toward the door, exaggerating every lift of her knees for fear of the returning agony to her back.

The woman reached the cup, took a deep, labored breath, and assumed a sitting position, leaning her back against the door for support. She sat that way for several moments until her breathing slowed and her thoughts leveled, and then closed her eyes in an extended blink. She then lifted the cup gently, cradling it from the bottom with both hands as if preparing to offer it in sacrifice, all the time feeling its cruel emptiness. She didn't bother to look inside, and instead placed the cup softly beside her before pushing herself forward and resting tall on her knees.

She closed her eyes again and bowed her head, thankful for the clarity that had presented itself. Her survival would not be dependent on whatever residue remained at the bottom. It would take faith and action. It was time again to accept what is and move on.

Of all the lessons she had learned in her long life, this one had come most grudgingly. But it *had* come, eventually, and once she embraced it, once she'd moved beyond just repeating the words to herself and had finally felt the power and truth of the phrase, it had been the greatest lesson of all. In the past, her reaction to this ruined batch of potion would likely have sent her into some uncontrolled rampage, screaming maniacally for hours, cursing the universe and destroying what few possessions she had. And then, once the fury subsided, she would conclude the episode by erupting into wild tears of self-pity, and then spending the rest of her precious day thinking of suicide and vengeful murder.

But that was in the past. Those futile thoughts of injustice and revenge were pollution to her mind and, for decades, had only weakened her. They were antithetical to what Life craved. She was still somewhat envious of those who had come to realize this fact in the span of a normal lifetime, but she was thankful it had eventually come to her. And thankful for her secret of immortality.

"I'll find it," she said softly.

She lifted her chin and stared out the window, as the sun's first rays provided just enough backlight to silhouette the multitude of lush trees that formed the spring forest. It was going to be a beautiful day. The sky would be clear, and the cool nip of the morning promised relief from the unseasonably warm days of the past week. It was perhaps a harbinger of a new start, she thought. The pain had vanished from her back, and her mind was as clear and unpolluted as ice. And silent. She reveled in the stillness, allowing every sensation of the surroundings to wash over her and soak into her skin. Yes, it was time to begin anew.

The old woman smiled widely, unleashing the large, jagged incisors and canines that crowded the front of her mouth. They were in need of replacement, but they were serviceable.

She stood from her kneeling position and walked to the makeshift wardrobe that anchored the rear wall of the small cottage. The wonder of faith now overwhelmed her, and she had no doubt that renewal loomed. It was only a matter of time—though time was leaking.

She removed the only piece of clothing that hung from one of a dozen wooden hooks that lined the back of the wardrobe's interior. The garment was a moth-ridden wool cloak, heavy and dark—a piece of clothing designed for frost and survival, from an era harsh and bygone. She placed the coat effortlessly over her torso and raised the oversized hood. She would undoubtedly be uncomfortable while the sun was up, since the day was likely to be warm and dry. But the cloak would protect her skin, which had become sensitive to direct sunlight—a thing she rarely received through the canopy of the forest—and if she were forced to camp overnight, the wool would keep her warm in the evening chill.

But such an adventure shouldn't be necessary, she thought. There was still time. Perhaps plenty of time. Going black was simply a sign that her moment had come to awaken and begin identifying the fresh source. To reconnoiter the landscape for the new point of supply. She had done it dozens of times since that first night so long ago, and, in fact, had become quite adept at tracking viable sources.

But identifying meant travel, a practice about which she had always been anxious and leery. Even as a young woman, before the Discovery, the unknown wilderness had always invoked feelings of dread and tragedy. By seven or eight years of age, her mother had so often explained the seemingly unlimited evils of men that she couldn't imagine any woman stepping off her property without being raped or beaten or enslaved. And she soon learned that the tales, though perhaps exaggerated, weren't simply cautionary. She had seen the truth of them first hand, and, indeed, had performed many of the cruel acts herself. Had those women she tortured been as cautious as she, they would have not been in that position, she often rationalized.

Yes, it was the quality of caution that had served her well and preserved her existence since The Enlightenment. But as always, caution was always overruled by necessity. It was time once again to hunt.

She stepped down gingerly onto the crude stone landing that served as a porch and settled for a moment without moving. She listened as a distant breeze pushed through the green of the forest, moving deliberately past each leaf and limb, before finally catching her in its wake. Yes, this would be a fine day. She lowered the cloak's hood, deciding she would begin the journey exposed to the wonders of the woods, figuring the sun would not be a factor for several miles, and the chances of encountering another person were remote.

She took another step on the porch and immediately recognized the adrenaline that had surged during her earlier moment of clarity was now waning. She could already feel the weakness of her joints and muscles returning. The sting of old age, a feeling she had forgotten, or perhaps never known, billowed down her spine and limbs, and the pain choked in a breath as she tried to exhale. Alarmed, she moved quickly toward the edge of the porch, convincing herself that by reaching the boardwalk at the bottom of the steps and beginning her journey on the overgrown pathway that led into the forest, she could somehow outpace the inevitable.

She reached the ledge of the stairs, barely, her legs giving out on the last stride, and narrowly avoided tumbling to the bottom. Only the stone wall that bordered the descent saved her from catastrophe. She held the barrier in a comic clutch, as if trying to keep a battleship from leaving port, and looked out at the seemingly endless timberland before her. She laughed aloud at the idea of venturing ten yards from home, let alone the ten miles or so it would require to reach the nearest source population. It was impossible. And rest was not the answer. Rest meant time and time meant decay. What the woman needed was help, and help—even more than companionship—had always been the greatest price of her isolation. The lack of companionship, or even the sound of another's voice, could certainly be brutal realities, but there were ways to deal with those. She had come to consider the trees and animals and insects important companions in her life and addressed them with respect and appreciation. And she had long since shed any embarrassment of speaking aloud or taking on different character roles. This, in fact—along with her baking—had become one of the few joys in her life, invoking the characteristics of women from her past that she had always envied or admired, playing the roles of huntress or princess or whore. Early on she had discovered that for even the most primal of human relationships there were always alternatives, as any thirteen-year-old boy could attest to.

But there was no substitute for the strength of men to remove an old iron stove, or fell a dying tree before it collapsed and demolish a house. Or for hands to help gather and hunt when the crops have failed and starvation is no further than a bad snowstorm away. She had paid for help in the past—and even kept slaves when the social climate allowed it—and though these servants had certainly alleviated many of the normal personal and practical burdens, the threat of loss had been too strong, and they never stayed on for long. Most of them she killed while they slept. Many were buried on this very property. Sadly, none of their innards were used for blending.

And now isolation would cost her immortality. The motif of so many legends and religions would evaporate with her last breath, as it may have done, for all she knew, with hundreds of other possessive hermits in the past.

She lowered herself down to a sitting position on the first step of the porch and rested her elbows on her knees. She coughed several times as if she had just finished a brisk winter walk and her lungs were struggling to adjust. She hung her head between her knees and watched as the wooden planks beneath her began to blur. She was about to go black again, perhaps permanently this time. Instinctively, she slid her buttocks to the next step down and continued this movement on to each lower tread until she reached the bottom. If she were going to die, she decided, it wouldn't be from a broken neck. There was one last impulse to get to her feet, but the message was never conveyed from her brain to her legs. Defeated, the old woman rolled onto her back and spread her arms wide, encouraging the world's embrace. She took in the bright blueness of the sky and wished that she could feel the wonder of rain one last time.

The blue canvas above her turned shadowy, not from the arrival of clouds, she assumed, but from her brain's lack of oxygen. She smelled the warm air rising from the ground, and tried to appreciate the last of life's sensory experiences. Surely this was death. She had escaped it for so long, but now here it was in front of her. The brew of life on which she had relied since the early times of the Northlands had finally failed her. Or she had failed it. It was true she trusted a source would come—her dreams had told her of its delivery—but it hadn't come, and she'd waited too long to move on. She'd trusted in her dreams and they had betrayed her, but it was *her* life, *her* responsibility. She had become careless and complacent. The supply was larger than ever these days, and she needed only to pull from it.

If only there was more time. A week. A day.

"I'm sorry," she whispered. "I'm sorry." She closed her eyes and slowed her breathing, as that relentless resistance to death which had dictated the bulk of her life now turned to acceptance. Without contention, she awaited sleep.

And then she heard the voice.

***

Anika Morgan was cold, and the mud that had gently cushioned the soles of her feet when she set out now enveloped her ankles and threatened to swallow her shins. Every step felt like someone was pressing down on the tops of her knees. She thought of quicksand. Was that a possibility? That this was quicksand? She knew—or at least had heard the stories as a child—about quicksand existing in the jungles of Africa and places like that, but not in the Northlands. Truthfully though, she couldn't be sure where it was found. Or if it was real at all. Was she really going to die such an improbable death as drowning in quicksand?

Anika cleared her head and focused. If she wanted to avoid death today, she figured it wasn't quicksand she had to worry about. Besides, quicksand was absurd, the forests of this territory were infamous for their swamps and mud; she had waded through much worse in her life. She had to stay on task.

"Just go," she scolded herself.

She wanted to scream the words, but her overworked lungs wouldn't allow it. Anika slowed her breathing and down-shifted her effort to an easy walk. The depth of the mud was making her progress comically slow, and trying to run through it was doing nothing but edging her closer to exhaustion. Adrenaline had its limits, and hers was almost reached. She would have to rest soon. In a few hours, the early morning chill would be giving way to the warmth of a typical spring day, and Anika could see the sun beginning its morning stretch upward. The sky was almost staggering in its clarity and blueness, and she was thankful at least to be dry; though had it been raining, she reasoned, she would never have attempted the forest to begin with, and probably would have been rescued by now.

But she *had* chosen the forest, and at the time had done so quite casually.

But why?

Why would she have made such an unconventional decision? Such a bad decision? She was normally much more conservative in her approach to problems, and the woods in this country, even on a clear spring day, were risky to explore for the most well-conditioned of men, let alone a thirty-eight-year-old mother of two. So why hadn't she just walked the road? Or waited for help at the place where the car drifted off the shoulder? It was true she wasn't thinking clearly after the accident—everything had happened so quickly—but she hadn't suffered any trauma to her head. In fact, she was miraculously uninjured.

So the question remained: why?

It didn't matter now, she thought, the decision was made; all that mattered now was finding shelter and a telephone. Besides, with her car nestled at the bottom of what must have been a fifteen-foot embankment, with little hope of being seen from the road, it seemed somewhat reasonable that finding a place to call for help on her own was a safer play than standing alone on the side of a quiet road in the southern Northlands. Not that this part of the territory was particularly dangerous, but one could never be sure.

Anika spotted a log about forty yards in the distance and decided it would be a suitable place to rest. She wanted to keep going, but she knew forty yards was about all she had left in her. If she pushed beyond that, she might not come across another place to stop, and would end up having to rest in the mud she was desperately trying to escape.

And she was getting scared. And fear, she knew, would only make her judgment worse.

She needed to stop and think, try to orient herself with what little she knew of the land here, and get out of these woods and back to her family. She could only imagine the fears they would conjure if they didn't hear from her soon. She should have been home by now, and it wouldn't be long before they started to worry. Soon they would call to check on her and learn that she had left ahead of schedule and should have been home even earlier. And that would be bad. She loved Heinrich, but for all his pretensions of strength and masculinity, he was emotionally weak. And combined with his injuries, he would be in no condition to comfort and reassure the children.

She reached the large log and climbed atop to a sitting position, throwing one muddy leg to the far side to straddle it. She sat this way for a moment, legs dangling while she caught her breath, and finally lay down on her back, bringing her legs together and linking her hands behind her head for support. Under the circumstances, it felt strange to be assuming such a relaxed position, and she imagined that someone looking in might conclude that she was on some spiritual journey—albeit one that was oddly messy—and had come to the forest to contemplate the meaning of life or something.

If only.

It was still early and she'd only been up a few hours, but the grueling hike had tired Anika and she had to be mindful to stay awake. She had to keep her eyes wide and her mind active. She thought of her children and how they must miss her. She realized now it was the longest she had ever been away from them, only a little over a week, but it was eons compared to what they were used to, and, with Heinrich in his condition, it came at a time when she was needed at home most. They were both wonderful, mature children, exceptional for their ages, but they had no business carrying the responsibilities she had left them with this past week. Why hadn't she just waited by the road?

Anika sat straight on the log and took the last remaining bite of a stale candy bar. It had been in her car for days—weeks maybe—and she was thrilled now to have grabbed it before setting out. At least she'd made one good decision today.

She swallowed the chocolate and then laid back down to fully replenish her lungs and examine her options. She supposed she could try to retrace her steps and get back to the original point where she had entered the forest, and then wait on the shoulder of the road until someone passed by. The roads were certainly desolate on the stretch where she'd swerved off—in fact, she couldn't remember passing a car once in her short trip from Father's house—but surely someone would eventually motor by and help. Even if it took several hours. At this point, the fear of some lascivious stranger with devious motives paled to the fear she had of still being in these woods come nightfall.

But the truth was it was too late for the road, at least at the part where her car now lay abandoned and invisible. Whatever it was that had compelled her into the wilderness had now taken her beyond the point where she had the will to make it back. It would be a disheartening trek of over an hour through the now detestable mud, and at this point she wasn't sure she would even be able to find it. The turns she had made along the way to avoid the deeper swampy areas and larger thickets had disoriented Anika, and though she was fairly confident that she could head back in the general direction she had come, with fatigue and fear now a factor, there was no certainty she would reach the road at all.

Her other option—only option really—was to continue on. She realized she may only immerse herself deeper, but eventually she would reach a boundary. This was the Northlands, not the Amazon, after all. She had to keep going and cling to the fact that possibility rested in every new clearing.

She stood up on the log and slowly surveyed the forest in each direction, hoping by some wonder of the universe her eyes would focus past the camouflage and spot something other than trees. It wasn't a particularly dense woodland, so even with the lush spring leaves there was quite a bit of visibility. But she saw nothing. She jumped down off the log and searched the forest again, this time at ground level, figuring she may have more luck at a different angle. Nothing. She climbed the log again and this time stood tall, straightening her back, and cupped her mouth with her hands. She breathed deeply and screamed as loudly as possible.

"Help me! Can anybody hear me!"

The words seemed to float through the trees, echoing off the branches and carrying downwind. With the additional height of the log, her voice felt forceful, and the decision to yell now seemed less an act of desperation and more of an actual rescue strategy. She paused and listened, not expecting a response, and, of course, getting none. She screamed again, this time feeling a strained burn in her throat. She couldn't remember ever having yelled this loud as an adult. Still nothing, and the subsequent silence was stark, only reinforcing her desertion. She couldn't know that the sound waves of this particular bellow deflected at just the proper angle, avoiding perfectly the large oak trunks and dense clumps of leaves that should have absorbed them forever, traveling instead just far enough from their source to reach the auditory canal of an old woman who lay dying on a weathered terrace less than four miles away.

Anika moved down to a sitting position on the log, broke off a dying branch, and began clearing as much mud as possible from her shoes and pant cuffs. It was a futile exercise she knew—they'd be covered again in a matter of paces—but she needed whatever boost she could get. At least she hadn't worn a dress today, she thought. It could always be worse.

She placed her feet back down on the damp dirt floor and was startled by a rustle beneath the log. She stifled a gasp and watched as two chipmunks ran past her and headed up a nearby tree. Anika unconsciously cataloged the vermin as a potential food source; though if it came to that, how she would trap such small, fleeting creatures she had no idea. She watched the tiny animals disappear into the camouflage of the tree's top branches and then continued her upward gaze to the clear blue sky. It was indeed a marvelous day, she thought, and then she started walking.

***

The old woman opened her eyes and searched her surroundings with the vibrancy of an infant seeing the world for the first time. The voice was faint—perhaps the faintest sound she had ever heard—but that she had heard it there was no doubt. It may be the voice of Death, she thought, but if it was, he was incarnate. That sound had come in through her ears, not her imagination. She replayed the words in her mind. Over and over. The voice was feminine—beautiful and distressed. Strong. Alive. Not the voice of Death. The voice of Life. Delivering again.

CHAPTER TWO

"Anika!"

Gretel Morgan flinched violently at the sound of her father's voice, somehow managing not to drop the ceramic plate she had been drying over the sink. He was awake, and, as was usually the case lately, unhappy.

"It's me, Father, I'll be right there," she called, turning her head slightly toward the back bedroom, trying her best not to sound aggravated. She certainly sympathized with his condition but had grown tired of the demands it came with.

Gretel sighed and placed the dish on the sideboard. She had hoped to finish the cleaning before he woke since her tasks seemed to multiply when he was conscious. Cooking his meals alone was a day's work; add in laundering his clothes (including ironing) and general fetching, and the assignment was barbaric. Thankfully, Mother would be home today, at least to bear some of the constant attention, if not the heavy lifting.

Gretel walked the ten or so paces to her father's room and paused at the door, softly clearing her throat and assuming the statuesque, confident posture her mother always seemed to have when she entered a room. At fourteen, her shoulders and hips had begun to forge, and early indications suggested she would have her mother's shapely body. She had no delusions of striding in and conquering her father's petulance in the same effortless way her mother did, of course, but hopefully she could disarm him if only for a moment.

She formed what she believed was a serious, business-like look on her face and entered the room. She could see that her father was sitting up slightly in his bed, but avoided his eyes and walked briskly to the end table, feigning irritation at the crumbs and empty glasses that littered its surface.

"Where is your mother?" her father grumbled, his deep, accented speech at once both intimidating and divine. "She was to be home by now."

"She's probably not coming home," Gretel replied casually, letting the words drift just to the edge of uneasiness. "I wouldn't blame her. If I was her I would have changed my name and run away to a village in the south." She kept her eyes down, serious, staying excessively focused on her father's mess.

Her father frowned and stared coldly at his daughter. "Perhaps I'll send you to a village in the south."

Gretel stopped sponging the table in mid-motion, and stared up at her father with a look of both disbelief and anticipation. "Would you? Please! Promise me, Papa!" She held his gaze for as long as possible before losing control of the charade and erupting into a snorted laugh.

Her father shook his head slowly and grinned. Gretel could see the flicker of joy in his eyes, proud of how quick his daughter had become with her banter. Yet another gift inherited from her mother.

"How are you feeling, Papa?" Gretel said, now straight-faced, unable to conceal her weariness. She sat on the edge of the bed and examined her father's bandages.

"Better than I look."

"Well, you look terrible."

"So better than terrible then." He waved an absent hand and began shuffling to get on his feet, having reached the extent of how much he wanted to discuss himself or his maladies. "Get me up."

"You need to stay in bed, Papa. You're not ready."

"Then you had better be ready with the piss pot."

With that, Gretel stooped and leaned in toward her father, offering her shoulder as a crutch. She could see him size up her position, and with a soft, guttural grunt he threw an arm around his daughter's neck, embarrassment no longer the palpable element it had been six weeks ago. His white bedshirt was badly stained with some type of red sauce, and his ever-growing belly extended over the elastic of his tattered long underpants. It had amazed Gretel the short time it took for a man with such a long-standing trademark of pride and masculinity to concede to the often cruel circumstances of life; in the case of her father, those circumstances had come most recently in the form of three fractured ribs—not exactly the bubonic plague in the hierarchy of ailments, but painfully debilitating nevertheless. Particularly for a man nearing sixty.

Gretel boosted him from the bed and shuffled him slowly to the threshold of the washroom, grimacing throughout the process, and from there left him to his own maneuvers. The doctor had explained to her mother that the injury would likely cause a decrease in appetite, since even automatic bodily functions like swallowing and digesting could be painful, and limited activity would reduce his need for the same amount of nourishment he was getting before the accident. The opposite, however, was proving true; he ate constantly and, as a result, had become quite heavy. She couldn't be sure, but Gretel guessed that her father had gained at least forty pounds in little over a month.

"So where is your mother?" The voice from behind the bathroom door was less demanding now and contained the subtle hint of concern. Gretel had lingered outside since she would have to bring her father back when he was done.

"Delayed, I guess. But she must have left Deda's already or else she would have telephoned."

"Then why didn't she phone to say she would be delayed?" His pitch was now higher and layered with obstinance.

"Perhaps she was delayed on the road, I don't know Papa." She paused and asked, "Are you going to be in there much longer?" Gretel was now annoyed, both at her father for his current weakness and at her mother for being late. There were still dishes remaining in the kitchen, and she needed a break—if only for fifteen minutes—to sit and rest. Not working or helping or talking. Just to rest.

"Maybe you should bathe," she suggested, offering the words in the tone of a helpful reminder so as not to offend him. "You'll call Deda's when you're out." Her father mumbled something inaudible from behind the door, and then a grain of joy arose in Gretel at the abrupt sound of water being released from the tub's faucet.

She sighed with relief and walked back toward the kitchen, her desire to finish housework now dwarfed by the urge to rest. She averted her gaze from the sink as she passed it, and headed quickly for the back porch, where she collapsed forcefully in a white, weathered rocker. She tilted her face up toward the ceiling and closed her eyes, thankful for the chance to relax, but understanding that what she really needed was sleep. Sleep had now become the default thought in her mind throughout the day, and, in fact, had become of such value since her father's accident, that over the past three weeks Gretel had started her mornings by staring at herself in the small nightstand mirror by her bed and listing in her mind the things that she would be willing to give up for an undisturbed day of slumber. A full day. Not one chore. Not one knock. Not even a voice. Just complete serenity. Of course, she possessed virtually nothing of her own, so this exercise basically involved the sacrifices of treasures she would never see and powers she would never have, the latest offering being a horse that could fly. Later, in the throes of the day, she would scoff at how little value she would have gotten from her imagined trade-offs; but she was convinced that, at the time, she would have made the deal.

Gretel could feel herself drifting, and decided not to fight. The dishes remained, but her mother would be home soon, and though she would be in no mood to finish her daughter's chores after a long day of travel, Gretel concluded that as a parent she would recognize when her child was spent. If her father needed help back to his bed she would help, but aside from that, she was done for the day.

***

"She's not home, Gretel."

Gretel opened her eyes and was greeted by the orange glow of the twilight sky above her. She was momentarily disoriented, but smelled the oil from the lamps and remembered she was on the porch. Her late afternoon catnap had metastasized into solid sleep. By her estimation, she was out for at least four hours.

Her thoughts immediately went to her father, whom, for all she knew, was in the tub dead, a victim of immobility, hypothermia, and a neglectful daughter.

She got up quickly from the rocker and felt the effect of her sleeping position in the form of a dull stiffness at the back of her neck. No question she would be dealing with that misery for the rest of the night. Tentatively, Gretel turned back toward the house and screamed at the sight of her father sitting at the porch table, dressed and shaven, his elbows propped up and his head buried in his hands. He looked as if her were in a library reading—the way one might read a dictionary or an atlas—but there was nothing on the table below him.

Her initial thoughts were of relief, that her father was alive and that she was not a murderer. Then, registering his condition, her thoughts became more selfish, assuming his apparent improvement meant she would now get real relief. Physical relief. More sleep.

She stood staring at him, waiting for him to speak, but he sat in position, silent.

"Papa?" she said, "What's wrong?" Gretel spoke softly, but her tone had no sympathy and was one demanding an explanation. Her father didn't move and she became uneasy, then scared. "What's wrong!" she said again, this time louder, panicked and quivery, the film of sleep and the surreality of her father sitting upright in a chair on the porch, functional, now completely wiped away.

"She's not home, Gretel." Her father lifted his head from his hands and looked out through the trees at the small narrow lake that lined their property.

Gretel could see where the tears had been on his freshly-washed cheeks and she noted that this was as close to weeping as she'd ever seen from either of her parents.

"Something's happened," he said, "I know something's happened."

Her father's words caused Gretel's legs to wobble, and she sat back down slowly in the rocker. She couldn't speak, and looked off in the same direction as her father, as if they were both trying to spot the same object on the water. "Did you call Deda?" she asked finally, in a whisper, already knowing the answer.

"Of course I called him. She left even earlier than she had told me she would. She should have been home long before we expected her." There was no anger in her father's voice, only defeat.

"Perhaps there was traffic then. A very bad accident...and the road is closed."

"I've called The System. There is no report of any accident along the Interways."

Gretel could hear in her father's tone that the bases had been covered. Heinrich Morgan was a man of routine, as was his wife, and any break from that routine would immediately incite him to make it right again. To look at all the possibilities and rule them out, one by one, until the answer to the problem emerged. And if the remaining answers were out of his control, and he couldn't reset the routine to its proper function, he shut down. This was the point he had apparently reached.

The tears in Gretel's eyes seemed to be dripping to the floor before she even felt the sadness, and her face flushed with hate for her father's weakness. Nothing was wrong! Her mother was fine! He should be ashamed, a grown man crying in front of his teenage daughter because her mother is a few hours late. For a month he had contributed nothing to the house—NOTHING—other than dirty plates and whines of discomfort. Gretel and her mother had worked the fields for six weeks while he moaned over a few broken bones in his belly. If only that horse had kicked his head! And now, when strength was needed—when he was needed—he was a clammy dishrag, like a woman who's just watched her son leave for war.

Gretel erupted from the rocking chair and ran toward her room, ignoring the sharp pain that burned through her neck the whole way. She stumbled in and fell face down on the foot end of her bed, nearly crashing her head on the bench of the small white vanity that sat only inches away. Almost immediately, she stood back up and strode defiantly back to the open bedroom door, slamming it harder than she thought she was capable of. For that split moment she felt better than she could remember in weeks, as if the suppressed grievances of her fourteen-year-old body and mind were instantly alleviated.

She went back to her bed and took a more conventional position, curled fetal-like at the head with her cheek flat on the quilt cover.

The heavy sobs finally ended and Gretel lay still until her crying stopped completely. She rolled to her back and gazed vacuously at the brown wood that made up the cabin ceiling. Her thoughts became clear as she studied the evidence of the situation and soon became hopeful. This is all certainly an overreaction, she thought. Papa's condition has unsettled him and I've let it influence me. There's a good chance—better than good—that Mother is completely fine. In fact, there was a much higher likelihood that her mother was stranded on the road somewhere waiting for help to arrive, than lying dead on a river bank or in a landfill. True, she should have been home hours ago—if she left early, then at least six or seven hours to be more accurate—and she had taken the trip up North dozens of times over the past four or five years since Deda had become sick, so she wouldn't have become lost. But none of that evinced tragedy. Gretel reasoned that if something truly terrible had happened, someone would know by now and the family would have been contacted.

But her father's words bore the texture of truth; if not because of the sure somberness of his words—"Something's happened"—than for the possible explanations available. Even if Deda had suddenly been rushed away in an ambulance and died suddenly en route to a hospital (which, of course, hadn't happened since her father had spoken with him earlier), Mother would have called as soon as she reached the hospital. Mother always called. If she didn't call, there was a problem. In this case, Gretel proposed, that problem may simply be a blown tire or some mechanical malfunction in the car. But the Northlands were no more than two hours away on a clear spring day, so it was unlikely she wouldn't have found a telephone by now if it were something so benign. There was no logical reason she could think of that Mother wouldn't have called, other than reasons she didn't want to imagine.

She began to cry again softly, and her mind became overwhelmed with thoughts of never again seeing her mother. It was unimaginable, and physically nauseating. Her mother was everything to her. Everything. Gretel's image of herself as a good young girl—exceptional even—was due solely to the woman she had studied thoroughly and tried for as long as she could remember to emulate. Though Gretel rarely noticed it in the environment which they lived, her mother had a finesse and dignity about her that always astounded Gretel, and only became evident—almost embarrassingly so—when it was contrasted with the tactlessness of most women in the Back Country. She avoided the crude speech that most of the Back Country wives used in an effort somehow to endear themselves to their husbands' friends. Instead she maintained an easy poise that seemed almost regal and out of place. Consequently, of course, her mother stood out among her peers, earning the attention of the men and, Gretel supposed, the backstage scorn of her fellow ladies. She was far from what most people would describe as beautiful, but despite the physical advantages they may have had, other women always appeared intimidated by her mother's confidence.

Gretel got to her feet and walked to the vanity, where she sat on the bench and looked at her distraught face in the mirror as the day's last few rays of sunlight entered her window. It was almost dark and there was no sign of Mother. She turned on the lamp and examined the framed picture of her parents that sat on the vanity top. Her father had gotten very lucky, she thought, and Gretel became sad for him. He was twenty years older than his bride, and in his marriage had always been decided in his ways, insisting on the traditional roles of husband and wife: provider and caregiver, tough and understanding, et cetera.

But in that tradition he had never shown anything but respect and love for her mother. When choices of importance had to be made, concerning her and her brother, or otherwise, Heinrich Morgan always insisted on his wife's opinion. He knew between the two of them she was the smarter one, and he never pretended otherwise.

And though Gretel couldn't remember a time when her father was what she would describe as 'sweet' toward Mother, he certainly never gave her any reason to be docile or frightened around him. He never complained about a meal—whether overcooked or late or for any reason—and he always thanked her when it was over, even offering compliments if he found it exceptional. And if Mother needed to leave him for a day or a week—as in the current situation visiting her ill father—there was never a sense of trepidation when she told him, and the news was always delivered as a statement, with the full expectation that it would be received without protest, if not encouragement. "I'll need to leave for the North tomorrow," her mother would say. "Father's doing poorly. Gretel will handle the house while I'm gone." And father's replies would be nothing other than words of concern for his father-in-law.

The memory of these exchanges suddenly awakened Gretel to the fact that she was not ready to assume this position of authority. The surrogate role of housewife that Gretel had taken on for the last nine days, and that she had begrudgingly admitted to herself was, on some level, enjoyable, was beyond her capabilities. Well beyond. She couldn't do this for five or ten more days let alone years!

Gretel was startled by the muffled sound of the cabin door opening and then closing. She sat motionless, not breathing, and looked at nothing as she shifted her eyes in amazement around the room waiting for the next sound to decipher. Mother! It was definitely Mother. It had to be. Tired and with quite a story to tell, no doubt, but it had to be her. She waited for the booming sound of her father's voice, joyful and scolding, to ring through her room. She wanted to rush out and verify her belief, but she was paralyzed, fearing that somehow by moving she would lose the sound and her hopes would evaporate.

At the tepid knock on her bedroom door, Gretel smiled and lifted herself from the bench, banging her knee on the underside of the vanity and nearly knocking the lamp to the floor, catching it just before it fell. The door cracked and began to open. Gretel looked toward it, waiting for the miracle, holding her awkward lamp-in-hand pose.

It was her father.

"No!" she said, the word erupting from her mouth automatically, denoting both fear and authority, as if she were repelling a spirit that had ventured from hell to inhabit her room. Her father looked at her with sadness and acceptance.

"Is she dead?" Gretel said, surprised at the bluntness of her question.

"I don't know, Gretel, we're going to look for her. Your brother is home."

***

Gretel let out a restrained sigh as the family truck pulled in front of her grandfather's small brick house, amazed they had made it. The truck, she guessed, was at least thirty years old, and probably hadn't made a trip this far since before she was born. And each time her father had made one of his dozen or so stops along the way, exploring the considerable land surrounding every curve and potential hazard that the back roads offered, he turned the engine off to conserve fuel. She was sure with each failed effort to locate her mother, the key would click ominously in the ignition when her father tried to restart the engine, and they too would disappear along the road. But it had always started, and here they were.

She looked across the bench seat at her father and was disturbed by the look of indifference on his face. Her brother lay between them asleep.

Her father opened the door and said weakly, "Stay in the car."

"I'm seeing Deda," Gretel immediately responded, opening the door quickly and storming out of the truck, taking a more defiant tone than was indicative of how she actually felt. She had every intention of seeing her grandfather though. It had been months since she'd seen him, and even though she often felt awkward around him lately, more so now that he had worsened, she loved him enormously, and still considered him, next to her mother, the most comforting person in her world. If there was one person she needed right now, other than her mother, it was Deda.

She ran toward the house and as she reached the stoop she saw the tall, smiling figure of Deda standing in the doorway. She screamed at the sight of him. He looked so old, at least twenty years older than the seventy-five he actually was, and his smile was far from the thin-lipped consoling grin Gretel would have expected. Instead his mouth was wide and toothy, as if he had been laughing. He looked crazy, she thought.

"Hi, Deda," she said swallowing hard. "How are you feeling?"

At the sound of Gretel's voice, Deda's face lit up, morphing to normalcy and becoming consistent with that of a man seeing his beloved granddaughter for the first time in four months. "Gretel!" which he pronounced 'Gree-tel,' "my love, come in! Where is your brother?"

"He's in the car sleeping," she replied, and with that her brother came running into the house and into Deda's arms, which Deda had extended just in time to receive his grandson.

Deda held Hansel's shoulders and pushed him away to arms length. "Ahh, Hansel, you look so big!"

"You look really old, Deda," Hansel said, as respectfully as an eight-year-old could say such words.

Deda laughed, "I am so old, Hansel! I am so old!" He placed his palm on the back of the boy's neck and led him to the small sofa which was arranged just off the foyer. Deda sat down and lifted Hansel to his lap; Gretel followed and sat beside him on the cushion.

"Hello, Heinrich," Deda said, not taking his eyes from the children.

Gretel's father stood at the door, silently watching the interaction between his children and his wife's father. "Marcel."

"Why don't you sit?"

"We won't be staying."

Over the years Gretel had grown used to this style of conversation between her father and Deda, terse and factual, completely devoid of style. It wasn't that they disliked each other exactly, but more that they had failed to reach the level of trust normally achieved between two people at this stage in a relationship. Her parents had been married almost twenty years.

"Have you contacted The System?" Deda asked.

"Of course. They won't do anything for days," Gretel's father replied. And then, "Unless there's evidence of a crime."

Deda nodded in understanding. "Gretel," he said, "why don't you and your brother explore in the cellar for a while. I've some new books you would both like, just at the bottom of the stairs, on the first shelf there. You'll see them when you go down."

Deda stood and led the children to the cellar door, opening it and pulling the ribbed metal chain that hung just at the top of the stairs, unleashing a dull orange glow of light. The cellar was an obvious suggestion so that Deda could speak to her father alone, but Gretel didn't mind, and played along for her brother's sake. Besides, they were going to discuss her mother—and the possibilities of what might have happened—and she didn't have the emotional stamina to handle that right now.

As she and her brother reached the bottom of the cellar, Gretel saw that the books Deda referenced were the same ones he had had for at least two years now: Reptiles of the Northlands, Sea Life, and a few others containing topics Gretel had long since lost interest in.

"These books aren't new," Hansel complained. "I've read these a thousand times."

"Your Deda's old Han, he doesn't remember" Gretel replied, "And, anyway, you still like them."

"Fine."

Hansel opened the sea creature book absently and slumped heavily into a dusty club chair, once the centerpiece of Deda's living area but now in exile, having been replaced by a chair more conducive to Deda's frail condition. The dust from the chair puffed into the dim light and then dissipated. Normally Gretel found places like Deda's cellar repulsing—the dust was as thick as bread and seemed not to be spared from any section of furniture; and the scurrying sounds that clattered from the corners of the dark room conjured in her mind pictures of things much larger than mice. And she was sure that the spiders she had seen over the years had to be as large as any in the world.

But for all the impurities, Gretel had no memory of ever fearing the cellar. Lately, in fact, she felt drawn to it, mystified by the shrouded hodgepodge of books and tools and bric-a-brac that coated the surface of every shelf and table. There were candles and candle holders next to decorative plates and stemware; prehistoric preserve jars being used as paperweights for pictures of men and women Gretel had never seen in person; and dozens of other trinkets and curiosities that as a small girl she had considered junk—nuisances that cluttered up what might otherwise have been a play room for tea parties and dancing and such—but that she had recently come to admire.

The cellar, however, for all its antique charm, was also dark and difficult to explore. There was no window, and the one low-watt bulb that hung by the door illuminated only the area a few feet past the base of the steps; beyond that, a flashlight was required to make out any details of an object, if not just to walk. Gretel never asked Deda why he hadn't put a working lamp in the area, and now assumed it was to discourage her and Hansel from playing back there, though he had never explicitly forbade them from exploring that part of the house. Besides, as large as the cellar was, certainly large enough to convert into an apartment if Deda had ever decided to take in a boarder, most children didn't need to be warned about what may lurk in such a place.

But by eleven, and certainly now at fourteen, the illicitness of the "dark areas" only enhanced Gretel's curiosity, and, frankly, made the jaunts to Deda's bearable. What enjoyments she got at eight or nine were now almost completely nullified by her grandfather's health and her own adolescence. So the cellar had become her entertainment, and specifically the magazines.

Gretel found the flashlight that always sat on the seldom-used workbench and turned it on in Hansel's eyes.

"Stop, Gretel!"

Gretel chuckled. "I'm going to look for something in the back, I'll be right here, okay?" Gretel knew to be playful and delicate with her brother; he hadn't yet fully accepted that something bad might actually have happened to his mother, and if it occurred to him now, she thought, she was in no condition to help.

Hansel didn't respond, but looked up from the sea creatures book and followed Gretel with his eyes to the far end of the cellar, making sure the light was always visible.

Gretel felt her way to the antique bureau she was looking for and found the knob of the right-side drawer of the middle row. She could feel the weight of the magazines as she pulled, careful not to force the drawer and tear one of the covers. She pulled the top issue off the stack and thumbed through it, suddenly feeling nervous at the sight of the smiling, underclad women flipping past her. She leafed through to the end and put the first issue in the stack face down on the surface of the bureau so as to keep them in order when she put them all back, and took out the next issue, passively thumbing through it, staring at the women who were pretty much all the same. They weren't nude, but they were certainly there to provoke men and not to sell undergarments.

Gretel wasn't exactly sure why the women fascinated her. She didn't like girls in that way—at least she didn't think so—she certainly didn't get the same feelings looking at these women that she got when talking with certain boys at school. It was something else, something about their expressions. The way they smiled so easily for the camera when, Gretel had to assume, they felt ashamed and sad the whole time. She wanted to hug them, befriend them, let them know that she was fascinated by them, by their strength to do what she could never imagine. And that they were beautiful.

"Gretel, what are you doing?" Hansel called from the stairs.

Gretel flinched, nearly dropping the magazine, before fumbling it back to its proper place in the drawer and stacking the first one on top of it. "Nothing Han, looking at some old magazines. I'm coming."

She shut the bureau drawer and turned back for the stairs, and as the flashlight turned with her, the beam strayed wildly, just drifting over the thick black spine of a book. The book.

There it was.

The thick hardcover tome had presided from the top of Deda's tallest bookshelf for as long as Gretel had a memory of the house, which was from about age four. At that time, of course, the book was as mysterious and out of reach as space, and she hadn't the slightest clue as to what it might contain. But its sheer size and blackness had fascinated her even then.

The cover was absolute in its darkness, with no shine or reflection, as if it were overlaid with black wool. And there was no text or pattern on the spine—which was the only part Gretel would ever see for many years—and she imagined that someone looking up casually at the shelf could easily have mistaken the book for emptiness, a large gap in the middle of other books.

By age seven she got up the nerve to touch the book, which was no easy task given the height of the shelf and the book's position. It required delicate stacking of furniture and the tip-toe balance of a ballerina, but Gretel was determined, and soon became quite adept with her scaffolding.

During those years Gretel visited Deda's house regularly—at least once every other month—and with every visit she made a point to feel the book, to physically touch it, rubbing her fingertips on the exposed area. It was always cold—as were all of the books in the cellar—and its lack of any real texture, Gretel believed, gave an indication as to its age.

But she didn't touch the book because of any particular enchantment, or even because she thought it was magic, she did so more as a gauge, testing when she would be able to move forward on her stalled curiosity. As she grew taller, and as her level of comfort on the far ledges of stacked stools and empty milk crates increased, she began trying to flip the book out of its snug resting spot, placing her index finger at the top where the spine met the pages and then pulling backwards. At seven it never budged, as if cemented down, and the effort only enhanced Gretel's wonderment. It would be two years later when she would finally free the massive text and learn a word that would eventually come to hold a high place in her lexicon forever.

Gretel turned and faced the bookshelf and centered the beam of the flashlight on the book, which was no longer in its normal far left position on the top shelf, having moved to one center-right. In ten years it was the first time she had ever seen it out of place, other than when she was perusing it of course. Had it been in its current position when she was seven years old, she noted, it would have been a much easier endeavor to pull the book down, since this particular side of the shelf was far easier to access.

Now, at fourteen, the trick was to grab the book without attracting her brother's attention.

Gretel could see Hansel sifting through some boxes on the shelves near the stairs, and knew that his boredom would draw him to her soon; but the book was just out of her reach, and she didn't want to risk arousing his inquisitiveness by struggling and groaning on her tiptoes. Careful not to make any sudden motions, she pulled a large bucket from under the old wash basin and tossed aside a crusty towel that had dried crumpled and deformed inside, probably sometime in the last decade.

Gretel then placed the flashlight on the workbench, beacon down, reducing her visibility to a small halo of light on the table surface, and blindly flipped the bucket on its rim.

"Hey, what are you doing?" Hansel cried, his voice dripping with suspicion.

"Hansel, don't come over here, you'll trip on something," Gretel replied, trying to sound casual.

The sudden darkness had alerted her brother and Gretel silently cursed herself. She could hear him making tentative steps toward the bookshelf and Gretel quickly stepped up on the bucket, nearly missing the bottom brim and toppling to the floor. She began feeling for the black leather. She couldn't even make out the shadowy forms of the books without the flashlight, let alone any of the writing, but there was no doubt she would know her book by touch.

"Gretel?" Hansel again, edging closer.

"Han, I'm very serious, there are a million things that you could fall on and hurt yourself."

"I'll hold the light for you so you can see."

"I don't need the light, I've got it."

Gretel continued to feel for the book knowing she must be close. If it were in its proper spot she would have gotten it already and been done with it, now all this commotion would force her to make up some story about it. It didn't matter, he couldn't read the book anyway. She couldn't even read it. In fact, she couldn't even read the letters.

Gretel moved her hand over from a thin laminated book, and as instantly as the forefinger of her left hand brushed the cold, dead leather, she knew she had found it. By now Hansel had reached the shelf and was looking up at Gretel on the bucket.

"Han, shine the light up here," she barked in a loud whisper. "I don't want to knock anything off."

Hansel placed his hand on the flashlight, but before he could lift it to aid in his sister's search, a large beam of light shone in from the stairs, illuminating her face and the goal of her quest.

"Ah yes," her grandfather said, pointing the hanging bulb toward Gretel, "that book. It fascinates me, too."

CHAPTER THREE

The first bite of chill came down just before the top of the red sun slipped behind the tallest cedars. Darkness was less than an hour away, and the waking moon was already visible, waiting to take its post in the night sky.

Anika Morgan hunkered in a small, weathered-out cavity that had formed in a hill bank and covered her face with her hands. She was lost and had not the faintest concept of where the treeline might be. The hope that had carried her through clearings and creeks, over countless bluffs and damp wastelands, was gone.

At least for today.

Her will had shut down and the prospect of death was now lodged tightly in her brain. What had she done? To her children? Her husband? Her life? In her unruliest imagination she wouldn't have seen herself like this! Dying in the woods of the Northlands. She lamented once again her decision to plunge unprepared into these strange woods, knowing full well that map reading and orienteering were a glaring weakness in her skill set.

But her instincts to survive—if not to navigate—seemed to be properly aligned. She knew she hadn't the skills to trap or make fire, but early on Anika recognized the unlikelihood of escaping the forest in the daylight, and had wasted no time seeking shelter. Hunger had come calling hours ago, and she had kept an eye out for anything that could pass for food.

But the elements, she knew, were her biggest threat, even in the midst of a mild spring day.

And she had been fortunate to find the 'cave,' which was how she thought of it, though it was really nothing more than a deep indentation in the side of a hill she'd been following for the last several hours. It was barely deep enough to sit in, let alone lie down, but it was shelter, and it would protect her from the cold night wind that was sure to come. The breezes she so welcomed during the heat of the day now terrified her.

A shiver scurried the length of Anika's back, the night again teasing what lie ahead, and Anika tucked her arms into the sleeves of her thin cotton blouse, gripping the bottoms of her elbows, her forearms layered across her abdomen below her bra. This was a bad sign, she thought: the sun had not fully set and the early stages of hypothermia had already begun. If she made it through the night, it wouldn't be without the help of God. Somewhere in the back of her mind she considered that her faith would help, but she would conserve her prayers for now, knowing the worst of the cold was still to come. What she wouldn't give for a blanket.

Anika drifted to sleep but was awake within minutes, the result of another short, epileptic shiver. She was wide-eyed and focused for a minute, and then drifted away again, repeating this cycle on and off for what may have been an hour, with her shakes each time becoming increasingly violent, as her muscles tried desperately to create warmth. She needed to move.

She crawled from the cave and stood outside in the open of the forest. It was dark, but not as dark as she would have imagined this far from civilization; the moon, thankfully, doing its part for her on this night.

She got to her feet and forced herself to run, at first in place, and then occasionally in short bursts to about a ten-foot radius, making sure not to lose sight of her shelter. She lifted her knees as high as possible, feeling the blood in them resist, and then start to come alive. The short naps had been frustrating and alarming—with death being the result of any deep sleep, she feared—but they had momentarily revived her, and Anika suddenly felt she could sustain the exercise long enough to get warm again. After that she wasn't sure, and she knew running around wasn't the long-term solution to her situation—after all, she was hungry, and her energy would fail soon. But for now running felt good, and she went with it.

The crunch of her shoes on the leaf litter and dry twigs sounded abrupt and panicky in the stillness of the forest, and the noise evoked in her some long-forgotten sense of urgency, the primal need to continue even under dire conditions and the harshest of circumstances. Though being lost in the woods in early spring, Anika conceded, hardly qualified as the 'harshest of circumstances.'

She felt suddenly energized, and desperately wished it were daytime so she could continue her lonely journey, ill-fated though it may be. She even considered, with the brightness of the moon, moving on at night; but her hunger, which was manageable now, wouldn't stay in the shadows for much longer, and if delirium was coming, she'd rather it arrive in the relative safety of her new burrow or in the light of day and not in the open of the forest darkness. Besides, if she did brave the forest tonight and was unable to find a cabin or some other artificial structure, it was unlikely she would again find natural accommodations like those she had now and would almost certainly freeze.

No, for now she would stay awake and keep her body moving as long as possible, conserving her water and resting when necessary. The night had a long way to go, but she felt she could make it.

Anika continued her pattern of light jogging, followed by short bursts of sprints, and then rest. As her legs began to tire, the jogging and sprint sessions became indistinguishable, and the rest periods became dozes. She resisted the urge to lie down, or huddle back in the cave, but sleep was inevitable.

***

The loud crunch of feet startled Anika, and with semi-cognizance she chuckled to herself, realizing she had fallen asleep while somehow walking in place. Wouldn't that be a great ability to have right now, she thought, and then realized she was doing it now, which inspired her in a groggy, abstract sort of way. Maybe she could figure out how to harness this newfound talent and sustain it.

The dreamlike concept turned to alert curiosity, and Anika opened her eyes to find herself lying in darkness on the ground in her "resting" spot. She wasn't sleepwalking, she was just sleeping. Mud and branches stuck to the side of her nose and lips, and something insectile quickly crawled its way up from the hairline at the back of her head toward the top of her scalp.

She scrambled to her feet and looked around, frantically ruffling her hair, trying in consternation both to rid herself of the parasite now nestled in her hair and to identify the potentially larger threat on the perimeter. Anika's slumbered eyes adjusted slowly to the night, and the once-bright moon had temporarily withdrawn behind a stray cloud cluster, making even the black forms of the trees virtually invisible. She was blind, and something was stalking her.

Her first thought was to climb, to locate the closest tree—fallen or otherwise—and get as high as possible. She was no great athlete, but she trusted her abilities given the situation. Besides, running was out of the question, since virtually any animal that she could think of would catch her easily before she took more than a few strides.

But if she were to get some height, Anika thought, maybe she could buy some time. Jab at whatever was after her with a stick or something and frustrate it until it gave up. Anika thought of wolves. Wolves couldn't climb trees could they? She'd heard somewhere that bears could, but were there really bears in these parts?

These initial plans and imaginings ran their course in a matter of seconds, and were quickly replaced with calmer, more reasonable thoughts. Anika now thought it much more likely that whatever was prowling her space was something more common and less deadly than a wolf or bear. A deer or fox perhaps. Maybe a moose. She stood her ground, motionless, now listening with conscious ears for the sound of steps to repeat.

She waited for what seemed like several minutes and then: Crunch. Crunch. Crunch.

The patient steps moved to Anika's left—perhaps ten yards away, maybe less—and then stopped.

Her guess of a deer now seemed most likely; the steps were heavy and deliberate—not the scurrying movements of a squirrel or rabbit—but not threatening either, secretive and apprehensive.

Anika breathed out for the first time in what must have been a full minute, and the passing thoughts of small game now made her stomach moan in hunger. She felt only slightly relieved, however, knowing the 'deer' could just as easily be one of a dozen other, less docile things, ready to pounce at any moment.

Anika slowly stooped down, blindly feeling for the largest stick in her immediate confines, which turned out to be a stray branch, two-feet long at most and no thicker than a billiard cue. She grabbed it and stood back up without moving her feet.

"Hello," she said softly, mildly aware that she was attempting to talk to what she had convinced herself was a deer.

The night answered back with only the distant chirping of crickets and the light rustle of the trees' topmost leaves. The moon had returned to the black sky, and Anika's eyes adjusted. She could now see the silvery reflection of the branches and rocks that crowded the area. If something large was still there, she would certainly see it when it moved.

Keeping as still as possible, Anika shifted her eyes from right to left, turning her head just slightly upon reaching the limits of her periphery.

Crunch! Crunch! Crunch!

This time the sound was plodding and aggressive with no pretense of stealth. Terrified, Anika turned toward the sound, and saw only a glimpse of something curved and dull smash down on her forehead, catching her brow above her left eye and splitting it like a grape.

CHAPTER FOUR

It was almost dawn when the Morgan truck pulled back on-to the gravel road that led to their cabin, and Gretel's doubts about seeing her mother again had grown stronger.

To this point she had been scared, and had concentrated this fear and directed it toward her father in a projection of overdue frustrations. But she hadn't really believed her mother was gone forever. Forever. She was too tired now to start adjusting to exactly what that meant to the rest of her life. And as much as her body pressured her to cry, there were simply no more tears.

The drive home from Deda's had been agony. Her father had stopped at every curve and intersection, every hill and possible hidden entrance, forcing her and Hansel out to wander the shoulders of the highways with him, branching off in opposite directions until he called them back with a barking "Let's go." They were the only words he spoke the en-tire drive.

And the searches were pathetic and hopeless in the vast darkness of the countryside, with only the narrow beam of the car's headlights to guide them. The only way they would have found their mother was if she happened to be sitting in the eight-foot wide stretch of light at the exact place where her father had pulled over. The ridiculousness of it made Gretel despondent and she cried nearly the whole time.

But as her father now pulled to a stop in front of their home, her sobs had been replaced with a more reserved depression and self-pity. If she had indeed lost her mother, then her loss, she knew, was greater than anyone's. Including her father. Whatever his weaknesses were as a man, he was an adult and was innately better built to deal with such losses. It was part of what separated adults from children, Gretel thought. She was sad for him, of course, but husbands lost their wives every day—or the other way around—it was an eventual fact of life. And with a home and a fair amount of land, he could marry again if that's what he wanted. Men with property rarely died alone in the Southlands.

There was Hansel, of course, who *was* a child, and Gretel did not discount the enormity of the loss her mother would be to him. Because of his age, he was more vulnerable than she was, and she knew there was no worse thing an eight-year-old boy could imagine than losing his mother. It would be devastating for her brother, of that she had no doubt. But she also knew that compared to virtually any girl born in the Southlands, a boy's life was charmed. And though his sadness would be deep and prolonged, his future would arrive unscathed. He would grow into a teenager and then a young man, and as he grew, so too would the respect of those in the community. Not that he would be any great pillar of society (it was the Back Country, after all)—or even a leader of men, she guessed—it's just the way it was here. Eventually Hansel would inherit the farm from their father, marry a girl, of which there would be several to choose from, and live as the Morgan men did for generations before him: long and average and in relative happiness. And it would go that way with or without his mother.

But it was different when a girl lost her mother. A girl truly *needed* her mother. It was true a girl's father protected her from physical harm, but her mother was her defender in the community, which, at fourteen, Gretel deemed far more important. And *her* mother was special, particularly suited for the task of raising a girl to womanhood. How brilliant she was! Having the ability not only to navigate the common pitfalls that consumed most of her friends' mothers, but also to float above all the ridiculous rules that most women accepted without protest. That role of an indentured servant, mothering unlimited offspring at her husband's command: that was never to be her mother's lot in life.

And until this moment, Gretel didn't think it was hers. She had anticipated and depended on her mother encouraging and reinforcing these values as she grew, molding her into something proud and independent. Not to lead armies into battle or found nations, but to become her own woman. And Gretel wasn't there yet. She wasn't ready to lose her mother.

She had, of course, considered another possibility: that her mother wasn't dead. That she had instead left them, fed up with domestic life on the farm. Perhaps she even had the intention of retrieving her and Hansel once she was settled into whatever new life she'd found, one that had been blueprinted and dreamed of for years. It wasn't an impossible scenario; her father was no prince, and though he was by no measure evil or abusive, charming and inspiring he was not. It was no great stretch to imagine a woman like her mother trading up when the opportunity arose.

But this prospect, though obviously a better, happier one, didn't fit, and provided little comfort to Gretel. Somewhere within her, she knew the news was grim.

Her father turned off the truck's motor and left the keys in the ignition. He opened the door of the truck and walked to the front door of the cabin where he stood motionlessly, his head hung, staring at the ground in front of his feet.

"We'll go again tomorrow," he said, "when there is light." He then opened the door and walked inside quietly.

Gretel sat in the passenger seat of the truck and stared bleakly through the open car door at the spot where her father had stood just seconds before. The thought of another day combing the emptiness of the Interways was unbearable right now, and she pushed the thought aside. She could only pray that he would change his mind by tomorrow morning and let The System do its work.

But what her father said wasn't as dispiriting as how he was behaving. For starters, he had left Hansel sleeping in the back of the truck, having made no effort even to wake him, let alone carry him inside: something he had done without thinking dozens of times in his life. Her father was still ill, Gretel realized, and his injuries were far from healed and were probably flaring as badly as ever right now, but he hadn't even looked at his son. Hansel was certainly no toddler, of course, he was in fact rather tall and stout for his age, having always been a hearty eater and eager farmhand. But her father had always relished carrying his son to bed, whether from the truck after a long road trip or the large sofa in the den where Hansel liked to sit and read his magazines. It was something Gretel had observed in her father with great interest, even early in her brother's life, since the act was so out of place within her father's overall character.

But she was being too hard on him, perhaps. His wife was gone, and whether through force or by choice, the result for the rest of his life was essentially the same.

Gretel reached down and picked the book off the floor. In the context of the dirt road that made up the front yard of her cottage, the black tome now seemed somehow smaller and incomplete, losing some of its fascination to Gretel. But not all.

The blackness and sterility of it were still mesmerizing—appearing as shadowy in the dim light of the truck as it did on Deda's shelf—and the feel of it, that leathery coldness, remained.

Deda had allowed her to take the book home, and she had only asked to do so because she had seen the look in her grandfather's eyes when he saw her with it, struggling to reach it from the precarious edge of the work bench. His face had burst into the same smile she had seen when they first arrived, only this time his eyes were alert, craving. Instinctively, she had asked for it, feeling that doing so was a preemptive strike of sorts, though what exactly it was she was preempting she didn't know. She had always wanted to take it, of course, but knew on some level that it would be out of place with her outside the realm of the damp cellar. And that now seemed true.

Deda had told Gretel that the title of the book was *Orphism*, and according to him it was older than The Bible; how he knew that fact was unclear, since he claimed to have no idea what the word 'Orphism' even meant or what the book itself was about.

"But your grandmother treasured it," he had told her while they both sat in Deda's small kitchen, having exited the creepiness of the cellar. Deda's smile had been warm as he reflected on his deceased wife. "And it's one of the few possessions of hers that remains. So I have come to treasure it as well." It had seemed so strange to Gretel to be openly discussing the book that for so long had held such mystery, and she felt a bit silly that she had never asked her grandfather about it before. It was only a book after all.

"Why did she love it so much?" Gretel asked.

Deda paused and then said, "It was special to her." His smile waned slightly as he looked away from his granddaughter, appearing disappointed that she had posed such a question. He forced a cough and rose from the table, making his way to the stove and picking up the teapot that sat on the back burner.

The awkwardness of the silence that followed Deda's non-answer was striking, and Gretel had been relieved when her father entered the room. His face was stern and tired. And he had made no acknowledgment of Deda.

"Gretel, we're leaving," he said. "Your brother is in the truck." He turned and walked out, and the subsequent sound of the front door opening and closing had been deafening.

The ride back to the Southlands would be tortuous, Gretel knew, but she had been glad to be leaving.

She'd grabbed the book—Orphism—with both hands and stood up from the table. "Bye Deda," she said and turned to leave, not really expecting a reply. She had come to accept these periods of moodiness and depression in her grandfather over the years, and though her feelings were often hurt by them, she mostly felt sorry for him.

"Your grandmother was an amazing woman," Deda said, his voice crisp and loud, as if he was standing right behind her.

Gretel turned back toward the kitchen and saw Deda standing at the stove, casually firing up the teapot as he was before.

"You, Gretel, would have loved her. And she you."

"Okay, bye," Gretel had managed to stammer, and then quickly walked from the house and into the front seat of her father's truck, which her father had wasted no time shifting out of park and driving away.

Deda's words had been eerie and out of place, Gretel now thought as she tried gently to stir her brother awake. But they were somehow comforting. She had never known her grandmother—she died when Gretel's mother was just a girl—but her mother had always spoken fondly of the woman, and that had always been important to Gretel.

Her mother. Gretel's eyes filled with tears once again. "Hansel."

"We'll never find her like this," he whined. "I want to go home!"

The fruitless searches had clearly traumatized her brother, and Gretel suspected there would be something akin to a revolution tomorrow morning when their father told him the plans for the day.

"We're home, Han. Let's go."

***

The next morning Hansel woke first, followed by Gretel, and they both performed their daily tasks as minimally and quietly as possible, making every effort to ensure their father continued sleeping. And he had, almost until lunchtime, before he finally ventured out to the main area of the house, clumsily fixed a plate of eggs and toast, and retreated back to his room. No mention was made of a search effort, and neither child reminded him.

But Gretel was now torn. With a full night's sleep, in the clarity of the day, she thought her father had been right last night: they had to look for their mother. Who else if not them?

Gretel had been exhausted after the ride from Deda's, and it had made her selfish, but if her mother needed help, and if her father was right about The System not doing anything for days, then of course they had to go look for her! Were they to let her die in a ditch somewhere in the Northlands? No, they had to go.

But go where?

The truth was they had looked in the only place they knew—along the Interways—and though the daylight could certainly be the difference between spotting a footprint in the mud or a stray piece of fabric lingering on a branch, Gretel didn't suspect this would be the outcome. By now, if her mother had crashed the car along that stretch of road—not a major thoroughfare, to be sure, but not empty either—someone would have noticed. Certainly there would be some indication of an accident. She or her father would have seen it. On the way back from Deda's it had been dark and impossible, but driving *to* his house there had been plenty of light, and they had stopped everywhere it seemed. And had found nothing.

What Gretel also knew was there was little chance of getting help from anyone personally. Her father had already made all the calls to friends and family, including even the most fringe members of both sets, and according to him no one had heard anything or was in any position to help. Of course not.

Her mother's extended family consisted of Deda, who apparently offered nothing new during her father's conversation with him (though her father hadn't told Gretel any of the specifics), and the few members left of her father's family were either far away, feeble, or on less-than-stellar terms with her father. In some cases it was all three. The Morgan family—that is, her father's kin—as far as Gretel was concerned, did not extend beyond her family's cabin's walls.

And then there was The System of course, who Gretel, like most children in the Southlands, rarely, if ever, saw. Her father had told her they never patrolled the Back Country unless there was cause or summons, neither of which, if it could be at all helped, occurred here. The land policed itself for the most part, and this value of self-reliance was well-met by The System, who preferred to stay tight to the cities where their oversight was much more condensed and efficient. Whether they were respectful of Back Country rules or indifferent to the plight of its people, The System stayed away.

But they weren't completely foreign to Gretel. She had, in fact, seen their cars on two different occasions, and one of those times had been in the Back Country when the Stein farm had caught fire and Jonathan Stein's grandmother was killed. Gretel recalled the sight of the blood red car racing past her cottage, its siren blazing loudly as the black ghost of the exhaust lingered in the coupe's wake. Gretel had been struck most by the car's color and its stark contrast to the Back Country landscape, and the dark black tint of the windows. She had never actually seen a System officer, but had been told they were men of enormous size.

The reputation of The System was one that inspired fear in the general citizenry, but The System itself kept itself in the shadows as much as possible. They relied on local law enforcement—and in the case of the Back Country, the people—to deal with the lower crimes and complaints, focusing instead on the more serious, complicated situations. This enforcement formula had given The System a somewhat mythical quality for Gretel, as it did for most of the residents of the Southlands, particularly in the Back Country. And Gretel understood very well that this was kind of the point.

But as far as Gretel was concerned, The System was also corrupt and inadequate, and she knew of no incidences when they had actually helped anyone she knew. In fact, if there was one thing she believed about The System, it was that they did not exist to help her, her family, or anyone in her community, though she had come to realize years ago that most of her viewpoints about it were based on her father's beliefs and not her own experiences.

And there was one other thing she now believed about The System: that ultimately she was counting on them to bring her mother home.

So Gretel clung to hope in The System and their rules, which apparently required at least another full day for her mother to remain missing before they began a search. And when they finally did, Gretel guessed, they would do so under the assumption that their mother had left them for bluer skies and a new life, and not that she was in trouble or dead. Okay. That was fine. At least they would be looking. It was more than she and her family were doing now.

Gretel's hatred for her father flared with this thought and again she became disgusted with his lack of masculinity and fortitude. She knew her mother would be doing more for him if the situation were reversed, and even if he was hurting physically this morning—which no doubt he was after the chaos of last night—his wife was missing, and he should never give up.

As if on cue, Heinrich Morgan opened the door to his bedroom and walked out, passing through the kitchen to the porch where Gretel had first heard the news of her mother's absence only yesterday. Yesterday. It seemed like weeks, and Gretel's spirit was momentarily buoyed by the brief time span.

Heinrich put on his boots, still muddy and wet from last night's search, and walked toward the door.

"Where are you going, Papa?" Gretel's voice was calm, sympathetic.

"Check on your brother in a few minutes, Gretel. He's in the fields."

"Where are you going?" she repeated, this time with more urgency.

"You know where I'm going. Check on your brother." Her father opened the door and walked out toward the truck, Gretel right behind him.

"I'll come with you, Papa. Let me help. Last night it was too dark, but today—"

Gretel's words were interrupted by a voice Gretel hadn't heard come from her father's mouth in quite some time.

"You will stay and check on your brother as I've instructed! That is what you will do!" Heinrich frowned and opened his mouth as if to say more, then gingerly stepped up into his old pickup and drove off.

As Gretel watched him drive away, the tears came again in force, though this time in silence. She watched until the truck was out of view, confirming that her father was indeed heading north to the Interways, and then walked back to the house where she sat down on the porch again and began to thumb slowly through her dead grandmother's book.

It was a rather ridiculous waste of time, she thought, looking through the book, since she couldn't read a word of it. But it comforted her and made her feel more connected to her family somehow.

According to Deda, the symbols and letters that made up the text were similar to Ancient Greek, and the book itself contained the practices and mythologies of a religion hundreds of years older than Christianity. How he knew all this without being able to read it was still a bit unclear to Gretel, and her grandfather had deflected the question during their powwow in his kitchen. Clearly he had some familiarity with the language, or perhaps her grandmother did, and had explained it to him. Either way, as Gretel now reflected, he had been holding something back.

Gretel tried once again to decipher the sentences, recognizing that many of the letters in the book were the same as they were in English—the 'A's' and 'N's' and 'T's' and such—but it was all gibberish, and her light-hearted stab at amateur cryptography left her brain sore.

Still, the age of the words and the feel of the book kept her rapt, and she looked through the pages slowly, as if actually reading. The book kept her mind off her mother—and her father for that matter—and she suddenly felt very grateful that her grandfather had encouraged her to take it.

Orphism.

She would research the subject the next time she went to town and could stop in the library. Or maybe she would ask some of her teachers when she returned to school, though she doubted any of them would be familiar with such an exotic text.

If she and her family had still gone to church she would have asked one of the nuns, or perhaps the preacher after Sunday service; certainly they would have some knowledge of a book older than The Bible. But the routine of church-going had come to an abrupt end several years ago, with little forewarning or explanation, and though it was something that Gretel welcomed at first, she had grown to miss church, if only for the gathering of friends.

Gretel read for an hour or so and then closed the book and placed it on her lap. She sat meditatively for a few moments, staring out the window toward the elms in the back, before deciding she had better check on Hansel. Her father had become far too overprotective of her brother lately, Gretel thought, but today she understood.

She took a deep breath and walked outside to the front stoop, leaving the book behind her on the chair. The air had quickly thickened with the emergence of the afternoon sun and the humidity stung her lungs instantly. Gretel looked off toward the fields and saw Hansel sitting in the dirt, playing with one of his many stick creatures that her father had made for him over the years. He was still such a young boy, she thought, and her eyes filled with tears.

Gretel cupped her hands around her mouth and lifted her chin, and as she inhaled to call her brother in from the fields, she noticed the cloud of dust that was rising from the end of the half-mile road that led past the fields to their cottage. It seemed to appear spontaneously, as if suddenly erupting from beneath the ground like a geyser of powder. The glare of the sun reflecting off the particles made it impossible for Gretel to see the source, but as the cloak of earth dissipated she saw the unmistakable red metal explode from the dust and go speeding insanely past Hansel toward the house. It looked as if the devil were coming, Gretel thought. But she knew better.

There was no mistaking it. It was The System.

CHAPTER FIVE

Anika fidgeted and grimaced, then rolled to her back and screamed. Reflexively, her left eye opened and the scream devolved into heavy breathing. She stared searchingly at the beams that ran along the ceiling above her, trying desperately to get her bearings. The daylight shone in from a small lunette window over her bed and illuminated the room, but nothing was familiar.

She touched her head where she had been struck and thought absently that it was probably a good sign of her condition that she even remembered the attack. The feel of her forehead made her dry heave. Her right eye was swollen shut and felt enormous; the entire area around it having the texture of a ripe plum, and probably looking about the same, she imagined. Anika pulled her fingers away from her head and looked at the white doughy substance that caked her fingertips. It had the consistency of batter, and she guessed it to be some type of moist medicinal powder.

Lying on her back, Anika surveyed the room and took note of the accommodations. They were far from charming, or even sterile, but they appeared fairly adequate—the wool blanket, sheeted bed, and apparent medicine on her wound even suggesting she was being nursed. It was a pleasant thought considering the attack she had received. Perhaps whoever assaulted her had done so mistakenly and was now atoning, believing perhaps that Anika was the wild creature she herself had imagined was lurking in the dark of the forest. Or maybe Anika had been unconscious for days and had already been rescued from her assailant.

Neither scenario seemed quite right to Anika, but whoever brought her to the comfort of the bed in which she now lay was certain to reveal himself soon. Her scream moments ago had been wild and echoing and, judging by the sounds of movement and clanging pots outside the door, there was definitely someone else in the house. And smells had begun to seep into the room, incredible smells that filled Anika's mouth with saliva and churned her stomach.

Despite the pain and fatigue gripping her head and muscles, she was eager to get up. Anticipating a rush of pain to her head, Anika lifted herself gently to a sitting position in the bed and pulled the wool blanket off of her lap. Surprisingly, there wasn't much protest from her body, though her head hurt badly, both inside and on the surface. But Anika was now confident she could get to her feet.

She swung her legs toward the floor and immediately felt the jolt of resistance on her right foot. Anika shrieked, immediately thinking someone had grabbed her from beneath the bed. But as she looked down to her feet she saw the black oval links running between the wall and the mattress before ending in a thick metal tube around her right ankle. She was chained.

She kicked her foot once, but there was little slack in the chain, and the effort was feeble. Now in a panic, she quickly cleared the blankets entirely from her legs and grabbed at the metal around her ankle. The clasp itself was fairly loose, but the metal was thick and appeared impenetrable to Anika.

She followed the chain from her ankle to the balled up quilt that had collected at the wall by her feet. She moved the quilt aside, looking down through the gap between the wall and the bed. There she could see a large metal plate with six thick bolts connecting the chain to the floor. She scooted down toward the foot of the bed, gripped the chain tightly with both hands and pulled up, again having no success as the length of the chain offered little leverage. The cold dark metal in her hand conjured thoughts of slavery and brutality, and only some primal sense of survival kept Anika from screaming again, though it was obviously no secret to her captor where she was being held.

A rush of pain shot through Anika's head, and she lay back down, supine, again feeling her wound and the mushy substance that coated it. It then occurred to her that she was indeed being nursed, but she was also a prisoner.

Suddenly the sounds outside the door—'kitchen sounds' is how Anika would come to know them—stopped, and Anika could hear the approaching rap of light footsteps followed by the creaking of her door as it opened slowly. The knob on the door rattled as it turned, and when the door finally opened, Anika could see the flat edge of something black and heavy—cast iron perhaps—emerge through the portal, followed by the white deformed hands that gripped either side of the object.

With only one good eye, Anika first marked the object as some kind of blunt weapon, different than the one that had put her in her current state, but just as medieval and menacing. Her heart began to gallop, and she instinctively got to her knees, raising her arms to shoulder height and width in defense, fingers spread, as if prepared for a Roman wrestling match. And then she began to scream.

Anika's one working eye stayed fixed on the shape in the doorway and, as it began to focus, she realized the object being carried was not a weapon after all, but was, in fact, a tray. With food. A large plate of food.

It was a meal.

With some effort, Anika forced herself to look up from the tray to the face of the person carrying it, but his head was shrouded in a dark hood that was much too large for the figure underneath. He looked like a monk, she thought, and the slow, silent movements through the room only reinforced the image. Anika could only see the tip of the nose and lips—she couldn't identify a face—but as she studied the shape in full, there was no doubt about it: the figure in the robe was a woman.

Anika let out a sigh, if not of relief, at least of the pressure built up in the previous few seconds over the prospect of being raped and tortured. Something bad seemed certain to be looming of course, but at least a sexual assault and murder didn't seem to be in the cards. At least not for now. Instead, it appeared, she was about to be fed.

"Where am I?" Anika asked as sternly as possible, "Why am I chained?" She kept her eyes riveted to the cloaked figure and watched intently as the woman walked toward the corner of the room opposite the bed and set the tray on a thin black wrought iron table.

The woman paused for a moment at the tray, making sure everything was just so, and then stood erect, turning toward Anika and lowering her hood. "Which question would you like answered first?" she said pragmatically, without emotion.

Anika was surprised at the normalcy of the woman's features, expecting something closer to a stereotypical hag from the fairy tales, decrepit and grotesque, slightly green perhaps. In fact, Anika guessed the woman was maybe only twenty years older than she, though her skin appeared more weathered-looking and hardened than that. Anika supposed she would have described the woman as homely, and rather unremarkable in every way, though with a little effort she would have probably cleaned up decently. She did notice, however, her mouth seemed a bit large for her face.

A glint of recognition flashed in Anika's mind, but it was subtle, and Anika hadn't the luxury to pursue it at the moment. "Why am I chained?" she answered.

Without hesitation the woman responded, "You are chained because I don't know you. And though, admittedly, you don't look like much of a threat, I have been robbed by nicer-looking creatures than yourself. With no intended insult of course."

Anika detected an aged quality to the woman's voice, and perhaps an accent that had diminished over time. "So you keep an anchored chain in your bedroom—just in case you meet any strangers?"

The sarcasm wasn't lost on the woman and she smiled, picking up the plate of food and carrying it to Anika's bedside. "This room was at one time used as a slaughterhouse. Some of the instruments remain."

Anika was skeptical of this answer, but decided she would be well-advised not to challenge it; besides, the approaching plate of food quickly became the main subject of her focus. She had literally never been this hungry before, and tears filled her eyes at the prospect of eating.

The woman set the tray down at the foot of Anika's bed and then turned and walked toward the door as if to leave the room.

Anika's eyes were locked in on the three small pies that sat neatly on the tray, the smells arising from them suggesting a combination of both meat and fruit. Anika's throat convulsed in hunger, but as the door opened, she resisted her desires for a moment and said, "Why did you hit me?"

The woman stopped at the threshold of the door, as if surprised at Anika's restraint, and turned back toward the bed. This time the woman did not smile, but instead looked sympathetic, caring. "We all need to eat," she said, and then walked out.

Anika watched her leave, and then dug her fingers into the pie closest to her, shoving irregular pieces into her mouth, barely swallowing between bites. The tastes were delicious, and though Anika realized her hunger probably clouded her judgment, she could think of nothing else she had ever eaten that tasted quite this good. Moments later, before Anika had devoured the last pie, the cloaked woman entered the room again, this time carrying a large black pot.

"Your toilet," she said placing it beside the bed. "Summon me when it needs emptying." The woman turned to leave.

"Wait." Anika shoved the last piece of crust into her mouth. She swallowed the last morsel without chewing it, and then, "Thank you, these were delicious. You're quite talented." Anika was still unsure of the woman's motives, but she figured flattery couldn't hurt. And the pies *really were* amazing.

"You're welcome."

"I'm feeling much better. Food and rest: what better medicine is there?" Anika paused, waiting for some reciprocation to her attempt at rapport. The woman stayed silent. "Perhaps you could show me back to the road." Anika looked down at the chain around her ankle. "Clearly I'm no threat." She snorted a laugh at this last notion.

"You'll need more rest; and your wound will need another application." The woman's tone suggested there would be no further discussion, and she walked quickly to the door, opening it and then pausing. "And the road," she said, "you can see it from here."

***

The next morning Anika woke to the sound of wood being chopped just outside her window. There was a deliberate, grotesque nature to the sound that she had never noticed before, no doubt now occurring to her because of her current circumstances. Her first thoughts were of her children, and then her ankle, and she immediately thrust her leg away from the wall to reveal what she already knew: the chain remained.

The fresh smells from the kitchen continued to drift into her room, and once again her appetite was activated, the memory of last night's pies momentarily nudging its way into her mind. But Anika had eaten heartily only hours ago, and now that her hunger—along with the other necessities of warmth and sleep—had been appeased, the idea of escape strengthened and quickly positioned itself to its proper place at the helm of Anika's concerns. It was clear the woman intended to keep her; what her intentions were beyond that was still the question.

Geographically, Anika was close to the Interways, that much the woman had revealed. In which direction she could find the road she didn't know, but working on that mystery was putting the cart before the horse. As long as she remained chained to the cabin floor, she might as well have been on the moon.

She had already assessed the thick clasp of metal that was wrapped around her leg, and it looked on its face that the only way out of it—other than cutting off her foot—was with a key. Or else an extremely hearty tool, which she doubted would be conveniently resting somewhere nearby.

Instruments from a slaughter house.

Anika knew her share about slaughtering animals, she had been killing chickens since she was younger than Hansel and had never seen anything like the set up in this room. And it wasn't just because of the furniture. A slaughterhouse attached to the main living area? Who would ever design such a thing? What type of person would allow the gore and filth and violent noises that accompanied the killing of animals to be only paces from her kitchen and sleeping quarters? And there wasn't even an entrance to the room from the outside. Why would a woman want to herd filthy pigs and goats through her home when a door built into the wall was a much easier solution? Anika told herself it was possible that the room was originally intended as a bedroom and was later converted to a slaughterhouse, but on some level that theory was even more frightening.

Anika's mind leaped back to the current situation. She needed to get her bearings and plan out what to do next. Was it two days since her accident on the road? That seemed right, but she couldn't be entirely sure. She'd taken a blow to her head—a considerable one—and it was possible she'd been unconscious for longer than a day. Either way, Anika figured the longer she stayed locked in the room, the more her chances of escape diminished. She had to figure something out soon.

She suddenly realized her vision was improved and once again felt the area above her eye. She was astonished at how small it felt, shrunken and compressed and immediately reconsidered the length of time she had been out. She'd received her share of shiners after all—they were an accepted part of life on a farm, particularly as a child—but the injury she'd sustained in the forest was blunt trauma, a deliberate strike with a weapon. And this injury appeared to be healing in a fraction of the time of any normal black eye. She couldn't see her eye, of course, so there was probably still some discoloration, and judging by her fingers, the white paste was apparently still being applied while she slept, but the swelling was virtually gone.

There was no longer any question in Anika's mind that she was being nursed back to health, so perhaps the woman's intentions weren't sinister, just incredibly cautious. Why else would she be healing her? Maybe she really was harmless. Mad and harmless.

Either way, Anika thought, she was being held prisoner, and whether it was for the rest of her life or a few more hours, she had a right to know why. No more stalling or cryptic answers: the next time the woman came to her room, Anika was going to find out what was going on.

A surge of replenishment suddenly filled Anika, and she felt the need to get on her feet. The chain on her ankle was too short for her to dismount and stand beside the open side of the bed, but she thought if she were able to push the bed away from the wall and create a small gap there, she might be able to stand on the inside.

Anika could tell the bed was sturdy and well-made; there was very little wobble in it when she shifted, and it felt dense to the touch. But it also wasn't very big, and she figured with some effort she could scoot the legs just enough.

Anika wedged her right foot in between the wall and the frame of the bed, and with less force than she had expected, was able to leverage her body enough to pry the frame from the wood of the cabin wall, creating a small space between the wall and the thin mattress. She wiggled her foot down toward the floor, the metal clasp just clearing the gap, and moved her body upright.

She was now standing on one foot.

She nudged the bed further away with her right knee and dropped the other foot to the floor. She now stood erect against the wall, the chain snaking limply on the floor at her right foot.

Anika felt the ecstasy in her legs, as well as the weakness and atrophy, and a sudden sense of claustrophobia nipped at her nerves, as though she would lack the strength to regain her position on the bed when the time came. With all the strength in her unbound leg, Anika drove the foot of the bed away from her, pushing out with her left foot and sending it toward the middle of the room. She let out a long steady breath of relief and gave an internal prayer of thanks.

There was now enough space for her to squat and get some stretch in her muscles, so she did this several times, limbering her arms simultaneously with wide, rotating movements. The burn in her thighs and chest was both harsh and relieving, and Anna could sense the blood flowing throughout her body, giving her the alertness and energy she was chasing.

She stooped down again, and this time grabbed the iron hitch that connected the chain to the floor, wriggling it to test its permanence. The fastening was as she suspected, heavy and tight, sturdy in its feel and look, and the eye bolt that connected to the chain was as thick as her finger. She studied the wooden floorboard to which the hitch was connected, judging whether or not—over time of course—she would be able to pry it up, and with it the iron attachment. Anika figured if she could secure any type of tool—a spoon perhaps that the woman didn't notice missing from her empty meal tray—she could hopefully work up the plank. She would still have the problem of a chain around her ankle, but at least she would be mobile. She just needed to reach the road.

But the floorboards seemed solid as well, and even if she were able to get hold of some kind of instrument, with her ankle bound, she wouldn't have the range necessary to jimmy the boards at the proper angles. It was as if the contraption were built for just this purpose, she thought, and with that image Anika gripped the chain tightly with both hands, her knuckles bulging taut and white. In a controlled panic, she began to pull up on the chain, hoping to summon the extraordinary strength that she had always heard existed in everyone, but only erupted at just the right moment during times of crisis.

Her biceps strained as she desperately tried to hold her hands stable around the metal links and lift the chain from its anchor. Or at least bow the floor board slightly, just to give her hope. Her effort, though, was feeble, as her palms, sweaty and slick from both exertion and fear, kept sliding up the metal cable. She needed leverage.

Anika sat down on the floor and faced the wall, her back straight, straddling the square bracket. She wedged her ankles at the juncture where the floor and wall met, the soles of her feet flat against the wall and her toes pointing to the ceiling. She wrapped the chain once around her right wrist and grabbed it with both hands near the anchor. It was a bit awkward with her ankle bound, but she now had the strength of her thighs. Anika pushed her body out with the last of the stamina that remained in her for now.

Nothing. She felt not the slightest movement from the anchor or wood boards.

Defeated, she leaned her head back gently to the bed which was now behind her and closed her eyes, fighting back the tears. The woman would be in soon, would see the bed in the center of the room and the exposed eye bolt, and she would know Anika was trying to escape. Perhaps she already assumed that, but this would be the proof. Maybe the woman would kill Anika right there on the floor, or maybe she would explain everything first, and then kill her. Or let her leave. Either way Anika would know her fate soon.

As if her thoughts had been screamed aloud, Anika heard the chopping sounds outside her window suddenly stop. She waited in fear, breathless, hoping for the sickening thump of metal on wood to resume, having not calculated exactly what the next step in her plan would be.

Other than to survive.

She wasn't ready to die. She thought of her children again, this time less abstractly, conjuring their faces in her mind. Hansel was only a baby, he wouldn't understand. And Gretel. All of the obligations that were Anika's, formed by decisions that she had made willingly since she had left home at seventeen, and that had ultimately shaped her life to this point, would fall to Gretel. It wouldn't just be unfair, it would be an atrocity. Her daughter's future promised value, significance; it wasn't to serve her elderly grandfather in the Back Country, or to spend the remainder of her youth as a surrogate mother to her brother and servant to her father.

This old woman seemed reasonable and lucid, Anika thought, though she was obviously a little askew. If she could maybe evoke some more information from her, possibly find some common ground with the woman to build on, she could buy a little time and figure an escape. Maybe convince the woman to let her go. Anika again thought of the accent. There was something familiar in it, the way the woman cut off the 'Rs', rolling them slightly. It wasn't a sound heard often in this country, but Anika was sure she recognized it, from her childhood perhaps. The memory, however, was faint and seemed to dissolve before she could approach it.

The cabin door thundered closed and the sound rang through Anika's room like a gunshot. She needed to arrange the room back to normal. She wasn't ready to die. Not yet. If she hurried she could pull the bed back to the wall and the woman would never know she was up, scheming.

The usual sounds of clanging pots and plates that seemed never to stop for long rattled outside Anika's door. The woman was cooking again, probably Anika's breakfast. There was still time. From her knees, Anika stretched her left arm toward the right rear post of the bed, and was able to grab it, wrapping her fingers around the adorning iron bulb. The chain on her ankle limited her reach, but Anika was able to use it for leverage to pull the bed back in. The bed was heavy on its return, but she was able to slide it slowly on the wooden floor, being careful not to make too much noise.

The sounds in the kitchen stopped, and the ensuing silence unnerved Anika, as if someone was waiting, listening. She had five or so more planks to navigate before the bed would be back to its original place, though even if she had all day she wouldn't have the leverage to get it flush against the wall again. She would have to leave a gap to get out and back on the mattress, and she certainly couldn't push the bed while on top of it. That was fine, it would be close enough.

The lull from the kitchen suddenly erupted into one last *Clang!*, as if a dozen dishes were dumped in a heap into a basin, and then the now familiar footsteps began to click quickly down the hall. Anika didn't have the bed repositioned yet, it was still slightly diagonal, and there were more planks to go; if the woman walked in now, the crookedness would be obvious to her.

Ignoring the noise it would make, and with her full effort, Anika yanked the top of the post, pulling the bed toward her like a rower on a Viking ship. It slid with less resistance than Anika had anticipated, leaving her off balance, and making it impossible for her to offset the effect of the clawed foot at the bottom of the right post catching on a slightly raised floor plank.

The bed almost turned entirely over on top of Anika, but instead rocked back to its side, forming a trench-like barrier in front of her, as if she had taken cover in preparation for a bomb blast.

Anika felt a fearful laughter well up inside of her, but resisted it, pushing the bed back on all fours, and missing by only inches the woman who now stood in front of her.

Anika screamed and recoiled, her back slamming forcefully against the solid wall.

The woman stood staring at Anika for a moment, expressionless, as if watching fish in an aquarium. There was no detectable sense of anger in her face, and Anika stared back at her, keeping eye contact and trying to gauge her next move.

The woman smiled slightly at Anika, and then made a peek over the bed, making sure Anika was still bound and hadn't somehow escaped the shackles. The look was warm and playful, and Anika felt a compulsion to smile back, but resisted. Instead she said, "I have to go. My children are—"

"What are their ages?" she interrupted. "Your children, what are their ages?"

Anika paused, weighing the consequences of revealing this seemingly benign fact. "Fourteen and eight," she replied. "My daughter is fourteen and my son is eight."

"Only two?" The woman looked away as if annoyed at this answer, and then rhetorically asked, "When did women stop having children?"

Anika was well past feeling insulted, and instead experienced a twinge of encouragement from the common ground they seemed to have found. "How many do you have?" she asked.

The woman's eyes seemed to flicker at the question, and Anika noticed the slightest downturn at the edges of her mouth.

"Certainly you have children?" Anika was almost challenging in her tone and knew it was a gamble; but the woman showed interest in *her* children, and whatever wound Anika may have opened on the matter she figured she could sew up on the back end. She wanted to keep the woman talking.

"I don't," the woman responded, clearly not interested in telling her own story.

"Really? When did women stop having children?" Anika forced a laugh, hoping to convey a sense of camaraderie and not insolence.

The woman turned back toward Anika, her eyes wide and focused, a slight smile forming at the edges of her mouth as if amused at Anika's boldness. "At one time I had six," she said. "They've all been dead many years."

Anika felt the blood rush to her face, a reaction indicative of both fear and embarrassment. Her stomach convulsed and she felt like vomiting."I'm sorry," she whispered. "I didn't mean..." Wide-eyed, Anika watched the woman's face, hoping she would say something—anything—to fill the empty space where Anika's words should have been, thereby letting her off the mat.

But there was only silence, and the woman continued her cold stare, forcing Anika to drop her gaze to the floor.

Finally Anika looked up and said, "Are you going to kill me?"

The woman considered the question for a moment, seeming to give it sincere thought, and then said, "Why are you here?"

Somewhat relieved, Anika digested the question, took a deep breath, and replied, "I was attacked...you attacked me and..."

"No!" the woman yelled.

The word was shrill and reflexive, causing Anika to flinch, and for the first time since she had been here, Anika saw in the woman the first real evidence of derangement. She'd assumed from the beginning it was there, of course, waiting restlessly underneath all the properness and hospitality, waiting for any imbalance to release it. And now here it was surfacing, from little more than a wrong answer.

"Why am I here?" Anika asked.

"No! No! I asked you, 'Why are you here?' Answer the question!" The woman was screaming now, enraged, her lips curling back from her teeth with every word, revealing the huge, dirty gray and brown triangles that clustered in her gums.

Anika coughed nervously and began to cry softly. She could feel the nausea again rising in her throat. What were those teeth? she thought. Oh my God, they were inhuman!

She felt hysteria coming on and realized she had to get control. Panic would just feed into the woman's outrage and that might just wrap things up for good. Anika thought again of her children. What answer was the woman looking for?

Anika took another deep breath and closed her eyes for a moment, and then opened them and said, "I was in a car accident."

She said the words stoically, looking directly into the woman's eyes, as if she had known all along this was the answer the woman wanted. She felt empowered on some level, though she couldn't have said why.

"My car went off the road," she continued, "and I went for help. I got lost in the forest."

Anika measured each word, each syllable, as if writing a sonnet, careful not to get the meter wrong. It was working. The woman was riveted, as if she were a child listening to a knight's tale. But there wasn't much more to tell without getting into the details, and somehow Anika didn't think the woman was interested in her muddy shoes.

What else? Just give the facts, she thought, and then said, "So I screamed for help."

The woman's eyebrows perked up at this last bit of the story, and a broad smile curved up her cheeks. Anika again shuddered and stopped talking. She felt lucky to have said this much without upsetting her captor. She didn't want to push it.

The woman's eyes softened on Anika, and she tilted her chin down slightly, cocking her head to the side, as if sympathizing with a petulant child who needed only to sleep to be right again. "You need more rest..." she began and then paused, "Angela?"

"Anika. How...how did you know my name?"

"Evidently I didn't."

"Yes, but...you were very close. How did you know?"

"I'll be in shortly with your breakfast. If you displace your furniture again, I will cut off your hands."

Anika felt a chill from the threat, but realized she had little to lose now. "You never answered my question. Are you going to kill me?"

"The proper word is 'Slaughter,' Anika," the woman replied. "One does not 'kill' an animal, one slaughters it."

CHAPTER SIX

Gretel finally exhaled, and then began to hyperventilate. She knew instinctively the car was not headed toward any fire this time: that car was headed for her.

"Oh my God," Gretel managed to whisper, and her eyes shifted desperately from the approaching red machine to her brother. "Oh my God! Hansel!" she screamed, "Hansel come in now!"

Hansel jerked up quickly, and Gretel could tell by his posture that he recognized immediately the panic in her voice. She regretted frightening him, but if she had been casual in her summons, she would have surely wasted time arguing with her brother about staying out for just a few more minutes.

Gretel wasn't quite sure why she was so afraid for her brother—after all, it was the police that were heading toward them, not a herd of buffalo—or why she wanted him to come home to begin with; if the approaching System officer was a real threat, Hansel would have been safer staying in the fields. But Gretel wanted her brother with her, instinctively, as a mother would her child.

Hansel watched in awe as the speeding blaze of metal passed him, barely slowing as it turned toward the house. He heard his sister's voice again and the spell was broken; he was now running with frenzy toward Gretel, leaving the homemade toys behind him in the field.

Gretel watched as the car pulled to a stop about twenty yards from the front of the house where it sat idling for several minutes. She realized she had never seen a System car from the front before, or from such a close distance, and she was mesmerized by it. It seemed massive to her. Not in its length or height, necessarily, but in its bulk, the way a cow doesn't look very large from the road—it's only when one stands next to it that its size is appreciated. And the headlights were like nothing she had ever seen, they were huge and elliptical, with the organic quality of staring eyes that Gretel guessed must have been the intention of the engineer. The grill was cased in solid black with silver plates running vertically along the front where, again, the resemblance to teeth on a living face was undeniable. The car reminded Gretel of a squinting dragon.

She stood motionless on the porch staring wide-eyed at the hulking red machine, only raising her arm slightly to take in her brother as he finally lumbered up beside her. The size of the car and the deep rumbling of the idling engine made Gretel think of a bull sizing up a bullfighter, only instead of the confidence of a matador, Gretel was frozen with fear. The System was there to help—to find her mother—that was their job; but it all felt wrong, and Gretel couldn't help feeling terrified.

"Who is that, Gretel?" Hansel asked, not taking his eyes off the car.

Her brother was fairly composed, Gretel thought, given the menacing mass of metal that loomed in his front yard.

"Is it The System?"

Gretel cleared her throat. "Yes," she replied with a feeble attempt at confidence.

"We should get Father. Is he awake?"

"He's gone. He went to look for Mother."

Hansel glanced toward his sister, who intercepted his look before he could draw some horrible conclusion.

"He'll be back soon. He just wanted to search again in the daylight. You saw how impossible it was last night."

This seemed to assuage whatever worry was brewing in Hansel, and he focused again on the current circumstances. After a moment he said, "Maybe they know something about Mother."

Gretel knew The System had come there about her mother, obviously, but she assumed it was to get information. A photograph, a description of what her mother was wearing, who her friends were, things like that. Information to help them in their search. Admittedly, Gretel even had a thought while she stood gawking at the car that they had come to question Father about his role in her mother's disappearance, though his alibi was indisputable. What she hadn't considered, however, was that they had come with news. "Yes. Maybe."

The prospect of answers turned Gretel's fear into tempered anticipation, though she realized that if the car was indeed bringing news, it almost certainly wasn't good. Otherwise, she figured, they would have called. Or brought her mother home. Wasn't that how it was done? She had seen bad news delivered that way in movies after a soldier had been killed in battle or a child had gone missing.

The eagerness for closure was now strong, and Gretel considered approaching the car. It was parked on her property, after all, and she would have been in her perfect right walking up to the cloudy black driver's side window and knocking delicately on the glass.

But that didn't feel right. It seemed rather dangerous in fact, and Gretel now imagined her face pressed down in the dirt driveway with the barrel of a pistol digging into the back of her skull. No, she would stay put for now. Even her father, Gretel suspected, wouldn't have been so bold as to approach a System car without being ordered to do so. If The System sent a car this far out to the Back Country, they obviously did so for a reason, and it wasn't for the purpose of parking outside her house to do nothing. Whatever they had to bring—whether it was questions or news—they would bring it eventually.

"Let's go inside."

Gretel put her arm around her brother's neck and led him back into the house, glancing over her shoulder at the snoring metal beast as she did so. Hansel clucked softly in protest but followed his sister, and once inside immediately dashed to the front window to continue his surveillance.

"Hansel! Get away from there," Gretel scolded.

Ignoring his sister, Hansel pressed his face against the glass and cupped his hands around his eyes. "Why are they not coming out of the car? What are they waiting for?"

"They're probably gathering papers and things," Gretel replied, "and reviewing our case. So they know what questions to ask."

Hansel pulled his face from the window, as if detecting a tone of insincerity in his sister's voice, and stared at Gretel. "Is she dead, Gret?"

Gretel could see the welling of tears in Hansel's eyes and the large lump that formed and then disappeared in his throat, and she knew this was the first time her brother had accepted the possibility that his mother was not coming home. She felt remorse at having triggered this truth in him, wishing her acting had been a bit better. But ultimately she knew this acceptance would help to soften the slamming news if it was indeed coming.

She reached out to her brother, beckoning him and took him into her arms, holding him as the muffled sobs erupted into her belly. "No, Han," she said, "I don't think she is."

Gretel closed her eyes and rested her cheek on top of her brother's head, rocking him gently as his tears poured into her shirt. She shushed him halfheartedly, but only to convey her compassion, not in any way to stifle his crying. She wanted him to cry as long as he needed.

The siblings stood embraced by the window for several minutes, and Gretel temporarily forgot about the mysterious officer watching their home. She considered instead the answer she had given Hansel: that her mother wasn't dead. Did she really believe that? Was her mother alive somewhere, unharmed? She had no reason to believe that, but in the pit of her heart, she knew it was true. No scenario had emerged in her mind over the past twenty-four hours to logically support that belief, but she believed it anyway. And if she was wrong—and the longer her mother stayed missing, the likelihood that she was wrong grew—then she'd be wrong. But until then, she'd go with her instincts and keep hope close.

Gretel opened her eyes and gasped at the figure walking toward her house. He was coming. Finally. She released Hansel from her clutches and placed her hands on his shoulders as he turned toward the focus of his sister's stare.

Gretel and Hansel inched closer to the window for a clear view and watched as the man approached slowly, almost leisurely, seeming to take inventory of the surroundings of the house. He was a law officer, of course, an investigator, so his interest in the house wasn't by itself unusual, but the insouciance of his mannerisms were so unlike anything resembling 'official' that if Gretel had seen this man walking on the street somewhere, or in a park, she would have guessed him drunk.

The two children watched the man disappear from view as he neared the front door and then waited in silence, listening to his footsteps on the porch stairs. The two loud raps on the door that followed, though expected, were startling, and Hansel couldn't suppress a yelp.

"Stay here," Gretel said, as she walked to the door, turning back to her brother before opening it. "Remember, he's here to help us."

Hansel nodded meekly to his sister, and then Gretel lifted her head, threw back her shoulders, and opened the door slowly. For the first time in her life, she stood face to face with The System.

The officer stood with precise posture in the doorway, respectfully distant from the entrance. He wasn't particularly large in stature, certainly not to the degree that the myths perpetuated System officers—Gretel guessed he was probably shorter than her father. And neither was there anything in his dress that inspired fear; in contrast to the car he drove, his clothes were rather customary. In fact, his overall appearance had a rather retroactive quality that was comforting.

"Good afternoon," he said smiling. "My name is Officer Stenson."

The words came out quietly, but unmistakably clear, as if he were disclosing very important information in the stacks of a library. He presented a small metal shield—which might just as well have been a dead fish as far as Gretel was willing to question his authority.

"I'm looking for Heinrich Morgan," the man continued. "Does he live here?"

"Yes," Gretel squeaked, somewhat pleased with herself that she was able to manage even a word.

"May I speak with him?"

Officer Stenson stood casually now, leaning slightly forward with his hands clasped behind his back. He was clearly making an attempt at coming across friendly, and Gretel thought he was doing an excellent job.

"No," Gretel replied. She stared unblinkingly at the man, on some level expecting him to eventually morph into the robotic giant that she had envisioned since her earliest memories.

The System officer held his smile and raised his eyebrows slightly, as if humored by the precociousness of the adolescent girl in front of him. "No?"

"I mean, he's not home. He left."

Officer Stenson frowned and stared to his right, as if thinking about what to do with such a perplexing answer. He turned back to Gretel and said, "May I ask your name, young lady?"

Gretel paused, and then with a bit of a defiant stare said, "Yes."

The officer stood waiting, and then realizing she had answered his question, threw back his head in laughter.

There was a glowing sincerity to the officer's face and movements, and Gretel couldn't help but smile herself. Something about this man she liked instinctively, but there was something deeper she remained cautious of. Perhaps, she considered, it was just his position as a System officer.

Officer Stenson composed himself, exhaling the last few chuckles from his chest, and then, nodding approvingly, said, "You're a smart girl. I should think you'll have all the boys under your command very shortly."

Gretel blushed.

"In fact, my son is about your age, perhaps I should drag him out of the car so you can help get *him* under control. I certainly can't seem to do it."

He laughed again at the answer the girl had given, and Gretel peeked behind him, amazed at the fact that there was both a boy her age in that devil-car in her front yard, and that this man in front of her was old enough to have such a child. He looked half her father's age.

The officer took note of Gretel's stare. "Ah yes, my son. That's why I was so long outside. He's had some trials lately."

Gretel detected a flare in the officer's eyes, but it evaporated as quickly as it rose.

"Now, more directly this time, young lady, what is your name?"

"Gretel," she replied with a smile of satisfaction. "Gretel Morgan."

"Gretel. Morgan." The officer wrote each name down with great concentration, maintaining a very formal demeanor, and this made Gretel laugh out loud. "Well, Gretel Morgan, do you know when..." Officer Stenson caught himself this time. "When will your father be back?"

"I don't know." Gretel frowned. "He went to look for my mother." Gretel looked away from the officer, suddenly flooded with the reminder of why he was here.

Gretel looked back toward the man, who had now assumed a slightly crouched position, bringing himself to her eye level. "Gretel," he said solemnly, "may I come in?"

Whatever fear Gretel had for the officer was now all but gone, and she figured that if he had come to hurt her, he could have done so at any time. She opened the door wide and stepped aside, and Officer Stenson entered, immediately catching sight of the anxious boy standing statue-like in the kitchen.

Gretel walked quickly toward her brother, framing her arms around him. "This is my brother Hansel."

Officer Stenson gave a delicate nod toward the boy, looking him squarely in the eye. The man reminded Gretel of someone who has encountered an unfamiliar dog and is trying to gauge its temperament based on the slight signals of posture and expression. There was an inferred tension in the silence, and Gretel could feel the distrust in her brother's body.

"It's all right, Han. This is Officer Stenson."

Hansel looked at his sister, and then back to the man. "Why is Officer Stenson all right?" he replied, maintaining the stare of a gunfighter, if not the confidence.

"Because he's here to help us," she replied, but immediately realized that the officer had not yet actually stated his reason for being there, and she was ready to get to the matter. "Isn't that right, Officer Stenson? You're here about our mother?"

The officer looked toward Gretel and then back to the boy. "I am," he said. "Is there somewhere we can sit down?"

***

Perched paternally on a weathered leather ottoman, Officer Stenson sat opposite the two children, who waited anxiously side by side on the sofa in the living room. Gretel recalled how she and her brother had sat this way countless times over the years, listening to their father's stories—or, occasionally, his scoldings—and Gretel felt a sort of comfort in this reverie. This man in front of her wasn't her father, but he was a protector by trade, and that was important right now.

The officer clasped his hands together and frowned, and then looked down at the floor, gathering his thoughts before beginning. "Normally I would wait for your father, but you both seem to understand the situation at hand, and I'll need to leave soon." Officer Stenson paused. "First of all, we haven't found your mother."

He stared intently at the children's faces, waiting, and Gretel could see the uncertainty in his eyes, realizing the news could be taken either way. Gretel instinctively reached over and grabbed her brother's hand, giving it a reassuring squeeze.

"We're searching the portion of the Interways that lead to your..." the officer lingered on the 'r' and pulled a small notebook from his breast pocket, flipping it open to the proper spot, "...grandfather's house. If something happened along that stretch, we'll know."

"You mean an accident?" Gretel said.

"Yes, an accident." And then, "Or if the car was abandoned."

"You mean like if the car broke down and she left it there? Why would she do that?"

"I don't know Gretel, she probably didn't. It's just a possibility that we need to think about."

"Do people do that a lot?" Gretel hadn't really thought about this as an explanation, but now that the officer had mentioned it the hope she'd kept ablaze flickered higher.

"No," Officer Stenson said without hesitation, "not a lot. But on that stretch of road there is very little traffic and there have been instances of people leaving to look for fuel or a phone to call for help."

The hope fire rose higher.

"But honestly, Gretel, we're not hopeful of that being the case with your mother. We've driven the route—I drove a large portion of it myself—we would have found the car."

Gretel closed her eyes and frowned. The scenario of her mother leaving for help wasn't completely unthinkable to Gretel. Her mother wasn't exactly what Gretel would describe as hearty, but she was a survivor, and if walking the countryside for help was the practical solution to a situation—like being stranded on the road—she would have pursued it. On the other hand, the officer had a point: if she had left the road for help, where was the car?

"Maybe the car was towed away?"

"The car would only be towed from the Interways under System direction, and no request was put in. Look, Gretel, we know what to look for and we're looking for it."

Gretel detected a hint of agitation in Officer Stenson's voice, and she blushed, embarrassed now that she had presumed to know more than the man in front of her.

Officer Stenson grabbed Gretel's hand. "You're obviously a very smart girl, Gretel, and I do need your help to find your mother. So perhaps I can ask you the questions and you can give me the answers?"

Gretel smiled weakly at the compliment and nodded.

"And Hansel, I'll need your help too." The officer took a masculine tone with the boy, curt and direct. "Will you help me?"

Hansel nodded bravely, seriously, eager to play a role in solving the puzzle.

Before the officer uttered the first syllable of his question, a voice boomed through the house, thunderously, as if God Himself had spoken. "Hansel, go to your room."

The voice was calm, even-toned, but the energy in the words nearly knocked the wind from Gretel's chest. It had come invisibly from somewhere behind the walls of the kitchen.

Father.

He appeared slowly in the entryway, locking his eyes on the stranger holding court with his children. He stood tall and still, his eyes narrowed. There wasn't quite rage in her father's face, Gretel thought, it was something closer to disgust. The way one might look at a person who has once again violated a recently regained trust. She was thankful that his hands were unclenched and visible at his sides; if there had been a gun in one of them, it wouldn't have surprised her.

Officer Stenson smoothed the creases in his pants and stood, and Hansel scuttled off to his room. Gretel shifted her eyes between the two men and began to follow her brother toward the back of the house.

"Gretel," her father barked, "stay here."

Heinrich Morgan stuffed his hands in his pockets and walked toward Officer Stenson, a passive-aggressive casualness in his demeanor, stopping only inches from The System officer. Gretel's jaw hung loosely at her father's boldness, both by his irreverence toward The System and the contrasting display of masculinity as compared to the withering he'd shown the day before. He had perhaps gone over the edge, Gretel thought, and this frightened her. She sat back down on the couch, a spectator to whatever would unfold.

"Mr. Morgan," the officer began, "my name is Officer Stenson. I'm with the fourth division of the Southlands System. I'm here about your wife, Anika."

Officer Stenson's voice was deep and clear, unaffected by the intrusion. The leisurely softness he had shown toward the children was now a sterile recitation of business. He stared directly into the eyes of the man before him, never blinking, and his mouth showed not the hint of a smile. This, Gretel thought, was The System of which her father had spoken.

"Really?" Gretel's father replied sarcastically. "You're here about my wife?" He laughed. "No doubt it was the first case on the docket this morning."

"Mr. Morgan..."

"Why are you here?" Gretel's father growled.

"You called us, Mr. Morgan."

Gretel recognized her father's smile at this response as one of sincere amusement.

"I was born in the Back Country, Officer Stenson, have lived here my whole life, and I've seen The System here maybe four times in those years. System officers don't show up to a person's home lightly—anywhere in the Southlands—never mind in the Back Country. I called you only yesterday because my wife went missing—not from here but from along the Interways—and yet here you are at my house speaking to my children? So I'll ask you again, why are you here?"

Gretel sat riveted as she watched Officer Stenson hold her father's stare and then look away, frowning. Clearly, there was more to tell.

The officer smiled sympathetically. "I understand how upset you must be Mr. Morgan, so perhaps this isn't the best time. And anyway, I haven't the time tonight to do a proper interview. I'll be in contact with you in a day or so—by phone. I'll show myself out."

He walked toward the door and then stopped with his hand on the knob, turning back toward the living room. "And Mr. Morgan, I may have some questions for you concerning the nature of your relationship with Mrs. Morgan. Domestic problems. Things like that."

"Leave my house, Officer Stenson."

Officer Stenson opened the door, looking past his newly-acquired enemy to the flabbergasted girl sitting on the couch. "Goodbye Gretel," he said. "You're a very charming young lady. I hope to talk with you again soon. Maybe you'll meet my son one day."

He left and closed the door behind him, the uncomfortable silence that lingered finally broken by the sound of Heinrich Morgan walking slowly toward his room, holding his side as he went.

The burping eruption of the engine starting outside made Gretel lurch: Officer Stenson awakening the sleeping dragon. Gretel examined again the mismatch between the demon car that approached her like a deranged Visigoth and the rather even-mannered man that controlled it. The opposition was almost comical. The officer had spoken to Hansel and her with such consideration and ease, without even the hint of an angle or condescension, while at the same time maintaining an authority that was without question. But Gretel had also glimpsed the nettles beneath the placidness, and intuitively knew to remain skeptical of anyone who could change his demeanor with such little effort.

She sat motionless on the sofa, waiting anxiously for the diminishing sounds of gravel crackling beneath rolling tires indicating the car's departure. But the idling rumble of exhaust endured for several minutes; evidently more business with the delinquent son. Or perhaps a transmission was being sent requesting backup for the arrest of one Heinrich

Morgan. Gretel hoped it wasn't the latter for the obvious reasons, but also because she knew her father wasn't well, and jail was the last place he needed to spend the night.

The soft knock on the window above the sink made Gretel shriek, and she covered her mouth with her hands. Her nerves were threadbare, and she momentarily doubted the prism of a face in the window over the sink. She stood and walked cautiously to the window, where the face of a dark-haired boy, frowning, came into focus. He lifted his hand to the window and pointed to the door.

Gretel walked toward the door and she could see outside that the boy was following her lead. She was more curious than apprehensive, and so opened the door, instantly meeting the eyes of, unquestionably, the most exquisite looking person she had ever seen in the flesh.

It wasn't just his face, which as far as Gretel could tell was flawless, it was that the boy seemed to be a perfect amalgamation of all the qualities one calculates in defining a person's attractiveness. His cheekbones and shoulders were high and broad, and the shape of his mouth and nose seemed to be transposed from a Roman statue. Even the way he stood was just right, with his feet shoulder width apart and hands behind his back, his head tilted slightly forward in cool humility. Even his clothes fit him perfectly. Only in magazines had she seen people of such beauty.

The boy gave a shy grin and rolled his eyes, embarrassed. "Sorry, hi," he said, "my, uh, Dad sent me to get his binder. He says he left it on the floor next to the ottoman."

"His binder?" Gretel remained locked on the boy, and her words came out robotic like she had been bewitched by an evil master and was repeating a benign test phrase to make sure the spell had taken.

The boy was her age, maybe a year older, and the exotic combination of dark curls and cold blue eyes were the stuff of key-locked diaries, so atypical in this land of straight blond hair and pink cheeks. She was transfixed.

"Yeah, you know, like his notebook thing." The boy mimed his hands in the shape of the object.

"Oh. Okay." Gretel opened the door. "Come in."

The boy shifted his eyes and looked back at the waiting car, and then stepped through the door; clearly he had expected the girl to just bring him the binder. Gretel noticed the action and blushed, but it was too late to rescind the invitation.

He took a tentative step inside the house and, spotting the ottoman in the next room, walked quickly toward it, recovering the binder and tucking it under his arm. He lingered a moment in the living room and looked at Gretel. "It obviously isn't any of my business or anything, but was he able to help you?"

"I'm sorry?" Gretel responded automatically. It was more a delay tactic than a misunderstanding of the question.

"My father. Did he help you with whatever he came here for?"

Gretel considered the question a moment. "He helped me feel a bit better, I suppose, but my mother's gone missing, and there's been no sign of her since early yesterday." Gretel glanced toward the back bedrooms and lowered her voice, "And my father told him to leave."

The boy nodded thoughtfully, and Gretel could see him mentally catalog her case. As the son of a System officer, Gretel supposed stories like hers were as common as the sunrise.

"I'm sorry," he said.

The words were unexpected, and they hit Gretel like an iron pan. They were the first true words of sympathy she'd heard since her family's recent implosion, and it took every bit of composure not to run to the boy, throw her arms around him, and pour her tears onto his shoulder.

"Thank you," she murmured instead, clearing her throat much louder than she'd intended. And then, changing the subject to thwart any oncoming wave of emotions said, "Do you ride with your father often?"

The question was a perfect change of pace, and a proud surge of butterflies danced in Gretel when the boy smiled. It was an adult comment, something her mother would have said.

"Almost never. And certainly not if I can help it." He paused, and his smile flattened. "I've had some trouble with schools lately...always really, and my parents are sending me off in the fall. Boarding school. Outside the city."

The boy shifted his eyes around the house, as if indicating its simplicity and rusticness.

"Not quite this far off, I guess, but near the edges of the Back Country. There's an academy for boys there—The Hengst Academy?"

Gretel shook her head and shrugged. Never heard of it.

"Well, anyway, I'll be starting there in the fall, I suppose. If my interview today was acceptable."

He stopped for a moment and looked at nothing, seeming to consider his life after the summer.

"So anyway, my father said he'd gotten a new case that was out this way and he needed to stop here before we went home. Though, truthfully, your house is quite out of the way."

That was the second jab the boy had tossed at Gretel about where she lived. The first she ignored, but now she was suddenly insulted and angry at the implications. That this land was somehow outside the borders of consideration. And how could anyone possibly survive in such territory? It was an attitude that was by no means new to Gretel—condescension toward Back Country folk, if not outright discrimination, was routine behavior from Urbanists. But she was in her own house and she'd be damned if she would take it here and—especially—now.

"What is your name?" Gretel's voice was steel, though her face showed no sign of bitterness.

"Petr," the boy replied, "Petr Stenson." He flashed his perfect smile at Gretel, pleased she had asked.

Gretel countered with a sarcastic half-smile of her own and said, "Well now that you've gotten your father's things Petr Stenson, please leave my home."

Petr's face twisted into an expression of confusion and humor, not quite sure if the girl was serious. "Did I say something..?"

"You don't know better, none of you do," Gretel clipped. "Goodbye."

Petr stepped past Gretel out the door, and Gretel followed him onto the porch, standing defiantly with her arms crossed as she watched the boy descend the porch, a look of bemused bewilderment on his face. He took a few steps toward the waiting car and stopped, looking back at Gretel.

"Just so you know, Gretel," he said in a way that Gretel could only describe as sad, "and I'm not sure why I'm telling you this." Petr paused, "but I don't think he's here to help you. I know he probably seemed that way. He does that very well."

Without hesitation, Gretel snapped back, "Well what is he here for then?"

Petr scanned Gretel's body, starting from her feet and working his way up. He then moved his head in a slow arc from left to right, up and down, studying the house and its surroundings, letting his eyes drift over each wooden beam and crooked branch and lowly piece of gravel, suspicious of everything, as if the answer to her question might be found in any one of the millions of insignificant objects that composed the Morgan property.

"I don't know," he said finally, shaking his head slowly, pausing for just a moment in the event the answer appeared at that last moment of surrender. "I don't know."

Gretel opened her mouth to speak but couldn't invoke a word, and she stood that way as she watched Petr Stenson walk back to the car and the red metal rocket speed down her driveway toward the Interways.

CHAPTER SEVEN

"You're looking much better Heinrich, but now it's time for rest."

The young nurse walked from Heinrich Morgan's room and gently shut the door, the smile on her face evaporating instantly. Gretel had witnessed this transformation in the woman's look almost daily since her arrival almost two months ago, and it made Gretel wince every time. It wasn't a cruel gesture—the frown—Lord knew that if anyone could sympathize with the woman's duties it was Gretel—but there seemed to be something beyond fatigue and frustration in her face, something measured. Maybe it was hate. But if it was, Gretel couldn't even say she didn't understand that.

Odalinde Merth had come to the Morgan house as a part-time nurse and had stayed well beyond the time Gretel originally imagined. She was certain her father would have improved to normal health by now, since that day Gretel had found him sprawled on the kitchen floor clutching his belly, blood streaming from his mouth. And though Gretel obviously appreciated the care Odalinde was giving her father, it struck her as unusual that the nurse remained with them. Not only had her work proven ineffective in recuperating her patient—a sign that it's probably time to move on—as far as Gretel could tell, she also wasn't receiving any pay for her work. As it was, the money wasn't enough for food to sustain the three of them, let alone pay for the services of a private nurse. Since their mother had vanished, Gretel and her brother usually went without at least one meal a day, and occasionally two. Perhaps a deferment arrangement had been made and Odalinde would collect payment for her nursing activities when times improved, but it was simply impossible that she was being paid now.

Heinrich Morgan's previously damaged spleen had flared and lacerated the first day Gretel and Hansel had returned to school after their mother's disappearance. Gretel had arrived home that day to find her father collapsed in a half-naked ball of flesh at the threshold between the kitchen and porch, and on first glance, seeing only the back of him, Gretel would have sworn he was dead. His motionless body was contracted, fetal-like, his arms clutched around his torso as if trying to stay warm. Gretel had stood staring at the lifeless heap on the floor, and almost instantly began preparing for her new life as an orphan, which she supposed would play out in the Northlands with Deda. It would be a hard adjustment, and Gretel knew that though he would take them in, Deda would be reluctant to assume the burden of children so late in life. But they would survive, and Gretel would take on the duties of raising her brother. There were worse lots in life to be sure, particularly for orphans in the Back Country, and Gretel swelled with an unlikely feeling of gratitude. She would take care of Hansel and Deda, and that would be the way it was.

The moan from the floor had frightened Gretel back to reality, and she quickly re-focused. Her father wasn't dead. She ran to him, stepping over his body and kneeling down to examine his face, which was bloated with pressure and contorted in pain. He was struggling to breathe, not because of any blockage in his windpipe, but because of the agony that breathing induced. Gretel could see the dried blood on his lips and chin, and when a weak coughing breath finally escaped his lungs, she could see the blood was coming from somewhere inside her father's body.

Gretel's next thought was that Hansel would be home soon, and she would have to mitigate the trauma caused by seeing his father in this condition, so vulnerable, sprawled unnaturally on the floor. Looking back on it now, she remembered that her instincts had been sharp that day, clear and unhesitating, and she was proud of the perfect steps she had taken: dialing the doctor's number from memory, repositioning her father and covering him with blankets, encouraging him to breathe. Hansel was certainly scared when he finally saw his father that day, but Gretel was all smiles and stoicism, and easily calmed him with the promise that everything would be fine.

And it *had* turned out fine, with Gretel the hero. The doctor later credited Gretel with saving her father's life through a combination of quick action and shock reduction. But, truthfully, she hadn't really surprised herself at all: the world had unleashed upon Gretel the most lethal of blows—taking her mother—and Gretel had endured. She had thrived, in fact, and the scar tissue of the wound now insulated her from both terror and hysteria. It was her role now, she realized, to be nurturer and parent, and what she had been consciously unprepared to do a few short months ago when her mother first vanished, nature had activated within her.

And that had been the difference: the newly-nested concept that something else in the universe was in control of such important matters.

Odalinde glanced up at Gretel and then looked away immediately. "Gretel," she said, the smile on her face unable to cloak the disdain in her voice.

"Hello, Odalinde," Gretel replied in a similar tone, keeping her eyes on the woman as if challenging her to a conversation. The exchanges between the women had devolved to become strictly perfunctory, and if the nurse remained much longer, Gretel knew they would cease entirely.

But Gretel had considered that end unacceptable—Odalinde had become far too friendly with Father in such a short time, and there were too many unanswered questions. "How's he doing?"

Odalinde looked up to meet Gretel's stare, a look of defensiveness in her eyes. She blinked slowly a few times and nodded, resetting her demeanor, and with a smile said, "Much, much better."

"Really? So not just *much* better today, but much, *much* better?"

Odalinde's smile straightened and Gretel felt her own stomach tighten. The words had escaped Gretel's mouth immediately, automatically, but it certainly wasn't an unusual thing for her to say. There was a new combativeness to Gretel that had started that day with The System officer's son, the day after her mother had gone missing. Gretel had become unrestrained with her challenges and often looked for a confrontation where none existed. And she needed—*needed*—to have the last word in any debate, no matter how explicitly her point may have been tested and discredited. This new quality had already resulted in more than one afternoon home from school, and kids who had previously spoken to her in class or on the walk home started avoiding her entirely. If she was honest, there wasn't one person—other than Hansel—whom she could truly call a friend.

At first she blamed it on a perceived awkwardness from others about her mother and Gretel's needing space to cope, and to some extent she thought that to be true; but those same kids spoke with Hansel quite easily, and even when they did speak with her, it wasn't with sympathy or deference, but rather with an abruptness that indicated a certain disapproval and hostility.

But that was a price Gretel had been willing to pay. She owed it to her mother to become the woman she was meant to be, that her mother had always envisioned. Strong and confident, controlling the situation when it was necessary and appropriate. Gretel knew that she still had a lot of refining to do, and that her mother certainly wouldn't have approved of her occasional rudeness or insubordination in school and otherwise. But if she had used her mother as an excuse to pity herself, to disappear into a tent of silence and demureness, that would have been altogether dishonorable.

There had been no official recognition of Anika Morgan's death. The System had instead 'Suspended' the case three weeks into the investigation. But according to the opinions of most, suspensions were rarely taken up again without the emergence of obvious evidence.

Similarly, Heinrich Morgan's dedication to his wife's disappearance lost momentum. He had driven the Interways for the few days following her disappearance, but his poor health, as well as an increasing build up of hopelessness, had left him spending most of the ensuing days in bed. Thankfully, he had been self-sufficient in the basic necessities, and Gretel had mostly avoided him. It wasn't until the day she found him on the floor that she realized how bad his state was, and Odalinde had shown up at the house only days later.

Gretel held Odalinde's look without blinking. If Gretel had been able to retract her last words, to erase the last few seconds of this scene, she would have. But it was said, and she would let the words play out. And besides, that feeling of instant regret had become typical to Gretel, and on some level it was comforting.

"Do you have schoolwork, Gretel?" It was a common play of Odalinde's to take the role of the mother. "Your father isn't been pleased with how it's been slipping of late."

And there the line was crossed. For the most part Gretel had not resisted Odalinde periodically slipping into the character of the maternal head of the house. She was the adult, after all, and performed most of the duties that role required—less one, Gretel hoped and assumed. But Odalinde had increasingly used her own intimacy with Heinrich as a weapon against Gretel, becoming the filter through which any expression of her father ran. "Your father is ready for you" or "Your father wants you to know that he loves you." And so on.

And indeed, even the disciplining and disappointments were now being contracted out. Of course, Gretel knew that Odalinde had to be lying in some of the cases, but Gretel had confirmed too many of the reports with her father to dismiss them out of hand.

Gretel clenched her teeth and glared at Odalinde, holding the look for a long moment before walking away, muttering as she left, "My mother would have hated you."

She spoke loudly enough that Odalinde certainly could hear her voice, though Gretel couldn't be sure she could understand the words. If she did, she didn't reply.

What Gretel was certain of, however, was that the words were true.

Gretel hurried into her room and closed the door, and immediately snatched the book from the top shelf in her closet, holding it to her chest as she lay down on her bed. She hadn't learned any of what the bizarre symbols meant since the day she brought the book home from Deda's, and she hadn't been able to find anyone who could translate it. Gretel had hoped that Deda would be able to tell her more about it, but she had seen him only once since that night, and on that occasion he had been distant and cold. The other candidates whom she had hoped would at least have knowledge of the book didn't, and, in fact, had never even heard of the term 'Orphism.'

But the book had become a security blanket for Gretel, and even though she didn't know what it was about, she always felt better with it in her hands.

Gretel lay still with her eyes closed and took deep breaths, imagining what she usually did during the quiet periods: her mother walking through the door, weary from her unbelievable ordeal, a wry smile of relief on her face. Occasionally, the image made her hopeful, but mostly it made her cry.

The creak of the bedroom door shattered Gretel's vision, and she turned to see Hansel slump in, his mouth slightly open and eyes half-closed. Gretel frowned at him and turned her body toward the wall. "What do you want Hansel?"

"I'm hungry," he whined.

"Odalinde is finished with Father; ask her to make you something."

"I did. She said there's no food."

Gretel turned back toward her brother, slightly alarmed. "No food? Is she sure?"

Hansel shrugged. "I haven't eaten today, Gretel."

Gretel's heart began to race, and she soon realized she hadn't eaten either. She, however, had gotten used to not eating much, and to share her portions with Hansel when she could stand it. But never had she not eaten all day. And Hansel! Hansel needed his food. He was a growing boy!

Gretel put the book aside and lifted herself from the bed, suddenly aware of her empty stomach. She left Hansel standing by the door as she exited her room and crossed the hall, opening her father's door without knocking. She heard him groan in his sleep as he shifted in his bed.

"Father," she whispered loudly. He moved again but didn't turn to her. Gretel registered the bowl on the side table, half-filled with soup. "Father," she repeated, her voice booming this time, commanding attention as if in preparation to scold him.

Heinrich Morgan raised his head with a grunt and turned wide-eyed toward his daughter. "Gretel? What is it?"

His voice was raspy and slow, his eyes cloudy and disoriented.

Gretel got right to the point. "There's no food, Father. Hansel hasn't eaten today. Nothing." She paused, debating whether to say her next line. "But I see you have." She stared at the bowl on the table. Heinrich followed her stare and studied the bowl, confused.

"No food?" The words came out clumsily, as if Heinrich were repeating a nonsense phrase, mimicking what he'd heard to make sure he'd gotten it right. Heinrich looked back toward his daughter and over her shoulder to the door. "Odalinde?"

Gretel turned to see the nurse standing behind her at the threshold, a smiling look of mock sympathy on her face, the way a mother might observe a crying toddler who has fallen after trying to take his first steps.

"I've only to go to the market, Heinrich. There's been so much to do around here, what with the children and your condition, that I'm afraid I've gotten behind on the shopping. There's not much money left, but enough."

"And the crops? Has anything come in?"

Odalinde looked away from her patient and down to the floor, embarrassed for him. There would be no harvest of any kind this year, and even she didn't have the stomach to say otherwise.

Why would father think a harvest was coming? Gretel thought. There had been no one to work the fields since his injury and mother's subsequent disappearance, and he couldn't possibly think Odalinde was tending them. As it was, their crops had been in decline for years, and without severe attention and care, it would have been impossible to keep them bountiful.

"Not yet," she said, and a more serious look enveloped her face. "But Gretel has no reason to worry." Odalinde placed a hand on Gretel's shoulder. "I'll head off now for some rice and bread, perhaps some sweets. I'll be back short-ly." She flickered a glance at Gretel as she began to walk out, and then turned back toward Heinrich. "Oh, and I'll take Hansel along."

The back of Gretel's neck tingled at the nurse's words, and for the first time she suspected Odalinde was more than simply unpleasant and coarse. Perhaps, Gretel thought, she was malevolent.

"I could go, Father. I can drive the truck—"

"Don't be ridiculous, Gretel," Odalinde interrupted. "It's part of my duties. And you've yet to do your schoolwork. Now let your father rest." She grabbed the knob of the door and shut it, corralling Gretel out to the hall in the process.

Gretel would have put up more resistance, but she saw that her father had laid back down and was again drifting toward unconsciousness. She would be surprised if later he even remembered the conversation. Something wasn't right with him lately, and it was more than his spleen.

"Hansel's staying here!" Gretel snapped after they were out in the hall, and she immediately walked over to her brother who had migrated to the living room. She stood slightly in front of him, protectively.

Odalinde raised her eyebrows, "Really? Perhaps we should let him decide."

Hansel locked eyes with his sister; there was defiance in his stare. "I'm going with Odalinde, Gretel. She's going to buy me a sweet bun with jam." A meager smile drew across Hansel's face as he looked timidly toward the nurse. "Right Odalinde?"

"That's right, Hansel. Or whatever you want." Odalinde turned to Gretel, "I'd ask you to come along too, Gretel, but what with your father's condition and your schoolwork and all."

Gretel looked away from Odalinde to her brother. She could see the fear on his face, but it acted only as a backdrop to his hunger, and she was suddenly glad he was going to town. Gretel knew Odalinde wouldn't hurt him—in fact, she was pretty certain that the nurse would buy him the treat that was promised. And if not, at the very least he would be offered a sample of fresh breads or pastries from one of the stalls at the markets.

But there was an obvious motive underneath Odalinde's gesture; whether it was simply to win Hansel's favor and divide the siblings or something more nefarious, Gretel couldn't be sure. As far as today was concerned, however, Gretel knew her brother was safe.

Gretel watched as Odalinde unlocked the cabinet beneath the sink and fetched her bag, squatting insect-like in the opening as she sifted through the satchel, inventorying the contents. The cabinet, tall and narrow in design, had previously been used as storage for household cleaning items and canned goods; but Odalinde had requested her own private depository when she arrived—'one that was secure from children'—and Heinrich had obliged her and cleared out the cabinet, customizing it with a lock. The reorganization had made for a messy kitchen at first, but as the canned goods and supplies dwindled, counter space was no longer an issue.

Gretel had kept a close watch on Odalinde's trips to this private space, and in particular to the time she spent huddled by the opening. As far as Gretel could tell, the bag was the only thing in the cabinet, or at least the only thing she tended to. And Odalinde always squatted, never sat, so as to always keep her bag completely covered and hidden while she shuffled and rechecked the contents. When she did finally take the bag out, it was always double-zipped and clasped, and clutched tightly to her breast or rib. And it was never left unattended—never—which for Odalinde's sake was a good thing. Because Gretel was waiting.

Odalinde shepherded Hansel out the door and down the porch stairs to the truck. Gretel followed them to the bottom of the stairs, leaving her brother with a look that said 'stay aware,' and then watched as the truck crept slowly away, disappearing over the hill toward town.

Gretel could feel the time until her family completely fell apart was short. They were starving and sick, their mother was missing and presumed dead, and now a stranger had come from nowhere and taken control of the household. Things were dire indeed. In the past, these realities would have overwhelmed Gretel and brought her to tears, but she now looked at them with pragmatism, prioritizing them as problems needing to be solved.

The first of these problems was, of course, her mother. Though she had promised herself never to give up on the possibility that her mother was still alive, there were few actions Gretel could think of taking to help find her. The System officer had never again come calling on her for help—help for which he had told Gretel in no uncertain terms he would need from her. Perhaps her father's invasion that night had dissuaded the officer. Or perhaps he'd never intended on returning, and had only told her that to make her feel useful.

And then there was the problem of her father, who apparently was not as far along as Gretel had believed. Or else his recovery had slipped. She knew nothing of medicine, but the doctor had prognosticated her father's recovery weeks ago, and indeed, based on the immediate signs, seemed to be accurate in his assessment. But there had been a slide in his recuperation—not in terms of his actual internal injuries, but in his overall energy and clarity. Even his intellect, Gretel thought. She didn't know what to do about the problem of her father, other than to wait it out.

As for Odalinde, this problem was becoming increasingly formidable, particularly after today's exchange. At the very least she was not to be trusted; at worst, she was a danger. Her threats were only passive at this point, however, and there was nothing specific Gretel could say or do to fix this problem right now. She would have to let that play out a bit more as well. And if the opportunity arose, she would get into that cabinet and see what mysteries lurked there.

That left the problem of food. It was the most pressing problem and the one that Gretel felt she had the most control over. Gretel didn't know where Odalinde's money had come from to buy the food for which she was now on her way to purchase, but it obviously couldn't be counted on to feed Hansel and her. With two children in the house, the nurse had let the supplies dwindle to nothing, having not fed either of them all day. But yet there had been a bowl of soup for Father. Had that bowl been from today? Or even last night? Gretel admitted to herself that she couldn't be sure, though she was fairly confident that if there had been enough for only one person, Hansel and Gretel would have been the last two names on the meal list. For the time being, and perhaps from now on, it would be up to Gretel to figure out where the meals would come from for her and her brother.

She mentally ran through the names of friends and neighbors in the Back Country, some of whom had helped out in one way or another since her mother's disappearance. Since most were poorer than Gretel's family, the help had come mainly in the form of labor and childcare. But since the arrival of Odalinde, it had mostly stopped, with the occasional visit of obligation to "see if there was anything they could do." There was certainly nothing in the form of financial help, the perception being, Gretel assumed, that anyone affording a private nurse could certainly afford food. Gretel could never quite follow this line of thinking though; after all, they were a farming family, their income depended on selling crops, and if no crops were being harvested and sold, how could they be taking in any money?

But Gretel didn't judge them too harshly. She supposed people had their own problems and usually looked only as deeply as necessary to satisfy their consciences. There may have been life insurance, after all, or a family grant to see the Morgans through. It wasn't the burden of neighbors to ask *how* they were making it with no crops or occupation to speak of—questions like those might easily be construed as nosy and intrusive. Apparently they were making it and that's all that mattered.

Besides, Gretel had always been taught it was the job of family to help navigate the straits of life, and Gretel's family was nothing short of conspicuous in their absence. Her father's side of the family had never been close to begin with, and they had drifted even further when Anika disappeared. And Deda, whom Gretel had barely seen since her mother vanished, had become, according to her father, 'a bona fide hermit,' and now refused to take calls or visits from anyone, including his own grandchildren.

Gretel walked around to the back of the house and continued into the small clump of trees that divided the rear of the house from the small lake that formed the back of the Morgan property. She walked to water's edge, absently picking up a small stone and tossing it in. Across the lake, Gretel could see the trees of the Klahr orchard approaching full bloom, the apple and pear trees perhaps a week away from perfect ripeness. In a few days the extended Klahr relatives and a dozen or so other workers would descend on the trees like caterpillars, furiously climbing and picking until the last of the fruit was sifted through and basketed, ready to be sold at market, or further processed into jam, bread, and wine.

The Klahrs were what passed for wealth in the Back Country, having a small stable of horses, a tractor, and two trucks, as well as, by all accounts, a profitable business. They were an older couple—Gretel imagined they were on the other side of sixty by now—and as far as Gretel knew they had no children of their own. At least none Gretel had ever seen. Presumably if they did have heirs, they were now grown men and women—men and women who had perhaps decided to see their land only as a future inheritance, pursuing instead a career more sophisticated than farmer. But Gretel didn't think this was the case. The Klahrs had lived across the lake from her family since before Gretel was born, and she had never heard of any Klahr children.

There was nothing at all ostentatious about the couple, but by all measures they were deeply proud of their farming operation, and ran it with great organization and efficiency. They kept to themselves for the most part—Gretel couldn't remember her mother or father ever engaging them in conversation—with her only interaction coming in the form of the occasional wave from across the lake. They seemed friendly enough, dealing with merchants in town or whatever, but work was always the order of the day, the exception being Sunday, of course.

So Gretel had no illusions that what she was planning was acceptable, and she justified it only on the most practical of levels: Her family needed to eat, and there was food in her sights.

Her decision made, Gretel walked back through the trees to the house. She wasted no time on preemptive regret or future plans of atonement, figuring those would only distract from what was required. If her family was to eat, focus and will were all that mattered.

There would be no school tomorrow. Tomorrow Gretel would become a thief.

***

Gretel awoke just after two o'clock in the morning, feeling well-rested and sparked with adrenaline. She had gone to her room just before Hansel and Odalinde returned from the market and had stayed there, forgoing whatever dinner had been brought home for her. More than food she had wanted to sleep, knowing she would need to be fully rested to take on the task ahead. And since Hansel hadn't come to her, Gretel assumed he had been fed, and that was her main concern.

As she had done dozens of times in her life, Gretel quietly slid open her bedroom window and slipped out, easing herself down the four-foot drop to the ground below. The sound of her feet in the overgrown garden bed was amplified in the serenity of the night, but Gretel didn't anticipate anyone investigating it. In a place where nocturnal animals were as common as weeds, rustling sounds outside your house rarely caused alarm in the Back Country.

She ran slowly on her toes until she was through the tree clump to the lake edge, and then stopped to get her bearings. It was darker than she'd expected; the light she had hoped to get from the moon was swallowed up by clouds. But her eyes would adjust, and she had the lantern.

After she'd made her decision yesterday, Gretel spent the rest of her time alone preparing for the early morning raid. She had fetched the lantern from the shed, checking the battery twice to make sure it worked. And the canoe, once a fixture along this sliver of beach, Gretel had untarped in the yard and dragged down to the shoreline. The skeleton of a mouse had welcomed her when she first pulled the covering from the small boat, and the accompanying oars had long been broken and discarded, but otherwise the craft seemed in decent condition. As long as it didn't sink, Gretel thought, that's all that mattered. If she had had to paddle with her hands she would have—the distance across was short enough that she could have swum it—but Gretel had been able to find a hollowed-out guitar among the ever-increasing junk in the yard, a fossil from merrier Morgan days when things like music were a part of their lives. It would do fine as a replacement for an oar.

Gretel now stood on the shore beside the boat and slowly scanned the water. She felt inside the hull of the canoe and found the lantern, lifting it out and lighting it. It was so bright! She was aware there wasn't a way to adjust the intensity of the lantern, unlike the oil lantern they'd owned when Gretel was younger, but in the daylight that hadn't seemed to be an issue. In fact, if she had any concern it was that the light wouldn't be enough. But now, in the cape of Back Country blackness, it seemed the light must have been visible for miles, as if a star had been born from the union of water and trees.

Gretel breathed deeply, trying to relax. The truth was there was no one out to see the light at this hour. These were farming folk, early risers; the only potential witnesses were likely to be either philandering or drunk—or most likely both. No one to worry about, Gretel thought. And in any case, witnesses or not, she was crossing the lake. Crossing the lake now. Life would decide her fate from there.

She moved the light over the canoe and checked again that both the guitar and buckets were intact. Gretel had decided on four buckets, figuring that four would hold enough fruit to last her and Hansel—and her father if necessary—for at least a week, more if she could keep it cool. She hadn't considered exactly how to store and preserve the fruit yet, or how to explain their origin if her father—or God help her, Odalinde—were to ask, but there were more immediate concerns at the moment.

With everything in order, Gretel placed the lantern in the front of the boat and shoved the canoe easily into the water, dexterously avoiding wetting her shoes as she grabbed either side of the stern end, and bounced in, landing in perfect sitting position at the stern seat. She moved the lantern to the bow, picked up the guitar and gently began to row across the lake toward the Klahr orchard.

In the daylight, the lake looked like hardly more than a large pond, but now, under the shroud of night, it seemed larger, frightening. There was a quietness to it that implied undisclosed secrets and demanded trepidation. Gretel thought she would have preferred raging rapids under sunny skies to the lake at this moment.

She distracted herself by trying to remember when she'd last been on the boat, but she couldn't recall, imagining it must have been when Hansel was just a toddler, and their father would row them past the entire Klahr orchard, down to the Stein mill where the lake ended. Gretel remembered being mostly bored by the trips, other than seeing the joy it brought to her brother and father. She would have given just about anything to have such stability and leisure in her life right now.

The canoe nudged into the silty bottom of the lake just a few feet off the shore of the Klahr side of the lake. Gretel was already across! She let out a breathy laugh at how quick the ride had been; she'd barely paddled the guitar more than a few times it seemed.

So far the plan was working as well as she could have hoped.

Gretel pulled the lantern and buckets from the canoe, and was now grateful for the lantern's brightness; she was completely unfamiliar with the landscape on this side of the lake, and began to imagine bottomless pits and angry dogs waiting for her just outside the circumference of the light's rays. She walked slowly up the slight slope of the muddy beach, focusing on the two or three feet that were illuminated just in front of her steps. Soon she crossed a threshold into a patch of wild grass and then saw the first of the trees planted closely together in the perfectly manicured row of dirt that formed the back of the Klahr orchard. She was there.

Gretel exhaled and then breathed in deeply, taking the clean, candied air into her lungs and holding it there, savoring it, before releasing it to the breeze. Her stomach reacted instantly, awakening from its slumber.

She lifted the lantern branch-high and her eyes were overwhelmed with pears. There were pears everywhere on the tree, bulbous and perfectly shaped, nestled in clusters, clinging to the leaves like giant green raindrops. There were dozens, maybe hundreds on the one tree, and Gretel's mind conjured a picture of the entire orchard, which ran as long and deep as human eyes could see, even from across the lake in the clear of day. She began to extrapolate out how many pears and apples there must be in the entire orchard and realized it was inconceivable. Millions, she thought.

Gretel's impulses stirred and she scrambled for a bucket. The trees were taller than she'd imagined, and Gretel would certainly have needed a ladder to pick one clean, but she only had four buckets to fill, and the low-hanging fruit would be just fine. Besides, there were hundreds—maybe thousands—of trees to choose from.

The buckets were filled quickly, and as Gretel began the first trip back to the canoe—one hand holding the lantern, the other lugging a bucket of pears—she lamented not bringing more than four. She could imagine sitting with Hansel and devouring all the pears in a single morning, and the Klahrs would miss four buckets of pears no more than the beach would miss four buckets of sand. But four was all she had, and she needed to stay on task. Besides, she could always come back for more.

With three buckets secure in the canoe, Gretel made her last trip back to the orchard for the remaining bucket when she heard a dull metallic click. She knew instantly it was the unmistakable sound of a round of ammunition being loaded into the chamber of a shotgun.

"Place the bucket on the ground," a voice commanded. The man's voice was neither loud nor aggressive. In fact, Gretel thought, there was a soothing, instructive quality to it.

Gretel did as she was told and now stood frozen, suddenly realizing the vulnerable position she was in. She had been caught trespassing and stealing—no small offenses, particularly in the Back Country—and was now being held alone by a man with a gun, a man who, Gretel assumed, was either going to kill or rape her. Or both. Property crimes in the Back Country were not turned over to The System—and they never went unpunished. She had never associated the Klahr family with anything other than piety and work, but the truth was she didn't know them at all. For all she knew they could have spent the bulk of their days offering sacrifices to Satan himself.

"Hold the lantern up to your face." The steady voice was coming from in front of Gretel, maybe ten or fifteen feet away.

Gretel obeyed, closing her eyes to avoid the glare of the light.

"Gretel Morgan."

Gretel opened her eyes in surprise, narrowing them, trying to force her vision through the darkness. She listened with both fear and anticipation as the heavy footsteps approached.

Finally, the figure came into view, but the light only illuminated his torso. The man was tall, and Gretel lifted the light over her head to try to see his face.

"It's all right, Gretel, let me have the lamp," the voice said, wrapping his long fingers around the handle. Gretel released her grip and dropped her hands to her sides, assuming a tall, penitent posture, as if waiting for a scolding.

The stranger lifted the lantern to his face and stooped to Gretel's height, revealing his face. It was Georg Klahr. "Let's go," he said.

***

Amanda Klahr placed the soup gently in front of Gretel, who instinctively grabbed the sides of the bowl and raised it just slightly off the table. She caught herself in time, but Mrs. Klahr had seen her, and Gretel immediately imagined how appalled her mother would have been.

"Here Gretel," Mrs. Klahr said, placing a spoon beside the bowl. The woman hovered for a moment, frowning down at Gretel. "I know the face of hunger child, and it's been many years since I've seen it as I do on your face right now. Eat the soup as you like; your bread will be ready soon."

Gretel's eyes filled with tears as she picked up the spoon and began ladling the soup into her mouth. "Thank you, Ma'am," she choked out between swallows, but the warm broth and the smell of the bread from the kitchen overwhelmed her, and the gratitude she felt yielded to eating.

The front door opened and closed, and Gretel looked up sheepishly from her bowl as Mr. Klahr walked into the kitchen.

"Anyone there, Georg?" Mrs. Klahr inquired, setting a steaming plate of bread beside the soup bowl.

"No," he replied, "seems not." Mr. Klahr placed his hat on the table and sat down across from Gretel, watching her as she dipped her bread in the soup and shoved it in her mouth.

Gretel kept her eyes on her bowl, afraid that lifting them and making contact with Mr. Klahr would somehow end the magic that was happening in front of her.

"You've a brother," Mr. Klahr stated. "Greener than you as I recall."

Gretel met Georg Klahr's eyes and hesitated. "Yes, sir."

"Did he eat yesterday?"

Gretel looked at Mrs. Klahr and then back to the man across the table, suddenly feeling guilty at her newfound bounty. "My father's nurse took him to town. She told him she would buy him something to eat there. I was in bed before they returned, but I guess she did."

The uncertainty in Gretel's voice was obvious, and she did nothing to disguise it. There was no point pretending things were just dandy at home when you've been caught stealing apples at four o'clock in the morning. The tone was not lost on Georg Klahr, and he glanced sideways at his wife.

"Mrs. Klahr will pack some food for you to take to your brother. Make sure it gets to him." Georg Klahr frowned and looked away, clearly disgusted at the abject position of the poor girl in his kitchen. Still looking away he said, "Is your father going to marry that woman?"

"No, sir!" Gretel snapped her head up from her plate and stared wide-eyed at the side of Mr. Klahr's face. Her voice was louder than she'd intended, and she repeated the words, this time more softly. "No, sir. She's his nurse, that's all."

Gretel hadn't known the Klahrs were even aware of Odalinde, never mind that she'd been with them long enough to ask such a question. But that's how it was in the Back Country: news about the arrival of strangers traveled with the speed of electricity, and often with greater detail than one would expect.

The thought of her father marrying Odalinde had frankly never occurred to Gretel, though now that the question had been posed it seemed like a legitimate possibility. Likely even. Gretel's stomach turned slightly and she put her hands to her mouth to suppress the nausea.

Mercifully, Mrs. Klahr quickly changed the subject. "How *is* your father?" She shot her husband a dirty look and Mr. Klahr looked away unruffled. "I know he was very ill for a while there. A mule kick, was it? To the gut?"

Still wallowing in the dreadful idea of her new stepmother, Gretel looked at Mrs. Klahr as if she had asked this question in Latin. "Ill? Uh...yes ma'am," she replied finally, "except it was a horse."

"Ah yes, a horse. But he's doing better?"

Gretel considered the question for a moment. "I don't really know. It seems sometimes that he is. Like he's fully recovered, though perhaps a bit sore still, and then later he's in bed for days. And sometimes when I talk to him it's as if he hardly knows me."

At this revelation, an awkward noiselessness enveloped the kitchen, and Gretel blushed at having disclosed so much in her answer to what was, more or less, a rhetorical question.

Mrs. Klahr had cleared her bowl and Gretel now sat with her hands hanging by her sides, suddenly feeling like a prisoner undergoing a soft interrogation who has just been coerced into willingly revealing everything about herself, without so much as a harsh word from her captors. These were her neighbors, yes, but as she reminded herself again, she didn't really know them at all.

She picked up her spoon again and began to scrape the bottom of the bowl.

"So what should we do about the apples you've stolen?" Mr. Klahr asked flatly.

Gretel glanced up at the man across the table from her, a look of regret in her eyes, though secretly she was thankful to be done with the personal questions and back on the topic of why she was sitting in the Klahr kitchen to begin with.

"I don't know, sir," she replied, and then thought a moment, her eyes glancing toward the ceiling. "I have no money to pay for them. I suppose my father will have to make amends." Gretel paused, perhaps dramatically she would later consider, "Unless you're to call The System."

The words blurted from Gretel's mouth with the tone of a hopeful alternative, and Gretel blushed immediately. It was true she was no longer afraid of The System, and in the context of the situation, she would have much preferred discussing this matter of the apples with Officer Stenson than with Georg Klahr.

But it was ludicrous to think The System would handle such a relatively petty crime as the one at hand. So why would she have made the suggestion? It wasn't to do with her mother's disappearance, Gretel thought. If The System did take the time to respond to this apple complaint, they would focus on the crime at hand—not on giving information about another case to the accused!

And Gretel knew in her bones that there was nothing about her mother for them to offer anyway. At least nothing they were willing to share.

So what then?

But Gretel knew the answer, of course. There was only one reason The System would have popped into her mind, and it was a reason Gretel had thought about on and off for weeks. It was The System officer's son. Petr.

Georg Klahr formed a quizzical smile at Gretel's suggestion of The System and sat studying her for a moment, as if he'd missed something in the story. "I think that might be a bit excessive. Don't you?"

Gretel shrugged shyly.

"And I'd also prefer not to involve your father...or that woman. What is her name?"

"Odalinde. Odalinde Merth."

"Or Odalinde Merth."

Georg Klahr rose from his chair and walked to the cupboard, taking out a ceramic mug and pouring himself a cup of coffee, mumbling to himself something about not going back to sleep.

Gretel frowned at the hint of blame.

"Instead Gretel," Georg Klahr continued, "I'd like you to repay me another way."

Gretel's eyes widened, and she eagerly followed Mr. Klahr as he paced back toward the window and looked out past the orchard to the first glint of morning sunlight. His words scared her slightly—Gretel wasn't naive to the deviant wishes of some (maybe all) men. But she also didn't sense evil in Mr. Klahr, neither in his tone or his character generally. And the fact that his wife stood not eight feet away comforted Gretel further (though she was not naive to the perversions of certain women either).

Gretel waited for the proposition silently, steeling herself not to speak, afraid that she might blurt out an offer beyond what was to be pitched—though what she would have volunteered she couldn't have said.

"As you obviously know," Mr. Klahr started, smiling and nodding toward the bucket of apples beside the table, "the orchard is just about ready for harvest. Starting Thursday in fact, I have men coming from across the Back Country, some even from the Northlands, to pick the fruit. They'll be here for the next several weeks."

Gretel sat riveted, still not quite sure what was coming.

"These men will need to be fed, and their clothes and linen will need to be cleaned. They're a quiet, respectful bunch generally, not very fussy, but there is still a lot to be done in regards to their care. It isn't easy work."

Mr. Klahr paused.

"Mrs. Klahr has been insisting on help with these duties for, what is it now dear, twenty years?" Georg Klahr looked at his wife and gave the same quizzical smile Gretel had received only minutes before.

"I lost count somewhere around year ten," Mrs. Klahr replied without looking up.

Mr. Klahr continued. "So...I'd like to offer you a job, Gretel, assisting Mrs. Klahr with these duties." He paused to let the offer penetrate. "You can work after school and on Saturday, even before school if you like. I'll pay you by the hour, the same wage as the pickers, and you can work as much or as little as you like, though if you say you will be here on a particular day I'll expect you to be. And you're not to miss school."

Tears began to form behind Gretel's eyes before Mr. Klahr had finished speaking. Her stomach knotted nervously and she couldn't contain the smile that fought through her pursed lips and spread as wide as her face. She couldn't quite believe what she was hearing, and said nothing in response, waiting for a 'catch' to the offer.

"So?" Mr. Klahr said, "Will I see you Thursday?"

Gretel cleared her throat and sat up straight in her chair. "Yes sir, you will," she said professionally, "Thursday. I'll be here before and after school. As early as I can."

Mrs. Klahr spoke up, "As long as it isn't as early as you showed up today."

Gretel blushed again, but her excitement instantly transformed it into a glow of joy. "Yes, ma'am."

With the deal in place, the Klahr's began hustling Gretel back home before the sun rose completely, so as not to raise the eyebrows of Odalinde. Generally, Odalinde didn't give much thought to Gretel's comings and goings, which would make her newly-gained employment not much of an issue, but there was no point inciting unnecessary suspicion. To be safe, Gretel and the Klahrs developed a believable story for how Gretel acquired her job, just in case anyone should ever ask. Though, truthfully, the only person Gretel could imagine caring much at all about the story was Hansel, and he would believe whatever his sister told him.

Gretel confessed to the Klahr's about the three buckets already in the canoe, and Mr. Klahr told her to keep them, along with the one by her side. "We've more apples and pears than we could ever sell or process in a season," Mrs. Klahr said, "Better you eat them than the pigs. And I want you to give that bread to your brother as soon as he's awake."

"Yes, ma'am." Gretel raised the wrapped hunk of bread to show she'd remember, and then thanked the Klahr's for what must have been the thousandth time as she stood in the doorway, the bucket of apples in the other hand. She soon realized this was the best night she'd had since her mother vanished, and she wanted to linger in it.

Finally, she turned from the house to leave when Mr. Klahr's voice struck her like an iron bar. "I'm sorry about your mother, Gretel," he said.

Gretel stopped but didn't turn back.

"We wanted to come so many times but..." his voice drifted off to a whimper, "...well, I'm sorry. We both are."

Gretel closed her eyes and sighed. "I'll see you Thursday," she said, and then walked away.

CHAPTER EIGHT

For weeks following that night in the Klahr kitchen, Gretel was as busy as she'd ever been in her life, and that included those weeks her mother had gone to care for Deda.

Each day, except for Sunday, began at five o'clock in the morning and ended close to eight o'clock at night. Ten o'clock if you included homework. And Gretel loved it. All of it.

She was learning new things every day from Mrs. Klahr, mostly about cooking, but other, less tangible things as well. And, most importantly, Gretel was making money. Mr. Klahr paid her in cash every morning for the previous day's work, and she was provided a meal for each shift worked, which basically meant breakfast and dinner every day, and lunch on Saturdays. Admittedly, Sundays were a blessing, and Gretel more or less stayed in her room and slept all day, but she was as enthusiastic and eager as a shrew come Monday morning, and often arrived at the Klahr house before Mr. and Mrs. Klahr had even dressed for the day. On these mornings, Gretel gave her sincere, albeit pride-laced apologies, but the Klahrs always dismissed them, rebuking themselves instead for their sluggishness.

Gretel's only apprehension about her new job was how it would play out at home and the effect it would have on her brother. Naturally, Hansel had become both dependent on and protective of his sister since their mother's disappearance and Gretel feared he would take her new schedule badly. He didn't have many friends to begin with, and the last thing Gretel wanted was for her brother to experience any additional feelings of loneliness on top of those which already gripped him. But he had been surprisingly calm about the news—nonchalant even—the buckets of ripe pears and apples no doubt contributing to his casualness.

And her father hadn't uttered a word of protest either. He was in fact relieved, both that his daughter was exerting her independence through the healthy outlet of work, and that desperately needed money would now be coming into the household. He hadn't asked about her salary, and Gretel hadn't offered to tell him, but the shine in his daughter's eyes had revealed to him that their worries could subside for a few weeks. In this exchange, which Gretel was determined to keep fresh in her mind for as long as possible, Gretel saw a glimpse of the man her father was before their mother went missing, before his injury even, and she laughed boisterously in his arms as he hugged her and told her how proud he was.

Gretel didn't know what would happen when the harvest eventually ended, or how they would continue to survive, but she wasn't ready to submerge herself into that concern just yet. She had done as she set out to do that night in the canoe: feed herself and her brother. Certainly, her goal hadn't been realized quite the way she'd intended, but that's how it usually went. Knowing what you wanted and then doing something—anything—about it was a big part of the battle.

And in this case, it turned out a hundred times better than she'd ever dreamed. She was now able to feed her entire family, keep some of her family's creditors at bay, and, since most of her meals were provided by the Klahrs, which meant less money was needed for food, she could even buy a few 'luxuries' like new dinner plates for the house and shoes for Hansel. To Gretel, it was all a miracle; two weeks ago such a scenario seemed far beyond impossible.

Even Gretel's school work had improved. Her grades, which had been dropping steadily, quickly began to trend upwards, and the combative behavior which had shortened so many of her school days over the past couple of months suddenly became agreeable and helpful. Gretel even became somewhat amicable with her classmates, and though her schedule allowed little time for outside socializing, she had made one or two friends.

Of course, she recognized many of these changes were due to her fear that any news of mischief in school might find its way back to the Klahrs, but it was also more than that: for the first time in months, Gretel felt happy. And it wasn't that fleeting kind of happiness which arrives seemingly from nowhere and then evaporates with the same lack of reason. It was a consistent happiness—that underlying peace that seems always to flow beneath the surface of certain people, subliminally repeating to them throughout the day that everything is okay. That no matter what happens, everything is okay. Those people who have never been without the feeling might label it 'contentment,' but Gretel was new to the feeling, and it was one she was now dedicated to for life.

"Gretel, the pies!" Amanda Klahr barked her raspy command at Gretel as she carried the oversized platter of biscuits out the front door to the waiting table of hungry pickers.

The men were mostly quiet and undemanding, particularly when it came to Mrs. Klahr, but she was as adamant as any city restaurant manager about having their meals to them hot and on time. Gretel surmised this came from a combination of pride and motivation, figuring the men would work hard for her if she worked hard for them. Plus, as far as Gretel could tell, the picking months were the only time of the year the Klahrs had company, and Mrs. Klahr enjoyed the entertaining part of the whole thing.

The Klahrs had long ago moved the daily meals of the workers outside where cleanup would be easier and space wouldn't be an issue. Georg Klahr had constructed a large wooden table for the purpose, with permanent benches on either side and a flat patio area made of clay brick. The giant table ran the entire length of the patio and was quite a marvel of construction. She had never measured it, but Gretel figured the table must have been twenty feet long. It was the length of a table that kings might dine at, Gretel thought, though its impurities and unfinished design made it suitable only for the environment in which it now stood. The whole area was actually quite beautiful, though Gretel couldn't imagine that the space was used much at any other time of the year. But it served its purpose well, and the scene of men seated around the table resembled something closer to a family reunion than a migrant worker lunch hour.

"I've got them, Ma'am! I'm right behind you." Gretel slipped on the oven mitts and took two pies from the oven, setting them on the stove top and grabbing the remaining two from the back of the rack. She placed the four pies on a large serving board and followed Mrs. Klahr through the door which, mercifully, she had left open.

Saturday: Gretel's favorite day of the week. And her busiest. She'd been at work for five hours now and it was only eleven a.m.

Gretel set the first pie at one end of the huge table and continued down toward the other end, spacing the remaining pies evenly so as to make them accessible to everyone. Gretel could feel the eyes of the men—not on her, but on the food. With great restraint the men sat sturdy, watching, waiting for the women to finish their roles and signal for them to begin. And when the signal came, the men wasted no time moving in.

They were courteous, of course, taking one biscuit at a time, or one spoon of potatoes or chili, and then passing the dish on. But when they began, they ate everything. Soup pots were bone dry when the hour was up. The boards of roast beef or game hens or whatever main course was served that day were cleaned by the workers as if they had come from the wash bin. The tea pitchers, the greens, and the seemingly never-ending bowls of apples and pears were drained without pause.

And then there were the pies.

Amanda Klahr's pies were staggering and had become so popular among the men that Gretel had suggested to Mrs. Klahr they be served first. Mrs. Klahr put up a mild protest at first but came around after testing the idea and receiving applause from the men when she placed them on the table at the beginning of the meal. From that point on, pies had been the appetizer at each lunch and dinner, whether they were made with fruit, meat or potatoes.

Gretel placed the last pie on the table and stepped back, placing her hands properly in front of her, waiting as a servant in a mansion might for any further requests. Gretel loved to watch the men as they began the feast. She reveled in it. There was such joy in that first moment, and the moments just after the first bites, from men who spent most of the day looking stoic and grim. The ear-touching smirks and agreeable nods that sprang up around the table when Mrs. Klahr finally said 'enjoy' in her ironic, understated manner made Gretel glow inside. She wanted to clap for the men, encourage them to 'take more, there's plenty!'

Of course, she said nothing and waited for Mrs. Klahr to flap her back to the kitchen for the next task.

"They're not children," Mrs. Klahr scolded amusingly. "You shouldn't watch them like that."

Gretel smiled, nodding toward the table. "I don't think they mind. In fact, I don't think they would notice if I was standing here naked."

Mrs. Klahr laughed and put her arm around Gretel, leading her back to the house where, once inside, Gretel went right for the kitchen and began cleaning the floors and range top. She worked fast, knowing that the dishes that awaited her after the men finished would take up most of her time until dinner, which she would need to help Mrs. Klahr prepare.

"Pace yourself child! My goodness! You'll be an old woman before you become a young woman!"

Gretel smiled conspiratorially and continued scrubbing. "With all the food I eat now, I'll get fat if I don't move this fast."

"Well I can't afford you getting sick, so don't overdo it."

And this was a truth Gretel had come to accept.

For the Klahrs, Gretel had evolved from a charity case to a necessity in only a few short weeks. She didn't know how they ever got through a harvest without her, though Gretel assumed they must have hired some kind of temporary helper, perhaps the wife or daughter of one of the pickers. The fact was: this day was a typical day for Gretel, and Mrs. Klahr's cautions to take it easy were simply courtesies. The work Gretel had been given was hard and heavy, and the pace at which she moved was what was required for it to get done. And Gretel was naturally suited for it.

At first, of course, the hours and work seemed impossible, particularly during those first two or three days; but Gretel's body adjusted quickly, not just in terms of her stamina, but also in her physique. The carrying of pots and baskets, as well as her newly-discovered love for rowing (the Klahr's had gifted Gretel a set of old oars), had quickly transformed her biceps and shoulders and thighs into those of an athlete. Gretel was accustomed to hard work on her land and household, but those duties had mostly been limited to feeding livestock, cleaning stalls, and mopping floors. The work she was doing now had made her lean and wiry, and she even seemed to have grown an inch or two.

She was becoming the woman her mother had always envisioned.

"Hi Gretel."

Gretel paused at the sink, trying to place the voice before turning around. It was young, male, and definitely one she had heard before. Not one of the workers—they rarely spoke to Gretel except to say 'please' or 'thank you.' Certainly never to engage in idle kitchen talk

Gretel flipped the dishtowel across her shoulder and spun toward the voice. A smile reflexively spread across her face at the sight of the boy in front of her. It was Officer Stenson's son.

For the moment, Gretel couldn't recall his name, which was odd considering she had replayed her encounter with the boy virtually every night for almost a month following their whirlwind meeting.

But so much had changed since then. She'd quickly began to rebuild her life—thanks almost entirely to the Klahrs—and had spent as little time as possible on the 'what ifs?' of the past few months. What if The System had found her mother? or What if Petr was her boyfriend? There was no room for fantasy in Gretel's life right now. Her actual life was working, and she wasn't going to waste it wishing she were somewhere or someone else.

Even with her mother, whom she still thought about several times a day, Gretel refused to descend the path of 'if only Deda hadn't gotten sick and mother hadn't gone to take care of him and...' She had learned at fourteen what most people never did: regrets were a waste of time.

But now, months later, here was the mysterious son of The System officer. Petr Stenson. That angelic face from the window was now appearing to Gretel in the center of the

Klahrs' kitchen, as if in a dream, looking as beautiful as she'd remembered him.

Gretel forced down her smile and shook her head quickly, blinking in confusion. "Hi," was all she could manage.

"It's Petr," he said, recognizing that perhaps his name had escaped her.

"Right, Petr. Are you...here with your father? Is there news about my mother or something?" There was only the hint of hope in Gretel's voice, mostly the tone was bewilderment.

"No, no, nothing like that. I'm sorry, I didn't mean to...I'm actually working here during the final weeks of the harvest. The academy agreed to accept me for the fall, with the condition I enroll immediately. They wanted to see if I'm suitable, I suppose. Anyway, the spring session has ended and the summer session doesn't start for a few weeks, and my father wanted me to work during my time off instead of staying home. I guess he thinks it will keep me out of trouble."

"So your father knows the Klahrs?" Gretel asked.

"I don't think so. But my roommate this spring at Hengst worked for them last season, and he told me they always need workers to finish up the season."

None of this sounded plausible to Gretel, but she continued with the conversation. "This isn't too far out for you?" she asked.

Petr laughed, "Of course it's too far, but what am I to do? I don't make the decisions." He bounced his gaze around the kitchen before his eyes landed back on Gretel. "Besides, I kind of like it out here."

Gretel blushed and looked away, swallowing hard, the sting of the boys piercing blue eyes lingering on hers. She composed herself and met the boy's look again, quickly running through the circumstances of this meeting, none of which added up, of course. That she had met Petr at all that first day was unlikely—he'd happened to be with his dad, and his dad had happened to leave his notebook behind in her living room?

And now she was expected to believe that this same kid had been referred to the Klahr orchard by a schoolmate at some snooty academy? Most of the workers in the orchard had never made it past grade school, let alone been to private secondary schools.

With these calculations, Gretel's defenses rocketed to the surface, with anger leading the way. She had little patience for lies—especially from teenage boys—and even less patience for those who looked to take advantage of the people she loved.

"What is his name?" Gretel asked.

Petr's smile dipped slightly and his eyes widened for an instant. "Who's that?"

"Who's that?" she repeated, mimicking the look on Petr's face and tone of his voice. "You know damn well who I mean! What is the name of your roommate? He worked here last summer, did he? Don't you think that's an easy enough thing for me to check?"

Gretel was close to yelling now, and had taken a step forward. She was now only a foot or two from Petr's face.

"What is his name?" she asked again, enunciating each word in staccato jabs.

"Gretel!" a voice barked.

Shaken from her hypnotic attack, Gretel turned to see Mr. Klahr standing tall in the foyer, his chiseled face expressionless and his eyes locked on hers. He had called her name the way a parent might to a disorderly child in a public place, whispery, with jaws clenched.

"Yes, sir," she whispered. She was breathing heavily now, her eyes blurred with a mixture of fear and anger.

"What has gotten to you, Gretel?" Mr. Klahr's voice contained more concern than anger. "This is how you speak to our workers now?"

"No, Mr. Klahr, but—"

"That's enough then."

Mr. Klahr walked slowly to Gretel, his eyes softening as he extended his arms and placed his hands on her shoulders.

"That's quite enough, Gretel. I want you to go home now. You've worked far too much lately, and with all of your schoolwork, I fear you're exhausted."

Gretel had plenty of words to come back with—how this outburst had nothing to do with work or school, and that Petr was suspicious, and that she needed the money—but she knew speaking them would be a waste. When Mr. Klahr made his decision, it was made.

Besides, she *was* tired, and a day of rest wasn't the worst thing she'd ever been told to do. She silently slid the dishtowel from her shoulder and placed it over the basin and then walked toward the door, glaring once more at Petr Stenson before turning the knob.

"His name was Francis," said Mr. Klahr.

Gretel looked over her shoulder at her employer.

"Petr's roommate, his name was Francis."

***

Petr's first week had come and gone with him saying little more than 'Hello' to Gretel, and she now regretted her tirade. It was more than just the scolding she'd received from Mr. Klahr, she'd completely overreacted, showing no grace in her behavior.

She still believed Petr's employment at the Klahr orchard to be an unbelievable coincidence, but apparently coincidences did happen, as was confirmed by Mr. Klahr himself. And now the result was that she'd alienated a potential friend. And maybe something more.

But what did it matter really? The harvest was ending soon and Petr would return to school. And Gretel had far more pressing thoughts to consider, the most important of which being her plans for after the harvest. Her family had come to depend on the money she was earning—for food, for medicine, for everything—and though the end had always been in sight, there was nothing in place for the future. But why was this her concern anyway? Gretel was just fourteen after all, and yet the primary adult in her life, her father, had become reliant on his daughter's temporary, part-time job. It was despicable to Gretel, and she had all but shed any remaining sympathy for his sickness. His recovery had plateaued, apparently, and though Gretel had been able to pay a doctor to reexamine him, he hadn't found any real reason for her father's lack of progress. 'Some people just recover more slowly,' the doctor told them, 'there's not much that can be done.' But he was bed-bound twenty hours a day, and Gretel began to regard him, fairly or not, as just plain lazy.

And frankly, Hansel was Gretel's only real concern now, though she saw very little of him lately; he certainly must have missed his sister just as she did him. But that was a consequence of necessity, and they would all be better off for it. In fact, her being gone was probably good for the boy's development, not having his sister around all the time to impart feminine softness into his personality. He needed to become strong, male, and, with an invalid as a father, Hansel would need to learn this from the world. And, indeed, Hansel was slowly making friendships with other boys in the community—not all of them Gretel's first choices, but safe enough. There certainly hadn't been adequate dedication and follow-through on his schoolwork—Gretel could only do so much—but Hansel had always been a solid student, and as long as he stayed away from trouble, she figured that part would work out fine. And so far, as much as Gretel could tell, her brother was keeping his nose clean.

It was Odalinde Gretel most worried about. She'd kept out of Gretel's hair for the most part, as it concerned her work and other things, but the longer she stayed on, working for free, the more Gretel distrusted her. The Morgan farm was no great land treasure—in fact it was slowly becoming ruinous—but it was property, and if Odalinde had her sights on it, who knew what intentions she had ultimately.

Gretel had been saving though, putting some cash away after each day's wages, leaving only enough for Odalinde to pay the creditors and feed herself and her father. Gretel had splurged some in the beginning, but she'd been frugal otherwise, and had saved up a decent stipend. When the Klahr gig was up, she would offer it all to Odalinde, with the condition that she leave quietly. She wasn't sure what she'd tell her father, or how she would care for him, but she needed that woman out of her house. Of course, Gretel had no illusions the payoff would work—she was old enough to understand that if Odalinde was the evil figure Gretel imagined her to be, the woman could have robbed them long ago—but maybe a lump payment was just what she was waiting for, and Gretel had to try.

Gretel finished her dinner duties and after the dishes were cleared and cleaned—and she herself had finally eaten—Gretel said her goodbyes to the Klahrs and rowed back across the lake, deciding to forego her normal routine of canoeing down to the Stein mill before going home.

She walked inside and instinctively put on a pot of coffee before checking on a sleeping Hansel, and then unpacked her schoolbooks and walked out to the porch, where she piled the considerable stack on the table. Among a few other assignments, she had her final biology test tomorrow. It would be a late night.

She dove right in, opening to a chapter on Mendel and his discoveries in genetics. She read the first page and then thought better of it, figuring such dry reading should wait until the effects of the caffeine had been fully realized. Instead she just sat quietly, reflecting on her day in the orchard and Mrs. Klahr's kitchen, feeding and cleaning and bantering with the Klahrs and the pickers. And Petr Stenson, with whom she guessed she should try to make amends.

The thoughts started well and then began to career again into the darkness of her future once the harvest ended. Gretel had visited the outskirts of this topic in her mind for weeks, but always backed away, not ready to face it. Everything had happened so quickly! The Klahr's, the job, the sudden abundance of food—it was all so wonderful that she hadn't really made any plans beyond. But it would come to an end when the last pickers left the orchard, and Gretel didn't know what she would do then.

The pot on the stove began to percolate, and Gretel walked to the kitchen and poured a cup of coffee. She immediately drank half of it—black—and then refilled the mug, flavoring it now with milk and sugar. Before her work at the Klahr orchard, Gretel had occasionally drunk coffee in the morning, usually on a lazy Sunday or holiday, but now she drank it habitually at night, and thanked God that He had blessed the Earth with such a miracle. She'd have never lasted the first week on the job without it.

The caffeine hit Gretel almost immediately, and the energy made her feel a notch better about the future. She was determined to maintain this life she'd made over the past few weeks, and if she had to knock on the door of every farmer in the Back Country to find work, she'd do it. She had experience now, and an apparent talent, and the Klahrs would certainly give a good reference to any potential employer. It wouldn't be easy, but that she would find work she had little doubt. She would make herself irreplaceable to the family that took her on.

Gretel now surged with inspiration and decided a row on the lake was exactly what was needed. She would study the biology chapter later; right now there was too much inside her to focus on the inherited traits of pea plants. Her canoe excursions were peaceful and cleansing and helped to untangle the thoughts that had silently built up during the day but which Gretel had not been able to tackle fully. She seldom missed a night on the lake, as she had done tonight, and now, with her mind overrun with thoughts of the future, she knew why.

When Gretel first started at the orchard, Mr. Klahr had offered to pick her up in the mornings and take her home at night—offers which Gretel had politely refused. At first she had done so because she didn't want to burden her employer or be bound by their schedules—she wanted to arrive as early as possible and leave when it was time to go. But eventually the rowing had become the reason. She cherished it. Every part of it. The smell of the wood and the water, the air on her face and neck as it drafted past her, and, of course, the results of her efforts, both on her mind and muscles. The short canoe ride home had become such a pleasure to Gretel that by the third day she had expanded her commute, rowing down to the Stein mill or up toward the abandoned cannery. Some nights the paddling was leisurely and calm, other nights it was as fierce as a slave galley. Tonight would be the latter. Gretel felt the need to be strong.

Gretel poured the last swallow of coffee into the sink and washed the cup out, turning it face down to dry on the towel next to the basin, and then walked to the front door.

"Gretel," a voice said from somewhere in the house.

It was her father, and though the words were calm and measured, they bit into the back of Gretel's neck as if they had been screamed.

Gretel stepped away from the door and walked back through the kitchen to get a view of the family room where it sounded like her father had spoken. And there he was, sitting on the couch smiling, Odalinde next to him with a similar look on her face.

"What's going on, Papa?"

"Sit down," her father said, pointing at one of the chairs that sat opposite the sofa.

Gretel walked slowly to the chair, never taking her stare off the couple sitting across from her. Her father looked misplaced on the couch, artificial, like a mannequin strategically positioned to showcase the couch in some bizarre showroom. Tears welled in Gretel's eyes though she couldn't have said why at the time.

"Gretel," her father said, "Odalinde and I have some news."

Gretel said nothing, waiting.

"We're getting married, Gretel."

There was a feeling in Gretel's body of collision and nausea, and she stifled a gag as her hand reached reflexively for her stomach. She had the sudden urge to release her bowels. Her face flooded with blood and adrenaline; somehow—incredibly—she kept her tears at bay.

Gretel immediately thought of Mr. Klahr's question that first night, and the look on his face at the time. He knew this was coming and had felt sorry for her. How naive she was! Of course they were getting married! It was obvious even to

Mr. Klahr, a stranger at the time, a man who saw her family only occasionally from across a lake. And yet Gretel hadn't seen it coming!

Instinctively, protectively, her thoughts went to the lake. She wished more than anything that she was drifting on it now, listening to the groan of the bullfrogs and the light *plop, plop* of jumping fish. Why hadn't she rowed tonight instead of coming straight home? Ultimately it wouldn't have made a difference, the revelation she'd just heard would have been told eventually, but maybe it would have been put off for the night.

"Married?" Gretel finally said, not able to manage even a trace of joy in her tone or expression.

"I proposed this morning and Odalinde accepted." Heinrich Morgan managed a dull smile and looked to his fiancé. "The wedding will be in the winter. Just after Christmas perhaps."

Her father's words seemed to be coming from somewhere in Gretel's imagination, as if she were playing a game in her mind, conjuring the most horrible scenes that could possibly occur in her life, just so that she may better appreciate what her life actually was. Her stomach tightened further and Gretel prepared to run for the bathroom, but the wave subsided.

"I'd like you to be in my wedding, Gretel," Odalinde said flatly, though with a mock formality that was appropriate for the occasion.

Gretel ignored her and said to her father, "Is she pregnant?

"Gretel!" her father snapped.

Gretel finally looked at Odalinde, stunned, realizing the hurtfulness of her question. But the inquiry wasn't meant to be mean-spirited; it was the only genuine reason Gretel could come up with for the engagement.

"I'm sorry," she said, and with those words the tears finally came.

Gretel ran from the family room and out the front door down to the lake. Tonight she would row as she'd never rowed before.

***

Though sullen and spiritless, Gretel rose the next morning and, as usual, arrived early for work. She tried to keep things to herself, but the morning chaos had hardly begun before Mrs. Klahr uncovered the source of her young apprentice's mood.

"Surely you must have suspected this could happen, Gretel?" Mrs. Klahr said. She spoke softly, in a tone intended to diminish the impact of her recent upset, not to point out Gretel's naiveté.

"Yes ma'am, I suppose I did," Gretel replied. "That first night, in this very kitchen, Mr. Klahr asked me if those were my father's intentions, so I must have had some idea. I tried not to think of it, I guess. I just wanted to go home one day and have her be gone." Gretel looked at the ceiling as she spoke, as if the feelings inside of her were suddenly organizing themselves in a way that made sense. "She doesn't love my father."

Mrs. Klahr let Gretel's words resonate, being in no position to confirm or deny the statement.

The two women sat without speaking for several moments before the sound of Mr. Klahr's boots striding thunderously in from the orchard fractured the silence. He sensed the mood instantly, and Mrs. Klahr filled him in on the relevant facts. He nodded thoughtfully, his discomfort palpable. "I'm sorry," he said, "I...I know how you feel about her."

Gretel mouthed an inaudible 'thank you', and sat frowning with her elbows splayed on the kitchen table and her fists screwed into her cheeks.

Mr. Klahr shot his wife a glance. "Gretel, we need to talk to you about something else," he said.

Gretel felt her stomach tighten and her eyes flicked up wide to meet Mr. Klahr's. "Yes? What is it?" She guessed maybe it was to do more with her behavior toward Petr and braced for admonishment.

"As you know, the harvest is ending. By the end of next week, we'll be done." Mr. Klahr paused for a moment and stared at Gretel intensely. "When we took you on, it was temporary, with the understanding that when the season is over, your work would be done here."

"I know," Gretel said. Her voice wobbled, pitching upwards on the word 'know.'

She sat up straight and closed her eyes, focusing whatever restraint remained inside her on not shedding tears. She'd done far too much of that lately. She felt a tear creeping over her bottom lashes and quickly caught it with her thumb. She squeezed her eyes tight and shivered once to clear any remaining sobs, then smiled weakly at Mr. Klahr, embarrassed at her fragility.

"Gretel, you don't understand." Mr. Klahr grabbed Gretel's hands. "We want you to stay on with us."

The words hung in the air, drifting around the kitchen like ghosts.

Gretel's smile fell straight. "What?"

It was Mr. Klahr's turn to smile now. "In case you hadn't noticed Gretel, we're old."

"You're the strongest people I know," Gretel said absently, irrelevantly.

"We do fine, Gretel, and we don't complain much. But we ache as much as the next people, and we aren't beyond needing help." He squeezed her hands tighter. "We'd have never made it through this harvest without you."

Gretel sat staring, stupidly she imagined, and as the reality of the offer set in, she couldn't restrain herself anymore, and the sobs came out in huge coughing waves. Her mother would have been mortified, but Gretel didn't care.

Then, as if possessed, she launched herself toward Mr. Klahr and threw her arms around him, his eyes widening in reflexive fear. He caught her and briefly held her at a distance, before bringing her into a full embrace. "It's true! You've been a godsend!"

Gretel pulled away and looked at Mr. Klahr quizzically, wiping her nose with her sleeve the way a five-year-old might. "But what will I do?" she said, almost panicking, "when the harvest is done?"

Amanda Klahr laughed. "Oh, my dear, there are plenty of things in your life to worry on, having enough work to do around here is not one of those things."

Gretel laughed at this and then stopped abruptly, suddenly awestruck by the strong, plump woman that sat before her. Gretel walked around the table to Mrs. Klahr and gently wrapped her arms around the old woman's neck, making a silent vow to take care of her for the rest of her life. "Thank you," was all she could manage.

"You're very welcome, love," Mrs. Klahr said, "but you don't seem to understand that this is not charity. We really do need you."

"Thank you anyway, both of you."

"And this also doesn't solve the problem of your father."

This fact sobered Gretel only slightly. "No, it doesn't. But one thing at a time. Right now I'm too happy to care. Besides, I haven't even started on breakfast and I hear the men mulling around outside already."

"Oh please," Mrs. Klahr said, "they're glad to wait. It only means they get to start working later. They get the same wage either way. But I imagine you are right, we should get going."

Mr. Klahr stood to leave. "Welcome to the family, Gretel. For good." And with that he walked out.

The rest of that day Gretel worked with an energy she'd never felt before. She took no break at lunch, instead grabbing a roll on the fly and a slice of pie while she waited for the dishes to come in. At dinner, she playfully teased the pickers as she placed their food on the table, and after, when the final plate was cleared, she alone wiped down the huge table and swept the patio clean (a chore that usually waited until morning). And when Saturday evening arrived, and her week was down to its final hour, the fierceness of her work endured, as she scrubbed the cabinets to a shine.

"I want you to take next week off," Amanda Klahr stated flatly, continuing to dry a bowl and not looking at Gretel.

Gretel giggled, wiping the pantry door down. "Yes ma'am, thank you. Perhaps I'll fly off to the tropics and catch up on my sun."

"I'm not joking, Gretel, I want you to rest. I've spoken with Mr. Klahr and he agrees."

Mrs. Klahr caught Gretel's stare, hardening her face to demonstrate the seriousness of her words.

"There's not enough work in the field for all the pickers anyway, so I'll put some of them to work in the house. Most of the meals have already been prepared so the cooking will be easy. It's just a matter of heating the food." She softened her tone. "Listen, if you're going to work here, you'll need to establish some balance in your life, and we're both concerned that you aren't focusing enough on being a young girl. I don't think I've ever even heard you mention friends."

This wasn't what Gretel had in mind with her new duties, and was speechless. And scared at the prospect of a week without pay.

As if reading Gretel's mind, Amanda Klahr said, "We'll pay you of course. It's our decision, not yours, so of course we'll pay you."

"I couldn't..." Gretel said weakly, still dazed by the order.

"You can and you will. I don't want to see you anywhere near this property until next Monday. We will give your regrets to the workers since most of them will be gone by then."

"Most?"

"Petr will stay for a few weeks longer, as a favor to his father."

Gretel tried to think of more reasons to protest her hiatus—some necessity the Klahrs hadn't considered perhaps—but she came up with nothing, and as the reality of a vacation slowly took hold in her imagination, she quickly warmed to the idea. Not only for the much-needed rest, but school was coming to an end, and with her final tests looming at the end of the week, time off would be an invaluable gift.

But perhaps the best part was she could finally reconnect with Hansel—at least enough to find out if there were any major problems that needed tackling. From afar things seemed fine with the boy, but a closer look wouldn't hurt.

And she could spend extra time rowing as well, perhaps take the canoe past the cannery one day and picnic in Rifle Field. Because of her schedule at the orchard, her leisure rowing was always done at night, in complete darkness or the gloom; and all her plans for Sunday jaunts to explore the lake always disintegrated into more sleep. Not this week. This week she'd row in the light of the sun every day.

Of course, time off from work also meant more chances to clutch horns with Odalinde. The two women had spoken very little since Gretel started working, and though to an outsider that might have appeared to strain them further, in Gretel's mind this was a mutual benefit. The edges of their relationship had sharpened severely in the days just prior to Gretel starting at the orchard, and time apart was needed medicine.

But if storm clouds did start forming this week, Gretel figured she had enough outlets to keep away from the nurse.

She also made the promise that this was the week she'd get into her future stepmother's cabinet beneath the sink.

CHAPTER NINE

As she did most Sundays, Gretel spent the bulk of her day in her room sleeping and reading. But by Monday afternoon, with the school day over and her body rested, she was eager to begin her vacation.

She was still struggling with the idea of so much free time, and all that was still to be done for the final week of harvest, but the order had been given to take the time, and she was determined not to waste it.

An appreciable relief had filled the room when Gretel relayed the news to her family—including Odalinde—regarding her newly-gained permanent employment, and she was proud to have provided that relief. Her father had wept at the news, as did Hansel (no doubt because his father had), and her soon-to-be stepmother gave a wide, quizzical smile that Gretel found unusual, almost as if she were reassessing Gretel, that she had perhaps underestimated her.

The other part of the deal—that Gretel would spend the upcoming week free from her duties (and would be paid for it)—Gretel decided to keep to herself, figuring it was no one's business but hers and would only result in requests for her time. She had a lot to do this week and she couldn't be bothered with other people's concerns.

Gretel's first order of business was figuring a way inside Odalinde's cabinet beneath the sink. This was, she reasoned, her house, and now that she was providing for the house, including paying for the food that filled the cabinets, she had every right to know what else was inside them. Even that one.

And if it turned out not to be the repository of danger and mystery that Gretel suspected it was, the nagging curiosity of the whole thing would at least be settled.

Odalinde's only routine outing each week occurred on Thursdays, when she left precisely at four in the afternoon and returned sometime around eight; this according to Hansel, who hadn't a clue where she went. Gretel mentally added the uncovering of that mystery to the list of things she would attempt to tackle this week.

But that was a problem for later. Gretel's concern now was to discover the contents of the cabinet, and how, if at all, they affected her family. If, in the end, it turned out Odalinde was only storing photos of her dead grandmother, or some ancient love letters from a teenage sweetheart, then so be it. But Gretel knew instinctively it was more than that.

The current lock on the cabinet was formidable, and, in fact, was a replacement for the one Gretel's father had put in originally when Odalinde first arrived—Odalinde declaring *that* lock to be 'perfectly unsuitable.' She had made some reference to 'Back Country burglars,' but Gretel had never heard of such a thing and concluded 'Back Country burglars' was just code for 'Hansel and Gretel.'

Gretel's first idea to access the cabinet was to go in through the side of one of the adjoining cabinets, removing it, or even cutting a small hole that could be glued back once the contents were known. But the walls of the cupboard were solid wood, oak probably, and to go through them would have required more destruction than she'd be able to cause and repair in one short evening.

Her other idea was to go in from the top, through the sink above the cabinet; but, similar to the walls, the basin was heavy, and would have been far too difficult for her to remove, especially with all the attached plumbing. And she hadn't the time to find someone with the skills to deal with all that. No, the only way in, she decided, was through the door. And that meant she needed the key.

This conclusion sat well with Gretel, and she was filled with hope. Getting the key would surely prove difficult, but not impossible, and she'd have to plan the thing carefully. But that it could be done, she was more than hopeful.

Gretel ruminated on the framework of a plan for a while before dropping the subject entirely and spending the remainder of Monday rowing on the lake, clearing her mind of any plans or plots or fantasies of the future. She'd only recently learned the sacredness of quiet, and the cleansing properties of it, and considered this new exercise in nothingness—she thought of it as having a 'white mind'—to be no less valuable than engaging her brain in the throes of work. The natural marvel of trees and water and untarnished air that had surrounded Gretel since birth were suddenly awakened to her, and she now basked in their stillness whenever possible. There was a time for designing and scheming, obviously, and she took pride in her industrious and conspiratorial inclinations, but she also had no doubt that peril awaited the unrested mind. And, in fact, it was often in the times of total clarity and peace that the ideas she needed most came to her.

And here it had come again, just as she began to turn the small boat that had become her sanctuary back toward home: the keys to Odalinde's cabinet were always kept in her bag, and her bag was never left unattended. If Gretel could pull her away from the bag, distract her for just a minute, she could grab them.

She had an idea, and she would need Hansel's help. It was by no means an infallible plan, but it was something.

***

The next day Gretel decided to walk with Hansel from school, which was something she hadn't done since she started working at the orchard. She needed to discuss the newly-devised plan with him, and this, she figured, would be the safest time. Other than her erratic shopping jaunts, and the Thursday night outing, Odalinde always seemed to be around, and had a knack for appearing from the shadows of a tree or the back of a dimly-lit room during a conversation, or entering a room just when the gist of a thought was being spoken. She was sneaky—it was always the first word that came to Gretel's mind when she thought of her future stepmother—and she, Gretel, was taking no chances of being overheard.

But Gretel also regretted the pretense of 'catching up' with her brother as the reason she was walking with him today, and despite her eagerness to construct the plan, and the reasonable explanation that she was off work for the week, she aborted the discussion for the time being. She realized the time together *should* be used to catch up with him, to rediscover Hansel's life; the plot against Odalinde could wait a few hours, even a day if necessary.

"Are you going to try for any teams next year? Soccer maybe? You like soccer, right?"

"I'm not good at soccer," Hansel replied flatly, "I'm not fast enough."

"What? That's silly! You're plenty fast for soccer! And besides, you don't need to be fast for all the positions." Gretel was giving it a go, but it felt forced. Clearly she was rusty at engaging her brother. And she really did want to encourage him to go out for a team!

"I don't like it anyway," Hansel said, and that was the end of that. The boy was going to play or he wasn't, and what she said wasn't going to change anything.

The siblings walked the road in silence for several minutes.

"Do you like her, Hansel?" Gretel finally said, "Odalinde, I mean."

Hansel looked over at his sister, trying to gauge the answer she wanted. But Gretel kept her face as casual and neutral as the tone of her voice.

"I don't know. Sometimes, I guess," Hansel answered.

Gretel nodded, maintaining her breezy air.

"I know you hate her though."

Gretel stopped walking and Hansel followed suit, sheepishly avoiding his sister's eyes in the process. She scrunched her forehead and smiled weakly at Hansel. "What? No. I...I don't...I don't really *hate* her." She glanced at the sky. "No, that's not the right word. I just...I guess I just don't trust her. And that's only because I don't know anything about her."

Her voice became shrill. "And now, all of a sudden, she's marrying Father, moving into our house for good, and we don't really know anything about her."

Gretel stopped, and then dropped her voice to its normal pitch and slowed her tempo.

"I know that Odalinde and I have had our conflicts, but we're both women, Hansel, and sometimes...I don't know, sometimes women take a little longer to get along. It doesn't really make sense, but it's true."

Gretel felt she was losing control of the conversation, and in doing so making Hansel feel more insecure, which was the opposite of her intention. If she wasn't going use this time to pitch her brother on being an accomplice to some future cabinet raid, she wanted at least to restore some stability to his psyche. Maybe even make him laugh a time or two. What she didn't want was to get him thinking that his future stepmother was out to steal their home and Father, and that she couldn't be trusted. And that seemed to be right where the conversation was headed.

They both started again toward home and Gretel stayed quiet the rest of the way, disappointed at her clumsiness. She decided she may not ask for Hansel's help at all. It meant she would have to come up with another idea since her original plan called for his diversion, but so be it. If he wasn't ready, then it wasn't fair to involve him. But either way, Hansel or not, Gretel still had every intention of finding out what was in that cabinet.

The children reached the long, dusty driveway that led to the Morgan house when Hansel finally spoke. "I know something about her," he said.

From the tone of her brother's voice, Gretel could instantly tell this 'something' was not insignificant, and she stopped quickly, grabbing Hansel's arm lightly and turning him toward her. She studied his eyes and could see that he had struggled with this knowledge for a while now, and probably had more than one internal debate about whether to share it. Gretel felt a bit angry at first—that he hadn't trusted her with this information—but the feeling fell away as quickly as it developed. The truth was if he had known this thing two months ago—this secret—there was no doubt he'd have confided in his sister. But Gretel's work at the orchard had abruptly snatched her out of his life, and with the new figure of Odalinde now tending to Hansel's daily needs, as cold and neglectful as that figure may have seemed to Gretel, Hansel's loyalties had become less defined.

"Is it something you want to tell me?" she replied.

Hansel nodded.

Gretel was careful to take it slow. "I understand if you're scared, Han, and if you don't want to tell me, whatever it is you know, or you want to tell me some other time, that's okay." She placed her finger under her brother's chin and lifted it to meet his eyes with hers. It was a move her mother had perfected with both her children. "But no matter what," she said, "I'll never let anything happen to you. Okay?"

Hansel nodded again, this time more contemplatively. "What about you though? I don't want anything to happen to you." He looked away, embarrassed.

Gretel gave a sad smile and sighed, a glaze of tears suddenly blurring her vision. She pulled her brother close and hugged him, resting her cheek on his dirty blond hair. Finally she said, "Do you still think about Mom?"

Hansel paused for a moment, thoughtful, and then said, "I used to think about her every day, "but now sometimes I don't."

"That happens to me too. That's okay. But then I remember to think about her and I get happy. So it's important that we don't forget her, okay? She loved us very much. So very much." And then, "And she wanted us to be happy."

Hansel let this sink in. "But what if thinking about her makes me sad?"

Gretel squeezed her eyes tight and the tears began to drop on Hansel's head. "Just don't forget her, Han," she said, and used all her will to stifle the sobs forming inside her.

The children stood silently embraced for a moment in the openness of the faded gravel driveway, like two figures holding on for their lives in the eye of a raging storm.

Hansel finally pulled away from his sister and stared coldly into her eyes. "I want to tell you what happened, Gretel. But I don't want to tell you here."

***

Rifle Field rested just past the Weinhiemmer Cannery and derived its name from the late afternoon sounds of factory workers, ostensibly drunk, finishing their shifts and then honing their marksmanship skills on those containers deemed unsuitable for market. The cannery itself, once a Back Country pillar of capitalism, had long been abandoned as a result of short-sighted management and a debilitating class-action lawsuit brought about by the families of dozens of botulism victims, several of whom had apparently died.

These days, in addition to being a blot on the landscape, the cannery, with its surrounding fence and sprawling rusted paneling, acted as a barrier to Rifle Field. And with the winding lake that swept past the opposite side of the large swath of land, the field could really only be reached by water.

When Gretel was younger, the Morgan family often pic-nicked in the field, and occasionally had even kept the name relevant by taking target practice at the side of the cannery. At one point, Heinrich Morgan had even taken steps to maintain the landscape of Rifle Field, hauling the mower out on the canoe to level the grass as well as by planting shrubs and flowers. The constant demands of the farm, however, saw this practice die quickly.

And now, after remaining deserted for so long, Rifle Field had been resurrected as an asylum for Gretel, her own private hideaway from the demands of family and employer. She had, in fact, only taken to land there twice since she began her rowing excursions (she usually couldn't spare the time and preferred to be on the water anyway), but she considered the field 'hers' now, and by all accounts, she was the only person to step foot on it in years. Until today, when her brother disembarked from the canoe and helped lay down the tarp on which they both now sat.

"It was a couple of Saturdays ago." Hansel began. "Not that long after you started working at the orchard." He paused. "I think it was Saturday...I know it wasn't Sunday be-cause you weren't home."

Gretel smiled, struggling not to pressure Hansel to the point. He was only eight, after all, and she didn't want to hurt his feelings or embarrass him by pointing out irrelevancies. They were in no hurry, and if it took all day, Gretel had every intention of letting her brother meander his way to the crux.

"Anyway, Odalinde was getting into her cabinet like she does; you know how she gets into that creepy stoop in front of it?"

Gretel smiled and nodded. Oh, she knew all right.

"I was on the porch watching her, and she knew I was there but she didn't know I was watching. But she was still covering everything up and staying really close to the door. And then when she was done looking at her stuff or whatever she does, and she was about to lock the door, right at that second Dad called out to her, loud, like he was hurt or scared or something. Right when she was about to lock it."

He stopped for a moment and his eyes widened. "It was like it was supposed to happen. It was weird."

Gretel was rapt with attention, not at all surprised at the timing of her father's call. "And then what?" she said gently.

"And then Odalinde jumped, and almost fell off her heels onto her back. But she caught herself, and then got up and ran to Dad's room."

Hansel stopped and looked at Gretel, waiting for the revelation to sink in.

Gretel stared back and finally said, "So?"

"I didn't think she locked it, Gretel. I could tell, just the way it happened and how she got so surprised. After Dad's scream, she took the key out of the lock, but I could tell she didn't turn it to lock the door. I could just tell. And then when she came out of Daddy's room, she rushed out the front door and drove off in the truck."

Gretel felt a pang for her brother whenever he regressed to 'Daddy,' but she kept silent and her expression fixed.

"I don't know if she went to get medicine or food or what," Hansel continued, "but she didn't say anything. Or even look at me."

Gretel could see where the story was going, and she hoped more than gold it arrived there.

"So I looked inside, Gretel. I opened it and looked inside."

Gretel couldn't believe what she was hearing. Was this true? A grin the length of the lake formed on her face. She was so excited she wanted to grab her brother and squeeze him until he popped. All the elaborate thoughts of taking apart the cabinetry, and her plan of using Hansel as a decoy to pull Odalinde away from her bag so that Gretel could somehow steal the key and...and do what? She didn't really know, and it didn't matter! Hansel. Beautiful Hansel!

But Gretel had to be realistic and temper her enthusiasm; what Hansel found only mattered to the extent that he could relay it to her. "What did you find, Han?"

Hansel focused his stare in concentration, trying to get it all right. "I thought there was going to be all kinds of junk inside," he said, "like loose papers and stuff. But when I opened the door, all I saw was that huge brown bag. You know the one?"

Gretel nodded slowly, hanging on every word.

"So I undid the clasp and started to open it, but then I saw the bag wasn't all that was inside the cupboard. Behind it, all the way against the back, there was a book. A black book."

Gretel stared at her brother in astonishment.

"It was your book, Gretel," he said flatly, "except it wasn't yours. I checked, yours was still where you always keep it."

Gretel's throat tightened and a true fear took hold of her senses. She was terrified, speechless, trying at once both to understand how what Hansel was telling her could be, and what was to be done about it. Finally she managed, "Are you sure?"

"I checked Gretel, your book was there. I know I'm not supposed to know where you keep it, but I..."

Gretel cut him off, "I mean are you sure that it's the same book? Maybe it just looked the same. Maybe it was just another big black book. About something else."

"*Orphism,* Gretel, I read it on the cover. And all those crazy letters inside. It was the same book." He stopped for a moment, remembering. "But there was something different about hers."

"What do you mean? Different how?" Gretel was losing her poise now and the shrillness in her voice was returning. She caught herself. "What was different, Han?"

"There was lots of writing in her book—like handwriting, with pencil and ink. It was all over the pages, on every page, in between the sentences and at the tops and bottoms. Everywhere."

"Writing? Could you read it? Was it English?"

"I could read most of it. It was definitely English, but a lot of it was sloppy and I didn't really pay that much attention to what it was about. I just flipped through some of the pages—a lot of the pages—and the writing was everywhere."

It took a moment—longer than she would later admit—to occur to Gretel what it all meant, but when it finally did sink in, she gave a throaty giggle and then started laughing. It could only be one thing. A translation! The words had to be a translation!

She quickly stood up on the tarp and walked off it into the tall grass where she began pacing in short laps, staring at the sky in wonder. Virtually every day for months she'd been looking at this book, trying to decipher a word here and there, hoping to get some idea what it was about. And had been utterly dreadful in doing so. And it turned out, apparently, that she'd been walking past the knowledge every time she entered or left the kitchen. Unbelievable!

Gretel's head was spinning with the fact that her father's nurse—whom she trusted no further than she could toss her—was somehow in possession of the same book her grandfather had given her, and which had fascinated her for years. But even that mystery was superseded by the idea of finally knowing what the book was about, and Gretel quickly paced back toward the tarp.

"Did you see at all what it said, Han, anything at all that might have told you what the book was about?"

"I told you, I just flipped through it. I was scared and I...I'm sorry, I..."

"It's okay, Han," she interrupted, sensing his fear that she was disappointed in him, "you did great." Gretel stepped toward her brother and stooped down to his level, taking his head in her hands. She smiled at him and repeated, "You did great."

Gretel stood up again and walked back onto the grass, this time continuing through the field toward the cannery. She needed a minute to consider everything. The plan was back on: she would still need to get into the cabinet—now more than ever. Whether Odalinde found out that she'd been snooping was less of a concern now that Gretel had probable cause; but at the same time, it was perhaps even more important to be discreet, and she revisited her plan, mentally tweaking the details. Hansel. A diversion.

After a few more moments, Gretel walked back to the tarp where her brother sat cross-legged, his face scrunched in his palms and his elbows propped on his knees. She stared at him a moment and detected a sadness in the boy that she hadn't noticed before. "Are you okay, Han?"

The boy looked up at his sister and sighed, catching her eyes for just a moment before looking away.

"What's the matter? Are you upset about the book? This is good, Han. I'm just excited to know what it's about, that's all. It doesn't mean that Odalinde is bad. I mean, it *is* strange that she has the same book that Deda had, but that doesn't necessarily mean anything. It could just be a coincidence."

"There's more, Gretel."

Gretel's face twisted into confusion. "More what? You said you didn't know what the book said."

"I'm not talking about the book." With that Hansel met his sister's stare and held it. "I'm talking about the bag."

The bag. Odalinde's bag! It was the main reason Gretel wanted to get into the cupboard in the first place, and now she had completely forgotten about it. She'd gotten so excited—elated—about the book she'd forgotten there was anything else in the cabinet and assumed the book was all Hansel would have cared about as well.

Gretel sat down next to her brother slowly, mimicking his Indian-style posture, and scooted close to him, resting her hands in her lap. She saw the seriousness about him and wanted to offset it by assuming a relaxed manner.

"What did you find in the bag, Hansel?"

Hansel looked down into his own lap and then looked over at his sister. "I found another book, a smaller one, with names and stuff on it. Like a phone book, but one you write your own numbers and names in."

Some type of organizer, Gretel got it. "And did you see a name in there that you knew?" she asked.

Hansel nodded.

Gretel waited for it, deciding to let her brother reveal the name without any further questions.

"There were lots of names on the pages in the book, and I didn't know any of them at first. Why would I, right?"

"Right."

"But then I was closing it, to put it back in the bag and be done with it, and I saw a name written on the inside cover, down at the bottom."

Hansel stared warily at Gretel, preparing her for the name.

"Officer Stenson, Gretel, that officer from The System who came out here."

"What?" Gretel's reply was a reflexive whisper, her mouth lingering wide, her eyes alert. Clearly not a name she was expecting.

Hansel nodded in confirmation. "I saw it written there, Gretel, with no first name either, just Officer Stenson. And there was a phone number next to it."

Hansel paused as his sister digested this latest morsel.

"I guess it could be another Officer Stenson, but I don't think it is."

Gretel didn't think so either. It wasn't impossible, of course, but neither was a spaceship landing on the roof of their house.

She conjured the image of Officer Stenson now in her mind—not the breezy, affable man she'd first met at the door, but the cold-mannered lawman that walked out of it, so completely unaffected by her father's demeanor and subtle threats. Amused by them almost.

And she also recalled Petr's words that day as she stood on the porch watching the boy walk away admonished: *I don't think he's here to help you.*

"Why do you think Odalinde has Officer Stenson's name in her book, Gretel?"

Snapped from her reverie, Gretel stood quickly, giving the indication that it was time to leave. "I don't know, Hansel, I haven't one clue," she said absently.

"Are you going to ask her?"

"No!" Gretel replied sharply, "and neither are you!" For the moment, Gretel was done with any fragile emotions still brewing in her brother. "Let's go."

Hansel helped Gretel fold up the tarp and they carried it back to the canoe before pushing the boat back into the water and paddling away from Rifle Field. It was the last time Hansel would ever set foot on that particular piece of land.

Gretel was quiet until they reached the shoreline of their property. "Hansel," she said finally, "I'm going to need your help."

***

Gretel stood with her hands stuffed in her pockets, the key on the tips of her fingers, and watched casually as Odalinde scurried about the kitchen, double-checking that she had all her things in order before her mysterious Thursday excursion. It was just as Hansel said: she was leaving for the evening, and the urgency of the woman's movements led Gretel to believe that the outing was not unimportant. She was shallow-breathed and fidgety, all the time having a whispered dialogue with herself as she glanced at the clock about every thirty seconds.

It was strange to see her in such a fuss, her default demeanor being one of such weariness and indifference, and Gretel played mentally with the possibilities. A lover was certainly not unreasonable—perhaps she had a standing tryst with some young ram from town, a weekly roll in the field to satisfy nature's insistence. Maybe it was even Officer Stenson who was on the receiving end.

But if that were the routine, Gretel would have expected Odalinde to be a bit more adorned than she was at the moment. She wasn't an ugly woman by any stretch—in fact Gretel thought she had the natural makings to be rather pretty—but there was a vacant, weathered look to her, and she always wore her hair and face with such plainness. And since her arrival, her wardrobe had gradually descended into outright sloppiness, with tonight being no exception. There was little to distinguish her appearance from any regular day around the house, her clothes wrinkled and large on her frame and her hair and face in need of washing.

The other possibility Gretel played with was that Odalinde was off to meet her lawyer or accountant, or perhaps some business-minded partner who would aid her in snatching the Morgan farm out from under the shoes of its familial heirs—namely Gretel and Hansel. It certainly fit with the impression Gretel had of Odalinde as cold and ruthless.

But that fantasy didn't quite make sense either. Odalinde and her father were engaged after all, and once they were married, the farm would essentially be Odalinde's anyway. And after father died, which he most certainly would before Odalinde, she would have full authority and ownership of the property. Why would she risk all the fighting and legal tanglings for something that would more or less belong to her in a matter of months?

But then again, patience didn't appear to be Odalinde's most renowned characteristic, and the more Gretel considered conspiracy as the back story behind her rendezvous, the more it felt like the truth.

The whole business of staging a diversion to steal the key from the satchel was far easier than Gretel had imagined, and all the planning she and Hansel had done for that purpose now seemed laughable. Odalinde had been so anxious and intent on leaving for the evening, that Hansel's scream from the bathroom, and the subsequent appearance of a two-foot garter snake in the tub, was more than enough to engage her long enough for Gretel to raid the bag and secure the key.

The only real issue had been the timing: Hansel had to be sure that Odalinde had already taken the bag from the cabinet before sounding his alarm, and Gretel had to be out of the room when it happened, since it was unlikely the woman would have left her alone with it.

But in the end it had all been synchronized perfectly, and by the time Hansel and Odalinde finally wrangled the reptile and secured it in an old hat box, Gretel had the key at the bottom of her pocket and was back outside watering the flowers.

"Will you be gone long?" Gretel asked.

Odalinde gave a measured look toward Gretel and held her eyes, all the time continuing with the details of her departure.

"I only ask because I'm usually not here at this time and I wanted to know if there is anything I need to do for Father while you're away. Medications and such."

"He's fine," Odalinde replied flatly, dropping her gaze and focusing it on Hansel, "and your brother knows what to do if he has any pain."

Gretel noted that Odalinde hadn't answered her original question and decided not to arouse further suspicion by pushing it. She'd really only asked because she thought it might appear suspicious if she took *no* interest in Odalinde's outing, being that Gretel had yet to see the woman ever leave the house for any reason other than to shop. Besides, Hansel said she was usually gone for several hours, and Gretel figured that if the answers she sought were to be found in the cabinet, she'd need less than a half hour or so to discover the real story of why the nurse had invaded her family.

"Have you and father set a date yet?" Gretel asked, silently cursing herself immediately after for continuing to engage Odalinde. It was in her own best interest to let the woman get on with her evening, but Gretel couldn't help herself. Her displeasure and suspicions about the marriage had been on full display over the past week, and she rarely missed an opportunity to highlight them with a snide remark or probing question. In this case, the question was innocent enough, but the suggestion of accusation was unmistakable.

"We've got a few in mind," Odalinde replied tersely, "I'll be sure to let you know the moment we decide."

The quick smile on Odalinde's lips was contrasted by the uneasiness in her eyes, and Gretel grinned, proud at the jab she'd landed.

Gretel stood tall in the kitchen and watched her step-mother-to-be glance at the clock one last time and then shoot a reflexive peek at her before leaving without another word. Just to be sure, Gretel loped to the bedroom window and watched the truck drive off. She was taking no chances.

Once the old Morgan truck was out of sight, Gretel immediately raced to the kitchen and found Hansel waiting eagerly next to the cabinet.

She had some concern that her brother's feet would get cold about what they were doing, that he would feel he was somehow betraying Odalinde and would then be saddled with this secret throughout his childhood. But his posture and expression indicated only that he was ready to get on with it.

Gretel fished the key from her pocket and kneeled in front of the forbidden cabinet. She slid the key gently into the lock and turned it clockwise. The click of the latch sounded refreshing in her ears, and she looked up at Hansel and flicked her eyebrows conspiratorially.

The light from the kitchen flooded the inside of the cabinet and Gretel saw instantly that it did not contain anything resembling the bulky tome that was *Orphism*. In fact, the cabinet was empty except for a small address book, presumably the one described by her brother.

Hansel stood behind Gretel, his head nearly resting on her shoulder, and he became immediately defensive by the book's absence. "It's not there!" he cried. "It's not there! But it was! I swear!"

"Of course it was," Gretel replied, "I believe you. She obviously moved it." Gretel couldn't hide her disappointment, and even though it obviously wasn't Hansel's fault the book was gone, she was annoyed at him.

"It was there."

Gretel had to bite her lip to keep from snapping at her brother to forget it and was glad when he didn't add on further to his deflated words. Besides, all was not lost. There was still the address book. It wouldn't be the Rosetta Stone to *Orphism* she was hoping for, but it might answer some questions about Odalinde and her business there.

Gretel's first observation about the book was that, though apparently well-traveled, it was rather new, certainly newer than she had imagined. Gretel had envisioned something more exotic—a homemade piece with a leather jacket and filled with parchment paper perhaps—something more closely resembling her *Orphism* book. But this book was ordinary, cheap, the type found in any dime store.

She flipped through the thin pages and found nearly every line filled with names, with only a few blank pages scattered throughout. She stopped randomly on several of the pages and scanned them, looking for any name that she recognized, but found none. There were, of course, several familiar names, but they were common surnames and no matches with first names that she could see.

Gretel finally dropped the wad of pages to the back cover and stared at the name "Stenson" on the inside of the front cover, just as Hansel had said. But it wasn't *exactly* as Hansel had said. There was the name 'Stenson,' and there was also a phone number, but instead of the word *Officer,* only an 'O' was written. It was understandable her brother would have made that connection, but it was possible there were other possibilities.

"Hansel, get me a piece of paper."

"For what?"

"Just do it! Hurry!"

Hansel fetched a small leaf of notepaper from the porch and handed it to Gretel, who checked twice the phone number of *O. Stenson* and then transcribed it to the sheet. She flipped through the organizer one last time and then placed it back in its exact location in the cabinet, checking one last time to see if, perhaps, *Orphism* had magically appeared in the meantime, which, of course, it hadn't. She then locked the cabinet and stuffed the key back in her pocket where it would rest until later in the evening when it would reappear for the presumably more difficult trick of being returned to Odalinde's bag.

But this first task was done. Easy enough. Gretel wasn't completely satisfied, of course since she still couldn't decipher her book, but something about seeing the inside of the cabinet and the seeming innocuousness of it made her feel better.

"Gretel?"

Gretel let out a yelp and snapped her head toward the deep rasp that blasted through the kitchen. It was Father, standing hunched in disbelief at the threshold.

"What in God's name are you doing?"

Gretel was silent and looked to her brother, as if he alone held the answer to their father's question. But Hansel only looked to the floor.

"Answer me, Gretel. What are you doing?"

Gretel closed the cabinet door and locked it, and then rose to her feet, locking eyes with her father, trying to gauge his anger and lucidity; but his face implied only a jumble of emotions which resulted in something closest to confusion.

He wasn't right—still—after all these weeks of convalescence from a common spleen injury—a serious injury to be sure, but certainly not one which normally resulted in such lethargy and feebleness. He looked as old and disoriented as the days following his collapse, as if he were healing from a stroke or some other brain trauma. Something was perverse about her father's recovery, and the lingering doubts that Gretel had about Odalinde's culpability in the matter were now erased.

"Nothing father," Gretel replied, "Odalinde let me borrow her book and I'm just returning it to her. Go back to bed."

"How did you get into that cabinet? You shouldn't be in there. I prepared that space for Odalinde, and you and your brother were never to go in there."

Her father's voice was low and weary, but far from calm, and Gretel saw that patronization wasn't going to work with him.

"I'm suspicious of her, father, and you should be too. Aren't you at all curious as to why you aren't getting better? You should be back working by now. Or at least not spending your entire day in bed. What's wrong with you?"

"I'm getting better," Heinrich Morgan replied, and then looked at the floor, unconvinced of his own words.

"You're not! And every time I mention it to Odalinde she says, 'All he needs is more rest.' Well, rest isn't making you better, and I've got money now. I'll take you into the city. Tomorrow. We'll have real doctors examine you. Good doctors that can run tests and..."

"No!" her father interrupted, "No more doctors, Gretel. Heinrich Morgan closed his eyes and took a deep breath, and then reached for the wall to crutch his stance. When he finally spoke again, his voice was barely more than a whisper. "You can't go into her cabinet, Gretel," he said. "You just can't." He paused again, as if he'd momentarily fallen asleep, and then said, "And that goes for you too." He nodded toward Hansel, his eyes still closed, and then turned and staggered back to his bedroom.

Gretel's anger at her father's weakness and her amplified hatred for Odalinde combined to brew the beginning stages of tears and fury, but she contained her emotions. It was a skill she hadn't yet mastered, but one she'd been working on daily.

In truth, she wanted nothing more than to run down to her boat and shove off into the lake and row for hours, sweating off the frustrations of her home while building her muscles in preparation for some impending showdown. Perhaps she would even dock at Rifle Field and spend the rest of the evening on her back staring at the stars, developing her strategy for making her life right again.

But none of that would be possible tonight. There was still the matter of returning the key, an operation that would require two people, and one that, even if it could be done alone, was too serious to delegate to someone as young and vulnerable as Hansel. Besides, Gretel would need to talk to her brother about what had just occurred with their father, assure him that although he was still sick, he would get better at some point, soon probably, and that he still loved them. And that he would keep to himself what he saw in the kitchen. Gretel couldn't really be sure that any of these things were true, of course, but reassurances like these were required of her now, and she accepted this responsibility with less reluctance as each day passed.

It was after ten o'clock when Odalinde finally returned, and though Gretel would normally have been sleeping at such an hour, especially on a school night, she was instead sitting at the kitchen table when the nurse walked in. Odalinde gave Gretel a curious look and grumbled her name in weary acknowledgment. Gretel saw this as a good sign that she was none the wiser about the key missing from her bag.

Now for the tricky part.

"Odalinde," Gretel said, rising from the chair, her eyes fixed on the woman, "I have something to show you. I realize it may upset you, and if it does, I would just like to say that I'm sorry in advance."

Now Odalinde's attention was rapt on Gretel, and she followed the girl's hands as she brought the figurine from behind her back into the light of the kitchen.

"I'm not quite sure how it happened, but..."

As if the script had been rehearsed for weeks, Odalinde placed her bag on the floor and took the porcelain swan from Gretel, cradling it delicately and holding it up to the light.

"What is it?" she asked rhetorically, without any of the alarm in her voice Gretel had expected.

Odalinde turned the fragile piece over gently with her fingers, squinting desperately to find the flaw, and as she examined the piece, Hansel appeared silently behind her, stooped with assassin-like grace, and nestled the cabinet's key down into the bottom of her canvas bag.

Gretel shifted her eyes to Hansel's squirrel-like movements, gave a slight grin, and then focused back on Odalinde and the figurine. It had, in fact, been Hansel's idea to use the swan as a diversion, and only to pretend that it had been broken, as opposed to actually breaking it, which had been Gretel's suggestion. Frankly, Gretel had barely noticed the figurine's appearance on the mantel, though apparently it had been there since the day Odalinde arrived; that the piece was important to Odalinde, Gretel hadn't the slightest idea. Whether it had any real value Gretel wasn't sure either, but Hansel insisted she cherished it, and had witnessed her take special care in cleaning it, even speaking to it on occasion when she was in one of her more airy, carefree moods.

"I knocked it to its side while dusting this evening," Gretel lied. "I'm sorry, but I think I've cracked it. Just there." Gretel pointed to the base of the swan's neck, placing her fingernail in a thin crevice at the point where the wing joined with the gray collar of the bird.

"There?" Odalinde squinted her eyes tighter.

"Yes. There, at the neck."

"That's no crack, silly girl! Those are its feathers, separated on the wing!"

Gretel took a deep breath and smiled, feigning relief, though in fact the smile reflected pride in her performance.

"Thank goodness!" she said, "I've never seen the figure close up before. I really thought I'd cracked it."

"Perhaps you should leave the dusting to me from now on." Odalinde sighed and walked the figurine back to the mantel and placed it in its proper spot, noting the dirty mantel. "Been dusting have you?"

"Yes, well…" Gretel snorted a laugh, "as you say, I should probably leave that to you."

With tragedy averted, Odalinde's fatigue returned, and she slinked back to the kitchen and grabbed her bag from the floor, fishing the key from the bottom. Gretel watched anxiously as the woman opened the cabinet door and went through her routine of restocking the space. But instead of simply shoving the bag in and locking the door as Gretel had seen her do dozens of times, Odalinde paused, suddenly, as if noticing something slightly off. It was only for an instant, the pause, and there was no suspicious glance back toward the kitchen, but that she paused was without doubt. Did she know? How could she know? Gretel had put the book back exactly as it had been. And there was nothing else in the cabinet to be moved.

At last, Odalinde closed the door and locked it, keeping the key in her clenched fist, and she walked slowly back to her bedroom. She opened the door, and just before she entered she turned to Gretel. "Gretel," she said stoically, "if you have any interest in my things, please don't be afraid to ask."

CHAPTER TEN

The concoction was coming along, but slower than the woman would have liked. The extractions proved painstaking—much more difficult than she'd remembered—and required every bit of the training she'd received in the Old Country. She had the book of course, which gave every detail of the procedures, but she still had to be precise with every slice and suture. No amount of instruction could correct for a shaky hand or poor intuition. Acquiring fluids from such delicate organs without killing was difficult, and the woman, to say the least, was rusty.

But she remained focused and disciplined, methodical with every incision and took only what was absolutely safe to keep the Source alive. The Source would die in the end, of course; once the liver was removed and the bile taken there was no chance of survival, but all the acids had to be just so, and that meant she would have to eat the pies for another week or so. If the Source was slaughtered too early, everything would be lost. It was always better to wait too long.

The woman re-read the instruction from the book that rested on the tray, and added the precise number of drops to the mixture, stirring slowly as she did so, folding the red liquid into the mash with a thin piece of flat steel she called a 'Fin', a tool she'd designed long ago for just this purpose. She was careful not to over-mix, and used a wooden spatula to gently scrape the excess potion from the Fin, sliding the utensils back and forth against each other until all the mixture was off. None of it could be spared.

Once properly combined, the woman placed a glass covering over the bowl and then draped a white cloth on top of the glass. It didn't need to be kept airtight, but the mixture couldn't afford the additions of dust or large insects either. Or, God forbid, mice. The white cloth prevented her from having to look at the vile broth all day.

A dull scream bellowed from the back room, signaling to the woman it was time for the evening feeding. She'd been expecting it would come soon. She'd learned by now to differentiate between the screams of sleep and those of confusion and fear, but either way they affected the woman's nerves little more than a clock striking on the hour.

The 'real' screams did mean, however, that the drug was beginning to wear off, and it was important the Source was kept as tranquil and unruffled as possible. The woman was convinced that adrenaline and hormones affected the potency of the mixture, more so even than the drug itself.

She filled a small cup with water and dropped in a pinch of the powder from the saucer next to the stove. She placed the cup on the feeding tray, which she'd already loaded with two small pies, and then walked with them back toward the bedroom where her victim lay chained. She opened the door quickly and entered, and was immediately hit with the smell of fresh urine. Again. An irritating side effect of the drug. She could only hope the Source had found the pot this time, as she was getting tired of cleaning and replacing the sheets. But that was just another part of it: she also couldn't risk the

Source being defiled from lying around in her own piss all day.

"Breakfast," the woman said coldly, not looking up.

The Source groaned and attempted to talk, instead only managing garbled nonsense. The drug made intelligible speech virtually impossible, since one of its functions was to boggle the part of the brain controlling syntax and tenses. It was amusing at first, the blathering, but now it just frustrated and annoyed the old woman, and she had wasted too much time already trying to elicit meaning from the subconscious ramblings. 'Hansel' and 'Gretel' came up a lot—no doubt the names of the Source's children—but the other words and names always stopped short of significance. Except for one.

It was tempting for the witch, living in such isolation, to ease up on the drug and allow some sort of dialogue with the girl, but the old woman knew nothing good would come of it. It wasn't that she feared feeling sympathy for the girl—she'd long since shed the ability for that emotion—but she was old, and she wasn't foolish enough to think she was incapable of being tricked by a mind more nimble than her own. She didn't know if this creature had such a mind—in fact, she doubted it—but there was no point in taking chances.

It had been months since the young gift lying before her had appeared, miraculously, as if fused from air and earth, a flower planted in the wood waiting to be plucked and drained of its nectar. Life had responded to her on that hor-rifying morning, almost instantly. Now it was her task to complete the work.

And that task would need to be completed soon. That morning on the stoop, when 'death' had been so close, had turned out to be nothing more than a bout of withdrawal, and it was only the hope and anticipation of a continued long life—and a new focus—that had seen her through it. But hope alone wasn't enough, and death would eventually come. She was tiring again, and she would need to drink soon.

The old woman rolled her eyes at the girl's garbled words and placed the tray on the end table, harder than she'd intended, almost spilling some of the powdered water.

The Source had figured out almost immediately after her capture that it was the water which was tainted, and at first had refused to drink it. But the slightest singe of a hot nail just below her left eye, along with the promise that the next time she refused it the nail would go an inch higher, had quickly reversed her resistance. There had been no 'next time.' The stress wasn't good for the hormones, of course, but a necessary evil to establish the rules.

"You're to drink first, then you eat."

The woman grabbed the chamber pot—which was full—and opened the door to leave.

"Tonight I'll take more," she said and slammed the door behind her.

* * *

Anika watched the woman leave through a cloud, and then registered the slam of both the bedroom and front doors. Two doors closing, she was positive.

The drug or poison or whatever it was, was wearing off, but it still lingered, and she had to be definitive in her thought process. The woman had left her room and then the house. That made sense. That had been her usual routine just after bringing the meals.

Anika figured out months ago that it was almost always the water that was drugged, but she also suspected it may sometimes have been the food as well, and as she lay staring at the knots of wood in the beams above her, she decided there would be no drinking tonight. She would have to eat—there was no real way to hide the food—but water was something else. She was banking it was in the water this time, and she needed to sober up.

In the beginning, the woman had sat like a barn owl from the vanity bench, ensuring Anika drank every drop of water and ate every crumb of pie. But it had been weeks since she'd last waited in the room for Anika to finish a meal, and after the tattoo had been branded on Anika's face, she hadn't needed to. The scar beneath her left eye and the memory of the pain kept Anika obedient to the regimen.

But Anika could sense the time left was short. Any day—any moment—could be her last. Something had to change. Soon.

As she recalled, her shackles were last removed only days ago after she'd wet the bed, but Anika was barely conscious at the time and had only a foggy memory of it now. She had a drowsy recollection of sitting against the wall naked, rubbing her legs with a wet cloth as the old witch changed the bed covers. But she couldn't remember changing into the clothes she now wore, and probably wouldn't have remem-

bered the episode at all if it hadn't been for the hag's screaming. She assumed the scolding was directed toward her, but it
didn't register that way at the time. In fact, Anika vaguely remembered laughing, which meant she was at the apex of the
drug's effects.

But Anika swore the next time the shackles came off the
scene would be very different.

Anika glanced over at the tray beside her and the waft of
plum hit her immediately. The smell disgusted her. All the
pies disgusted her now. She wasn't sure if it was a reaction to
the drugs or what the food now represented—or perhaps the
recipe for the pies she found so delicious in the beginning
had changed—but her stomach now immediately lurched
even at the sight of them. The ones with meat were the worst.
She ate them, she had no choice, but Anika promised herself
if she was still alive at the end of this ordeal, she would never
again eat another piece of pie.

She scooted to the end of the bed, threw the chain over
the post, and pushed herself over the foot and onto the floor.
Her legs wobbled a bit, but she steadied them quickly. They
were getting stronger, at least compared to a month ago.

Anika stood still for a moment, feeling her muscles adjust to standing and focused her mind again. She took a deep
breath and bowed her back, forcing her legs and spine to
stretch as far as they would go. The cracking of joints and
tendons reverberated through the room, adding to the exhil-
aration of the maneuver.

Following that first day on the floor, when the old
woman had caught Anika testing the room for weaknesses—and told Anika about her morbid intentions—Anika

was reluctant to leave the bed; and, in fact, she had not gotten out of it for several weeks. But her body's craving for motion had eventually won out over her fear, and she now got up at least three times a week. Sometimes for only a minute of two, but usually closer to an hour.

The movements were a blessing and seemed to be making her stronger, though with the shackle on her ankle she was mostly limited to stretching and isometrics. And, of course, Anika did this only when she was certain the woman was gone, though truthfully she began to doubt the necessity of that. On the one other occasion, the woman had caught her up and about she had only given Anika a mild scolding. Anika reasoned the woman needed her to stay healthy, and healthy did not include atrophied muscles and bed sores. But still, she didn't want to push it.

The other thing Anika figured was that the woman meant to eat her.

She had never told her this explicitly, but the fact that she considered Anika an animal to be slaughtered was as obvious a clue as one could expect to gather. As was the constant supply of pies. Too much food was better than starving, Anika supposed, and she couldn't have cared less about her appearance, but Anika could feel herself getting fat, particularly in her legs and feet, though she probably singled out those extremities because those were the parts of her anatomy she was forced to stare at most of the day. She wasn't anywhere near obese, but she was significantly heavier than the day she arrived. She labeled this fact as bad, since she needed to maintain some level of fitness on the off chance a window of escape opened. At this point, knee bends and back stretches weren't keeping her weight down, and she felt a lot like a turkey the week before Thanksgiving. And unless she did something soon, she'd end up like one.

Anika laced her fingers together and raised her arms over her head, pressing her palms toward the ceiling. She raised herself up on her toes and lowered her head with her eyes closed, holding that position for as long as she could.

When she opened her eyes, she saw a red patch of gauze attached to her gut and blood pouring down her side. Another incision. By her count, that made a total of five that she could see, and she was almost certain there were at least three on her back, near her spine between her shoulder blades. This one was fresh though—from when she couldn't say for sure—but it was probably from early this morning. The drugs had hit her hard this time and now she knew why: they'd been dosed up to serve the purpose of both anesthetic and pacifier. Anika recognized the feeling from the other times.

The patch of gauze was about the size of a cracker and was taped to the side of her abdomen just below her ribcage. It was bright red, but not entirely soaked through, which meant the sutures had probably just opened during her stretches. Quickly Anika climbed back on the bed and, on her back, gently pushed her way back toward the head next to the night table. She had to stop the bleeding before the woman returned. If there was one thing Anika had learned about the woman since her capture, it was that she disliked instability. On the occasions that she had lost her temper, either with Anika or otherwise, it stemmed from things not working out just as she'd planned. Anika ruminated that this was probably the source of most anger in the world, but a deranged person's anger was a bit more to deal with.

Anika picked up the napkin from the tray—the old witch usually forgot to include it, but not today—and dipped it in the water. Looking at the glass, Anika now realized if she didn't drink the water the unnoticed cut on her belly would be all too noticeable to her in a few hours when the anesthesia wore off. Hopefully, she thought, the stuff works as a local anesthetic as well.

She reclined slightly and then placed the wet napkin on the incision, wiping away the excess blood. The cut was relatively small, about three inches she guessed, and the stitchwork looked precise. She'd need to be more careful with her stretching.

Anika sat up and reached to dip the napkin again, but this time froze, her eyes locking in on the large black book lying next to the pies. She'd completely missed it before. Even now, as she focused on the form, it looked more like the shadow of a book than an actual book, and she considered the drugs may still be working their charms.

To be sure what she was seeing was real, she reached over and touched the tome, feeling the dull, cold leather. Certainly real.

She turned the tray toward her, hoping to get a better look at the cover, but whatever words or symbols may have been etched during the original printing had long since faded. She had to restrain herself from instantly picking up the book and opening it. The woman may be back any minute, and who knew what the punishment would be for snooping. And there remained the more urgent matter of her cut.

Still, this seemed like some form of an opportunity, if not for an escape, then at least to gather information which could help her.

Anika moved the pies from the tray to the night table and as she did, spotted a thin piece of straw sticking from the top of the book. A bookmark. She wedged a finger between the pages on either side of the straw and pulled the book open, gravity thumping the weight of the first three-quarters of the book down to the tray, nearly spilling the glass of water. Anika clenched her teeth and whispered a curse.

She stared wide-eyed at the pages and instantly saw that the writing was foreign to her—Greek perhaps—and that the surrounding margins were littered with handwritten notes. In fact, she noted, all of the white space was taken up with pencil and pen marks, including above and below the type. The space between the lines was wide, so the letters were perfectly legible, and as Anika studied the text further, she saw this writing was in English. Cursive, sloppy, and grammatically atrocious, but definitely English. In some instances there were just single words, often capitalized and underlined or with exclamation points. But most of the words seemed to be a translation of the text and not the aimless writings of a lunatic. And as Anika continued to read, she now realized one thing was certain: there wasn't much time left.

CHAPTER ELEVEN

Gretel's first week back at the orchard was bittersweet; she was happy to be with the Klahrs again, working and feeling productive, but there was an anxiety that nagged, lingering in her belly, reminding her that things at home were tenuous and unresolved. That her father may be dying. Perhaps being murdered slowly.

She thought of Hansel almost constantly, imagining the unbearable guilt she would forever live with if anything happened to him. There hadn't been any further mention from Odalinde concerning the swan figurine, and apparently father had kept the cabinet breach a secret, but Gretel perceived a difference in Odalinde since that night in the kitchen, a new sort of quietness that implied restraint and plotting.

Still though, it was nice to be back at work, and compared to the madness of the weeks during the harvest, Gretel had it easy. All of the workers were gone, having migrated to further corners of the region where various other crops were about to be born, so Gretel's work mainly consisted of cleaning the Klahr house to the point of sterilization, dividing the newly picked fruit for their various uses, and helping prepare the meals for Mr. and Mrs. Klahr.

Petr was staying on for a few weeks more, but apparently would only be making appearances on Fridays, as well as the weekends. So in addition to not being particularly busy, Gretel's first week back was also quite lonely.

But she worked hard and tried to stay occupied, and Mrs. Klahr, bless her heart, seemed to make the point regularly to Gretel that her presence was critical to keeping the Klahrs out of the graveyard and the house from crumbling to splinters. Still, she wasn't used to the downtime and boredom that filled much of her day, so when Friday finally came and Gretel saw Petr standing on the bank of the orchard as she eased her canoe to the shore, she couldn't help but smile and wave. She was instantly embarrassed by the act, of course, and was still blushing when she walked up to the boy, who himself wore the look of giddy unease.

She'd barely spoken to Petr since that day in the Klahr kitchen—she'd been so focused on her work and the harvest—but she had always been keenly aware of his presence at the house and felt a nervous comfort whenever he smiled at her or offered to help with a chore, only to be told "No, thank you" in a way that implied everything was exceedingly simple to Gretel and in her complete control.

Now, though, having spent a mostly restful week away from the orchard and returning to find the feverish regimen of the place substituted with an almost placid routine of thorough maintenance, Gretel regarded Petr as an old friend, a domestic soldier like herself, who'd fought beside her in some recent battle and now waited for her in the clearing dust.

"You're here early," Gretel said, arching her eyebrows to show she was mildly impressed.

"I got in last night. Something came up and it was the only time my father could drop me off."

Gretel nodded, still smiling, and stared at Petr, measuring him, until finally he looked away, embarrassed.

It was strange. As beautiful as Petr was physically, Gretel was not at all intimidated by him. Of course, she didn't really know him well, so there was still a certain self-consciousness she felt around him; but whenever they met, within a minute or two she always felt like she had the upper-hand. Even on that first night in her kitchen, when she first collided with those sky blue eyes and dark curls, she had been more stunned by his looks than threatened by them. Not that she normally came unhinged in front of boys anyway, but she would have thought a boy like Petr would have made her far more uncomfortable than he did.

"It's good to see you, Gretel."

Gretel's smile widened with this brave revelation, as if she was proud of Petr for his boldness, and she let out a good-natured laugh. "It's good to see you too, Petr. Are the Klahrs awake?"

Gretel and Petr split the chores evenly that day, with Petr taking on most of the outdoor duties and Gretel minding the interior of the house. But by Saturday, the two children decided the work could be done in the same amount of time if they tackled the tasks together, and they would enjoy the added pleasure of companionship. Mrs. Klahr met this suggestion with a thin smile, and then an exaggerated nod signifying the resourcefulness of the idea. Petr and Gretel both knew what she was thinking—that love was blooming or some such thing—but they initiated no corrections to this assumption, as they were both just happy to have a friend to work with and conversation to fill the day.

And if love blossomed, that was fine too.

"What do you do on your days off?" Petr lifted a full bucket of pears onto the flatbed of the Klahrs' truck, wiping the sweat from his forehead.

It was an unseasonably hot day for the Southlands, even for early summer, and though he'd only worked two full days that week, Gretel could see the boy was tired and looking forward to Sunday. Unlike Gretel, Petr technically had to work on Sundays, but the work was laughably light, and even he understood his pay for that day was mostly charity.

"I sleep mostly. And row. That's the bulk of it. The two things that keep me away from my...my father's nurse."

Petr stared at Gretel for a moment and then heaved another full bucket to the unhinged tailgate. "Is she cruel?" he asked bluntly. "Your father's nurse, that is."

Gretel glanced sideways at Petr, not really wanting to get into her home affairs. She liked Petr, and they seemed to have enough in common to become real friends, if not more, but her instincts told her it was too early to fully trust him. Especially with his father's name (maybe?) etched in Odalinde's address book.

"Maybe," she offered, "I'm not sure yet."

Petr nodded as if understanding not to push it further, and then changed the subject. "Well, I was thinking...if you...if you are going to be around tomorrow...I only work until noon, and my father won't pick me up until around four." The boy looked away and swallowed hard. "So I was wondering if you wanted to have lunch tomorrow. With me. A picnic maybe."

The corners of Gretel's mouth turned up slightly, reflexively, and she cocked her head in a move indicating both flattery and delight. "I...sure...I would love to."

"Okay! That's great! Do you want to meet somewhere here in the orchard?"

Gretel thought for a moment and then said, "Do you know Rifle Field?"

Petr shook his head.

Gretel was suddenly embarrassed for Petr, and realized she had just hijacked his plans by inserting Rifle Field into the date. "I'm sorry," she said, "it doesn't matter. The orchard is fine.

"No, it's okay. I'm not sold on the orchard. What's Rifle Field? It sounds great."

Gretel smiled and recognized a new sweetness in Petr. She saw a mature quality, one that just wanted happiness for the ones he cared about and didn't need to control the feeling or be credited for bringing it about.

"It's just on the other side of the cannery. From here you can only get there by boat. If you want I could pick you up and we could go there."

After the suggestion had left her mouth Gretel realized how forward she must have sounded, but she felt comfortable in the offer. "Or, again, the orchard's fine too. Wherever."

"No! No, it's fine. Rifle Field sounds perfect. I'd really like to see it."

"Okay then, I'll pick you up at noon."

CHAPTER TWELVE

Anika's mind spun as she read the gruesome recipe in front of her, the matter-of-fact tone in which the steps and measurements were explained only adding to the horror.

She frantically began to investigate her incisions and scars more closely, desperately craning her neck over her shoulders, trying to figure out what had been taken already. And what surgeries were still to be performed. Surely she wouldn't survive these procedures much longer! Specifically the removal of her liver, which, apparently, judging by the bookmark and what she could decipher of the markings, could occur any day. Maybe this day. The woman had said she'd 'take more tonight,' and though Anika didn't get the sense that the 'more' she was referring to would be the death blow necessarily, she simply couldn't risk waiting any longer. Even if the woman 'only' tapped her spine for a few driblets of fluid, she could easily sever a nerve or crack a vertebra. And what good would survival be at that point? She had to get out of there today.

As Anika read further, she saw that the book also contained ingredients for the pies she'd been eating.

As she suspected, those pastries indeed seemed critical in making the final product (which is how Anika now thought of herself) and contained a bizarre assortment of things. Some of the ingredients hadn't been translated, and others Anika had never heard of, but even the sounds of them had a sinister quality. Goose Proventriculus. Aged Lynx Bladder.

Baneberry. Not exactly the stuff of Christmas desserts, she thought. And where this crazy old woman even found such things or knew where to look for them, baffled Anika.

But really, what was the difference? The ingredients could have been candy canes and jellybeans for all it mattered. The planned conclusion was for Anika to die, painfully, and if she wanted to thwart those plans, she had to move soon.

Anika closed the huge black book, poured the glass of water into the bedpan, and began on the pie.

As she ate, her thoughts surged with the idea that this was the last pie she would ever eat in her life, whether that life ended today or fifty years from now.

The taste of the thing was horrible, of course, but she took down every shard of crust and sludgy finger scoop of black saucy meat, using all her will to suppress her constant gags. As she finished and wiped her mouth and hands on the bed sheets in long streaks, Anika mentally finalized her plan.

The inside of the bowl was still slick and hard to hold, but she resisted cleaning it—when it dried it would become sticky and create the perfect grip. She placed the heavy ceramic bowl by her hip beneath the sheet and waited. The woman would be home by nightfall, Anika presumed. There was nothing left to do but wait.

***

The old woman had waited for just such a morning to make the journey. A cool day at the end of a long dry spell. It had been eleven days since the last rainfall, so the floor of the forest was well-parched and navigable. With her strength as it was, long morasses or wide creek beds would have been impassable. But on a day such as this, she felt confident about the trek. As long as she could find what she sought quickly.

Most of the signs that her Source traveled these parts only recently had long since eroded or been covered by leaves. But one clue had endured, miraculously, to quite literally light the way. A food wrapper, small and rectangular, used for enclosing something store-bought and processed. The casing was silver, highly reflective, and like a beacon it flashed just a glint as it caught a renegade ray of sun that had maneuvered past the canopy. It winked at the woman, beckoning. The woman considered it afterward and determined there must have been two hundred feet between her and the small discarded foil, but it had pointed the direction exactly, and without backtracking a step, the haggard woman found the abandoned car.

Life again delivering.

There were no signs that the car had been discovered by anything other than Northland fauna, but the old woman opened the passenger door warily anyway, as if suspecting a trap had been set. But if indeed they were responsible for sending her Source, certainly there'd be no point in trapping her. It was she who made the potion. Not them!

And there was no trap. Instead the door creaked lazily open, and the leaves which had perched between the door and the roof frame fell harmlessly to the ground. The woman stood back from the car and stared inside, searching.

There wasn't much, other than an empty mug and the balled remains of what appeared to be an old newspaper.

Cars had certainly changed quite a bit since her last experience, but the compartment below the dash—the glove box they called it, for storing a driver's gloves in case the day was cold—remained.

She pulled the lever and dropped open the door of the small box, and was instantly greeted with a stack of papers, along with a set of miniature tools and a near-empty container of what appeared to be some type of lotion. The woman fished out the papers and shuffled through them, tossing those she found useless to the floor until she found what she was looking for: Anika Morgan's identification card.

Anika Aulwurm Morgan.

The Source had given her first and last name on that first day in the slaughter room, when she still held a small level of trust—and even gratitude—for the old woman. It was a common enough name, Morgan, and not one she could attach to him in any way.

But another name had emerged, six nights ago, in the fever of poison, during the woman's routine room inspection. The young Source had let slip the name *Aulwurm*. She'd said the name twice, groggily yet distinctly, but had attached it to no other name. The old woman had frozen at the sound of the word, and the tingle in her eardrums had cascaded down her back.

Aulwurm.

It was a name the old woman knew well: a surname that formed branches not far from her own on her family's tree.

And beyond just her recognition of the name, Aulwurm was unusually distinct. It was the maiden name of her grandmother and, as the old woman recalled, her Aulwurm uncles and aunts had taken great pride in the rarity of their name, claiming that it was born and existed in only a very segregated section of the Old World.

She'd heard the name only once since she'd been in the New Country—during that one night over a year ago when the men had come. Other than that time, over the centuries now that she'd been alive, the old woman couldn't remember ever hearing the name outside of her family. And certainly never in the New Country.

But just as the woman suspected, upon hearing the name ring from the lips of her Source only nights ago, Aulwurm was the middle part of Anika Morgan's full name—as it had been the middle name of her mother, no doubt—having been passed on through generations to all girls born to the family, by parents who wished to keep Old Country traditions and birthrights alive not only in their male offspring, but in the females as well. Certainly young Gretel's middle name was no different.

The moment she'd heard the name the woman wanted to wake her Source immediately, and use all her means to coerce the girl into revealing her family's full history. But since learning of her fate, the Source talked very little now and was explicitly silent on the issues of her personal life. She asked and answered only those questions that dealt with her most basic needs, and there was little doubt in the old woman's mind that her Source would die before exposing her children any further. She had considered torture again, another branding to the face perhaps, but she was too close now and didn't want to risk an infection so close to the end.

And besides, she wanted to explore for herself the truth of what happened. If indeed this was the Source of her dreams. If the memory was real. If the men had indeed come to her—in the flesh—and not in the dementia of her mind. She wanted to know if they *had* sent the girl—as her imagination dictated. She wanted to know if it was time for her to pay.

She recalled it all again: it was evening, cold, and the old man had sat relaxed in her kitchen, with the younger one beside him, anxious. The old one had explained how it would happen: there would be an accident, and a woman would be delivered to her. She would need to trust in the powers, allow them to guide her, but the Source would come to her, and she needed only take in the prey.

And then prepare it. Perform the blending which she had mastered.

How they had known of her cabin—or even her own existence—was a mystery to the woman, and she uttered not a word that night, feigning feebleness and madness, as well as a language barrier. It was the first men she had seen in ages, and she was terrified by the intrusion and aggressiveness, particularly of the older one, as well as the overall surprise of their arrival.

But the older one had been undeterred by the woman's condition, and he had simply laid out his plans—as well as his expectations—as she stood quivering, panicked, hunched by the window which overlooked the cabin porch.

And as quickly as they arrived they were gone; the sound of the departing car engine had roared in her head for days.

But then the weeks passed and the encounter faded, until soon the woman believed it hadn't happened at all, but was instead a dream, or one of her many fantasies she played out in the absence of intimacy. It was a strange fantasy to be sure, but so were many of them.

But then Aulwurm brought it back to reality.

This strange, surreal meeting *had* taken place, and now, as the old woman stood beneath the huge Northland trees breathing in the warm autumn air, the entire one-sided conversation flooded back to her, and she knew her time was even shorter than she thought.

CHAPTER THIRTEEN

Gretel was on the lake by eight o'clock the next morning, which was two hours earlier than she'd been awake on a Sunday in as long as she could remember. Her lunch with Petr wasn't for several hours, and though she'd get some rowing in on her way to Rifle Field, the type of rowing she'd use for that excursion wasn't the effort Gretel was accustomed to on her day off. Sunday was her day of rigor on the lake, the day she sweated out those frustrations and grievances that couldn't be expressed through words or work. On some days the brutality of her catharsis was so severe that Gretel imagined any onlooker would think she was in the midst of some desperate escape, fleeing the bonds of slavery or the eager jaws of a crocodile, perhaps.

But to Gretel the feeling was nothing short of wonderful, and once she finally reached exhaustion, usually somewhere just beyond the last scattered stretch of the Klahr orchard, a substitute feeling of peacefulness slipped into her body, as if filling the gap left by her concerns. Gretel would drench herself in the feeling, at once studying and devouring it, always knowing on some level that she was experiencing the sensation of normalcy: the natural state of being where God had intended humans to dwell.

She dipped the blades of the oars into the water and gave a long exaggerated pull, propelling the boat forward down the middle of the narrow lake, closing her eyes to experience the full pleasure of the draft on the back of her neck.

She repeated these long, slow strokes, gradually building up speed while stretching the muscles of her chest, shoulders and back. She focused on the strain of each tendon, visualizing as they stretched and contracted, slowly unloading the buildup of anxieties from the previous week.

And then the fury began.

Gretel thrust the shafts of the oars from bow to stern, pivoting them at breakneck speed on their fulcrums, the blades slashing the surface of the water in hypnotic ferocity. She puffed her cheeks with each exhalation, and focused the air back into her lungs with every breath, watching absently as the banks of her property diminished. She was two hundred yards or so when the film of sweat began to form on her cheeks and forehead, and the world of confusion and problems began to drift steadily away. How laughably easy it was, Gretel thought, to simply leave a situation, to simply turn away and run, or row, as the case was here. When she was home, chest-deep in the chaos and responsibility of what her life had become, constantly being forced to decide on this and argue her points on that, she seemed utterly trapped, hopelessly surrounded by walls so tall and thick they could never be scaled or penetrated. But from the distance of only a hundred yards or so, surrounded by the vastness of earth and water, the truth was uncovered. The walls were a mirage. Escaping her world was no more difficult than thrusting a rowboat down a lake and leaving, and then watching with cold detachment as her house and property faded around a bend. She could never *actually* leave it of course, there was too much at home that she loved and needed to see through, but if she really wanted to, if she could ever summon the boldness and courage, she was free to just keep going.

The other part of rowing that Gretel had grown to love was the utter blindness of it—that feeling of never being sure, not entirely, what lie in wait. Of course, after all these weeks, she now knew this lake as well as anyone on earth probably, but there was always that possibility that some unknown log or critter had surfaced just up ahead, or even that another boat, heading just as blindly in the opposite direction, was on course to collide with Gretel and plunge her unconscious into the water. And when those fears didn't satisfy her adventure, Gretel would create other fantasies: imagining hazarding some exotic river perhaps, all the time being watched by cannibals; or unknowingly bounding toward the shelf of some plunging waterfall.

She watched as the trees in the orchard began to diffuse, signaling the end of the Klahr property, and she summoned what remained of her reserves, ferociously clenching her jaws while ignoring the burn in her triceps and thighs. When her muscles had nothing left to serve, Gretel stopped abruptly and unleashed a scream that started deep in her belly and ended in a fit of hoarse, violent coughing. The burn in her chest was cold and harsh, but it lasted only a second or two, and her breathing steadied quickly.

Gretel flexed her biceps and stared down at them, rubbing them with her open palms, the sweat and oil accentuating their definition. She loved the thin, wiriness of her body now, and she figured she was at least as strong as any boy she knew her age, including Petr. She thought of her mother and how she would be in awe of Gretel if she could see her now.

Gretel stared at the sky and thought of what that encounter might look like. Her mother would first hug her desperately, of course, but then she would push her to arms length and examine her, laughing incredulously at the transformation that had taken place in her daughter. Gretel looked at herself in a mirror everyday and couldn't believe the change; imagine what her mother would see!

Gretel turned the boat around and headed back for home, this time taking the long easy strokes one would normally expect to see from a Sunday morning oarsman. As she reached the plush, perfect lines of the orchard, she heard the sounds of light work from somewhere beyond the treeline. Petr, no doubt, passing the morning with busy-work.

Gretel was tempted to pull to the bank and visit, but it would only be a few hours before their lunch date, and even though she imagined Petr would be more than happy to see her beforehand, she didn't want to seem pushy. She liked the boy, he was friendly and funny, and certainly he was handsome enough, but she wasn't ready for the complexities she imagined would accompany having a boyfriend. And she wasn't even sure she liked him in that way. She had always remained fairly demure in his company, but she never felt that nervous, chest-gripping sensation that she'd had around a handful of boys in the past. Maybe she'd been hardened by the loss of her mother and the unnatural burden of taking care of her family, but Gretel felt instinctively it was more than that. It was him. It was Petr. She couldn't pinpoint the component exactly, but some chemical or current that naturally combined to form that swell of passion wasn't being properly received by her or transmitted by him. Maybe it was that ever-elusive component of trust, she thought, and figured this might be her lot with men for the rest of her life.

Gretel drifted into the bank behind her home and hopped out of the rowboat, pulling it up far enough onto the shore to keep it from floating away. She then turned and sprinted toward the house, burning off the last of the energy that remained in her from the morning.

As she reached the porch stairs leading to the front door, Gretel dropped her head in concentration, placing her feet on each step just right, so as not to tumble during her ascension. And as she reached the top of the steps, Gretel plowed the top of her head into the center of Odalinde's chest, barreling her over as a bull might do to an overconfident matador.

Gretel's first thought was that she had just run over Hansel, the force of the impact was so solid and the body had put up such little resistance, but when Gretel looked to see Odalinde on the ground at her feet, staring back at her with such astonishment and fear, Gretel couldn't hold back the grin on her face.

"What...Gretel watch where you're going!" There wasn't anger in Odalinde's voice; her tone was more instructive, as a mother teaching manners to her child.

Gretel's grin flattened, though it was hardly replaced with the look of concern. "I'm sorry. I didn't see you there."

"Well, I should hope you didn't see me! You could have killed me!"

"I think that's a bit of an exaggeration. Are you all right?" Gretel didn't wait for the reply as she stepped over the fallen woman and past the threshold into the house.

"It's not an exaggeration! What if I had been knocked down the stairs?" Odalinde asked rhetorically. There was a shrillness now to her voice that teetered on yelling, but it remained motherly, as if combating the petulance of a child. "You need to pay attention when..."

"I said I'm sorry!"

Gretel now stood back on the porch at the woman's feet, staring down at her as a fighter would to his fallen opponent. It was a posture of intimidation and warning.

Gretel waited for a response from the nurse and, receiving none, walked back into the house. She wiped the sweat from her face with a towel and poured herself a drink of water, and then began making the lunches for the picnic. She listened attentively for the opening of the truck door, signaling Odalinde was leaving, or else the sounds of her coming back into the house. Several minutes passed with no movement from the porch. Finally the front door creaked open and Gretel heard Odalinde walk slowly into the kitchen. Gretel didn't look up.

"Gretel?" Odalinde said softly, as if waking her from a nap.

Gretel looked up.

"I'm leaving for the market. I'll be home in an hour or so." Odalinde paused for a moment and looked down at the floor before raising her head again and making eye contact with Gretel.

"I'm sorry for my tone on the porch. It was an accident, I know that, and my screaming at you was uncalled for." She paused again. "While I was outside I was thinking, perhaps we could talk later. There are some important things—very important things—I've been wanting to tell you. You and Hansel. And I think now is the time."

Gretel looked at Odalinde suspiciously and then returned her attention to the picnic lunch. "I suppose that will be okay," she said casually, "but I'll be having lunch with a friend today, so I won't be home until this afternoon."

"A friend?

Gretel glanced at the nurse and dropped her eyes quickly, as she wrapped a loaf of bread in a damp towel. "Yes," she said, "a friend. You know, someone whose company you enjoy and they enjoy yours."

Odalinde didn't respond to the jab. "Is it that boy from the orchard?" she said flatly.

Gretel ignored the question. "As I said, Odalinde, I'll be back this afternoon."

Gretel placed the remaining items for the picnic into a shallow woven basket and left it on the counter by the door, and then walked toward her room to begin changing for lunch.

"If Hansel is around later, I'll be happy to participate in that wildly important talk."

"He's The System man's son, correct?"

Gretel stopped frozen in stride.

"That officer that was looking for your mother, right?"

"How do you know him?" Gretel whispered. "The System officer, how do you know him?"

Gretel had mentioned to her father that a new boy had come to work at the orchard and, as she now tried to recall, had perhaps even told Odalinde. But she had never mentioned his name, and certainly had never told them that he was Officer Stenson's son. In fact, Gretel had never told either of them about that first night when Petr had come to the door for his father's binder. She had even kept it a secret from Hansel. She couldn't have said why exactly, but Petr's cryptic statement on the porch that night, as well her general instincts, impressed upon her to keep Petr in the shadows. After all, if she had remarked to her father that next morning that Officer Stenson's son had stopped by just after he'd gone to his room, and oh, by the way, implied that his father, whom Gretel's own father had bounced only minutes before, was less than genuine about his intentions to find their mother, that may have pushed her father over the edge. He may have even tried to find Officer Stenson, or filed a complaint to The System itself, which certainly wouldn't have improved the chances of finding her mother.

"I don't know him," Odalinde replied, "not really. But I did meet him. He stopped by one day when you were at school, not long after you began working at the orchard."

Gretel was floored by this revelation. "What did he want?" Her breathing was now frantic and labored. "Was there something found?"

"No, no, nothing like that. It was more of a courtesy visit, I suppose. He said his son worked at the orchard, just like you, and since he was in the area he wanted to see how all of you were getting on. He asked for you."

Gretel said nothing as she digested this news.

"He left his number with me and wanted you to call him if you felt up to it. I wrote it down. Stenson, I believe his name was. I wanted to tell you, I had every intention in fact, but your father forbade it."

"Did father talk to him?" Gretel asked.

"Your father was in a very bad state at that time. He had no idea the officer was even here."

"Well, what did he say? Was there any news at all on my mother? He had to have said something?"

Odalinde frowned and her look softened. "I'm sorry, Gretel, he didn't. He just wanted to know how you were getting on."

Gretel searched the room with her eyes, trying to place the meaning of this revelation.

Odalinde watched Gretel silently, until finally she said, "I should have told you sooner."

"Yes," Gretel replied, "you should have."

CHAPTER FOURTEEN

The rustling of leaves snapped Anika to attention; despite focusing all of her will to stay awake, she'd drifted off to sleep.

But early on in her captivity the sounds of the forest nestled in her subconscious, and now, after...months (?)...she could detect the nuances distinguishing the crackle of the witch breaching the treeline and the sounds of a deer trepidatiously grazing outside her room.

The old whore was back. Finally.

The crunching steps quickly turned to clicks as the ancient monster reached the boardwalk and made her way toward the porch steps and front door. Anika's mind suddenly flooded with doubt. The woman would sense her plotting. Smell it maybe, or taste it on her tongue like a snake. If nothing else she would notice the bowl missing from the tray, or even see the bulge beneath the sheets. And then what?

Anika reached beneath the blanket for the bowl she'd stored next to her hip, but felt only linen. She felt lower, down to her thigh and past her knee, but still nothing. She spread her fingers wide and pressed the mattress around her frantically with both hands on either side of her legs. Where was it! She arched her back and felt under her torso. The sugars from the pie had cemented on her fingers and palms, and the sheets stuck to them as she hunted the bowl, making the search more difficult. The bowl was nowhere!

She sat up in fear and lifted the sheets over her head, hoping that the ceramic container had just rolled to a blind spot in her grasps, but she saw nothing.

She was now overcome with panic and her vision began to blur with tears. How could she have let it go? After having it in her grasp for so many hours! Waiting. Preparing.

Anika steadied her mind and made the rational assumption that the bowl had to be close. Perhaps it had rolled to her feet. Or off the bed. She slowly leaned her head over the side of the mattress, closing her eyes as she did so, sensing the importance of what she might see when she opened them: the bowl shattered on the floor would mean it was all over. It would mean she was to die in this room at the hands of a madwoman—this woman who intended to harvest Anika's body for some demented concoction. It would mean she had botched her last chance.

It meant she would never see her children again.

Anika opened her eyes and exhaled, seeing nothing other than the bedpan full of poisoned water. There was still a chance. For another day at least. For another plan to be formed. She couldn't give up now.

The door of the cabin closed with a gruesome thump, and the hurried steps of the witch marching toward the bedroom were immediate. There was no more time to look for the bowl.

Anika twisted her body into a sleeping posture, her back to the door, making one last fruitless search beneath her pillow in the process. She closed her eyes and prayed silently.

The bedroom door creaked open and Anika could sense the witch hesitate before slowly walking in. She listened carefully to the woman's steps, trying to gauge her location as she stalked the room surveying the scene. The woman had been gone for longer than she'd ever been before, and Anika could sense her uneasiness at what may have transpired in her leave. But other than the missing bowl, Anika was pretty sure she'd kept things as they were.

"Get up!"

The scream was deafening, and Anika's eyes shot open in panicked surprise.

"Get up now you filthy pig! This will not do! This will not do at all! Filthy, filthy pig!

Anika's mind erupted in terror, and tears filled her eyes as she braced herself for the weapon—perhaps the same one used to hunt her in the forest—to plow down upon her. The woman's rage certainly meant the end this time. She must have seen the bowl (and the book! Anika had forgotten about the book!) and was finally going to kill her.

"I leave you alone for only a few hours, a few hours longer than usual, and you...you scat yourself! Filthy pig! Get up. Get up now and get off the bed. I will not have you lying around in your own filth!"

At first Anika had no idea what the woman was screaming about, but as she turned to the woman and obediently started off the bed, she looked down at the sheets and saw the long brown streaks. The pie stains where she'd wiped her hands. The woman thought Anika had foregone the bed pan and defecated on the bed.

"Get up!" the woman shouted once again, this time hunching toward the bed in short quick steps, her eyebrows sloped at a cartoonishly angry angle.

Anika slowly but deftly scooted to the front of the bed and pushed herself off, almost catching her chain on the bedpost in the process. She should have still been groggy from the poison, incapable of such a move, but the woman made no sign of noticing, focusing instead on the mess of linen before her.

"There can be no impurities for the last step," the woman murmured to herself, carefully removing the pillows from the bed as she assessed exactly what she had in front of her. "It's almost ready. Almost ready and look at this filth!"

Anika stood statue-like, removed from the scene, watching the old hag lament as she began to strip the sheets. The words "almost ready" didn't sound promising.

The woman shuffled the wool blanket to the dusty floor and then snatched the top sheet from under the bed corners, gathering it into a ball and walking it back to the door.

And Anika saw it immediately, resting in the crease between the mattress and the wall.

The bowl.

With the woman's back still turned, and without thinking, Anika grabbed the ceramic hollow off the bed and shoved it beneath her gown, holding on to it through the fabric, trying to appear as casual as possible.

Did the woman notice the move? Or hear it? If she did, she didn't care, and without looking at Anika, the witch walked back to the bed, still grumbling about the mess. There was still the bottom sheet to contend with, and that contained the lion's share of the clean-up challenge.

Starting at the foot of the bed, not twelve inches from where Anika stood frozen in uncertainty and anticipation, the woman began to remove the fitted corners of the bottom sheet. It was a struggle at first, the sheet perhaps a bit small for the bed, but eventually she released it and moved toward the head of the mattress to unbind the other end.

And then, at the midpoint of the bed, she stopped.

She didn't look back at Anika, but instead looked down at the brown streaks that marked the white sheets. With barely a turn of her head, the witch peeked back toward the tray with which she now stood parallel, and then back to the mattress again. Casually she placed two fingers from her left hand on the edge of the brown stain and then brought them to her nose, smelling the mistake she had made.

The witch never saw the girl fumble frantically beneath her gown, nor did she hear the whispered word 'Die' as the clay bowl smashed onto her left cheekbone. She did, however, feel the collapse of her eye socket and the ensuing rattle of splintered bone in her sinus cavity, as well as the stiff, mercilessness of the wooden floorboards on the back of her skull.

She had felt it all before she blacked out.

***

The old woman woke in a panic, coughing and gasping for air. Her windpipe was blocked with what had to be a shattered piece of her own skull.

She tried to stand, but her legs had been bound at the ankles and thighs, and her arms at the wrists and behind her back. She fell back to the floor face down, her eyes bulging, wheezing in terror. She tried again to stand, using the leverage of the bed, and this time made it to her knees, desperately trying to take air into her lungs. The lack of oxygen began to fog her head and blur her vision. She was dying.

Behind her she felt the bed frame brush her back, and she reached for it with her elbow, trying to gauge its exact position. With a last act of will and survival, the old woman leaned her torso forward, almost touching her head to the floor, and then rocked back violently, slamming her upper back against the steel of the bed.

There was a simultaneous flash of pain and light as the bone shot from the witch's throat like a prehistoric bullet. She closed her functioning eye and collapsed back to the floor, now lying on her side, replenishing her cells with precious gasps of air.

She lay in that position for several minutes until her breathing steadied and then focused on her body as the pain set in. Her face was destroyed. The left side felt as if someone had removed her cheekbone. She had no sight in her left eye and had to assume she would never regain it. That was okay; it was her weaker eye anyway.

The throbbing ache that now filled the space between her shoulder blades where she'd smashed her back to the bed added slightly to her misery, but it was the mildest of her physical problems at the moment. It was the sickening looseness in her head that concerned her most, and she feared that without the attention of a skilled surgeon her brain would begin to leak from its cavity. She could deal with the pain—that would go away in time—but she needed to know that her body was stable and that she wasn't going to hemorrhage slowly over the next few days.

The potion. If she could complete the last stages of the mixture, she reasoned, adding the liver parts, specifically, she could mend enough of her body to carry on. It wasn't quite perfect yet, the mixture, there was perhaps another week of aging and feeding that needed to be done to get it exact, but it was close enough. She'd never tempted it before, always fearing the worst if it wasn't precise, but certainly the recipe allowed for slight degrees of error.

As for her permanent injuries, she could always find a doctor later to fix her face—if not her sight—and continue living for a hundred more years. Longer.

But first she needed the Source.

That the young girl left her alive didn't surprise the witch. She'd met very few people in her long life that could kill mercilessly unless it was in direct defense of themselves or their children. It was no small feat to slice the throat of an old lady lying unconscious on the floor, or even to chain her and leave her to starve, even if it that old lady's intentions were to harvest your organs.

Undoubtedly the Source hoped the blow she'd struck would kill her captor, but if it didn't, she hadn't the will to make sure. And for that she would pay.

The woman wiggled her way back up to a sitting position and leaned gingerly against the bed. She tested the strength of the rope on her wrists and could tell the girl had done a competent job with the knotting. The witch pushed her back hard against the bed now and screamed, extending her knees out and sliding her shoulders onto the mattress. She took three heavy breaths, accepting the pain in her back, and then slithered the rest of her torso onto the bed. She was now able to stand.

There was enough slack at her ankles that she could shuffle to the kitchen, and once there she began looking for something to slice through the cords at her wrists.

There was nothing accessible that she could see immediately, but if she could open the front door, there were plenty of items in the yard that would serve the purpose. With the height of the doorknob, however, that would be a challenge all its own.

As the witch's mind began to construct a way to wedge a butcher's knife between a drawer and the counter, her eye caught sight of a brown shard of pottery at her feet. Her heart raced, and as she stumbled too quickly past the kitchen counter, nearly collapsing from her bound ankles, she instantly saw the rest of the pot along with the soupy mixture splattered across the floor.

The potion.

It was destroyed.

***

The road was indeed close to the cabin and Anika found it quickly. Thankfully the witch hadn't been lying about that. Anika was coughing and wheezing as she reached it and collapsed hard on her buttocks, her back finding a tall, roadside evergreen to lean against.

She'd not stopped running since leaving the cabin, and despite the relatively short distance, her lungs—and legs—were exhausted. Anika was frustrated by her fitness level and wanted to continue farther down the road, but will alone wasn't going to overcome months of muscle atrophy. She would only rest a minute though, and then would start walking; she wasn't going to risk being missed by a passing car. If she had to, she thought, she would strip naked and run to the middle of the road.

She rubbed her lower leg just above her ankle where the chain had been clasped. The gesture was part massage and part reassurance that the shackle was really gone. The sensation that it remained was still strong and Anika imagined she'd be feeling it for some time. Maybe for the rest of her life.

She replayed the events of the last hour in her head, wondering if she'd killed the witch (she doubted it) and thought of all that could have gone wrong. What if Anika hadn't seen the pie bowl in time? What if the blow hadn't knocked the woman unconscious? What if the woman didn't have the keys with her? This last thought was most frightening, since Anika would have been forced to kill the old woman—if she hadn't been killed already—and then solve the puzzle of escaping the chains before starving to death alone in the slaughter room. Perhaps she would have gnawed off her foot, though what good that would have done she didn't know since she was still in the middle of the forest and she doubted there was a phone in that cabin.

But none of these thoughts occurred to her at the time—at the time it had all been instinct. Even her decision to slide that bowl of unspeakable broth to the floor was impulsive, though one she was now glad she'd made. Had the cauldron not been sitting out in the open, so easily accessible, Anika wouldn't have risked the time to find it.

She stood gently, unsure of her thighs' ability to make such a movement, and was encouraged by the result. They seemed to relish the motion, aching for long steady movements. Well, they would certainly get them, Anika thought, maybe for the next several hours, though she hoped it wouldn't be quite so long.

She began to walk the Interways toward the Southlands. With any luck, she'd reach the Back Country by nightfall.

***

Once the ropes on her wrists were free the woman dropped to her knees, leaned forward on her elbows, and began lapping the liquid from the floor like a cat. The ropes, it turned out, were old and brittle, and escape had been fairly easy. Four or five strokes against an exposed wall beam and she was free. The adrenaline induced by the sight of the wasting concoction drying at her feet didn't hurt either, and her sawing motions had been frantic and fearless.

Much of the soupy mixture had congealed, forming a protective, awful, skin-like film. But the hag didn't have the luxury to care, and she scooped the broth up indiscriminately, splashing it into her mouth like a wanderer in the desert who's just stumbled upon a lone puddle of water.

The taste was far from good, but nothing like it had tasted in the past. Perhaps it was the bile that gave the potion its putridity, she thought, or maybe the direness of her situation was muffling her taste buds.

It didn't matter; as it was, there was no guarantee that drinking it would render any benefit at all. In fact, it was more likely to sicken her, she thought, since all of the ingredients weren't included.

But she had nothing to lose. She could feel herself slipping. It was a feeling similar to the one she had that morning, just a few months ago, before Life had brought her back.

The woman stopped drinking only to breathe, the burgundy mess slogging down from her chin in thick webs. She leaned in to drink again, and as she pooled her hands together to scoop she felt the first tingle. It was like the sprinkle of water from a distant splash, tickling the left side of her skull where her former prisoner had shattered the empty pie bowl. It was slight at first, the tingle, and then quickly crescendoed into something nearing an electrical surge. Initially, there was *only* the feeling, and then the old woman recognized an ease and slowness to her breathing. It was as if her nasal passages had suddenly doubled in size. She gluttoned for the air, taking giant, vacuumed breaths through her nose and exhaling through her mouth, the huge swallows of oxygen as refreshing as any drink she could ever remember tasting.

She took another deep breath and then stopped in a gasp when she spied the open door to her left. The front door to the cabin. Wide open. Had it been open this whole time? Or was her Source back to finish the job, deciding she had the will to kill after all, and was now hiding somewhere in the room, armed and cocking some organic weapon?

Confused, the old woman turned suspiciously toward the door and jumped as the kitchen and back hall suddenly appeared in her periphery. And it was then she understood what was happening.

The door had indeed been open all along—open at least since her Source had escaped—it was just the woman hadn't been able to see it. Until now. Until the potion. She could see. From both eyes.

She was being healed.

The old woman untied the knots at her feet and moved slowly, delicately, to the lone chair in her cabin, afraid any jarring movements might impact the potion's effects. She sat upright in the chair, stiff, anticipating what was to come, just as she had done only months ago in the same spot. This time, however, she knew instinctively there would be no blacking out or painful contractions; this combination was fresh, beautiful (perhaps with the bile it would be perfect!), and it was going to make her whole again.

The electric tingle moved from her skull to the space between her shoulder blades, tightening the muscles there and then loosening them to just the right tension. From there it moved swiftly past her legs to her feet—drained from so much hiking through the restrictive forest—and lavished them with warmth and health and nutriment.

The old woman sat for what must have only been an instant, basking as the potion stormed everything from her complexion to her toenails, inundating her body with minerals and magic, cleansing each cell of decades of decay and pollutants, to regenerate a physique many generations past its intended time and purpose.

Nausea entered her stomach briefly but was quickly invaded and tamed, the potion not allowing any form of discomfort or disease to sustain itself. From her gut the magic formula flowed downward, stimulating her between her legs, moistening her crotch and evoking a smile and shiver. It rushed the length of her body to her teeth, at once filling cavities and filing incisors. The feeling swarmed upward through her newly-repaired skull and rippled over her scalp, vaccinating each follicle and patch of dander. Reflexively, the witch finger-combed through her hair and closed her eyes in ecstasy at the ease in which her hands glided through. Her tangled locks had existed for so many years she'd forgotten what healthy strands felt like.

This feeling was different. All of it was different. She'd taken the potion for close to two hundred years, she guessed, and had never experienced anything like what was happening today. It was as if decades of mixture had been concentrated into one pot, accelerating and magnifying all of the potion's wondrous effects.

She'd heard of this before—this exceptional regeneration—eons ago in another world and language, when knowledge of the potion itself—if not the ingredients—had been known by many, and witchcraft and magic weren't the metaphors and caricatures they were today. And though few ever had the will and stomach to explore it then, there were plenty of stories from The Ancients that implied its truth.

Even the book, of which she was told several still existed in the world, did not mention this rumored secret, for reasons even the old hag could understand on some level. It was said, she recalled, that the fluids of a kinsman could produce what she was now experiencing. That the closer the relation of whose blood and fluid was being extracted, the more magnificent the effects would be to the one ingesting it. It was obvious now; she understood it all. Life never failed its end of the deal.

Aulwurm.

Anika Morgan was her blood.

CHAPTER FIFTEEN

Gretel was late meeting Petr at the orchard and had considered not showing up at all. Odalinde's news about the visit from Officer Stenson—Petr's father—had left her melancholy, and though she didn't necessarily feel required to act bubbly for Petr's sake—they were just a pair of friendly coworkers meeting for lunch after all—she also didn't want to be a downer.

But by the time noon rolled around the walls of the bedroom started closing in on Gretel, and she decided a picnic was just the thing she needed. Besides, it was about time to push the elephant out of the room and talk about that night on the porch—and Petr's declaration that his father was not really there to help. Maybe there was nothing substantial to Petr's ominous words, but she felt she knew him well enough now that he owed her an explanation.

"You're late," Petr said, holding the boat steady as he stepped apprehensively onto the wooden bottom. Gretel thought he looked like an old lady as gingerly as he was stepping.

"You're not afraid of the water are you?" Gretel said playfully.

"No. Not really. Not as long as I'm on top of it and not in it. I can't really swim that well. And when I say 'not that well' I mean not at all."

"Can't swim?" Gretel was floored by the revelation. "Whoever heard of a boy in the Back Country who can't swim?'

"I may be *in* the Back Country, but I'm not *from* the Back Country. Just in case you forgot. And there aren't many lakes and rivers in the Urban lands."

Petr maneuvered his way to the center of the boat and reached blindly for a seat.

"You'd better hope the Klahrs keep you in the orchard and never ask you to fish for them," Gretel teased, gripping a single oar with both hands and launching the boat from the bank.

Petr, who now sat only a few feet away on the bow seat facing Gretel, grimaced at her and she smiled back.

Gretel liked her current position of power, helming the vessel, responsible for the life of her passenger as she gently glided them both toward the cannery. If there was ever a time to ask Petr about that first night they met, she figured now was it. "So how is your father?"

Petr held tightly to the sides of the boat and kept his stare fixed on the water, clearly uncomfortable with his current location so far from shore. "Uh, he's fine, I guess. Do we need to go this far out?"

"There are some shallow dunes that form close to the bank," Gretel lied. "We need to stay out far enough to avoid them." Realistically, they could have stayed twenty feet from the bank and been just fine, but Gretel wanted to keep Petr vulnerable for as long as possible, and hopefully get some answers.

"He came by one day to check on me," Gretel continued, "a while ago. I wasn't there. Did you know about that?"

Petr didn't hesitate. "Yeah, I think I remember him saying something like that." And then, "Is it much further?"

Gretel ignored the question. "Speaking of your father, do you remember that first day at my house, when your father sent you back for his binder?"

Petr looked up at Gretel and nodded. "Yes, of course."

"Do you remember what you said when you were leaving?"

"You mean before you kicked me out?"

"Okay, fine, before I kicked you out," Gretel repeated coldly. Now that the subject was afoot she was in no mood for bantering, and her words were curt and focused. She kept her gaze on the boy in front of her and steered the rowboat around the bend in the lake, intuitively heading for Rifle Field.

"I don't remember exactly," Petr replied, this time more serious in his tone. "I think I asked you why my father was there. Why he came out to your house in the first place." Petr's eyes were now back on the murky water and he was shifting slightly back and forth on the seat, trying to find the true middle.

"Wrong!" Gretel barked, snapping Petr's head to attention. She locked on his eyes and held them steady. "You actually said, 'I don't think he's here to help you,' those were your exact words." Gretel lowered her voice and then continued. "You already knew why he was there because I had told you in the house. And then when I asked why he *was* there if not to help us, you said, 'I don't know,' and, by the way, you looked very suspicious while saying it."

"I...I guess I don't..."

"We're here," Gretel interrupted, slipping off her sandals and hopping into the shallow water bordering Rifle Field. "Help me pull it in."

She'd, of course, pulled the boat on the bank dozens of times by herself, but she felt barking orders would keep Petr off his guard and manageable. Gretel slung the blanket over her shoulder and grabbed the loaded basket and walked off alone while Petr finished docking the boat. He sprinted to catch up with her, and the two children silently acknowledged a spot in the field and spread the blanket.

Gretel sat on her knees and unloaded the basket, arranging the bread and fruit on the blanket in her own private categories.

"So, do you remember now?" she said finally, after several minutes of speechlessness.

"I remember," Petr replied.

Gretel broke off a large piece of bread from the loaf and handed it to Petr. And waited.

"Okay," Petr said, absently crumbling the bread piece as he searched for the words to his confession. "The truth is my father sent me to the door and told me to talk to you. I think he left his binder on purpose."

"But why? What did he want you to talk to me about?"

"I really don't know. He didn't say anything specific. I think he just wanted me to meet you. When he came back to the car that night he described you to me and told me that you made a good impression on him. He said you were very sophisticated or something, and asked me why I couldn't be as mature and polite as you."

Gretel felt a flush in her cheeks. "So why did you say he wouldn't help me?"

"I was just mad at him for insulting me, I guess, wishing I was more like some stranger he'd just met for only a few minutes." Petr dropped his eyes and smiled. "And a girl to boot."

Gretel couldn't hold back a smile and she shook her head in playful irritation.

"Plus," the boy continued, "I was already unhappy about the meeting at the boarding school. It was just a long day. And by the time he sent me to your door—and then you threw me out—I ...I was trying to scare you, I guess. I'm sorry."

Petr gave an epiphanic sideways glance and then nodded. "My father was right, I'm not as mature and polite as you are. Your mother had just disappeared. I should have been more understanding."

Gretel's look was hard as she stared at Petr's shamed face, but she wasn't mad at him. She put herself in his position, and though she wouldn't have behaved exactly as he did if the roles were reversed, she certainly would have acted out in some way. Not to mention that, as she recalled, he had remained incredibly cordial and sophisticated throughout the encounter.

"And I want to be honest with you about something else," Petr said.

Gretel stared in anticipation, swarming with relief that she had finally reached this point with Petr.

"My father knew that you were starting at the orchard, and that's why he asked the Klahrs to take me on."

On some level Gretel knew this fact, but she was stunned to hear it admitted. "So Mr. Klahr was lying about your friend from school?"

"No! Of course not! Mr. Klahr would never lie to cover me. He'd choose you over me any day."

This fact was so self-evident Gretel didn't even bother disputing it.

"My roommate really did work there last summer. That was just a coincidence, and a good excuse to use for finding the work in the first place."

Gretel stayed quiet for several moments, and then started giggling softly.

"What's funny?"

"Your father sure thinks highly of me!"

Petr laughed. "I guess."

"I mean, I only met him for ten minutes!" Gretel was in full-blown laughter now. "Maybe he wants you to marry me someday!"

Petr's laughter had crescendoed to match Gretel's.

"Maybe," he replied "but I don't think your father would approve!'

This last quip sent Gretel into hysterics, and the laughter and joking continued throughout the better part of lunch, at one point causing Gretel to spit out the apple she'd been chewing, nearly causing her mortal embarrassment. It was the most fun she'd had in months, and maybe longer.

Finally, when the chortling subsided, Gretel said, "I'm sorry too."

"For what?"

"Mainly for being mean to you that day at my house—and most of the days during the harvest—but also for your dad getting you involved that day. That wasn't fair of him." Gretel watched the boy closely to see if he became defensive about his father, which he didn't seem to, and she pressed him. "Why do you think he would have done that? Really?"

Petr shook his head and shrugged.

Gretel decided to let the gesture suffice, and then asked, "Do you get along with him?"

"As much as most kids get along with their fathers, I guess," Petr answered. "I don't see him that much anymore since the academy, and now with work and everything. Plus he's not home much."

Since Petr seemed open to conversation, Gretel plowed on, asking about his home and the rest of his family, what it was like to live in the Urbanlands, and the benefits and drawbacks of having a System officer for a father, of which there seemed to be plenty on both accounts. Petr was vague on the subject of his mother, who had died when he was six, but was otherwise candid about his life, and by the end of the conversation, when Gretel had formed her image of what he'd told her, it all seemed fairly ordinary. Not quite boring, but certainly nothing like she'd have guessed only months ago.

She watched his expressions throughout the lunch, recognizing the shine of pride in his eyes as he recounted the pistoleer award he'd won when he was ten; and, alternately, the devastation at the loss of his grandmother—the woman who had raised him—only the year before. Gretel was rapt by his voice, so lush and sincere, and when the discussion lagged, it seemed the most natural action in the world for her to lean over and kiss him. He kissed her back, awkwardly yet gently, and when Gretel pulled away Petr remained puckered and shut-eyed for just a moment too long, and this made Gretel giggle and Petr blush.

After the kiss, neither child said a word until time dictated they begin the process of leaving. Gretel would have stayed until nightfall if she could have, and she knew Petr felt the same.

In blissful silence the two teenagers walked back to the rowboat, occasionally stealing glances and smiling, though Petr's smiles possessed something more than Gretel's. Gretel had enjoyed the kiss—later, what she would always consider her first—but it was being with Petr that she enjoyed more. It was friendship that she wanted most from him right now, and though their relationship had certainly crossed into something more since this morning, Gretel wasn't in love. At least not yet. Not in the holding hands, having babies kind of way.

The silence continued for the entire ride back to the orchard, with Petr in his same position on the bow seat and Gretel at the helm. When they finally reached the bank, Petr lingered for a moment, staring at Gretel and smiling. She thought he was going to kiss her again, which would have been perfectly appropriate, she thought, but he didn't, and that was okay too.

"Thank you," he said finally, "for the picnic. I had a great time. I wish I could stay longer."

"Me too," Gretel replied softly, smiling. And then, as if needing something to segue from the mushiness, said, "And good luck on the ride home with your father."

"Thanks."

Petr disembarked with a hop, displaying a confident acumen not seen during boarding, and Gretel watched with a sympathetic smile as he jogged up the bank into the first cut of grass lining the orchard.

At the tree line he turned back toward the water and called with a wave, "And good luck with your stepmother. Everything's going to be fine."

Gretel waved back and watched the boy as he ran on air toward the Klahr house. When he was out of sight, she shoved off toward home, pressing the oars back and forth with steady deliberation. She had considered an afternoon rowing session, but decided to pass. It wasn't that she was tired—in fact she had more energy than she'd had that morning—but her talk with Petr had created a longing for her family—Hansel mainly, but father as well—and she decided to go directly home to see them.

She was halfway across the lake when the knot formed low in her belly, and by the time she'd reached the bank of the Morgan property something akin to panic had set in. She stepped from the boat and stood statue-like on the rocky shore, her eyes wide and searching, her breath shallow as she rummaged through her memory, replaying each of the encounters she'd had with Petr over the last few weeks: today at the picnic, that day in the Klahr kitchen when he'd reappeared like a vivid memory, the past few days in the fields and in Klahr house working as partners and forming a real friendship. She even thought about each of the dozen or so perfunctory conversations they'd had during the harvest.

And she was sure.

Gretel knew the answer to her internal question: she'd never referred to Odalinde as anything other than her father's nurse.

She'd never mentioned to Petr that Odalinde was going to be her stepmother.

CHAPTER SIXTEEN

The car presented itself to Anika first in a dream, as a low sustained thunder somewhere miles off on the horizon, a benevolent warning to an inevitable storm.

The dream itself was almost an exact replica of Anika's current situation: she had escaped from an isolated cabin in the woods and was now desperately looking for help along the Interways. Only in her dream she was not alone, Hansel and Gretel were with her, and Anika's desperation to find safety for her children was a burning sickness in her abdomen. And in her dream, unlike in reality (thank God), rain was apparently on the way.

On any other day the rumbling thunder would have been inaudible to Anika, or unperceived, a white noise drifting above the trees until simply vanishing into the atmosphere. But Anika's senses were heightened, and even in her sleep her mind indexed the sound, cross-referencing it with latent experiences of the past. Her mind told her the sound was an impending storm, but the rumble was continuous and growing, unlike the crescendo and decrescendo of thunder. And, as she recalled, the sky had been clear before she'd fallen asleep.

Anika opened her eyes and glanced around, instinctively keeping the rest of her body still, afraid that moving would somehow expose a secret hiding spot in which she'd been hunkering. But she hadn't been hiding. In fact, her position was rather exposed and precarious, less than four feet from the pavement of the Interways. She quickly got to her feet and breathed deeply, rubbing the confusion from her eyes while giving silent thanks that her children, though she missed them terribly, weren't actually with her.

Anika realized now that her energy levels were lower than she originally thought when she first started her journey home—she'd only walked a few miles by her estimate, and already was asleep. Exposed.

She peeked toward the horizon for storm clouds and saw nothing but dusky blue clarity. She was mostly pleased with this sight, though thirst was beginning to factor in, and the thought of rain triggered a lumpy swallow in her throat.

Then, as if keen to Anika's inquisitiveness, the wind brought forth the low rumble of thunder from her dream. But the sound, she now realized, wasn't thunder, it was the mechanical growl of an engine—a large engine by the sound of it—and it was getting louder. A car was coming. Finally.

Anika stood and began to walk down the middle of the road toward the oncoming sound, and then broke into a slow lope, her arms hanging at her sides. She hadn't the strength to run properly, but she needed to get to that noise and confirm her miracle. Her mind was shrouded by hope to the actual danger of running toward oncoming traffic, but she absently figured that at the long stretch of road she'd started down, any car headed toward her would see her well before reaching her.

Anika squinted in desperation, trying to adjust the lenses of her eyes to the dimming afternoon light, hoping to catch the first flicker of metal heading toward her. She knew she'd been right about the sound. There was no question it was the sound of a car motor, or perhaps a motorcycle, and it was growing louder every second. In less than a minute she could be rescued, on her way home to Heinrich and her children, beginning her life again. She started to cry and began running faster. 'Thank you! Thank you, God!' she sobbed.

She ran another thirty yards before the sound that began as a subtle reverie finally materialized into reality. Anika stopped running and leaned slightly forward, hands on her thighs, measuring the distance and the validity of what her eyes were seeing. It was true. A car was headed straight for her.

She started laughing hysterically and waving her hands in front of her face in a frantic, scissor-like motion. The headlights grew larger as the car neared, and Anika could hear the downshifting gears as the car began its deceleration. Exhausted, she dropped to her knees and put her palms flat on the street, her head hanging as she simultaneously laughed and coughed and spat. It was implausible that she had made it to this place, free and unbound, seemingly in good health with her sanity still intact, though this last part she knew was yet to be fully determined. At no point had she ever completely given up hope, but, if she were honest with herself, at her core, she assumed she was going to die in that cabin.

Anika tried to will the muscles in her neck to raise her head to the approaching stranger, but it was useless; her exhaustion was almost absolute. A whispered 'thank you' was all she could manage before collapsing face down on the street, her arms no longer able to support her torso. She listened as the footsteps quickened and she elicited the trace of a smile when she felt the blanket fall across her shoulders and back.

But the cover didn't warm the chill that flashed in her neck and spine when her rescuer spoke.

"Anika Morgan," the voice said confidently, "so you're not dead after all."

***

Anika sat quietly in the front seat of The System officer's car and held the woolen blanket tightly over her shoulders, sweeping it across the front of her neck and chest. The constant speed and steady hum of the tires on the road caused her to drift in and out of sleep, and with each brief awakening she brought the meticulously clean blanket under her nose to inhale the scent. She'd forgotten the smell of cleanliness, so accustomed had she become to the slaughter room's gradual descent into filth and disgrace; and now, as she held the blanket to her face, the fresh fragrance of laundered fabric made her think of summertime as a small girl.

Anika felt the car slow dramatically and then turn sharply to the left, and she woke instinctively to brace herself from toppling toward the driver. She opened her eyes and glanced at the window where a wall of daylight confronted her.

Out of the front windshield Anika could see a narrow dirt road which had been divided down the middle by an overgrowth of grass and weeds. With some reluctance, she shifted her attention to the figure on the seat beside her, expecting either to be met by a face familiar to her, or else one not quite human, signaling she was in the midst of a dream. Instead, the smiling face she saw in the driver's seat was as normal and unintimidating as any she'd see on a busy Saturday in the local market, though she supposed a bit more handsome. And not one she recognized.

Anika sat straight on her portion of the bench seat and rubbed her palms down her face to clear the grogginess from her head.

"You're the man who helped me I suppose," she said, her voice sounding raspy and timid. She cleared her throat. "I can never thank you enough."

"You're welcome," the man replied, not taking his eyes from the road in front of him.

Anika vaguely remembered that the man had spoken her name as she had lain in the street, just before her last memory of the blanket being draped across her shoulders. "Do I know you?"

The man smiled quizzically and finally looked at Anika. "I don't think so," he said, "do I look familiar to you?"

"No, it's just that...back on the street...I think you said my name. At least I think I remember that."

The man's smile straightened and a serious look emerged on his face, an expression which hovered between interest and concern. He looked back to the road. "Yes, Anika, I know your name. Every System officer in this area knows your name."

Anika flinched at the man's words, and an icy tremble trickled the length of her nape and dispersed across her blanketed shoulders.

With her eyes now adjusted, Anika slowly surveyed the car's interior and immediately noticed the bulbous metal switches and steep buttons, as well as the standard two-way radio, which indicated she was indeed among a man of The System. This wasn't the first time she'd been in a System vehicle, and she was deluged with thoughts of her childhood when, as a girl of twelve, Anika rode quietly in the back of a cruiser as she was shuttled behind an ambulance carrying her father to the hospital following a rather severe traffic accident. At the time that short trip had seemed like a dream—Anika's mind protecting her from considering all the possible fates of her father, she supposed—and she'd been unusually distracted by the car's interior. She'd seen nothing like it in her world before, the stark leather of the seats and door panels, the chrome lines outlining every hard feature, and the various multi-colored blinking lights that spanned the dashboard. There was an alien feel to the car that made Anika feel both helpless and safe, and now, as she sat rigid and wary in the passenger seat of this more modern, yet still familiar cruiser, that same feeling possessed her again.

"The System." Anika was suddenly flooded with hope as she recognized her good fortune, and her mouth exploded into a huge grin. "You're from The System! But how did you know it was me? On the street?"

The officer chuckled. "I know everything about you Mrs. Morgan: your age, your hair and eye color, even how you were dressed the day you disappeared." He glanced at her again. "Which doesn't seem to fit with what you're wearing now by the way."

Anika started to respond, but held back, deciding that an explanation regarding the difference in her attire wasn't the proper place to begin her story.

"Besides, Mrs. Morgan, how many possible women do you think one would expect to find in the middle of the road, especially in this part of the country?"

Anika processed this reasoning as sound, though slightly off, but explored that notion for only a moment before the reins on her instincts snapped. "My family! You must have spoken with my family then? How are my children?"

"We have spoken with your family, Anika, on several occasions, and everyone is fine. Though your husband was quite ill for a while after your disappearance."

"Ill? In what way? Who's been looking after the children?"

Anika realized the rather one-sidedness of her concern, inquiring about her husband's condition only to gauge the impact it had on Gretel and Hansel, but at the moment her children were all she could think of.

The officer stopped in front of what appeared to be a small warehouse and shifted the car into park. "As I said, your family is fine, including your children. In fact—and I don't tell you this to upset you in any way—but your daughter seems to have thrived since you went missing. Shall we?"

Anika hadn't noticed the warehouse or even that they'd stopped, and she stared baffled at the officer for a few moments before finally understanding his suggestion to enter the building standing before them.

"What? What is *this* place?"

"It's a place for gathering information. Yours was a very complicated case, Mrs. Morgan, and there's a lot we need to investigate concerning what happened. You'll just need to stay here for a while, and I promise to get you home as soon as possible."

"A while? How long is a while?"

The officer sighed impatiently. "I don't know exactly, Mrs. Morgan. I suppose until we have the information we need."

Anika glanced toward the stark building and then back to the officer. "Does my family know that I've been found? Has anyone contacted them?"

"Yes, certainly. Of course. We had an officer visit them as soon as I was able to verify your identity. They've been contacted."

Anika noticed at a fairly young age that most men of power were poor liars, she imagined it was for the simple reason that they usually reached their ends through force or intimidation, and lying wasn't a skill necessary to master. And she recognized this lie at once. The shift of the officer's body, the loss of eye connection, the change in pitch and excessive affirmation: all obvious signs of deceit.

She could now feel the rise inside her toward hysterics, but fought the emotion, catching it in her chest and driving it back to her belly. Her nerves had been shredded in the slaughterhouse, and her psyche going forward in life would be as fragile as butterfly eggs; but the ordeal had also assured Anika that within her was an involuntary prowess of survival, a fundamental determination to keep her heart beating and blood flowing, at least until that final moment when it was no longer hers to decide. She'd always believed everyone possessed this strength to some degree, and over the last several months it had been revealed that hers was exceptional.

"I'll take all the time you want to answer questions," she said calmly, "of course, every detail. I would just like to see my family first."

The officer stared at Anika for a moment, as if considering her request, and then said flatly, "Let's go."

"No!" she screamed, and then as if speaking an echo, "No." Anika sat hugging the blanket around her torso, staring forward, looking as petulant as a four-year-old who's been told to eat her vegetables. She could sense the officer considering whether the time had come to use force, but then, with a sigh, he continued the act.

"Listen, Mrs. Morgan," he said, "the longer we wait to get the information from you, the better chance whoever did this to you will go free. Is that what you want?"

"What makes you think someone did anything to me?" she replied, her eyes wide and crazed. "I never told you anything about another person. Maybe I was just lost."

The officer frowned. "If you had just become lost in the woods, Mrs. Morgan, you would have died weeks ago. Only the most skilled survivalist would have been able to find food in those forests. And I assume you didn't sew a new set of clothes for yourself while wandering through the wilderness."

Anika looked away, slightly embarrassed at her 'Aha!' attempt.

"Besides, some of the injuries I've seen on you don't come from tree branches or a slip on a wet rock. Or even a wild animal. A person caused those wounds."

"Then if I can't see my family yet at least let me see a doctor. I definitely do need a doctor." Anika softened her tone, sensing she had struck a chord of sympathy within the man.

"Your medical needs will be taken care of promptly. Once we're inside."

It was obvious The System officer's intentions were deeply anchored, and that going anywhere other than inside the building was not a possibility for Anika. And though her will was steel, she simply hadn't the physical strength to fight or run; that would have been tantamount to suicide. Her only choice was to obey.

The absurdity of the scenario nearly caused her to erupt in laughter. It was nearly impossible to imagine: not a full day had gone by since she escaped the most atrocious nightmare she could have conceived—being slowly harvested by a monstrous hermit for some obscene recipe—and now here she was again, being held without choice, and this time by a public servant under oath to protect her!

Anika tossed the blanket to the backseat and exited the car without another word, and then walked ahead of the officer to the front of the structure. The building wasn't much bigger than a large house, but the design and lack of windows suggested it was used for something other than living, and its modern, utilitarian appearance was in complete opposition to the rustic road they'd just traveled. The officer followed Anika to the metal door which stood at ground level and then fished a single key from his pocket, inserting it into the deadbolt above the knob. Anika had one last thought to flee, but the bleakness of the perimeter was daunting and hopeless.

With a push, the door opened to a large, brightly lit room with high ceilings, though several rows of overhanging fluorescent lights made them feel much lower. Stacks of empty metal shelves lined the side walls, which were made of unfinished concrete. The floor was wood and dusty to the point of slick, and the holes between the planks were so gaping that Anika could see through to the natural ground on which the warehouse stood. And perfectly centered in the room, a couch and two brown, leather chairs had been placed on top of an area rug, and a small table and lamp set was positioned beside the couch.

"Have a seat, Mrs. Morgan," the officer ordered.

Anika walked to one of the chairs and sat down, the dust exploding into the air and clouding her face. At this stage she'd resigned herself to do as she was told, at least until the request became unreasonable. When that time came she hoped to still have the resolve to put up some iteration of a fight, whether verbal or otherwise. She still left room for hope that the officer's intentions weren't sinister, that he really did just want to ask her questions and get some answers about her disappearance. Maybe he didn't trust her, she thought. Maybe her case had caused him to snap, and now his fanaticism was leading him to inappropriate, or even illegal, procedures. That certainly made him a bad System officer, but it didn't necessarily make him dangerous.

But that didn't change the fact he was being less than truthful about something. About that she had no doubt.

The officer locked the door behind them, walked toward Anika, and stood behind the couch, facing her. "Mrs. Morgan," he said, his tone now very official, "my name is Officer Oliver Stenson. I was assigned to your case soon after you were reported missing by your family."

Anika leaned back in the chair and placed both arms on the rests, assuming a look of comfort that contradicted the feelings inside her.

"After your father told us you'd gone missing along the Interways, a team of several officers was dispatched that day to find evidence. What we found instead was..."

"My father?"

Officer Stenson stared at Anika for a moment, confused. "Yes, Mrs. Morgan. Your father, Marcel Gruen."

"Yes, I know my father's name, I was curious that my father called you and not my husband. Or my daughter. My father wouldn't have known that anything was wrong once I left him. How would he have known to call The System?"

Officer Stenson glanced away, searching, as if the explanation lay somewhere on the warehouse floor. He looked back at Anika and then smiled. It was a full, toothy smile, one Anika hadn't seen before.

"Perhaps your husband called your father and then he called us," Office Stenson said, "I suppose I can't be certain of the telecommunication pattern exactly. Are you suggesting that I'm lying?"

Anika locked the officer's gaze, resisting any displays of the fear she felt. "I didn't mean that at all. It's just that it's odd to me. My father reporting me missing, that is."

Officer Stenson dropped his stare and started walking toward a door at the back of the warehouse. It seemed to Anika to be an interior door that led to some unseen backroom of the building. The door appeared solid metal on the bottom with a framed mirrored window on top. A one-way mirror she supposed, of the kind she'd seen in police movies.

"I'll return in a moment for questioning," he said flatly, "please wait for me here. The door to the outside is locked securely. In case you were wondering."

"When do I see a doctor? You said I would see a doctor. And I need to eat something. And can I at least have water?"

"Of course. I'll bring you something now. The doctor should be arriving shortly."

With that Officer Stenson walked into the back room of the warehouse and closed the door behind him. Within a few seconds Anika could hear talking behind the door. Though she couldn't make out the words being spoken, the conversation seemed somewhat confrontational. There was a moment of quiet, and then the door opened slowly and a taller, much older man emerged from the back room. It was the last man she'd seen before she was seized and tortured.

It was her father.

***

Gretel lay motionless in her bed, the sheets to her chin, searching the ceiling above her as she considered the picnic and what Petr had said to her on the bank. Her mind was exhausted of explanations, and Gretel was now virtually certain she'd never mentioned the engagement to Petr. Which left only one explanation: someone else told him.

Gretel quickly eliminated the Klahrs as the source, since they had never offered any personal information about Petr to Gretel, and she couldn't imagine them acting any differently when it came to her private affairs. On the one or two occasions when Gretel had asked something about Petr, they either didn't know or told her to ask him. That's how they were: very respectful of a person's personal business.

So who? And why?

Gretel was startled by a knock on her bedroom door. "Who is it?"

"It's me." Odalinde. "You've been in there quite a while Gretel. I figured you would be on the lake by now. Are you feeling okay?"

"Yes, I'm fine." Gretel tried to keep the irritation out of her voice but fell short. "I just didn't sleep well last night, that's all. I'll be out in a minute."

This was the price of routine and dedication, Gretel thought: once you falter even slightly, everyone's eyebrows shoot to the ceiling.

She willed her feet to the floor and within ten minutes was twisting the knob of the front door. She made no eye contact with Odalinde, but could feel the woman shifting glances toward her.

"Do you think you'll be on the lake long today?" Odalinde asked for the first time ever.

Gretel paused at the threshold and then turned toward Odalinde, squinting, confused by the question. "What?" she asked.

"I was just asking if you planned on spending a lot of time rowing today, or if you would be home a little earlier." Odalinde's voice was eager, nervous.

"Why would you want to know that?" Again, there was no bite in Gretel's reply, only confusion.

Odalinde frowned and her eyes softened. "Remember earlier when I said there were some things I needed to tell you and your brother?"

Gretel nodded.

"Well those things can't wait much longer, Gretel." Odalinde walked to the kitchen table, pulled out a chair, and sat. "And if you're ready," she said, "I'd like to tell you now."

***

"Hello, Anika."

"Father?" Anika whispered.

Anika had never been one to believe in ghosts and magic, but seeing the form of her father, now, at this moment and in this setting, could only be the result of a force supernatural. Or perhaps she was hallucinating—the workings of her brain stressed to its limit.

"I suppose I'm the last person you expected to see come through that door, eh?" Marcel forced a sad smile and nodded slightly, answering silently for his stunned daughter.

"Father...What...Why are you here? Are you being held here? I think I'm being imprisoned! Again! I don't know what's happening. Who is that man?"

"It's okay, Anika, it's okay. He is who he says he is. He is a System officer."

Anika's father turned back toward the door and yelled for Officer Stenson, calling for him as simply "Stenson," before erupting into a rasping cough. The episode subsided for a moment, and then continued again, this time more violently, forcing the old man to double over, hands to his knees. He stumbled around the sofa, using the back as a crutch, and then dropped to the cushion, bouncing comically and nearly toppling to one side. As if prompted by the act, Officer Stenson walked back through the door carrying a plate and a ceramic cup of water. He kept his eyes to the floor, brooding.

Anika stayed focused on her father, watching him with a mixture of concern and terror, both at his condition and his apparent knowledge of the situation. In fact, she observed, he seemed not just knowledgeable, but in control.

"This was not the plan, Marcel," Stenson said through tightly clenched teeth, "what are you doing?"

Anika's father tried to speak but was still in the throes of sickness, and waved a dismissive hand instead.

"What is happening?!" Anika screamed, rising like a piston from the chair. She walked to the couch and sat next to her father. "Give me the water! Now!" she barked at Stenson, reaching her hand behind the couch but keeping her eyes to her father.

Officer Stenson handed the water to Anika and she put it to her father's mouth, gently tipping a steady sip over his lips as she'd done dozens of times over the past year.

He swallowed the water and then pushed the glass away, gulping down several frantic breaths, trying to fill his lungs as fully as possible before the coughing resumed.

"I'm dying, Anika," he said, "and...I don't want..." was all he had managed before the hacks started again.

"You're okay, Papa, don't talk," she whispered, stroking the back of his head. She glared back toward the officer who was standing alone, away from the oasis of furniture, awkwardly watching the domestic scene play out as if he'd stumbled upon it accidentally.

"My father is not well. He should not be here!"

"Your father is here of his own will, Mrs. Morgan," Stenson replied. "In fact, it is your father who..."

"No!" It was Marcel. He stood, precariously and with some effort, but much quicker than Anika would have thought possible given his condition, his chest bowing forward, his shoulders high and receded. "No. If she is to hear it she will hear it from me."

"I don't *want* her to hear it, Marcel. There is no purpose served by it. That was never the plan and it shouldn't be the plan now."

"I want her to hear it, Oliver," Marcel said, his words soft now, a plea for understanding.

The officer shook his head disapprovingly, but remained quiet.

Anika's father closed his eyes for what must have been twenty seconds, and then breathed deeply, exhaling comfortably, the coughing fits mercifully over for the moment. "I know what has happened to you, Anika," he said finally. "I know where you've been."

Anika shook her head in a combination of confusion and denial. "What?" The word was barely audible, and the tears in Anika's eyes felt poisonous.

"I know all that you've been through. At that cabin."

"You have no idea what I've been through! How could you know! What is happening here? Papa, what did he mean that you want to be here? What does that mean?"

Anika looked back and forth between the two men, hoping the pieces would suddenly come together and the answers to her questions made apparent. She watched as Officer Stenson walked toward her and set the plate on the table beside the couch. The dish contained an assortment of cheeses and surprisingly fresh-looking bread, but Anika's appetite was lost.

Officer Stenson said nothing more as he strode to the back of the warehouse and disappeared through the interior door.

"I'm trying to tell you, Anika," her father continued, "I'm dying. Soon. I can feel it in my chest and hear it in my cough. You know it as well as anyone. You can hear it too. And you've seen how I've rotted over the years."

Anika cringed at the word choice.

"You know I'm dying. You do. But the problem is my girl, I am a selfish man, and I don't want to die." He paused, and his eyes widened just slightly before saying, "And I don't intend to."

Marcel sat down again on the couch, this time easily and controlled.

"I had always hoped, Anika, and at times even prayed, that as the years piled on me and my body began failing that I would accept death as everyone does, as people have done for thousands of generations: ideally, with grace, but if not grace, then at least concession." He paused, calculating the words. "But once I learned of it, of the miracle, and the truth of what it meant, I..."

He stopped suddenly, recognizing the frenzied crescendo of his voice. The volume and tenor reminded Anika of a carnival barker.

"I could never unlearn it, Anika," he continued slowly, "I could never not try." He paused again, and this time stared intently at his daughter. "That is where you come in."

The words drifted in the room, each molecule of air now saturated with the solution to the riddle of why Anika's father was sitting before her in a warehouse at the end of the world. Anika shook her head in disbelief, the tears now streaking steadily.

"I don't understand," she lied, "what are you saying?"

Marcel's look was rigid, but his voice had the tone of kindness, "You know what I'm saying, Anika."

"But why? Why me? And how could you have...It was just an accident. I wandered into the woods. What you're saying doesn't make sense!"

"Sit down, Anika, the story is a long one."

"I don't want to sit down!" Anika screamed, now teetering on hysterics, but her father's look was fierce, and one Anika had known since her earliest memories. It was a look that, even under the circumstances, she'd been conditioned to obey.

She moved backward to the chair and sat, waiting for her father to begin the story of why her life had been shattered.

CHAPTER SEVENTEEN

Gretel stared at Odalinde, who was now seated in the kitchen, her shoulders and chin high, her back stiff against the chair. Gretel's hand was still firmly wrapped around the door knob, her expression mixed with fear and confusion.

"I don't mean to be rude, Odalinde, but I really had plans to row today. I..."

"Sit down, Gretel. Please."

Odalinde's stare was hypnotic, and Gretel could see in the woman's eyes that whatever she had to say was not insignificant.

"It's about your mother."

Gretel relaxed her hand and let it slide from the knob, the feeling of urgency now replaced with one of anxiety. "What is it? What's happened?"

Gretel walked to the kitchen table and sat down next to Odalinde.

"And I want your brother to hear this too."

Gretel quickly called for Hansel, who emerged from his room moments later. Seeing his sister and guardian seated together instantly made him curious, and he too sat down, facing his sister from across the table.

Hansel and Gretel stared unwaveringly at Odalinde, waiting for her revelation. Gretel could sense the woman's nervousness as she looked to the floor, studying her thoughts and trying to figure where to begin.

"I've wanted to talk to you both for quite some time now. And it's taken me much longer than it should have. And before I begin, I just want to say I'm sorry—for many things really, but most of all I'm sorry for that. For waiting so long."

Neither child said a word in response to this preamble, and Odalinde continued.

"I'm going to tell you why I'm here, why I came here at all, to your home." She paused a moment, waiting for any interruptions that may come, and hearing none said, "and to tell you what I believe happened to your mother."

"Mother?" Hansel said, the word coming off his tongue as if only generally familiar to him.

"That's right, Hansel, your mother."

"What do you mean 'why you came here?'" Gretel backtracked, "you're a nurse, our father was...is ill."

Odalinde's mouth turned down in a guilty frown, and she sighed deeply through her nose. "Yes Gretel, but there's more. Much more. Now I want you both to listen to me carefully."

She stopped and looked back and forth between the siblings, making sure she had their attention.

"What I'm going to tell you must not be discussed with anyone. Not with your friends, not with your teachers, or even the Klahrs. No one. You'd be wise even to keep it from your future husband or wife. Do you understand me?"

Hansel nodded, rapt with intrigue.

"Okay," Gretel said, "but why are *you* about to discuss it with *us*?"

Odalinde smiled. "Because Gretel, you're at the center of this story. You were always to know."

"Know what?" Hansel asked.

Odalinde began.

***

"Your mother was born during a time of enormous upheaval and discontent in the Old Country. The kings and emperors of the assorted lands—men who had known the greatest power ever held over humankind—were abruptly and successfully being challenged by their people. The uprisings were fleet and merciless, and within a decade each had watched helplessly as his power receded to the past like broken waves. In their place chaos and strife emerged."

Marcel was settled back on the couch now, motionless, his eyes barely slits, his mouth effortlessly and eloquently unleashing the story to the ether.

"Most in the nobility and clergy were killed during this time, or banished to the wilderness to die a much lonelier death, one filled with cold and hunger. Those of the tradesmen and peasant classes fared only slightly better though, since once their rulers fell, they were essentially leaderless and naturally distrustful of anyone who tried to assume a position of authority. And this distrust fractured not only regions and villages, but neighbor and family as well. The ultimate result was a continent of borderless nations and mob rule."

Anika hung on every word, both fascinated by her father's fecundity and frightened by the delusions that had apparently infected him. He'd obviously been sick for a long time—and *very* sick lately—she'd never been in denial about the truth of that, but it was a sickness that until now had seemed not to affect his mind. Where did this depiction of her mother's childhood come from? Old kings and emperors? Peasant classes? He was describing a world hundreds of years before her mother was born.

"But there were other peoples in these lands," he continued, "groups that existed outside of the classes—villages whose families could trace their ancestors as accurately and distantly as the pharaohs of Egypt. They lived beyond the kings' reaches mostly, in the hills and forests or other grueling geographies abhorred by soldiers and uncharted on most maps of the time. These were places thought to be strategically and culturally irrelevant, and so were largely ignored by leaders and forgotten by historians. Even tax collection was considered folly in such lands, since the cost to reach them was often far more expensive than what could be seized. Those clans that made their homes in these regions were considered at the time to be primitive, tribal, unlearned in the modernity of things like architecture, weaponry and fashion; and indeed, by the standards of the ruling classes and those beneath them, they were comparatively uncivilized in those subjects.

"But in many areas they were genius, intensely curious of the world, scientifically sophisticated and meticulous in their calculations. And perhaps more importantly, they were literate, and therefore able to pass on their discoveries not only through speech and pictures, but through the invention of hundreds of unique written languages, each containing uncommon alphabets and symbols, languages that were frequently known only to the tiny society in which they were formed, where members often lived and died having never spoken a word to a person outside the territory. It was in a place like this that your mother entered the world."

"That's enough!" Anika screamed, rising to her feet once again. "You've gone mad, Papa! I won't listen anymore!" She stifled the sob boiling in her chest and breathed deeply. "I don't understand, Papa, your mind was well when I left you, your memory as nimble as ever. What's happened to you?"

Marcel gave a patient look to his daughter and offered a subtle gesture for her to sit, a command she obeyed with a sigh of aggravation.

"I won't argue that I'm not insane, Anika, to you the evidence must seem quite staggering at the moment. But what I've told you, and everything I'm going to tell you, is true."

"You're speaking of Mother as if she were born in medieval times! What...what are you saying?"

"I'm telling you now, Anika. If I may continue?"

Anika gave a permissive nod and listened.

CHAPTER EIGHTEEN

"I'm not here to nurse your father," Odalinde began, "not primarily anyway."

Gretel studied the woman's face, which seemed now to have become softer, more innocent. But Gretel's wariness remained, and she even left open the possibility that this conference was a trick, though intuitively she knew it wasn't. "I don't think I ever believed that," she replied, "I don't think I've believed most of what you've said since you came here."

She could feel Hansel's eyes on her, wide and disbelieving, but Gretel's eyes stayed fixed on Odalinde.

"I've tried not to lie to you, Gretel, to either of you. I've been brusque at times, I realize that, but..."

"Why *are* you here then?" Gretel interrupted, not interested in rationalizations or anything resembling an apology.

"To put it concisely, I'm here to protect you."

"Protect us?" Gretel snorted, her eyes wide with astonishment. "*Protect* us?" She repeated the phrase, as if offering Odalinde a chance to rethink her word choice.

"I know that seems odd to you right now, but..."

"No, Odalinde, it doesn't *seem odd right now*, it actually seems insulting and deranged right now! Protect us. How have you protected us? By starving us? By threatening us?"

"I've never..."

"You've done nothing to protect us! Hansel and I have been protecting ourselves since the day father got sick. And every day after. And you coming here has made it all worse!"

Gretel stopped abruptly and stared at Odalinde, waiting for her to fire back with shouts of her own, or perhaps with one of her moderately concealed threats. Instead the woman stayed silent, her hands folded in front of her as if encouraging Gretel to finish.

"Why is my father still sick?"

Odalinde nodded, as if understanding this question was inevitable. "Your father is a good man," she said, "and I've grown very fond of him."

"*Very fond of him*? Have you grown fond of him? You're marrying him! I should hope you're fond of him!"

Odalinde looked away. "Yes, well, we'll need to discuss that as well." She looked back to Gretel and waited for another barrage, but Gretel had, for the moment, said her peace. Odalinde then leaned forward conspiratorially. "But to answer your question, I'm keeping your father sick to protect you from him."

Gretel's face again twisted in anger and disbelief at the woman's brazenness, and all the blood in her body seemed to hurtle toward her head, flooding her brain with the energy it would need to defend her father from this villainous slanderer.

"As I said, Gretel," Odalinde added, holding up an open hand in anticipation of Gretel's eruption, "your father is a good man. A good father and husband. I know that. And so do you. And what you also must know is, that above all else, he loves you both. Very much."

Hansel was now crying, the combination of fear and love and anger too much for him to contain all at once. Gretel put her arm around his shoulders and offered a reassuring shush.

"Then why..." Gretel could no longer arrange her thoughts into a rational sentence.

"But your father is also weak. Weak emotionally, temperamentally, and, increasingly so, physically. He would never withstand the temptation once offered. There are few men who could, and your father is not one of those men."

"Temptation? What temptation?" Hansel asked, "I don't understand what you're talking about."

"It's a very long story, Hansel—centuries old—and most of it doesn't concern either of you. Or me for that matter. But some of it does. Some of this story involves you both quite directly. So I suppose the place to start is at the beginning. Or at least at the beginning of when it matters to you."

"And when is that?" Gretel asked.

"It's the day I met your grandmother," Odalinde said.

She paused a beat and tilted her head slightly forward, narrowing her eyes, making sure the children understood that what she was about to say was true, and that she, Odalinde, recognized the preposterousness of how it sounded.

"Long before your mother was born."

***

"By the time your mother was born the elixir was already discovered and, as your mother recounted to me many years ago, it was spoken of throughout her early childhood, though apparently none in her particular village knew the precise recipe at that time. Or even if the stories were true."

Marcel seemed adrift in his chronicle of an era to which he'd never belonged; Anika thought he looked almost melancholy, sad that his experience of the time would never be more than vicarious and obscure.

"It was a bit of legend at first I suppose, the elixir, but most believed in it, believed at least that there was some truth to it, though the full extent of the power was surely doubted."

Anika's skepticism was unshaken, but she listened carefully, resigning herself to hearing the tale. Besides, she'd never known much about her mother's youth, her schooling and adolescence and such, and even considering the setting in which she now found herself—imprisoned for the second time in as many days—there was comfort in the idea that even a portion of what her father was telling her might be true.

"It was not until your mother reached sixteen or so that the magic was revealed to her explicitly." Marcel paused and stared intensely at his daughter, as if considering whether to continue with the revelation.

Anika could see in her father's eyes that he believed every word he was saying. And that his madness was rampant.

"The magic came in the form of a book, written in a language spoken by so few people that the number could have been measured in dozens. And among those who spoke it there were even fewer who could read it. Your mother was one who could."

The excitement had returned to Marcel's voice, signaling the impending climax to his tale.

"It was true magic, Anika. Of the kind you've always read about in stories. It was, in fact, the unearthing of the most quested possession since the birth of humankind. Truly! And not one whose value was found only in the sentiment of religion or culture, like the Holy Grail or some Pharaoh's sarcophagus," Marcel grimaced at the insignificance of such things, "but one of true power. Life unending, Anika. Immortality."

Anika sat stone-faced, disinterested, a complete opposite reflection of her father's face across from her, which was alert and grinning maniacally, his eyes carefully searching his daughter's face for the look that conveyed, due to the marvel of his story, that she now understood his motives and forgave him his actions.

"Anika. Did you hear me? There exists the formula to let me live forever."

"So for you to live forever requires me to die?" Anika retorted. Her voice was low and clear, her expression never changing.

"Yes, well, it is..." Shame returned to Marcel's face and he looked away from his daughter quickly. He rubbed his hands together in a nervous gesture and then covered his face with them. He sat motionless for a few seconds, and then removed his hands and soberly answered his daughter's question. "Unfortunately, the answer is yes," and then almost as an afterthought, "you or one of your children."

Anika was now at full attention, but she stayed balanced and icy. "And what is it about me...and *your grandchil-*

dren...that makes us so perfect for this priceless recipe of immortality? Surely the pollution that *your* blood contributes can't be it."

Marcel attempted no defense. "There is nothing about you or Gretel or Hansel that is particularly unique, for the formula that is, except that you *are* my blood, and therefore a necessary match for what I need."

Anika glared hatefully now. "I don't understand."

"According to your mother, virtually any human under the age of sixty or so can be used to create the mixture. The measurements must be exact and the timing perfect, but those parts contained within the natural anatomy of any normal human being are all that is required. Only those with the rarest of deformities or genetic conditions are exempt. In other words, any transient on the street can be harvested for the miracle."

Anika closed her eyes and turned away in disgust at her father's morbid detachment, then breathed deeply and resumed her confident stare.

"If I had decided earlier in my life to participate in this evil, I, of course, would have used the degenerates of society—the criminals, the molesters—all of the monsters that feed on the weak and drag humankind toward the sewer. Of course I would have done that!' Marcel stifled a cough and then softly said, "It is what your mother did for all those years."

Anika wanted to interrupt, pursue this off-handed charge by her father that his wife—her mother—was in fact some kind of serial killer, albeit one utilitarian to society. Instead she stayed silent, not wanting to veer the story away from the substance.

"But I resisted, Anika. Steadfastly! I kept a vigil for my soul. I knew that even immortality wouldn't last forever. And when that final day came, even if millennia in the future, I would face the judgment awaiting all of us and would have to answer for my actions. It is this belief that kept me unaddicted. And when your mother finally died, my sobriety was only reinforced."

Marcel sighed, and his mouthed turned down in sadness.

"But the truth is this, Anika: when death is upon you, when the horizon is no longer an abstraction, when morbidity is no longer a passive thought but rather a place you can feel in your belly and taste in your mouth, your decisions waver. The concept of death and the reality of it are two very different things. And death is upon me now, and I plan to fight it. I..."

"You haven't explained where I come in," Anika interrupted finally. Her words were curt and emotionless, intended to be in harsh contrast to her father's dramatic explanation and tacit plea for sympathy.

"The concoction is not a potion of youth; it does not undo disfigurement or trauma or disease. A man with one leg could not drink the mixture and suddenly grow a new one. Nor will a cripple walk or a dwarf grow. The potion simply feeds those healthy cells that exist, and, more importantly, arrests their natural march toward degeneration."

Anika could tell it was the first time her father had ever explained the details of the potion, as he knew them to be, and now that he'd begun the words spilled from him with ease.

"Oh, there have always been stories of course, according to your mother there were certain additives that would strengthen bones and taper teeth, perhaps even make them grow larger. And of course there are always the vanity claims of clearing complexions and strengthening hair. But even if those rumors are true, Anika, by the measure of rumors, they're rather benign. It is a well-accepted, centuries-old truth that the restorative powers of the potion are limited. It is not a cure for death. It is a prevention."

He paused then, signaling the import and relevance of the words that were to follow.

"Unless the subject is close kin. In that case, there may be the exception. There the possibilities may become more variable."

Anika nodded slowly in disappointed understanding. Then she smiled softly and shook her head. "So this is why I've gone through all of this? This is why my family was destroyed? My children made to suffer? My husband left to raise them alone?"

"Anika, Heinrich is..."

"Shut your mouth! Don't you dare speak aloud the name of anyone in my family!"

Anika gave her father the chance to challenge her command, and when he didn't, she continued.

"Not even the promise of youth? You'll have me tortured—and my children if necessary—to live a few more decades—a century maybe—as a deranged old man?"

"Not Gretel and Hansel! I did not..." Marcel broke into a desperate bout of coughing. He stood awkwardly, attempting to get leverage on it.

"And what is it about life that you so cherish, father? Tell me. Is it the loneliness of it? Or perhaps it's your lack of contribution to the world? And lifelong lack of ambition. Yes, that must all be it. Who would want to forfeit such a meaningful life as that?"

"I was good to you, Anika." Marcel extended his arm and formed his crooked hand into an accusatory point. His other hand he kept pressed to his mouth in anticipation of another coughing bout.

"Yes, father, you were. But what now? Your children are raised. Your wife is gone. And even if you can be cured by my death, you're old and frail. What will you do with your immortality other than hoard and treasure it for its own sake?" The edge had left Anika's voice now, as if she were offering her father one last chance to recognize how horribly wrong all of this was.

"My new life will be different." Marcel's eyes shifted in doubt. "I will make it into something valuable."

"Your life *was* valuable father. To me. To Mother. And to Gretel and Hansel. But it's become rotted. Nothing good will come in the future. Death is necessary, father, for everyone."

Marcel sat back on the sofa and stared into his daughter's eyes. "No, Anika," he said, "today only your death is necessary."

CHAPTER NINETEEN

"But my mother is...was older than you."

"No Gretel, she's not," Odalinde replied. "Not by quite a bit."

The woman hesitated a moment and then strode the few steps to her secret cabinet behind her, simultaneously fishing something from her pouch. Without seeing it, Gretel knew at once it was the key she and Hansel had 'borrowed' only days ago. She plugged the key into the lock casually, with no concern of the potent little spies that ostensibly surrounded her. It was so unlike the times Gretel had seen her in the past, hunched and secretive, a compact wall of back and shoulders.

Both children sat mesmerized as they watched Odalinde reach into the cabinet, fumbling only briefly before pulling out the large black book that Gretel now recognized, without an ounce of doubt, as *Orphism*.

"I told you!" Hansel whispered.

Odalinde frowned and gave Hansel a narrow sideways stare, which the boy received and dropped instantly. "I suspected it was you, young man," she said.

"I'm sorry. I didn't..." Hansel's tone was more pleading than whimpering, but he was teetering on tears.

"It's okay, Hansel. It really is." Seeming to sense Hansel's descent toward a breakdown, Odalinde walked slowly to the boy and kneeled by him, resting her upper arm across the back of his chair, keeping her forearm raised to gently pet the back of his head with her hand. "It was never either of you I was worried about."

It was the first act of real warmth Gretel had seen from Odalinde since her arrival, and the gesture comforted Gretel in a way she hadn't felt since she'd lost her mother. But the scent of the ongoing mystery was strong, and she had no intention of losing it.

"How is it that you can be old enough to remember my mother being born?" Gretel asked. "That's not possible."

Odalinde looked squarely at Gretel and then stood straight, gripping the book with both hands so that the front cover faced forward. She framed it against her chest and said, "As I said, the story is long, but the short answer to your question is this book. This book is how it's possible."

"*Orphism*?"

Odalinde's eyes sparkled at the sound of the word, and a sad smile drifted across her lips and then receded. "Yes, Gretel, *Orphism*."

Gretel shook her head slowly in disbelief, blinking several times. She realized now that she hadn't truly believed Hansel's story about his discovery in Odalinde's cabinet. Particularly after searching it herself and finding it empty. If pressed for the truth, she would have said she even considered that Hansel had made the whole thing up to get her attention, and that she was willing to entertain him, thankful for the fact that he was talking to her at all, thankful that he had weathered the loss of his mother with such courage. It was true she had hoped the book would be there, but wasn't so surprised when it wasn't. It couldn't have been her same book.

"Is that...is it the same as the one I have?"

Odalinde nodded. "It is."

"I told you," Hansel said again, this time to no one in particular.

"How many copies are there?"

Odalinde smiled again, this time fully and warm. "It's an excellent question, Gretel. An excellent question. There are a handful maybe. I know of at least two others. But the truth is I don't really know for sure."

Odalinde straightened her smile now. "Your book, it was given to you by your grandfather? Is that right?"

Gretel nodded.

"When was that?"

"The night my mother disappeared. When we drove to his house trying to find out what happened to her."

"Before that day, the day he gave it to you, did your grandfather ever talk about the book? Or mention anything about it that you might remember?"

Gretel didn't need to think about the answer. "No. Nothing. I don't think he knew that I'd ever even seen it until that day. I used to look at it all the time though. Up on the shelf in the basement. And when I got older and could reach it I used to read it—well, look at the words anyway. But I never let him know that I'd found it. It always seemed like a thing to keep secret."

At this last remark Odalinde nodded again. "Yes, it does seem like that type of thing."

"But when he saw me with it," Gretel continued, "that night in the basement, he just gave it to me. Like he wanted me to have it and was waiting for me to ask. So maybe he did know that I'd found it. I guess I can't be sure."

"Did he tell you anything about it after he gave it to you?"

"Why? What does it say?" Hansel chimed in. "What's the book about?"

"In a moment, Hansel, okay? I'll tell both of you. I promise." Odalinde's voice was calm and reassuring, and she stroked the boy's head as she stepped toward Gretel and kneeled in front of her, waiting for the answer to her question. "What did he tell you, Gretel?"

"He just said that it was very old. That not many people could read it. And that my grandmother liked it. 'Treasured it,' I think he said."

Odalinde nodded politely and then asked slowly, "Could *he* read it, Gretel? Did he say whether *he* could read it?"

Gretel immediately shook her head. "No. He couldn't read it. At least that's what he told me."

Odalinde let out a sigh and stood up again.

"But..." Gretel stopped.

Odalinde froze, her eyes encouraging.

"I think he was hoping that *I* would be able to read it. Or that I could learn to read it. I don't know exactly. He wanted me to have it, that's for sure, but he was strange about it. Sad or something."

Gretel thought back to the scene in Deda's house and then shook her head quickly.

"But he's sick—dying I think. He was probably just having a spell. That's what my mother always called it when Deda acted strange."

Odalinde nodded and let this last piece of information sink in.

"This book is bad, isn't it?"

Odalinde's eyes searched the room for an answer to the question, a signal to Gretel that the woman had never thought about the book in these terms. "Yes Gretel," she said finally, "it is bad."

"And it's bad because..." Gretel's eyes darted furiously as she was suddenly flooded with the rain of discovery. "...it's some kind of black magic book, right? A book that tells how to live forever. That's how you knew my grandmother. And how you were there when my mother was born. That's right isn't it?"

Odalinde gave a tired grin. "You have amazing intuition, Gretel, as I knew you would."

Gretel said nothing, her look never wavering as she dismissed the compliment and waited for actual confirmation. She couldn't have said exactly how she figured everything out so quickly, but she suspected Odalinde was right, she did have exceptional instincts.

"Perhaps not forever," Odalinde admitted softly, "but yes, in essence, that is what the book does."

"How old are you then?" Gretel asked, and saw instantly in Odalinde's face that this question was one that tortured her, one that she fought every day to keep her mind from exploring.

"I don't know exactly, but very old. Much older than I should ever have allowed myself to become."

Hansel smiled, almost laughing at this exchange. He looked to Gretel for the whimsical reveal of a teasing punchline, a wink or a punch to the shoulder perhaps; but he saw only cold seriousness in his sister's eyes.

Reflexively, he reached for his face, forming a dome over his nose and mouth as if ready to sneeze. Gretel at first took the gesture for one of shock, the stifling of a gasp, but her brother then lurched forward from his chair, his hands fixed in place as he dashed toward the front door, fumbling with the knob until finally turning it just in time to direct his cascade of vomit away from the kitchen floor and onto the porch. He stumbled a few more steps until he was fully out of the cabin and in the sanctuary of cool Back Country air. He descended the stairs until he reached the gravel driveway where he could freely release whatever sickness remained. Gretel listened to her brother retch once again and then heard his breathing steady as he let out some hybrid of a wretch and a scream.

Odalinde retraced Hansel's path across the kitchen floor, following it to the threshold of the open front door. She paused, submitted a brief check of the situation in the driveway, and then closed the door until it was open just a crack.

"He'll be fine," she said, "everyone is frightened the first time they hear about the book. It's not an easy thing to digest." Odalinde rolled her eyes and smiled weakly at her unintended pun.

"Is it really true though?" Gretel asked, now fully realizing the significance of what was being revealed here. She wasn't worried about Hansel; it wasn't the first time nerves had caused the reaction she'd just witnessed. "Is it true anyone that can read this book could live forever?"

"Well, it's not quite that simple."

Odalinde walked back to the table and sat across from Gretel.

"Even if you know the language, or it's been translated for you, there are delicate skills you'd need to master—medical skills among them—and there are several quite obscure ingredients you'd need to be able to recognize and find." Odalinde paused and then nodded. "But, yes, eventually you could figure it out. More practically though, you could find someone who already had all of these skills."

Gretel was curious about the "medical skills," but she put it aside for the moment.

"So then I don't understand," she said, "why is the book a bad thing? I mean, I know people have to die to make room for new people, but...I don't know...life is good, right?" Gretel lingered on the last word, not sure exactly what she was trying to say.

"This is not about life, Gretel, this is about death: what happens to your physical body after it's been born into this world and then deteriorates from time or is ravaged by trauma or disease. We are meant to die. All of us. Avoiding death is unnatural. It's the opposite of nature, in fact."

Odalinde spoke quickly, never taking her eyes from Gretel. She stopped and searched the girl's face, looking for a sign of understanding that the truth she'd just heard should never be doubted. Odalinde took a slow breath and then continued, this time with less frenzy.

"Life, however, is something else. Life is always with you. Even after your body dies. Life is energy, and energy can't be destroyed. Life is your spirit or soul or a dozen other names that have been given to that thing—that force inside of you—which lets you know you're alive. It's the force that comforts you and motivates you, makes you love and sympathize. You, Gretel, have a strong awareness of Life. Stronger than most. That is part of your heritage and it will never go away."

"My heritage? What does that mean? I don't understand."

"The energy of the universe is available to all of us, Gretel. It flows through everyone and makes us who we are. And, if we wish, often with much trial and persistence, we can manipulate this energy to make things happen for us. To direct things toward us. For some, like you—and me, I suppose—that ability comes much easier."

"So is it some kind of magic?"

"I suppose that's a way to look at it, except that magic implies something otherworldly and exclusive. This isn't witchcraft. The energy of Life is the most common force in the universe. So common, in fact, that most of us ignore it. The way we ignore sunlight or oxygen."

"So this book, *Orphism*, explains this power? How to use it?"

"In a way that's what it does, yes. But the truth is the power of Life can't fully be explained in a book. It must be felt, experienced, individually harnessed for whatever purpose a person wishes to use it. Most people, even if they could read the language in the book, wouldn't have the discipline or insight to understand—on the deepest level—exactly what the book explicates. But the people who wrote the book, Gretel, they understood these things quite well. They were a group very strongly aware of the world and the offerings available to them."

"But you said the book was bad. So people can use this power to do bad things?"

Odalinde gave a tired sigh and rubbed the heels of her palms against her temples. "I don't believe the intention of the book was bad. Not originally. It was just the result of natural curiosity and exploration. And to answer your question: Oh yes, Gretel, people can use Life to provoke a great number of bad things. Unbounded really. You see, Life doesn't distinguish between good and bad—those are human adjectives that we assign to things based on an accepted set of social values. If a man were to inherit a family, for example, and then kill the children so that he may bear and raise only his own, we would consider that man bad, and our system of justice would likely deem it so bad he would be killed as a result. But when a lion does the very same thing—kills the offspring of other lions so that only his genes move on—we distance ourselves from judgment, accepting that the world of the lion operates by different rules. Well, in a way, Life sees the world the way we see the lion: objectively, without prejudice. If a person is knowledgeable of this Life power, he can use it however he sees fit. Even in a way that we would describe as bad."

Odalinde stood and walked back to the door, opening it just wide enough to check on Hansel again, before walking back and sitting at the table.

"I know this is a lot to hear right now, Gretel, and much of it you probably don't believe. That's okay. Where this power comes from and how it's used is not important right now. All of that is something you'll need to explore and come to believe on your own."

Odalinde stretched her arms across the table, her palms facing up, beckoning for Gretel's hands. Gretel offered them freely, and the touch of the woman's hands again awakened some hibernating memory of her mother.

"But the power of this book is real. And I have the feeling it has to do with your mother's disappearance."

Gretel's breathing shortened, and she could feel the muscles in her shoulders tighten. She squeezed Odalinde's hands tightly. "You think she's alive, don't you?"

"Honestly, Gretel, I don't know, she may *not* be. But I think if *you* believe she's alive—truly believe it—that's a very good sign. Do you believe she is?"

Gretel could only nod.

"Okay then," Odalinde said, "Okay."

"But how? Where would she be?"

"The whole process of creating the formula is complicated; it takes time. The source needs to be healthy and strong to start, and then it needs to be fed correctly. And the extractions can often take months depending..." Odalinde's eyes had grown wide, and the first two fingers of her right hand instinctively went to her lips as if giving an emphasized signal to a child to stay quiet.

Hansel now stood in the doorway, frozen, listening to this impossible conversation. His mouth hung wide and Gretel thought he looked a bit like a nutcracker.

"What are you talking about?" Gretel asked, nearly whispering. "Extractions? Fed?"

"I'm so sorry..." Odalinde began.

"What are you talking about!" Gretel violently recoiled her hand from Odalinde's.

Odalinde closed her eyes and exhaled. "The book—*Orphism*—is about a lot of things, much of it to do with what we discussed earlier, controlling the powers of Life and all that."

"But it's also about living forever," Gretel added, her impatience brimming.

Odalinde opened her eyes. "Yes. It's about that too. The first part—the part about Life and spirit and the ways of the universe—is not only powerful, it's also quite beautiful. The people who wrote it were unusually synchronized with the world. These were an ancient people, untraceable to any known descendants. Perhaps as old as those of Asia and Mesopotamia."

She paused, signaling a transition.

"But there is the other part of the book. The part on solving death." Odalinde gave a deep, nervous swallow. "This part was written by your people, Gretel. And yours, Hansel."

Odalinde waved for Hansel to come back and sit, which he did, reluctantly.

"This part is not beautiful. In fact, it's quite horrifying."

"Hansel, maybe you should go," Gretel snapped, her tone signaling she would have no tolerance for any more weak-stomach distractions.

"I'm fine," he replied, unconvincingly.

Gretel glared at her brother with a "you'll be sorry if you're wrong" look, and then immediately shot her attention back to Odalinde.

"It's a recipe, essentially, for a potion that stops the dying process. The brew is ingested, in small amounts at first, and then gradually, over decades, the doses need to increase for the formula to continue working. I don't think anyone knows exactly how it works, and it isn't like it's ever been studied properly in a laboratory."

Odalinde stopped for a moment to arrange her words, and Gretel tried to appreciate her aim to be delicate.

"Many of the ingredients—not all, but many—are derived from the human body."

Hansel brought a fist to his mouth but quickly composed himself. "That's disgusting," he said.

"Yes, it is, Hansel. It's despicable. But what is even more despicable, and what you would correctly assume, is that people don't usually give of their body parts willingly." Odalinde dropped her eyes ruefully. "There are victims."

"So they're killed?" Hansel asked, each word coming out with a beat in between.

"The final part is always fatal. Some die sooner than others. Those are..." Odalinde stopped and shook her head as if to strike the beginning of the sentence.

"Those are what? What is it?" It was Gretel this time.

"Those are the fortunate ones." Odalinde frowned and bounced a sad stare between the two children. "The true horror is the torture. The mutilation. It's abominable."

Gretel narrowed her eyes and sneered. "But you've done this," she challenged, unable to pitch down the shrillness in her voice. "You *are* one of the people who has tortured. You *are* someone who has eaten people. You must be, right?! You've lived for what? Centuries!"

"I have killed and tortured people, Gretel. Yes, I have done those things. More times than I could ever count or wish to remember. And the shame that I feel now—not just for those deaths, but also for the lack of feeling that I had for them at the time—I will feel that shame until I am buried."

Odalinde stood again and walked away from the table, her back to the children.

"And that time will come. I haven't blended for several years now. And I won't do it again."

"So you've decided to die then," Gretel stated flatly, with satisfaction. "Why?"

Odalinde turned back toward Gretel.

"For all the reasons I've explained. This discovery is a mistake. It's monstrous. I understand that. I've always understood it but...I couldn't stop. I just couldn't. If Hell exists I will burn there for what I've done. But it has been done. And I can't undo it. All I can do is try to help you and Hansel. And your mother."

The fury in Gretel was rising, and she clenched her teeth, struggling not to leap at the murderer standing in her kitchen.

"So if you made this decision, why did you wait so long? Why did you not help us right away! My mother could have been saved!"

"I didn't know your mother's disappearance had to do with any of this. At least...I wasn't sure. I truly wasn't. My reason for coming here wasn't to protect you from your father, it was just to take care of you because of a promise I made to your grandmother. A promise that I would take care of your mother—or her unborn children—if they were ever in need."

"But you're not making sense. You said you were here to protect us from our father," Gretel said, quick with her challenge.

"Protecting you from your father was not the reason I came here, it was the reason I stayed."

Gretel closed her eyes and spread her hands across her face, and then quivered her head back and forth in a short, vibratory twitch, trying to shake the mountain of puzzle pieces in her head into something flat and orderly. "None of this makes sense," she said, "what does my father have to do with this?"

"I didn't think anything at first. But then..." Odalinde paused and looked away.

"What?"

"On your bed, soon after I got here, I saw the book, the copy of *Orphism* your grandfather gave you. I didn't know if your father could read it—I still don't actually—but if he could, he was a danger to both of you. A sick man, in the last quarter of his life, that is the most dangerous man of all to know this secret. So I've kept him as he is, just sick enough to...make him weak."

"Why didn't you tell me about any of this? You knew I had this magic book the whole time and you never told me? Didn't you think everything was connected? My mother's disappearance? All of it?"

"No, I didn't. Not necessarily. Your grandmother had a copy of the book, I knew that, so it wasn't impossible to think your grandfather had simply handed down her copy to you or your mother as a keepsake."

Gretel was quiet, considering the possibility there may be logic in this reasoning.

"And I don't know if any of this *is* connected, Gretel, it may not be."

"It is," Gretel replied without hesitation, "I know it is."

Odalinde frowned and nodded, offering no challenge to the teenager's intuition.

"I handled all of this badly. I'm sorry to both of you. I didn't know what I was doing. I haven't raised a child or nursed a man in...I don't know how long. A very long time."

"You're not good at it." The words had left Gretel's mouth before she had a chance to consider them.

Odalinde smiled. "I know I was hard on you, Gretel, and neglectful to both of you, but I didn't want either of you to grow fond of me. When I left, I wanted you to be glad for my riddance. Plus it was how I was raised, and how I was taught to raise children, building them for survival. If your father were to..." She stopped suddenly, rethinking her words. "If he were not able to care for you, if he didn't get better, you would have to grow up quickly, on your own."

A lump grew in Hansel's throat, and the first tear bubbled in the bottom of his eye. "So you're not staying?" he asked. "You weren't going to stay?"

"No Hansel, I can't stay."

"So you never planned to marry him?" Gretel asked, the sadness in her voice conveying sympathy for her father and not sorrow at the news that she was losing a stepmother.

"No, Gretel. I have another life, other commitments. People I care for. That is where I would go in the evenings on..."

"Thursdays," Gretel finished for her.

Odalinde smiled again. "Yes, on Thursdays. But when your father asked me to marry him it was a very awkward situation. If I had said 'no' I would have had to leave immediately. It would have been too uncomfortable. And even though I never really knew if your father had to do with this, I believed something was wrong. And I was right, something *is* wrong."

Gretel sat quietly for a moment, and then she rose slowly, locking eyes with Odalinde, her chest burning at the question she was about to ask. "And how do you know Officer Stenson? How do you *really* know him?"

The confusion on Odalinde's face was instant, and Gretel trusted it.

"Who is..? You mean that System officer that came to check on you? I *don't* know him, Gretel. As I said the other day, he came by to check on you and you weren't here."

Gretel stared coldly into the woman's face, searching for the tell, the flicker or swallow or shift of the eyes. "Hansel saw his name in your book," she said finally. "And I saw it too."

Odalinde glanced toward Hansel and frowned and then looked back to Gretel.

"I told you, he gave me his name and number and told me to give it to you. I wrote it in my book where I keep all of my other numbers. I didn't give it to you because I didn't trust him. There was something insincere about him. I still believe that to be true."

"You told me father wouldn't allow it. You said that was why you didn't tell me."

"That was a lie. Your father never knew he was here."

"So you never told Officer Stenson about your engagement to Father?"

"Of course not! Why would you think that?"

Gretel dismissed the question with a quick head shake.

"He was here only a few minutes, we barely spoke at all, let alone that I would disclose anything like that. Particularly that topic. I just wanted him gone."

Odalinde's answers were coming to Gretel quickly, logically, in a way that only the truth could. She sat back down and took a deep breath, and the buzz of nature filled the otherwise silent kitchen.

"So do you think he knows where my mother is?" she said finally, wearily. "If she is alive, do you think he knows where she is?"

Odalinde opened her mouth as if to answer, but instead took a deep breath and then pressed her lips into a thin, sad smile. "Honestly? Yes, I think he knows something about what's happened. But if Officer Stenson is part of this, he's only one part."

"So who else then," Hansel asked before Odalinde could get to it.

"You're not going to like my answer. Neither of you."

Hansel's eyes widened and his mouth dropped in a short gasp. "Father?" he said.

"No Hansel," Gretel said, her voice deep and controlled, "she means Deda."

CHAPTER TWENTY

Oliver Stenson's red System cruiser turned sharply down the hidden path leading to the old woman's cabin and then abruptly stopped, its tires skidding across the dirt driveway, leaving a haze of dust that hovered effervescently for a moment, and then deflated to the ground. It had been months since he'd come here, as a skeptical neophyte on the subjects of witchcraft and magic potions, terms for which he was always chided by Marcel for using. This wasn't wizardry or spell-casting he was told, this elixir was natural, accessible to everyone.

In the beginning, of course, at the very center of his beliefs, he doubted nearly all of what he'd been told about the bizarre brew; and the fulfillment of the promises that were made to him for his part in the scheme he accepted with equal doubt. But if it *was* true, even in part, even if it was something akin to a vitamin that allowed him twenty years beyond his natural life—or fifteen—his investment in the plan seemed worth it, especially if those years proved strong and healthy. After all, his role would be minimal: to monitor the case of a missing Back Country woman who would vanish along the Interways one spring morning; and then to make sure any leads in the case were steered in a direction away from certain sections of the Interways and this cabin. It sounded simple. It was simple. With his System experience and knowledge of the area, his part required little more than rigging a few clues here and there, and maybe leaving off a few more off the reports. Simple.

And in fact, as it turned out, it had been rather simple. Stenson wasn't even needed for the actual crime. Marcel had told him exactly how it all would happen: that Anika Morgan's car would drift off the road, and she, in a foolish search for help, would stumble directly into the clutches of the old woman. And it had happened just that way!

The poor woman, Anika, had somehow—impossibly—disappeared from the Interways and ended up in this time-forgotten, wooden shack in the bleakest part of the Northlands. Untraced. Unwitnessed. And he, Stenson, hadn't needed to do a thing! Even the car was virtually invisible, almost perfectly camouflaged at the bottom of that embankment. Only the most basic of additional cover had been necessary to keep it from being seen by anyone walking along at more than eight or ten feet away. And when the day came that it was finally discovered—if that day ever came—the obvious assumption would be that Anika Morgan had simply wandered into the woods after an accident looking for help and then died, her body overcome by the elements before being ravaged by some hungry animal (and in a way, Stenson thought, that is what happened), her clothes rotted and buried forever beneath countless layers of mud and leaf litter. Yes, finding that car now would do no good; it was far too late to find the connection between Anika Morgan and this cabin.

But there was a problem now: Anika Morgan was still alive. Recaptured, thank God, but still alive.

Marcel had known immediately that she'd escaped—*had felt it*—and within hours Stenson was rumbling his cruiser up to a defeated Anika Morgan lying prostrate in the middle of the road. It *was* magic. It was the only explanation. If anyone else had found her, the whole plan would have collapsed. She would have been taken to a hospital or barracks, or perhaps even home, and the whole story of her nightmare would have been unfurled. And by this time, instead of standing quietly outside the door of his cruiser, debating whether to walk to the front of the cabin door ahead of him and knock, or to investigate around back to keep the element of surprise intact, he and the rest of the Northlands unit would be ransacking the old shack for clues, of which there would be plenty. Perhaps even enough to connect him to the case.

But it hadn't happened that way. *He* had found Anika Morgan, just one more of an increasing number of fortuitous events that fell in his favor, and another example of why Oliver Stenson had steadily grown to become a believer in the potion. Devout. He'd yet to see any actual proof of the elixir's life-giving effects, but still, all of what Marcel had told him would happen had, from the accident, to the capture, to the hiring of the woman's daughter at the orchard. He hadn't predicted the escape, of course, but even magic contained some degree of variability, Stenson supposed. Yes, Stenson was a true believer now, and over the past few months he had become vigilant in his role of protecting the secret.

But he was also ready for the payoff. He was ready for that feeling that had been described to him by Marcel as described to him by his wife. And he was ready to bring Petr home from that school and, more importantly, to get him out of that orchard for good. 'We need to watch her,' Marcel had told him, referring to his own granddaughter. 'Gretel knows more than she knows.' Stenson had no idea what Marcel was talking about at the time, and after his visit with the girl he understood even less. Gretel seemed like a typical teenage girl to him—mature certainly, but typical—naturally distrustful of authority, and devastated that her mother had gone missing. But ultimately Stenson had deferred and agreed to position Petr at the Klahr orchard to act as their unknowing spy.

But it was time for all of this to be over. It was time to become untangled from all of this villainy.

Stenson exited his cruiser and stood tall, surveying the surroundings, squinting for any sign of the old woman. "Hello," he called out. He wanted to follow with the woman's name but realized he didn't know it. He wondered if even she knew it at this point. "Hello," he called again and closed the cruiser door, deciding to take the direct route to the front of the cabin.

Stenson imagined a flurry of scenarios as he approached the front door—an exercise that, as a System officer, was automatic to him. He didn't conjure any images that were particularly dangerous, especially since the escaped prisoner had already been caught, but the quietness made him wary. The most likely scene, he thought, was that the woman was dead, or else severely wounded. The prisoner had escaped after all, and Stenson could only believe that she'd done so using force. Perhaps the story was even known by now, revealed to Marcel by his daughter in some gleeful rage. He suddenly wished there was a way to contact the warehouse.

But what did it really matter? Stenson's only real concern—besides keeping his own freedom—was the potion. The beautiful potion. He realized now that he was addicted to it without ever tasting a drop! Ha! That was madness, of course, but it was true. It was the first and last thing he thought about each day. Every day. He'd risked his career, farmed out his son, and been an accomplice to kidnapping, torture and attempted murder. What more evidence was needed to show he was a slave to it? And the more he thought of it, the worse the addiction grew.

And now, with months of images of the brew stirring slowly in the middle of his mind, he almost couldn't stand it. His respect for Marcel on this matter was immense; how had he had resisted it all those years? But this respect was somewhat offset by Stenson's hatred about the fact that the old man never learned the recipe himself, that he had never taken the path of his wife. Of course, Stenson never considered that if Marcel had known the recipe, Stenson's role in the whole plan would have been unnecessary and he would have been left out. But that was addiction.

He forced his mind back to the top concern on the docket: The potion, and the fact that it wasn't completed. The Source was still alive, which according to Marcel meant, at the very least, the final ingredients had not been included. Stenson was pretty sure he'd been told that piece involved the heart, but it could also have been the liver. Whichever. It was close to finished. Very close. It had to be!

He knuckled five aggressive raps on the cabin door, the thick, solid design of the structure muffling the sound into something dull and impotent, like knocking on a tree trunk. He waited a moment and then walked a few steps to the porch-level window, bending over at the waist and cupping his hands around his eyes as he put his forehead to the glass to peer in. But he could see only vague outlines and darkness, the result of decades of built-up grime and dust.

The System officer walked back to the door and this time turned the knob slowly. It twisted easily, ironically almost, considering the daunting mass of the door itself. He pushed the door open about three feet and was immediately assaulted by the unmistakable stench of flesh. Old and rotten. Dead. He turned back to the air of the porch and breathed deeply, instinctively lifting his uniform shirt to cover his nose and mouth while blinking out the film of water that had formed protectively over his eyes.

"Oh my God," he whispered.

His mind instinctively formed a few additional, more precarious, scenarios for what might be in the cabin, and after processing them almost simultaneously, the officer pushed the door firmly with both hands so that it opened as wide as possible, offering the awful odor an undisturbed route of escape. The width of the doorway allowed Stenson to see most of the inside of the cottage from the porch, the only exceptions being the two bedrooms off to the side. And with this expansive vantage point, his conditioned brain went through the progressions. A disturbance had occurred. Violent. In the kitchen area. The escape had been through the back door (it was open). And there was something else. Something much worse.

Stenson's breathing became rapid and his throat tightened at the sight. Something had been shattered, something ceramic—a bowl or plate—and the dark mixture that it had contained was now splattered grotesquely across the floor.

"Oh God, no!" The words came out in something resembling a whine, and Stenson raced into the cabin, now completely unaware of the foulness in the air. He reached the scene on the floor and knew instantly—not with magic or witchcraft (screw you, Marcel!), but with the knowing instincts of a seasoned detective—that his chance at immortality was finished.

Oliver Stenson stood with his legs slightly apart and his head hung, his eyes closed as if saying a prayer in front of a gravesite. He opened his eyes and stared absently at the dried black puddle, making sure to keep his boots clear, just in case...just in case it was still...viable.

With his index finger extended, he began to kneel toward the floor. He needed to touch the black sludge, to feel for himself whether there was truly power there. The tip of his finger was only inches away when a sound from the back of the cabin broke the stillness. It was rustling and quick, and Stenson's hand instinctively repositioned itself away from the puddle to his sidearm. He knew it was unlikely to be anything too concerning, probably just an animal, lured by the sickening promise of decaying flesh. But he was cautious anyway, as he'd been trained to be in even the most seemingly benign situations, and he unholstered his weapon as he walked toward the open kitchen door.

More noises came from the back, this time heavier and more methodical, though still quick. Stenson reconsidered his original assessment and now thought the sounds were footsteps. Human footsteps. He stood in the doorway and faced the outside, his toes just across the threshold. He gripped the gun tightly and laid it close to his chest.

"Who's there?" Stenson called, deepening his voice an octave. He waited a few beats for an answer, sensing attentive ears just outside the door. "My name is Officer Oliver Stenson. I'm a System officer. If there is anyone there show yourself or respond to me now."

"What can I do for you, Officer?"

The words imploded the silence almost before Stenson had finished barking his commands. The voice was clear and robust, young and feminine, and for a moment Stenson felt like a child, seven or eight maybe, whose mother has just caught him sneaking sweets before dinner. It was almost comforting. But not quite. There was something else in the voice, in the tenor perhaps, something vibratory in the pitch that was ancient and unfriendly. And the words had come not from the backyard but from inside the cabin, near the front door in fact, on the opposite side of the house from where he'd heard the footsteps.

Stenson spun toward the voice and raised his weapon. His eyes were wide and locked, not with fear exactly, but something close to it, uneasiness perhaps. Enhanced uneasiness.

"And what is your answer to my question, officer." The words were slightly playful and challenging. "Again, in case you weren't ready for it the first time, the question was 'What can I do for you?'"

Officer Stenson lowered his sidearm and stared at the figure which stood rigid and motionless; the dusky gray robe it wore gave it the appearance of a shadow, faded and strayed from its source. The eyes and cheekbones were blanketed by a large hood which draped forward several inches past the figure's face; the only features Stenson could see with any clarity were the nose and lips. It was the old woman, he was sure of that, the general outline matched, and she had worn the same robe on the other occasion they had met. And besides, who else would it be?

But she was different now, transformed in some way. And it wasn't just her voice, which had lost all trace of the off-key, aged hoarseness he remembered from the few words she'd spoken that day. She was...taller, sturdier. Imposing even. Or maybe it was just that her posture was better—perfect in fact—that she appeared taller. And from what he could see of her face she was younger, judging by the smoothness of the skin on her nose and color of her lips, by at least a decade. Maybe more.

"Were you outside?" he stammered finally. "Did you hear me call you? How did you get in here so fast?"

"I *was* outside and I *did* hear you call," the woman challenged in a tone conveying the question 'and what are you going to do about it?'

The woman stood waiting for a reply to her implied question, but Stenson stayed silent.

"And I'm fast, Officer Stenson," she continued, "that's how I got in here so fast." At this remark her eyes flickered.

"Now, one more time: What can I do for you?" The old woman's words had lost their airy edge and were now sardonic and impatient.

"What can you do for me? *Do* for me?" Stenson's voice rose considerably on the second sentence, and he opened his eyes wide, presenting that slightly crazed look signifying that a punch in the nose for asking such a question wouldn't be unreasonable. "Perhaps you hadn't noticed..." Stenson again wanted to address the woman by name but remembered, once again, that he didn't know it. "The young woman who was sent to you, that was arranged for you to...blend...or whatever it is you call it, is no longer here! So maybe the first thing you can *do for me* is tell me *why* she isn't here anymore and, instead, is sitting alive in a System holding house. And she's there, by the way, only because *I* found her lying in the middle of the Interways! That's what you can do for me!"

The old woman stood motionless for a moment, staring at him, and though he couldn't see her eyes, Stenson knew it was a look of hate. She then formed her lips into a pleasant smile, while at the same time raising her hands and gripping the flopping edges of the oversized hood. Stenson noted again the smooth unblemished skin, this time on her hands and wrists, as she pulled the hood back slowly, revealing the truth about what the officer had thought may have been just a trick of the shadows and sunlight. She *was* younger. By twenty, even thirty years, he guessed. For a moment he thought he may have been wrong about his initial certainty that this was the same person; but no, it was definitely her, the woman he'd conspired with to murder a young mother in order to use her innards for his own youthful quests. But how? The woman in front of him now looked barely older than a young mother herself. If he was being honest, he would have described her as attractive. Beautiful maybe. Her skin was taut and unblemished, and the dullness of her eyes was replaced by the alert glitter of a schoolgirl's. And her hair. Her hair erupted from the hood of the cape in a mane of auburn silk, pouring down her shoulders and chest like diluted honey.

Stenson opened his mouth to speak but stopped, not knowing exactly what to say. Then, suddenly, he made the obvious connection. It was the potion. And it was better than what he'd been promised. Younger. It could make him younger!

The woman again stood still, as if showcasing herself for the man. But Stenson stared for only a moment. He knew the woman was studying him, and he'd seen her lips, barely splitting apart, revealing the stark whiteness of her newly polished enamel. The twitch of her mouth was slight, unnoticeable by the average citizen, but to Stenson it was a common tell, and it snatched him back to the moment. He took a breath and gripped his fingers tightly around his firearm, anticipating action. He was in that stage of an encounter—he'd been there dozens of times, he figured—when a perpetrator is weighing the options of whether to flee or attack, and by what means he'll carry out the decision. In almost every other case, Officer Stenson would have guessed correctly as to which move this perp was going to make. Given the two choices, a child would have guessed the same. First of all this was a *woman* in front of him, and an older woman at that (though not as old as she used to be). And, ostensibly, she was unarmed, as well as uniquely familiar with the environment having lived there for what, a hundred years? This suspect was no threat to him. This suspect was a runner ('and I'm fast, Officer Stenson, that's how I got here so fast'). It was System Work 101.

These calculations were processed in the mind of Officer Stenson automatically, only seconds before the witch glided across the room, as if carried from behind by a blast of sudden wind, and slammed against the torso of The System officer.

She's flying! he thought, *like a real witch*. It was the last conscious thought of Officer Stenson's life, just before the enormous fingernails of the woman entered his gut below the ribcage, piercing his stomach and severing his large intestine. With her other hand she gripped the back of his head and pulled it close, like a lover overcome by passion. But instead of a kiss, the woman exposed her fangs, newly filed and razor sharp, and tore out the left side of her victim's neck with the ease of an African lion. She clung tightly to the man, her mouth open in anticipation of a struggle, but the attack had left the officer instantly paralyzed.

She was stronger now, much stronger, and it would take some time to learn the appropriate effort needed to kill her prey in the future. But she had time now. So much time.

She spat the hunk of flesh toward the sink and discarded the body of Officer Oliver Stenson to the floor with the care of sock tossed to a hamper. His skull popped against the countertop on the way down before joining the rest of his body in a puddle of bodily fluids—a mixture that included both his and those of the woman he'd helped capture. His chest lurched in its last few attempts to get oxygen to his lungs, but his mouth hung agape, frozen, unable to suck any air past the shroud of blood and saliva that had built up on his tongue and in his cheeks. And with his windpipe shredded, the air would have never made it anyway.

"You're rather lucky," the old woman said absently, "in another life I would have kept you to die much slower."

***

With blood dripping from her chin, the woman walked outside through the back door and looked to the place where she'd been digging. Interruptions! She'd been expecting the officer of course, especially since the girl's escape, but she had work to do; there was no time for distractions. She needed to recapture her prisoner, somehow keep her alive and remake the potion. It would take time, certainly, and there was no guarantee the prey would survive the ordeal again. But if she didn't, all was not lost. There were others. Others who were nearby with perfection in their blood. Other Aulwurms.

The cabin, however, was no longer safe. If only she'd sampled the mixture earlier! She'd have her prisoner without this hassle! But she knew that wasn't completely true either. Even if she still controlled the girl, the old woman knew the extorting thieves would be coming. The mixture was overdue: she could recall the schedule perfectly now in her revived brain. And it was 'Marcel.' Yes, that was his name. That was the man who had sent the lovely Source to her, and she reveled in the purity of this truth. But it was she alone who could make the brew. It was she alone with the knowledge of the recipe. Not them!

And things took time. There was no patience in this modern world; everyone needed things now. And this System officer, Stenson, he seemed particularly hasty. She could see in the way he leaped for the spilled potion that he'd grown addicted to the idea of it. To the idea of immortality. It was a pattern she'd seen dozens of times in her past. No temperament to handle the wait. And as she'd also witnessed, the pursuit of the broth had caused his early expiration, an irony never lost on her.

But Stenson's death was unimportant. Nothing more than a mess to clean. Her aims were different now. She'd found the true serum. The one she'd heard whispered of in the Old Lands by her ancestors. The myth sought by all. She could stay young. Forever. She was strong again, of mind and body. And Life. She would reconnect with It. Control It as she once had when she was young and zealous.

She walked back to the kitchen and stood over the twisted body of Officer Stenson, which now lay still, dead. The witch's feet were planted irreverently in the remaining mixture on the floor, and she almost chuckled at the locked expression of fear and pain on the officer's face. She kicked the left side of his body and heard the sound she was listening for—the jingle of keys—in his right pocket. She reached over and pulled the ring of keys free, and then dangled them in front of her face, smiling at the confidence she felt inside of her. It was almost impossible to believe what she was considering—no, not considering, what she was *going* to do. The world now seemed a platter to her, a buffet of opportunity and treasure. Every second in this cabin now seemed a waste of the eternal time she now possessed. If even yesterday she'd been granted this opportunity, the opportunity to drive off in this machine, she would have certainly hidden from it, afraid of the technology she'd shunned for so long. She'd driven a car in the past, in the days before secrecy and privacy had taken over her life, but it had been years, and she'd certainly never controlled anything like the monster parked outside. Yes, her old self would have spent days, weeks maybe, figuring out some method to dispose of the car without ever starting the engine or even getting inside. But now the machine excited her and the thought of driving released a burst of saliva across her tongue. The energy under her. The power and speed at her control. And, most importantly, the utility of the thing. There were more sources to find before this day ended, and the car would help her find them.

It was time to hunt.

CHAPTER TWENTY-ONE

"So it was you who arranged for the Klahrs to hire me."

Gretel's statement came out sad and robotic, not quite a question. She kept her head still and her eyes forward, watching the pavement pass beneath the truck. They were on their way to Deda's, and the sickening memory of the trip she and Hansel made with their father on the day her mother disappeared regurgitated in her stomach.

Everything Odalinde had told her in the kitchen was too much to process: that her mother may be alive and that it was likely Deda who stole her away to begin with. That it was Deda who was the villain in this mystery. This possibility was devastating, and Gretel wasn't ready to explore her true beliefs about the tale just yet. Instead, she circled the issue, attempting to talk her way in from the edges until she reached a point in the middle where everything came together to make sense.

"No, Gretel, that was you," Odalinde said, "you alone." Odalinde took her eyes from the road and stared hard at Gretel, searching for a signal of belief that what she'd just said was true. She looked back to the road and frowned. "But I was also wrong. I was wrong to have forced you to that point—the point where you were scared and stealing food. I was just...I just wanted to instill in your heart that you were strong. Stronger than you believed. And that if you were pressed to survive—forced to save yourself and your brother—you would find a way."

She turned to look at Gretel again, this time giving a look that was softer, sympathetic.

"And you did, Gretel. You found a way. I knew you would. I could tell that resolve was in you the second I met you." Odalinde paused and then said, "It was like I'd met your grandmother all over again."

Gretel felt the swell in her throat and she turned quickly toward the window. It wasn't that she cared about crying in front of Odalinde necessarily, but crying at the mention of her grandmother seemed to negate the strength for which she'd just been commended. Besides, she didn't want to trust Odalinde completely, and crying at this point would make her vulnerable. And, of course, there was Hansel. She had to stay strong for him.

"I'm sorry, Gretel. For everything."

Gretel stayed quiet, with her forehead and nose pressed against the side window. She gave a hard blink to wring out the last threat of tears, and when she opened her eyes, she could see in her periphery that Hansel had fallen asleep in the back. She sat straight again, now feeling encouraged to continue questioning Odalinde more directly.

"Petr referred to you as my stepmother." Gretel paused, setting up the blow. "But I never told him about you and Father getting married. Why would he have said that? How would he have known?"

Odalinde furrowed her brow and smiled, nearly snickering. "I don't know, Gretel. I told you, I never said anything about marrying your father to anyone. And certainly not to Petr or his father."

"So how then?"

"Maybe he just made a mistake. Or..." Odalinde paused, "is it possible you *did* tell Petr and just forgot?"

Her tone was delicate, one intended to encourage Gretel to explore this explanation more deeply. But Gretel *had* explored it exhaustively and was positive she'd never mentioned the engagement. The whole affair had weighed on her far too heavily to have one day tossed it out casually and forgotten about it.

"No, it isn't possible."

"So you never told anyone then? Not even at school?"

"No," Gretel hesitated, "except...Well, I told the Klahrs. But no one else."

Odalinde's eyebrows flickered up and she cocked her head slightly, her eyes staying focused forward. It was a gesture that said, 'Perhaps there's your answer.'

"They wouldn't have told Petr," Gretel protested.

"No? And why is that?"

Gretel started in on her defense of the Klahrs, but decided too much time had been wasted already on the illfated marriage of Heinrich and Odalinde, and she instead changed the subject entirely. "That figurine-thing, the swan on the mantle, that was my grandmother's wasn't it?"

Odalinde smiled and nodded, again fascinated by Gretel's instincts. "She gave it to me when your mother was born. It's an old custom for a mother to give a gift to the godparents upon the birth of a child. I've treasured it for a long time. And when I came here it seemed proper to bring it along." She paused. "I'm going to leave it for you, Gretel. It's yours now."

Gretel was touched by the gift, and wanted to ask a thousand more questions about how Odalinde came to the responsibility she now owned. And about her grandmother. And how she died.

But the subjects felt out of place to explore at the moment, as if they were stories from a different book to be read later. So instead Gretel asked, "What will we do if my grandfather is there?"

The sympathy returned to Odalinde's face, and she reached out and stroked Gretel's hair. "I've thought about that. Obviously we can't simply walk into his house and accuse him of kidnapping your mother. I do believe he's involved in this, but I don't have proof. So, we'll say we're there to visit, that's all."

"What about Hansel? I don't know if he'll be able to stay quiet."

"I won't say anything," Hansel chimed from the back, "I promise."

And for the rest of the trip to Deda's, no one said a word.

**

Anika awoke in the chair and saw her father sitting on the couch in the same position he was when he told her of her impending death. It hadn't been a dream. Anika hadn't suspected as much, but the soulless man next to her now left no doubt.

She tried to gauge how long she'd been asleep, but without windows, she had no idea. Clearly her body was still recovering from its ordeal, and she was thankful for the rest.

"Who is the woman?" Anika asked coldly, "The woman whose face I smashed?"

Marcel was sober now, no longer convulsively trying to sell the merits of his diabolical decisions. It seemed to Anika that he'd recognized his daughter was right—he was deranged—and that continuing to advocate for what he was prepared to do only amplified that assessment.

"She's your kin, Anika," he answered, "distantly related, but your blood."

Anika nodded at this, the truth of her father's words obvious to her now that they'd been spoken.

"She, however, didn't know of the relation. At least your mother didn't believe so."

This too made sense to Anika—she'd never gotten the sense the woman viewed her as anything other than a common animal. If she *had* known, based on what her father believed about the potion, Anika suspected the woman's ferocity and precision would have been even greater.

"Your mother had known the woman was in this country the day she arrived, so many years ago. She was young then, the woman, and alone." Marcel looked to the floor. "And not yet inoculated with the potion."

"Was she looking for Mother? Why did she come here to begin with, to the Northlands?"

"The Northlands have always been a common refuge for Old Country folk, surely you know that. Just think of all the like surnames in these parts. The reasons for coming are always changing—when the woman came it was probably for opportunity and adventure, a drive far less coercive than the persecution from which your mother fled. But in any case, it has never been unusual for ancestors to settle in common areas."

Anika had never been close with her relatives, but it was true there were many around. "So Mother welcomed this woman when she arrived? They bonded?"

"No, Anika, that's not how it was. I don't think they ever met. Your mother had been here long before the woman arrived. Long before she was ever born."

"So how did she know this woman was coming at all? If people arrived regularly, and she had no real connection to her, why was her coming here of any note to Mother? I don't understand."

"It was the book, Anika. It was, of course, the book. Your mother knew she had the book."

"That doesn't help me to understand."

"The copies were tracked carefully back then. There were only a few dozen or so in existence, most of which were kept by members of your mother's family. When a copy traveled, so did word of its movement. Your mother learned of the book's voyage to the Northlands and she took it as her duty to make sure the secrets it contained stayed safe."

"But how did she know the book was coming? Who relayed that message?"

Marcel rubbed his brow with the tips of his fingers and closed his eyes. He inhaled slowly, careful not to trigger another fit of coughing. His exhaustion was palpable to Anika.

"I don't know every detail, Anika. Your mother told me this story long ago. I just know your mother was afraid—terrified—that the secret would become known, known here in a land that lacked the context and history to respect it. It's why she never taught it to me."

Anika was relentless with her questioning, leaving no room for her father to change the subject. "But the woman knew the secret. How would it stay safe if that woman knew?"

"You mother knew she had the book, but it was possible she didn't know of the black secrets it contained. She thought it quite unlikely actually. And that was the primary reason your mother stayed away from her. She was afraid if she befriended the woman, and made their common ancestry known, that eventually the secret would be revealed. So instead your mother kept her distance, watching for signs from afar, listening for news of unusual deaths...murders."

"May not have known the secret? Why would Mother have assumed she didn't know?"

"Many of the inheritors of the books, even in those days, revered the document only for what it symbolized, the beauty of life and the powers of nature. Things like that. But they never *truly* believed or attempted to practice all that was inside. Not most of them. They didn't believe in the practical nature of the book. Much the same way millions of people own Bibles but don't live their lives by the letter of The Word. Some do, but most don't. These books eventually became keepsakes, family heirlooms, an inheritance with a medieval backstory that few believed."

"But there is..." Anika paused suddenly and closed her eyes. She exhaled slowly and continued. "There's the recipe. I don't recall in the Bible a menu for cannibals." Anika could see her father draining further, and knew he had no energy for banter or argument.

"Once the books became two or three generations removed from their original scribes, there were few people in the world anymore who could read them. There were a handful of families who kept the language sacred and passed it on, but most didn't. The world was moving on, on to the one we live in today, a world of enlightenment and science—things like *Orphism* were suddenly viewed with fear and contempt—and ultimately mythology. It was why your mother left her home."

"So Mother didn't know if the woman could read the book? Is that what you're saying?"

"She doubted it but had no way of knowing for sure. But even if she could, your mother thought it unlikely the woman would ever attempt to practice it. Not the blending part."

"But Mother was wrong."

Marcel leaned back in his chair and frowned. "It so happens that, yes, she was wrong. In many ways I wish she hadn't been but...well, there it is."

Anika stared at her father and said nothing, and then stood suddenly with her cup of water and walked to the main door of the building, twisting the handle for good measure, but showing no surprise when it didn't turn.

"You didn't think it would be that easy did you?" Marcel's tone was mild, as if trying to soften the natural sinisterness of the phrase.

"I suppose not," Anika said as she began to stroll the interior perimeter of the warehouse. "But what now, Father?

Your plan failed. I'm here, alive, and as far as you know I've killed the woman, leaving you with no one to complete the recipe. You're a dead man after all."

"The woman isn't dead, Anika. I know she isn't."

"How can you be sure of that?" Anika's tone was challenging, almost cocky, and she continued sauntering the warehouse floor, clutching her mug nervously in both hands, passing the empty metal shelving until she reached the back wall and the interior door where Officer Stenson had ducked out.

"Your mother never taught me the secret to immortality, but the book contains more than that. Much more. There are things inside—lessons—powerful and wonderful things which your mother did teach me. Ways to connect with the life force inside of everything, and to feel that force, intuit it, guide it when necessary. It took years to learn and control it, but I have done it. And I feel Life in the old woman. I feel it as strongly as ever."

"So is that where your slave has gone? That System officer? To bring her here? To kill me?" Anika tried the knob of the interior door but it too was locked, and though she hadn't expected anything different, she let out a disappointed sigh.

"They'll be here soon, Anika." Marcel paused and then said, "I know it means nothing at this point, but I truly am very sorry."

Anika let out a sound that was a mixture of laughter and scream. She stood bewildered at the back of the warehouse, staring wide-eyed at the tall ceiling, resetting all that had happened since she'd been found on the road this morning. It didn't seem possible.

"So why did you never teach me any of these great lessons, Papa?" Even now, Anika knew the sarcastic lilt she attached to 'Papa' would sting her father.

"I tried, Anika, when you were very young. But you didn't grasp it. It didn't come naturally to you. I always intended—when you were older—to resume the lessons, but your mother died and, well, I just didn't. I'll admit I was disappointed you weren't naturally able to feel it, feel it the way Gre..." Marcel stopped, as if speaking his granddaughter's name was forbidden.

"Gretel? The way Gretel does?"

Marcel nodded slowly. "Yes, Anika, the way Gretel does."

***

Gretel wasn't surprised to find Deda's house empty when they arrived, nor was she surprised that an aimless search for clues as to Deda's whereabouts rendered nothing.

Odalinde and Hansel took the main floor while Gretel searched the basement. At once the musty smell of the cellar transported her back to the last time she'd been down there, the night her mother disappeared, the night she and Hansel waited anxiously as their father and grandfather discussed what could have happened to the only woman in the world that loved all of them.

Gretel rummaged again through the drawers of the old desk—including the one that held the dirty magazines—and was momentarily amazed that she and the girl who had mischievously perused those pictures only months ago were the same person. It seemed almost impossible, and she nearly giggled at the embarrassment she felt at the time. Such innocence.

She scanned the dusty bookshelves where Orphism had sat for so many years, that empty slot now as vacant and black as the book itself. A montage of all the times she'd constructed makeshift scaffolds and had secretly leafed through the book's pages instantly flashed through her mind. It was all so distant now. How she wished that book was still there. How she wished everything was still here.

As for clues, the basement contained nothing tangible, a fact Gretel knew to be true before she touched the first step down. But there *was* something—an inkling—a memory to pursue maybe, something peculiar about that night that went unnoticed. At the time it didn't stick—there was far too much to process about that night— but there was something. Gretel couldn't quite find it, however, and if it was still in her brain, whatever that "it" was floated mockingly out of reach, and Gretel didn't feel she was very close to it. Deda was involved, however, about that she was convinced, and her impatience to find him—and her mother—was festering.

"Let's go," she said to no one in particular as she reached the top of the cellar stairway, "we're wasting our time here."

"Okay, but where?" Odalinde asked.

Gretel knew the woman's question wasn't rhetorical. Her ex-stepmother-to-be believed in Gretel's intuition, and she, Gretel, now felt the pressure of that belief. "I don't know! I just know there is nothing here and we have to hurry!"

"Stop yelling, Gret!" Hansel snapped, the boy once again precariously close to tears.

"Gretel, it's okay," Odalinde said, her voice soft and measured. "I think you're right. I don't think we're going to find anything here."

"Then why did we come here at all?"

"Your grandfather is involved, Gretel. I was being delicate about that before, but you know he's involved."

"Yes, I do know that. But he isn't here. I knew he wouldn't be here."

"Where is he then Gretel!" Hansel's voice was as loud as Gretel had ever heard. "I need to find Mother!" The boy slapped his hands to his face, covering his cheeks and eyes, while deep, guttural sobs exploded from him. He dropped down to the floor like a sack of flour and cried, his back and head convulsing with each bawl.

Gretel frowned at her brother and walked to the front door. "Let's go," she said coldly, as she turned the knob on the door.

***

Gretel sat rigid in the front seat of the truck while Odalinde, ostensibly, consoled Hansel. She brushed aside any feelings of guilt about her treatment of her brother, and instead used the time instructively, focusing her intuition. She closed her eyes, squinting them in concentration, and placed her hands flat on the top of her head. She was missing something.

She sat this way for several minutes, still, waiting for the answer to arrive from the ether, when, finally, the front door to Deda's opened and Odalinde stepped out holding Hansel's hand.

"I'm sorry, Gretel," Hansel said as he climbed into the back of the truck, "I didn't mean to yell at you. I just miss her."

Gretel sighed and had to fight the reflexive eye roll that surfaced. "I miss her too, Hansel. And don't be sorry. You didn't do anything."

Hansel was quiet for a moment, and then said, "I guess I just never believed it, you know? I always thought she was coming back. Especially on that first day, the day she didn't come home. I was scared just like you and Papa, but I also thought you were both wrong. I thought when we came here that night that...that Deda would know. I thought Deda would tell us everything was fine, that Mother had just been delayed or...I don't know. Something."

Gretel's eyes welled at the sincerity and eloquence of her brother's words, and she turned toward him, awkwardly pulling him close and hugging him. "It's okay, I know."

With Odalinde sitting unobtrusively beside them, the siblings remained embraced momentarily when Gretel's eyes flashed open.

"Wait a minute," she whispered, pushing her brother away. She turned her eyes to the roof of the truck, exploring her memory.

"What is it, Gretel?" Odalinde asked.

"That night—that night Hansel and I came here, when Mother went missing—Deda had nothing to tell us that could help. He never told us anything."

"We already know it's Deda, Gretel," Hansel said, "We know he's involved in this."

"But that's just it," Gretel shook her head as if fanning away her brother's obviousness, "Deda didn't tell *us* anything. Remember Han? We were shooed to the basement. Deda and Papa wanted to talk in private. Why in private?"

"So we wouldn't hear if something bad had happened. They didn't want us to get more upset. Deda wanted to protect us."

"But protect us from what? If Deda didn't know anything, what could he have said that would have upset us any more than we already were? And yet, he wanted to talk to Father alone."

"What are you saying, Gretel?" Odalinde's voice was low and clear.

"I don't know exactly," she replied, "we need to talk to Father. And we need to go now."

CHAPTER TWENTY-TWO

The old woman sat motionless in The System cruiser, her eyes closed, a long, thin smile drawn across her face. Her breathing was slow and rhythmic and her mind was clear. The smells accompanying her meditation were foreign and wonderful, and the feel of the leather on her palms, so lithe and cool, calmed her even further. And the sound. Those sounds which had surrounded her, which had imprisoned her for generations, were now virtually extinguished by the insulation of this perfectly built machine.

Resting on the seat beside her, contained securely in a bowl no larger than the one she'd been assaulted with, were the remnants of the broth, salvaged with great effort from the floor of her kitchen. There was no need to bury it now, she wouldn't be coming back.

Almost instantly after turning the ignition, the old woman heard a voice. "Hello officer," the female voice said, "where would you like to go?"

The old woman instinctively spun her body toward the back seat, teeth bared, looking for the intruder. But the back of the cruiser was empty, and the old witch quickly realized it was not a woman, but rather the car, that was speaking. A robot. To assist her.

The old woman glanced fervently about the cab of the cruiser, looking for some clue, a note perhaps, containing the magic words that would unlock her destination. Did the words have to be perfect? Would there be some alert if she spoke errantly? Or worse, would she trigger some self-destruction mechanism?

No.

This was her new life. Her Orphic life. A life without paranoia, only perfection. A life where only the powers of the universe worked for her, constantly thrusting her forward toward her ever-evolving completeness.

"Anika Morgan," she said. "Take me to Anika Morgan."

The robot was silent for several beats, every one of which pulsed through the old woman's blood as she sat wide-eyed, anticipating.

"There is no match for Anika Morgan," it said finally. And then, "Do you mean Gretel Morgan?"

"Yes," the old woman said, almost laughing, her face as cheerful and alive as a child's on a playground, "take me to Gretel Morgan."

CHAPTER TWENTY-THREE

Before the truck was at a full stop, Gretel had opened the passenger-side door, hopped out to the driveway, and was racing toward her house and the boy sitting on her porch steps.

It was Petr.

She had no idea why he was there, and why his father hadn't come to pick him up, but she didn't care; a fury had overtaken her, and now that he *was* here, it was time he filled in his part of the mystery.

The boy stood quickly, a weary smile on his face; it was a look that showed both surprise and pleasure at Gretel's apparent excitement to see him. "Hey Gretel," he called, "since I guess my..."

"Who told you?" she demanded, braking the last steps of her run just before slamming into Petr. She was gasping heavily and had to bend at the waist to allow the air in. "Who told you?" She wanted to say more, berate the boy really, but she had to catch her breath, and the three words were all she could manage.

"What? Who told me what? Gretel, what's wrong? Where were you?"

"Who told you!" Gretel was now only inches from Petr's face, eye to eye with him, screaming. Over the boy's shoulder, she could see what appeared to be the outline of a car. It was covered by an old faded tarp, and for a moment Gretel's mind flashed to her canoe and thoughts of rowing.

"Gretel I don't know—"

Gretel snapped back to attention. "About my father and Odalinde getting married! You know Goddamn well what I'm talking about!" Gretel took a deep breath and lowered her voice. "I never told you about them getting married, Petr. So who told you? Was it the Klahrs?"

"No!" Petr chirped, quickly, a clue to Gretel that Petr hated even the suggestion that the Klahrs were somehow involved in any of this. But it also signaled that Petr was hiding something, and it was time to come clean.

Odalinde parked the pickup truck and had now arrived with Hansel to stand beside Gretel. Petr Stenson had an audience now, and they were rapt with attention.

"It wasn't the Klahrs," he began, and then quickly veered into an apology. "I'm sorry, Gretel, I..."

"I don't care, Petr. Later I might, but not now." Gretel's eyes shifted again to the tarp. What *was* that?

Peter nodded and continued. "My father told me, Gretel."

"Your father?" she whispered, and then glared at Odalinde. "You said you never told him."

Odalinde frowned. "I didn't Gretel." Her voice was low and weary, disappointed at Gretel's continued skepticism about her. She turned back to Petr. "Who told your father, Petr? Do you know?"

Petr looked to the ground and kicked a stray pebble. "I can't be sure, but I..." he paused for a moment, considering his speculation, and then blurted, "I don't know. I don't know who told him. I'm sorry. And what does it matter anyway?"

"Dammit, Petr!" Gretel barked, her patience exhausted, "It *does* matter, and you *do* know! Now who told your father!?"

"I told him."

The voice of Gretel's father boomed down to the huddle below, startling it to attention like a herd of deer stumbled upon by hikers. Heinrich Morgan stood tall at the top of the porch stairs, his posture healthy and majestic, as if addressing peasants from his chamber balcony.

Gretel stared disbelieving at the man, her face now flush and her throat and mouth as dry as the ground she stood on. "Father?" She couldn't remember the last time she'd even seen him outside. It had to be months she guessed.

"Papa!" Hansel whimpered.

Gretel turned to the boy in fear as he began walking toward his father. She couldn't speak, and then almost vomited as she watched her brother nearly bare his teeth when Odalinde grabbed his shoulders to restrain him.

"No, Hansel," Odalinde said calmly

Hansel's wild stare lingered on Odalinde for a moment, and his breathing was panicked and wheezing. Gretel knew what he was imagining. Their father was back. Finally. And now they had to go to him and reunite. After all, what was the point of all these months of suffering and neglect if they were only going to shun him upon his recovery? What were they doing all of this for?

But Gretel now realized what her brother did not. Things had changed. Her father, it seemed, was the enemy.

"I don't understand, Father," Gretel said. "Why...how..." Her thoughts were coming too quickly and they jumbled into incoherence.

Heinrich took his first step down when Odalinde froze him in stride. "We'll hear your story, Heinrich—from the porch."

Gretel's father smiled at what he clearly inferred as brazenness, but he obeyed, and Gretel took this as a good sign. Perhaps he knew of Odalinde's secret and feared the powers that it implied.

"I think on some level you do understand Gretel, just as you always have. Since you could talk, you always understood things very quickly."

There was nothing menacing in her father's tone, but his words now left little doubt in Gretel's mind that he had participated in her mother's disappearance. Petr had now turned toward Heinrich, and the group of four stood in anticipation. Gretel's instinct was to get back in the truck—with Petr and Hansel—and drive away, but she stood hypnotized.

"I didn't plan any of this, Gretel, not initially. When your mother disappeared that day, I was as grief-stricken and devastated as you were. More perhaps. I loved her very deeply."

Gretel glanced over at her brother and felt a sense of pride in his attempt to control his emotions. Tears had begun to stream, but he was silent, listening to every word. She looked back to her father. "Then why?"

"This explanation, Gretel, you would not understand. You wouldn't believe any of it. I don't suppose I believed it, not truly. Not until today."

Gretel's eyes were locked on her father. "What happened today?" she asked, her words slow and suspicious.

"Magic, Gretel. True magic."

A smile formed on Heinrich Morgan's face, and as his lips parted, Gretel screamed at the teeth that emerged through the opening. They were larger than before, inhumanly angled.

Petr began backing away, instinctively pulling Gretel's hand, which she snatched away. "What in...your tee..?"

"Odalinde what is that!?" It was Hansel, his voice resonating with a sound of terror Gretel had never heard from her brother.

"It's okay. Hansel, it's often part of it. Your father has the potion. I don't think it's much but...Oh my God, he has the potion." Odalinde was speaking as if to herself, trying to understand how any of this could be happening. "I don't know..."

"I thought he couldn't read the language!" Gretel cried. "You told me he couldn't!"

At this Heinrich boomed out his voice again. "So perhaps you *would* understand what has happened." He stood for a moment, silent, studying his daughter curiously, a bemused smile on his face.

"You murdered your wife—our mother—for this?"

Heinrich turned his head quickly to the side, as if slapped, and then returned his focus to his daughter. "I had nothing to do with it," he said flatly. "It was only after that I...participated."

"Who did then? Who killed her?" Gretel waited, and then, receiving no answer asked, "Was it Deda?" Gretel could sense the tension in her father, restraining his reflex to look away once again. She was like a boxer offering quick, stinging jabs. "Or maybe you're lying; maybe you did kill her."

At this last suggestion, Heinrich became very still, almost frozen, and then, almost impossibly for a man of his age and condition, set off down the steps in a rage, like a rodeo bull ungated. He reached the landing area at the bottom of the porch and turned in the direction of his daughter. Instinctively, Odalinde and Petr both stepped forward, flanking Gretel, preparing to meet the deranged attacker head on. That encounter, however, was averted by the woman now occupying Heinrich's position at the top of the porch.

"Heinrich!" the woman shouted.

Heinrich Morgan's feet stopped instantly, as if programmed, but the momentum of his body did not, and he fell forward, putting his hands in front of him to brace his fall and breaking his left wrist as a result. His screech of pain was ignored by everyone. The group instead stood gazing, incredulously, at the stunning woman in the cloak above them. Her heavy robe and clear, white skin gave her an apparition-like appearance, and it would have surprised no one if she simply vanished into the forest—a memory to be doubted later in life. But the figure remained, unmoving, a serene image at the top of the porch, seemingly incapable of the command she'd just barked at Heinrich.

"You'll not move again, Mr. Morgan until you are instructed." The woman's eyes lingered on Gretel's father for a moment, ensuring he'd understood his orders, and then she looked back to the woman and the three children on the driveway beneath her. "Gretel and Hansel," she said, "I've heard about you."

Gretel strode forward, pushing past Odalinde and Petr. "Heard about us from whom?"

"Why from your mother, of course. Your lovely, delicious mother."

"Murderer!" Hansel screamed, and Odalinde again had to snatch the boy back by his collar.

At this accusation, the woman raised her eyebrows and frowned. "I am that, yes, many times over. It's a title which your guardian, no doubt, assumes as well. Am I wrong on that count?" The witch cocked her head toward Odalinde.

Odalinde stayed silent and looked away, one hand still firmly on the back of Hansel's shirt and the other ready to restrain Gretel if necessary.

"Yes, well, perhaps that discussion is for another time. As far as your mother is concerned, however, I cannot quite claim her as my victim. At least not yet."

"She's alive?" Gretel knew the answer to the question before she'd asked it, and her joy quickly turned to fear when she realized why the woman had come. She took a step back and glanced again at the tarp-covered car beside the house.

The old woman caught the glance and grinned. "My new toy," she said, "perhaps you'd like a ride?"

"No thanks," Gretel replied quickly, "unless you want to take me to my mother."

With this statement, the old woman threw back her head and laughed. The sound was awful to Gretel, much closer to the cackle of the witches of myth than of the relatively attractive woman at the top of the porch.

"If I knew where your mother was, I wouldn't be here with you." The witch pondered a moment and then said, "Well, again, at least not yet."

"What do you want then?" It was Odalinde who spoke now. "We don't know where she is."

"Oh, I know you don't." She paused. "But," the woman continued, now pointing at Petr, "I was hoping that perhaps he does."

Gretel looked back at Petr, and could see by his expression that he didn't know what the woman was talking about—or at least he didn't *know* he knew. "Petr?" she said.

"I never met Gretel's mother. I don't know her and I don't know where she is."

Petr's voice was bordering on panic, and Gretel knew he was still shaken by the crazed look on her father's face only moments ago. And the teeth.

"Oh, but you may, Petr. Certainly your father showed you things. Took you places. Yes?"

"What places? How do you know my father?" Petr's words were now spoken with nothing less than terror.

The old woman descended the porch stairs slowly, gracefully, and when she reached the bottom, she turned sharply and headed toward the side of the house where the car was parked. Without breaking stride, she clutched the tarp where it covered the hood of the car and walked it back toward the trunk until the full view of the machine was revealed. As Gretel suspected—or perhaps knew—it was The System cruiser.

Petr's mouth fell open slightly, just parting his lips, and he shook his head in a short rhythmic spasm of disbelief. "That's my father's car," he said, his voice vibrational from fear, as well as the shaking of his head.

"Why yes it is, Petr, and he keeps a lovely picture of the two of you right there on the ...hmm...I'm not sure what it's called! But it's wonderful at shielding the sun!"

"Where's my father?" Petr asked, nearly in tears.

The old woman walked back to the front of the car and stood centered in front of the grill. She narrowed her eyes and steeled them on Petr. "Your father is dead. He's been dead for several hours now." The tone was aggressive and menacing—nothing less than a dare to the five sets of ears in the range of her voice. "And unless you want to join him—along with your girlfriend and her brother—I suggest you tell me where I can find Anika Morgan."

"Don't you dare threaten them!" Odalinde snarled.

As fast as Gretel's thoughts could process what was happening, the old woman's feet had left the ground, effortlessly, and she had flown—literally flown—from the front of the cruiser to the spot where Odalinde had stood only a second before. The cape of her cloak was flattened by the wind as she flew, giving her the appearance of some evil super villain from the pages of any number of comic books. The old woman's hands were raised above her as she flew, with her fingers pointing to the ground, sharp, spearlike nails protruding from the tips. She looked like a wizard attempting to cast a midair spell on some poor peasant or toad perhaps. As she landed, Gretel could see the woman's teeth bared to the top of the gumline, wolf-like; except instead of the wide canines and blunt incisors of a dog, the teeth were severe and jagged, like those of a shark.

The event happened in an instant—Gretel hadn't time even to scream. Instead she stood silently, paralyzed, her mind reflexively beginning to cope with the loss of Odalinde.

But Odalinde was fast too. She'd moved off her spot, two feet or so, just far enough to avoid the slashing fingers and fangs of the flying demon. The old woman's momentum carried her forward on her landing, and as she stumbled forward, Odalinde clutched both of her hands together and hammered the back of the witch's head, sending her face-first onto the gravel. "Run! Odalinde commanded. "All of you run!"

"Odalinde, I can..." Gretel began to protest.

"Go Gretel. Now. Take your brother and your friend and go." It was Gretel's father this time. He stood tall, clutching his wrist to his chest, a look of sadness and disgust on his face. "Go to the Klahrs. Tell them what's happened."

The old woman had returned to her feet, her serene, ghost-like appearance now diminished by dirt and rage. "Heinrich!" she shouted and took several steps backward, trying to keep her enemies in her periphery. She regained her poise. "I'll find them, Heinrich, no matter what. The only difference is now you'll be dead too." The old woman then turned to Odalinde. "But first, you."

Heinrich Morgan looked at his daughter one last time, the sadness in his eyes was a look Gretel would remember for the rest of her life. "Now," he repeated.

Gretel grabbed her brother's hand and barked at Petr to follow, and listened in agony as Hansel screamed, "Father!" while the three children made their way down to the lake.

CHAPTER TWENTY-FOUR

The old woman hadn't expected a challenge, not really, not on a physical level anyway. She had arrived cautious of Gretel, of her ostensible intuition and fortitude—particularly being that she was the daughter of the woman who had nearly killed her. But she hadn't counted on this mystery woman who apparently had her own reservoir of courage. This woman who reminded her of herself in many ways.

"So you're an Orphist," she said, as a statement, not a question. "I sensed that in you the moment I looked at you. I could see it in your eyes. It stops the aging, but it does little for the weariness."

"I will die now, quietly, at your hand if you prefer," Odalinde replied.

Apparently the woman's fellow Orphist had no interest in camaraderie.

"I've done this life as far as I wish," Odalinde continued. Then, perhaps overplaying her hand said, "You can use me for blending. Just leave them alone. All of them. Heinrich included."

Ignoring her compromise, the old woman said, "How long have you lived—'Odalinde' is it? How long have you lived Odalinde?"

Odalinde stayed quiet, the old woman recognizing her reticence to reveal anything capable of weakening her position.

"It doesn't matter," the old woman said, "I'm sure it's been long enough. Far too long in fact. Certainly you know your body will do me little good at this point. And besides, I've found it. I've found the treasure. The Prize of Prizes if you will. And I'll never let it slip away."

Had it been only a few days earlier, the old woman would have been killed by the stone in Heinrich Morgan's hand. It would have landed solidly on the back of her skull and sent shards of bone into her brain. At the very least she would have been rendered unconscious, with no chance of a second clemency, as there certainly would have been additional blows that followed.

But her senses were heightened now, and she could "see" the rock at its apex just before beginning its descent. Like a dervish, the old woman took a step to the side and then back, and then spun three hundred and sixty degrees, easily avoiding her assailant while assuming the position of strength. She was now behind Heinrich Morgan, restraining his arms to his sides, her breasts flat against his back and her mouth just inches from the man's neck.

The woman knew instantly after arriving that it would end this way for the Morgan father. He'd been part of Marcel's plan after all, a fact she'd uncovered so easily with just a taste of the broth; but as a result of his ongoing poisoning—no doubt being administered by the Orphist woman—he had temporarily forgotten his commitment.

And so it had been a dangerous play for her to strengthen him, allowing him that tiny, delicate taste; the woman knew it the moment she'd touched it to his lips. But it was only done as a temporary measure, an aid to learn what she could from the feeble man. Certainly he'd have some clue as to his wife and daughter's whereabouts. Besides, whatever strength he regained was meaningless; the amount of brew was trivial and the effects wouldn't last the day. It was nothing at all compared to what she'd lapped up. And, of course, Mr. Morgan wasn't a blood relative of his wife. That was the main difference.

The old woman turned her right hand so that her palm faced outward, away from her body, and then she plunged her nails into the side of Heinrich Morgan's neck, letting them glide naturally through the flesh. She flushed in excitement again at her newfound strength, admiring the ease at which her fingers penetrated the skin and muscle. She let her hand rest for a beat, relishing the sounds of asphyxiation and screams ("NO!" from Odalinde), before flinging her hand violently forward and tearing out the man's throat. With her other hand, the old woman held up the corpse of Gretel's father for a few seconds, showing off her strength to her next opponent, and then tossed the body to the dirt. "Are you ready to die?"

CHAPTER TWENTY-FIVE

"How are they, Papa? Do you even know how your grand-children have been doing?"

"They're fine, Anika, but it's best we not speak about them now. It will only upset you further. Please." Marcel nodded with a smile and waved a hand toward himself, beckoning his daughter to come and sit.

Anika kept her distance, remaining instead at the back door of the warehouse. Ready. For what, she wasn't sure. Perhaps when the officer returned—if he returned through the same door from which he left—she could make a run for it. Or maybe ambush him. He and that horrible witch. It was no plan at all really, a wild grasp at survival, but whatever happened, she wasn't going to surrender again. And she was done obeying her father.

"And how do you know they're fine?" she asked. "Have you seen them? Or spoken with them?"

"Oliver..." he paused, "Officer Stenson, the man who found you, he has seen them. He tells me they are well."

Anika bit her upper lip to restrain a scream. The thought of that hideous officer looking at or being anywhere near her children sickened her.

"In fact, if I'm not mistaken, he spoke with Heinrich just a week or so ago. Everything with your children is fine."

"Spoke with Heinrich? Why?"

Marcel peered at his daughter across the room, squinting her into focus, pausing long enough to give her time to come to the answer to her question.

"No," she whispered.

"I'm sorry, Anika."

"No!" Anika screamed. "No!" And with that final scream, a foreign rage erupted in Anika, a rage she hadn't felt even at the moment she'd crushed the skull of the hag. In one fluid motion, Anika gripped the mug of water tightly by the handle, spilling its contents to the warehouse floor, and then, torquing her body violently for leverage, smashed the bottom of the cup against the door's mirror.

At first the sound was electrical in nature, sharp and piercing, and then it turned heavy and liberating as the shards of silver glass rained to the floor. Instinctively, Anika shielded her eyes from the exploding shrapnel, and then, re-alizing there was nothing else to do now but keep going, she floated her arm slowly through the new opening in search of the knob on the opposite side. The cup had left a sizable hole where the mirror had been, but jagged shards from every di-rection of the perimeter still threatened. She would obvious-ly have to hurry, but she needed to avoid shredding her arm if it could be helped.

As she groped for the doorknob, Anika could also see through the opening to a small room which contained an ex-it door leading to the outside, the unmistakable neon beacon shining red on the wall above.

Her hand found the opposing doorknob and then felt its cruel resistance as she twisted it. That should come as no surprise, she thought, the door *is* locked. She continued her blind search, fine-tuning it, using now the tips of her fingers to locate the locking mechanism. Within seconds, she'd found the dial and unlocked the door, and then pulled her arm back through the opening. She was free.

Having not wasted any precious time worrying about what her father was doing during her escape, Anika turned back now to gauge him. Perhaps he was letting her leave.

As she considered this possibility, she felt the palms of her father's hands plunge into the middle of her chest, knocking the air from her lungs, the sound like a baseball bat on an old pillow. Her body spun slightly to the right before crashing against the cold metal scaffold behind her. The metal shelving held her upright for a moment, and then she slumped to the floor, dropping slowly before coming to rest on one knee. With her head bowed in a look of prayer, Anika blinked several times at the floor, reflexively taking inventory of her condition. She wasn't seriously hurt. Luckily, her right arm (which would have a nasty bruise later but wasn't broken) had taken most of the impact; had her spine taken the brunt, she thought, she may have been finished. Just survive, she thought. Just keep surviving.

"I can't risk you anymore, Anika," her father spoke, this time making no pretensions at niceness. "When they arrive, she'll have to use you as you are."

Anika turned her eyes to her father, glaring. Any trace of love or sorrow for him was gone. There was only hatred, a searing contempt for the man who'd raised her.

And as this transmutation took place—from sympathy to loathing—everything in front of Anika crystallized. The shard of mirror. The side of her father's neck. The resolve.

She'd felt this before, at the witch's cabin: a focused rage—a rage unlike the wild fury she'd released on the mirror minutes before.

***

Anika had known every move before it happened. It almost wasn't fair, she thought. And as she was walking through the door, pebbles of glass crunching beneath her shoes, she fixed back on the body lying frozen on the floor. As she stared at the corpse, the shard of mirror that protruded neatly from her father's neck, just below his right ear, caught the light and seemed to wink at Anika. Anika winked back and walked out.

***

Gretel hauled the canoe toward her, backpedaling up the bank, making certain to keep the boat from drifting, and then raced behind Petr and Hansel through the orchard to the Klahr's house. Every gram of her body wanted to go back and fight, to help save Odalinde and her father—but she couldn't risk Hansel and Petr following her. And she wanted to see her mother again.

"What is it, Petr? Gretel?" Mrs. Klahr was on the porch, welcoming the children as she untied her apron at the back and then crumpled it into a ball. It was Amanda Klahr's version of preparing to fight, Gretel thought absently.

Gretel spoke rapidly, breathing heavily and stuttering. "Mrs. Klahr, it's my father, and...and Odalinde...and my mother...and a woman...she's a monster...or..."

"Gretel, slow down." Mrs. Klahr twisted back toward the house. "Georg!" she called. "Come out here, Georg! It's the children!" She turned back to the kids, this time addressing Petr. "Petr, what's going on?" Mrs. Klahr's tone sounded almost amused as if suspecting a prank.

"It's true, Mrs. Klahr. There's a woman...she...I think my father..." Petr stumbled, not sure how to relay anything that could make sense in only one or two sentences.

"Okay, settle down Petr. My goodness!" Mr. Klahr had arrived on the porch next to his wife. "Georg," she said to him, "scamper over to the Morgan house and see what all's happening there. These children are quite hysterical."

"No! Mr. Klahr, no!" Gretel's face twisted in terror. "Don't go over there! She's dangerous!"

"But Gretel," Hansel cried, "someone needs to help them!"

Hansel was right, of course: it was likely her father and Odalinde needed help (the woman had flown!). But the thought of losing Mr. Klahr was too much for her to imagine. Gretel knew her father was gone—dead or alive she couldn't know—but that he was a man who had passed the post of redemption, about this she was sure. And Odalinde. Odalinde had come here for them, exclusively, almost as a sacrifice—or salvation even—for the horrors she'd brought upon the world. Gretel felt she was meant to die protecting Hansel and her. Perhaps she's dying right now, she thought.

But the Klahrs played a different role in this story. They weren't part of this twisted history that her grandmother brought here so long ago. They were of *this* world. Back Country folk. Righteous and charitable. They had saved

Gretel when her mother went missing (not dead, Gretel remembered again, her mother wasn't dead). Even when Odalinde suggested the Klahrs had betrayed Gretel, in the car on the way to Deda's, Gretel knew she was wrong. She knew they were as pure a people as she could ever expect to know, and Gretel would never bear losing them. Even if she found her mother—when she found her—Gretel would always need the Klahrs.

"It's okay, Gretel, I'll be extra careful. Got my companion, you know." Mr. Klahr unhinged the twin barrels of his shotgun and loaded the chamber. "I'll be just fine."

Gretel's fear hadn't shaken Mr. Klahr, but Mrs. Klahr's face was now serious and concerned. "Be careful, Georg. If something's happening you can't handle, you come back here."

Mrs. Klahr's tone left no space for discussion, and Mr. Klahr simply nodded, then walked briskly to his truck and drove off.

***

Anika opened the exit door and could see instantly that night would be arriving soon. She had freed herself from captivity, but her struggle to get home remained, and darkness would present a formidable obstacle. She had no idea where she was, and The System officer would surely be back soon, likely with that savage witch in tow. Wandering these foreign parts in the dark seemed all but suicidal.

But as Anika stepped on the ground outside the bleak building, a flood of recognition overtook her. The smells and landscape, and even the siding and structure of the building itself, all became familiar. She knew this place. Perhaps not the exact earth she stood on, but for certain, she knew this ground. Or at least the area surrounding it. She looked to the sky and inhaled deeply, attempting to coax a memory from her senses. It was there, this memory, bulging at the surface of her mind; and from what she intuited, it wasn't some stray thought from a single moment in her distant past—this memory was close, with a feeling of security and routine. It was a memory of Home.

As Anika stood recollecting, she absently took note of the land extending before her at the back of the property, and how it proceeded quite differently from that in the front. When she'd arrived at the warehouse, she recalled the road leading to the front of the building had been long and flat, innocuous and rural and had ended rather lazily at the front door. But the back sloped steadily away from the house until, at a distance of perhaps thirty yards or so, the land dropped off dramatically, sloping at such an angle that she couldn't see the ground below. The building, it seemed, was atop a large hill.

Anika walked toward the edge of the slope, not knowing exactly what to expect, and at about halfway to the drop-off could see another building enter into view. It was just the roof at first, and then, as she proceeded closer to the edge, the whole of the large industrial complex below came into view. And the memory was complete. Anika knew exactly where she was.

She jogged zombie-like the rest of the way to the edge of the hill and looked down, breathing spastically in disbelief, consciously slowing her inhalations to keep from hyperventilating.

It was the cannery.

There was no mistaking it. The rusted out factory shell and overly secure barbed wire fencing that strangled the grounds were as recognizable to Anika as her own reflection. She'd seen it a thousand times. It had been years, but her family—and at times, before the children, just she and Heinrich—had spent countless hours at Rifle Field picnicking and playing games, or, in their somewhat wilder and more adventurous days, shooting their guns through the fence at the broadside of the building. She was staring down on the Weinheimmer Cannery. It was impossible, Anika thought. Her house was right across the lake! She'd no way to get to it from this spot, of course—even if she were to get over the fence she'd need a boat to get across the water—but if not for the trees and cannery, she would be able to see her house from where she stood! She wouldn't speculate as to why her father would have held her so close to her home until much later; her thoughts now were soaked of her children.

During the times she'd spent at Rifle Field she'd barely even noticed the hill upon which she now stood, and she'd certainly never dreamed there had been a warehouse at the top. It made sense now of course, this warehouse—maintenance workers and others would have needed a place to store supplies and tools or whatever—but it just wasn't something you thought of, particularly since the cannery had been closed now for so many years. And with the dense foliage of the Backwoods and its location so far from the main road, the warehouse simply wasn't visible from any place she'd ever

been. She supposed that had the imposing fence that surrounded the cannery not existed they may have explored Rifle Field further, but the fence *had* always been there, and
they'd never even considered what was beyond it.

Anika's initial instinct was to scream for help. Their
neighbors with the orchard, the Klahrs, lived on this side
of the lake, had for decades, so it was possible—probable
even—that *they* were aware of this place, and would have
heard her voice if the sound carried right. Perhaps she'd even
be heard at her own house. But Anika was disoriented and
felt wildly insecure about her judgment of the distance. She'd
never been great with directions and ranges to begin with,
and after all she'd been through, she felt even less certain of
her internal gauges. Besides, even if someone were to hear
her, the noise would be faint and directionless, likely to be
dismissed as far off children at play, or perhaps a bird. And,
more importantly, for all Anika knew, the officer and the
witch were rolling to a stop in front of the warehouse at this
very moment, and the yelling would be as good as wrapping
a chain around her neck and locking it to one of the warehouse shelves. Never again, she thought, I'll die before ever
being a prisoner again.

But could she make it over the fence? As fences went,
it wasn't particularly tall, and the portion of it that formed
the barrier was standard chain link; she assessed it would be
easy enough for her to scale to the top. But it was at the top
where things got problematic. Four or five rows of gruesome
barbs formed a wide V-shape that ran the entire length of the
fence, making it as difficult to get on top of it as across it.
From where she stood now, the jagged steel canopy appeared

as some giant metal crocodile, waiting for her entry into its agape jaws, perhaps promising to take her across the lake—a painful retelling of the fable about the mischievous gingerbread boy, Anika thought, only this time she would star in the ill-fated title role.

But Anika knew a choice had to be made, and there were really only two options: head back down the long, dirt road on which she'd arrived, risking imminent darkness and the openness that seemed certain to expose her to The System officer; or, scale the fence in front of her and take her chances with the barbs and the awaiting lake beyond. She hadn't swam in years, she suddenly realized, but she was comfortable enough in the water, and she trusted that instincts and desperation would take her the distance she needed.

It was the fence that would be the challenge though, and if that was to be her choice—the fence—she would need to move quickly.

Anika descended the hill and walked up to the fence, pushing the weight of her body against it and gripping her fingers through the links like a prisoner of war. It felt strong, stronger than she would have suspected after so many years. She could see through to Rifle Field the exact spots where she and her family used to lay out their blanket and set the picnic platters, Heinrich always meticulous in his combing of the patches to avoid settling on an ant hill. The grass was wildly overgrown now though it appeared certain areas had been recently trampled and used.

This scenario, her precise position standing at the fence, reminded her of something from a nightmare: pursuing some elusive goal—in this case, her freedom—yet ultimately able only to observe it in silent frustration as the monsters steadily moved in.

But this wasn't a dream; here she was able to make choices, and Anika's mind instantly sharpened as she assessed the fence and the possible ways over. The barbs atop were even more imposing at this close angle, and a panic started in Anika's chest at the sight of the rusty aluminum thorns. She could bear the pain, she thought, but if she got caught—stuck—it would almost certainly spell the end.

She walked the length of the fence to the front wall of the cannery which stood only a few feet from the barrier. Rifle Field stared at her, mocking her with its closeness. Anika surveyed everything, not sure exactly what she was looking for, but loosely hoping that, perhaps, time had created a gap at the base of the fence, some opening wide enough for her to squeeze through. She wasn't as thin as she'd ever been, that was certain, but even if she were as thin as Gretel it wouldn't have mattered, the spaces between the bottom of the fence post and ground were sound, and not big enough for her even to put an arm through.

She dropped to her knees and raked her hand into the grass, clawing it like a badger. The earth was surprisingly loose, and Anika came away with a mound of wet dirt that left an ample hole just to the side of the fence post. With the cannery situated so close to the lake, the ground below the fence was essentially mud, and could be removed without much effort. But who knew how deep the fence went, and even with the ground being damp, her fingers would be numb in no time. If she had a day to dig, or even several hours, and if she were rested and nourished with the morning sun above her, and if virtually every single thing about how she felt right now was different, she was sure she could tunnel under using her hands alone. But Anika figured she didn't have that time, and her strength was dwindling.

Once again Anika stared up at the evil barbs above her. It was impossible, she thought—over or under—she simply didn't have the energy.

Anika slowly dropped her head to her chest and, for the first time in months, after all she'd seen and been subjected to, after all of the betrayal and cruelty that had become her daily life, she began to cry. Her weeping was almost silent as she stood and turned to face the cannery. Her eyes remained closed while she tilted her face to the darkening sky. The bout of tears lasted only a few seconds—Anika would later consider this burst of sorrow was somehow necessary, physiologically, as a means of cleansing her mind, ultimately allowing to enter the thought that would free her.

With her head still angled up toward the roof of the cannery, Anika opened her eyes. And she saw it. A window.

At first Anika rejected what she was seeing as an illusion, a mirage, a cruel trick of her desperate mind. But her memory instantly reacted, assuring Anika the window was real. She'd seen it before, of course, during any number of the Rifle Field visits, but each time it had gone unregistered: an unnoticed speck on the landscape.

Anika bolted toward the foot of the hill to the cannery entrance on the opposite side of the building, nearly losing her footing on the grass as she navigated the corner and then braked, almost instantly, in order to avoid passing the thick metal door. She stood tall and looked indifferently at the threshold, and then let out a disbelieving chuckle at the un-latched door before her. The rusted metal ring that normally, presumably, would have been looped through with the steel shackle of a thick padlock, was empty. Anika unfolded the latch, which barely resisted despite its worn, corroded look, and opened the cannery door.

The interior of the cannery was mostly empty, except for the large canning tables and various-sized tubes of copper piping—some as large as tree trunks—which ran in maze-like fashion from floor to ceiling along the walls. There was little else, however, to indicate that this building had ever been a cannery. There was no heavy machinery or shelving, no stacks of cans or old Weinheimmer signs, and Anika assumed everything had either been gutted by the failed owners or repossessed by the State.

But there were tools strewn about the facility, everything from hammers to pickaxes, which, Anika presumed, had been used to extract sealers and conveyors and whatever else of value existed from their moorings. She figured she wouldn't need much to get through the window, and she scooped a thick, wrought iron claw hammer from the dusty floor. There was also a wide barn shovel leaning against the far wall, and Anika briefly reconsidered the tunneling-under plan. She decided to stay the course and head to the window, but she grabbed the shovel anyway. You never knew.

From there everything moved like a storm. She scaled the steps leading to the second floor of the cannery and then stopped in front of the window—the window she'd taken notice of, remarkably, for the first time only minutes ago. The glass panes were missing almost entirely, probably broken out decades ago, but the frame of the window remained. It was weak-looking and well rusted, but the grid which once divided the panes was intact and would need to be broken out. But Anika was sure in her plan, she had seen everything play out the moment she spotted her escape route from the ground below, and knew the frame would pose little difficulty. She gripped the iron hammer and banged once on the cross grill of the window and then again. Anika suspected the window would be frail, but when it virtually disintegrated on the second gavel-like blow, she was incredulous.

She placed her first foot on the sill, and then her second; her body was still plenty thin enough to fit between the jambs, though she did have to crouch slightly to avoid the head of the window. She looked just beyond the fence to her landing spot, and then back to the floor of the cannery.

The shovel.

Without really knowing why, Anika stepped down from the sill, grabbed the spade, and tossed it out of the window and over the fence to Rifle Field. She then climbed back up and re-squatted, and with both of her hands gripped to the sill on either side of her feet, Anika took one last breath, and jumped.

CHAPTER TWENTY-SIX

"You can't live forever." Odalinde's words were weary, a desperate attempt at reason with the mad woman who now stood above her, measuring the setting, timing the moment for her final, fatal attack. She was so strong, Odalinde thought. Hopelessly strong.

"In theory, that seems not to be true." The witch's reply was quizzical as if lightly considering the concept for the first time. "Though practically I'm sure you're right. But, my fellow Orphist, these types of philosophical dialectics have never been of interest to me, in any area of study really, but particularly in the subject of..."

She paused, and Odalinde noted the trepidation in the witch's voice in the words that followed.

"...the subject you've presented," she continued. "My role is only to take the opportunities as they are presented to me. And as I've promised to those Universals who are greater than the sum of us all, I shall never reject one again."

With a squint, Odalinde locked eyes with the remade woman, and then, never losing the gaze, shook her head slowly in disgust. "You're no Orphist. You believe yourself one, talk as one, but you are not. Just as I was not. But what I know now is that you are much worse than I am, or ever was. You care nothing for life—you're not even human."

Odalinde had given up on survival, and this type of banter would all but guarantee her death. But there was no discomfort in that thought—her time had arrived to forfeit what she should never have possessed. And as this judgment became realized, a feeling of warmth drifted over her. She'd done what she could for Gretel and Hansel, and her only goal now was to draw out this moment, to stall—for as long as her heart forced blood through her veins—the infandous demon above her.

"You're a common being. Like a tree." Odalinde laughed at her somewhat childish analogy. "Destined to live on for centuries, alone and soulless—loveless—with nothing to offer the world." Odalinde looked away in confusion, a visible display of her rethinking the comparison. "So, to be accurate then, you're much lower than a tree. A tree is an object which lavishes on the world fruit and habitation, air to breath and shelter from heat and rain. You give nothing. You're a parasite. An immortal parasite. What worse thing could ever exist on this earth?"

The witch's expression stayed frozen. The confident smile, which emerged instantly after sending Odalinde to the ground with the force of a stallion's kick, remained. But Odalinde could now detect the effort behind the smile, and the rage bubbling beneath it. Would she kill her now? Odalinde prayed not, not for her own life, but to give the children just a bit more time.

"I was like you. For years. I know the addiction as well as anyone who's ever been in its grips." Odalinde's tone was softer, now trying slowly to unreel the witch, just enough to keep her on the line while still maintaining the attention she'd won. "But I returned to Orphism—true Orphism—not the horrid recipe that has become its legacy. I rediscovered—or perhaps found for the first time, it had been so long I couldn't remember—the remarkable book of The Ancients. The beauty and truth of a spectacular people, who informed of a message that, had it been widely read, was potent enough to catapult humanity centuries forward. Perhaps further. I felt the pride in that, the responsibility." Odalinde smiled flatly. "And I changed. It took some time, but I changed."

Odalinde paused, hoping the witch would give her some measure of reply, some morsel of conversation which Odalinde could latch onto and steer into a dialogue. But she stood frozen above her, her teeth bared in that insidious smile, fingernails protruding down to the ground.

"You've enough now to live for as long you'd ever want to," Odalinde continued. "Look at you! You're...quite stunning really. I imagine you were rather old once—old!—and now you've replenished. You've found that elusive fountain of myth!" Odalinde lowered her voice, sensing an impact of her words on the witch. "Look at you. You don't need more. These aren't animals of the forest, these are your kin."

Odalinde knew any word she uttered could topple the delicate interest she'd acquired, and she measured each carefully.

"You don't want to be a destroyer forever. You've already taken this gift—despite what you've done to get it—it's yours now, and there's nothing that can be done to return it. So take it, live a long life, and then, centuries from now, let your spirit return to the universe, the way Life has intended it always to be. For all of us."

Odalinde reveled in her eloquence, not out of pride, but because she recognized that her filibustering words and the truth of what she was saying were one and the same. Yes, if it was time to die, she was ready; she had never been as certain of anything in her long, damaged life. She would welcome it now, the moment she believed the children were safe, she wanted not another second in this world.

But she would never know if her words would have been enough to change the witch, or if another few minutes could have made any difference at all for the children. The scene was broken, interrupted, as the sound of popping gravel cascaded from beneath the truck of Georg Klahr.

CHAPTER TWENTY-SEVEN

Anika stood looking back at the cannery window and the fence over which she'd just vaulted; she had no clue if she'd cleared the deadly barbs by five feet or five inches. Before she jumped she told herself only to look forward, to the tree-tops in the distance, and to focus on landing as soundly as possible. And the strategy had paid off. The ground, soft from overgrowth, cushioned the soles of her feet—as well as her knees and shoulders on the subsequent roll—and she'd touched down on the other side uninjured. She was free once again, and the thirst to find her home was now primal.

She walked slowly across Rifle Field to the edge of the lake—the latest hurdle in Anika's seemingly endless maze of obstacles—took off her shoes and rolled her pants to her knees, and then waded to the middle of her shins, gauging the depth of the water and the amount of swimming that would be required. Once she left the grounds of Rifle Field and started up the lake, she knew there would be no bank on which to rest, not until she reached the Klahr orchard—or her own property on the opposite side. Was that a quarter mile? A half? Surely it wasn't a mile! Really she hadn't any idea. She could wade much of the way she supposed, and at no point would she be required to swim at breakneck speeds or fight currents; but once she was out there, beyond plod-ding distance, there was no going back.

And darkness had arrived.

The night was clear and the moon, not yet high, was a solid gibbous that in little over an hour she estimated, would offer a beacon to follow. It wasn't visibility that worried Anika, it was her stamina. Even the numerous nocturnal critters, some of which were potentially harmful, never even entered Anika's thoughts; had she found herself in this situation a year ago, having never endured the ordeal that would now shape her life forever, thoughts of snakes and eels would have paralyzed her. But she trusted herself now, trusted her instincts and decision-making. And there was little choice besides.

She stepped back to the shore and disrobed to her underwear, figuring the weight of her clothes would only add to her burden, and then waded back into the lake, this time pushing forward, feeling the cold murkiness of the lake seep over her crotch and hips before settling at her midriff. She looked back to the shore, briefly regarding her shoes and clothes, considering whether the smart move was to toss them into the water, erasing evidence that she'd been there at all. She quickly decided against it—if she were to drown, she figured, those may be the only clues to finding her body and eventually punishing the guilty. The System would certainly crack the case! she thought, smiling in spite of the dreadful truth of her cynicism.

Anika began sidestepping slowly down the bank toward her destination, careful to have one foot planted firmly before lifting the other, and thankful for every inch she made closer without being forced to swim. At the onset, the going was steady, and the ground at her feet was sturdy. Maybe she could walk most of the way, she thought. It wasn't likely, but not impossible. Perhaps the water levels affected the bed beneath and deposited dirt and gravel at the borders, making this trip achievable by foot alone! She was getting carried away, she knew, particularly since she knew as much about lakes and tides and submarine sediment as she did about the mating habits of the striped polecat. Nothing. But her mind was occupied, and though the waterline had risen since her departure—closing in on her breasts—the rise was gradual, and she was confident in her progress.

Her foot set down on something hard, Anika assumed a rock until it moved slowly away, and then she assumed a turtle. If the only thing she encountered in this lake tonight were turtles, she thought, she'd label herself happy. She'd been lucky to this point, not just in the lake but since she'd left the warehouse.

Since she'd killed her father. (This was not the time to explore that part, she thought. Later she'd be happy to run through the emotions associated with that act, but not now.)

Of all the scenarios, things had fallen into place for her. Finally. She'd escaped the warehouse before the officer returned, had found her escape route through the cannery window before nightfall, and, miraculously, found herself no more than a short boat ride from home, though this last part, she supposed, would have been luckier with the provision of an actual boat. But, all in all, things could have gone much worse.

And when the report of the shotgun exploded over the lake, she assumed they were about to.

***

Gretel screamed at the sound of the blast, turning sharply toward the window that looked out on the orchard and the lake beyond.

Reflexively, Petr draped his arm across Gretel's shoulders, pulling her close to him. She moved into his clutch, but her eyes were wide with shock and focused on Mrs. Klahr, whose look was akin to Gretel's.

The four of them—Gretel, Hansel, Petr, and Mrs. Klahr—stood frozen, breathless, waiting for the next shotgun blast to erupt. Did Gretel want a second shot or not? She couldn't decide. Did one shot mean Mr. Klahr had killed the witch? Or did it mean the witch had descended on Mr. Klahr, flown across the lot as she'd done to Odalinde, and the one blast was just an aimless discharge? She was suddenly praying for the second report, but it never came. Gretel's eyes darted crazily from the window to Mrs. Klahr to Hansel and back to the window again.

"It will be all right, Gretel," Mrs. Klahr stated flatly, without conviction.

Gretel pulled away from Petr and walked briskly over to Hansel. She kissed him gently on the forehead and then pulled him close. She held him that way for just a moment and then turned and walked to the door, opening it wide.

"Gretel, no!" It was Petr

"I have to go, Petr. I should have never left them." And then, "And he needs me."

"He tried to kill you, Gretel," Mrs. Klahr said sharply, without apology. "And may have helped murder your mother."

Gretel stood still, hesitating, her back to Mrs. Klahr and the others. "I love you, Mrs. Klahr. Until my last day on this earth, as long as my mind is sound and my body able, I will do anything for you. And when I said, "he needs me," I meant Mr. Klahr."

Gretel could hear the sounds of Mrs. Klahr crying as she walked down the steps of the porch toward the lake and the waiting canoe.

CHAPTER TWENTY-EIGHT

No! Odalinde thought, as she turned to see the headlights of the weathered pickup. It was Mr. Klahr, the man who had saved Gretel, the man who, along with his wife, had given the girl a job and a purpose, and thus a new hope about what her life could be. She was relieved at first, knowing that the children had obviously made it to the Klahrs and reported on the madness presently unfolding, but then panic set in. She'll kill him, of course, Odalinde knew, but worse, she'll torture him, use his pain as a path to the children.

"Go away!" Odalinde screamed the instant the truck door opened.

The man inside ignored the command, and instead stepped to the driveway, a twin-barreled shotgun steadied upon his shoulder before his second foot touched the ground.

"I'll go away when you're in the truck 'side me, ma'am," replied Georg Klahr, his voice slow and gentle. "Not before then, however. You there, locksy lady with the chompers, I'll need you to step away from the children's guardian. Now!" Mr. Klahr slid the fore-end of the shotgun back and then forward, stripping the shell from the magazine and loading the chamber.

The witch did nothing at first, standing completely motionless, and her pause seemed aggressive to Odalinde, calculating. And then, as if finally comfortable with the plan she'd formulated, the witch obeyed, and stepped away from

Odalinde, slightly forward, toward the threat before her, her eyes remaining fixed on the man.

"You know the children? Those two in her charge?" the witch asked. Her words sounded intrigued and pleased.

"Be quiet!" Odalinde shouted from behind the woman, "You don't know me, or anything about my children. You're just that old fool from across the lake! Get out of here! This is none of your concern!" Odalinde tried to sound demented and fierce; she'd never met the Klahrs, but from what Gretel had no doubt told them about her over the last several months, the man was likely to be convinced of her madness.

The witch moved quickly back toward Odalinde, like a large spider scurrying to a cricket, and, using a single hand, reached down and snatched Odalinde by the hair, standing her straight and positioning her to act as a shield.

The moment for Georg Klahr to shoot was then, Odalinde knew, there wouldn't be another opportunity. But the witch's movements were lightning fast, and with the natural stress of the situation, combined with the incredulousness of the overall scene—including the dead body of his neighbor Mr. Morgan, bloody and shredded on the driveway—it was no doubt Mr. Klahr couldn't squeeze the trigger. It was likely he would have missed, of course, or even shot the wrong target, Odalinde thought, but it was a chance, and though the woman was still at bay, in that few seconds the advantages had turned dramatically.

"What do you know of the children who were here?" the witch said calmly.

"I know I can see the older boy's father's cruiser parked there behind you," Mr. Klahr replied in a similarly calm tone.

"And I know if you make another move without being told, you'll wish you hadn't. Now tell me now about where I'd find that boy's father."

"Why, I'd be happy to do more than that! I'll take you right to him! I know just where he is!" The woman paused, and Odalinde could imagine the hate emitting from her eyes as she glared at Georg Klahr, a wide, mocking smile lifting her cheeks. "But I believe I asked you for some information first. You see, after I'm done slaughtering this one," the witch glanced at Odalinde, who was stagnant, doll-like in the grip of the woman, "I'll need to find those children. The siblings especially. I just have some questions, of course." The woman's voice then dropped an octave, becoming serious and threatening, as if she'd tired of the pretense. "And as she's just reminded you, this has nothing to do with you."

"Well seeing as the children you're so eager to talk with's father's corpse is growing cold behind you there, I'm thinking I won't tell you where they've gone. No, instead, I'm going to leave it up to you to decide whether to release your claws from that woman right now, and then rest quietly until The System gets here, or to have this conversation end with your face full of buckshot and your brains scattered about this property for the scavengers to feed on. I don't mean to rush you, ma'am, but I'll need a decision soon." Mr. Klahr's tone was steely and the squint of his eye through the sight steady and focused. The next time the witch moved any faster than a tree sloth, the trigger would feel the squeeze. Odalinde knew it, and no doubt the witch did too.

Odalinde could feel the woman's breath and heartbeat quicken, and the grip on Odalinde's neck tightened. The witch was ready to attack.

Almost before the thought had formed in her mind, Odalinde felt herself lifted from behind as if a large condor had swooped down and snatched her in its talons. "Shoot!" was all she could manage to scream—though she couldn't be sure it was audible—as she catapulted through the night, the woman attached to her from the back. They were barely two feet off the ground she guessed as they hurled directly toward Mr. Klahr. She could see the surprise in his stillness as they approached him, a frozen disbelief at what he was witnessing. Odalinde tried to scream again, but upon opening her mouth felt a pinch just above her collarbone. The last thing she heard before collapsing in the witch's grasp, unconscious, was the sound of the shotgun.

CHAPTER TWENTY-NINE

The narrow ledge that ran along the bank at the bottom of the lake had run out, and Anika was now forced to swim. She'd been fortunate to this point, and was now trying desperately to stay calm, positive, knowing her energy would deplete much more quickly if she let her thoughts descend into panic. But the gunshot had been close, and judging by the direction of the report, it had come from the other side of the lake. Anika didn't want to admit it to herself, but if she'd had to guess, it had come from her house.

The swimming had come naturally to this point and she'd felt remarkably capable in the water—she'd kept her strokes long and smooth, keeping her head above the surface and stopping every minute or so to tread water and rest. She'd make it, she now believed—based on her assessment of her strength and pace thus far, she'd make it. At least to the orchard. But once there—at the orchard—she'd have to stop and rest before heading home. Home—where a gun had been fired only minutes ago. Why was there a gunshot? Certainly no one was hunting in the dark, she could be sure of that, and knowing what she did now about her husband's role in all of this, Anika's mind invoked its most awful scenarios.

She tried desperately to banish the thoughts and focus on the progress she was making, watching the stripe of moonbeam on the lake approach. But thoughts of tragedy became pervasive and soon merged with a weariness Anika never thought possible. Anika was now crying and coughing in fear. She stopped again to rest, to rein in her hysteria, but she was struggling now just to remain afloat, her arms were weakened by fear and exhaustion and her breathing was spastic.

"Don't panic!" she scolded herself, aloud. "You've come too far to die here!"

She pushed off again, trying to breast-stroke her way forward, but was forced to stop almost immediately. Her energy was crippled now, and evidently Anika was much weaker than she'd believed herself to be. Adrenaline could fuel someone for only so long, she knew—at some point a person needed real strength and actual energy. And hers was spent.

She stretched one leg as far down toward the bottom of the lake as possible, reaching with her foot and toes, hoping to feel the cold slime of the mud floor, indicating she'd be reaching the bank soon. But she felt nothing, and though she wanted to stretch farther, dipping her head under until she felt exactly how deep the water was, she decided against it, fearing she might never resurface.

Anika's eyes filled with tears, not at her impending death, but at her failure to complete her journey to find her children. To save them. Were they dead already? Every cell in her body told her no. So why couldn't she summon the strength!

She was now paddling laboriously at the surface, and her feet beneath were kicking down frantically, running and stepping furiously just to keep her nose above the water line. She stared out at the ribbon of placid moonbeam, coughing out the lake water that was now lapping over her lips and into her mouth. A beautiful night, she thought absently, the water in the distance as still as pavement.

Anika's nostrils filled with water, forcing another reflexive, gasping effort from her to stay alive. She pushed herself back above the water line, squeezing her eyes shut and snorting the water from her nose. And as she opened her eyes, Anika saw the beam on the lake waver, rippling only slightly at first, and then a bit more. A gust of wind, Anika thought though she'd not felt it herself. And then she saw the real source of the disturbance. It wasn't a mirage—she wouldn't allow herself to consider that possibility—it was real. There was only the tip of the vessel at first, and then a silhouette of oars, slapping machine-like at the water, blended into view.

Anika filled her lungs with air in one last stab at survival, and then screamed, "Help me!" at the canoe cutting through the moonlight.

CHAPTER THIRTY

The old woman could feel the warmth of blood on her neck and face and instantly knew she was hurt—perhaps badly. It had been a dangerous strategy using the woman as a shield the way she had, but in truth, she hadn't thought about it at all; the strategy had chosen her more than she it. It was pure instinct.

But now, with the armed man in front of her preparing to reload his weapon, she needed to make a decision: attack again, unprotected and weakened—her new gliding ability was wonderful, but afterward left her temporarily exhausted—or retreat.

Without looking back, the witch rose to her feet, stumbling badly at first but somehow maintaining her balance and began running to the back of the house and down the slope toward the lake. She kept her body crouched all the while, like a soldier avoiding sniper fire, and her eyes focused on the porch steps which would provide some measure of cover.

The witch ran past the porch and grabbed one of the wooden steps, the momentum swinging her body left and underneath the open staircase. She paused for a moment, listening, and then continued down the gravel slope of the Morgan property toward the lake. If the man decided to pursue her, which she'd no doubt he would, she'd be trapped at the water's edge. She had no aversion to swimming (in fact, she imagined, it was likely she'd now be quite adept at the activity), but even if she were as quick as a porpoise she'd be an easy target for a shooter on the bank.

The woman stepped down onto the mud of the lake bank, noting the footprints of the children who had fled the property earlier—as well as the drag marks of the boat they'd set off in. In an attempt to limit visibility, she ducked low behind a clump of small trees that were skirted in a patch of ivy. And listened. But it wasn't steps she heard, it was the sound of an old truck engine starting and the dusty growl of spinning tires. He was leaving, and seconds later, he was gone. Out of fear for himself or to return to protect the children he'd spoken of, the witch didn't much care, she knew only that she was safe for the moment. And moments she could not waste.

Her first thought was of the Orphist, Odalinde. She assumed she was dead. That the shotgun blast had ripped her apart; after all, *she'd* been hit—and hurt—how was it possible her human shield survived? But there had been no time to check to make certain.

Reluctantly the woman raised her hand to her ear and neck, and, finding the source of her gruesome injury, winced with nausea. Her right ear was gone and her neck was missing a chunk, though apparently one not vital to her immediate survival since she wasn't feeling the encroaching blackness of death's approach that she'd felt in the past. She had the potion, of course, which would certainly heal her. The thought kept her calm for the moment, but she'd need to attend to her wounds soon.

But first the woman. It was time for the woman—Odalinde—to die.

The witch stepped from behind the tree cover and looked out across the lake at the orchard—the orchard owned by the man who had just attempted to murder her, she assumed—and mentally listed it as her next stop. It would be more difficult now—with the home fortified and the element of surprise now gone—but guns or not, she'd need to get to Gretel and Hansel. Perhaps there was a gun in the cruiser, she thought, certainly the officers kept weapons in the trunk. She wasn't so confident as to count on it, but she hadn't checked before, and securing her own arms was a possibility that was strong. If only she'd thought to take the officer's weapon before leaving her cabin! But she hadn't, and there was no point ruing the decision. And in her own defense, she'd never envisioned these difficulties. She had never counted on a struggle.

She turned back to the house and took two steps up the slope toward Odalinde when she heard the scream.

It was a scream she'd heard a dozen times before.

CHAPTER THIRTY-ONE

Gretel screamed in reply, reflexively, and slammed the oars to the water, adroitly rotating the canoe toward the sound. At first she didn't believe what she'd heard—the 'voice'— and decided it was nothing more than a combination of night sounds and her imagination.

"Help me!"

This time the voice was clear and belting, but also desperate, struggling. Drowning, Gretel thought.

"Wait...wait for me. I'm coming!"

Gretel dunked the oars and gave one long thrust. There was nothing but darkness in this direction, and she could easily row right over the floundering soul if she wasn't careful. But her stroke was perfect, and Gretel saw immediately the shape bobbing just above the surface.

"I'm here," Gretel said nervously. "Give me your hand."

Without looking up, the drowning woman lifted a feeble hand from the water. Gretel grabbed it with one hand and with the other reached down past the thin woman's elbow to her triceps, gripping it firmly. The woman reached up with her free hand and grabbed the side of the canoe, and with a manic tug from Gretel, pulled herself into the boat. She lifted her head and met the eyes of her savior, and there was nothing left in her to restrain her emotions.

"How did you get so strong?" The question blurted from Anika's mouth in a fit of laughter and crying. It was a benign question, an act of maternal instinct aimed at calming her daughter.

Gretel was hysterical in her joy, and couldn't lift her sobbing head off her mother's shoulder. Anika wasn't much better in her composure, but knew the proper reunion would have to wait.

"Where is your brother, Gretel?" Anika stroked the back of her daughter's head, coaxing her to lift it and speak to her.

Gretel had a look of bewilderment and terror on her face as she lifted her head. "I think Father's dead. I don't know for sure, but..." she kept herself stiff and upright, but unleashed another fit of tears at the sound of her own words.

Anika turned away and closed her eyes, squeezing them tightly in an effort to keep stable.

"But Hansel is fine," Gretel continued. "He's at the Klahr's. He's safe."

"Oh, thank God," Anika sighed and pulled Gretel close, relishing the warmth of her daughter's body.

Gretel sniffled like the child she was. "Where were you, Mother? How did you...? What happened...?"

"It's too much for now, Gretel," Anika said. "Far too much for now." Then she paused and looking in the direction of her home said, "What was that gun shot?"

Gretel's eyes flashed wide, suddenly reminded of why she was out on the lake to begin with.

"What is it, Gretel?"

"Mr. Klahr. And Odalinde."

"Who?"

"There's no time, Mother, we have to go!"

CHAPTER THIRTY-TWO

The old woman could hear the voices—female voices—on the lake, but the whispers were faint and she couldn't make out the words. But she'd heard those first two words that had snared her attention and recognized them instantly. Those familiar words contained in the scream. The first time she'd heard them was all those months ago, when she lay dying at the base of her porch, debilitated, anticipating the approaching clutch of death's grasp. And they had rung through the forest like the song of an angel, to save her—quite literally—and to draw to the surface a reserve of power she'd never dreamed existed inside her.

Help me!

The witch gave one last glance to the front of the Morgan house, mildly considering the option to continue up the path to the front of the house to ensure the children's guardian was indeed dead in the driveway. But this detail suddenly seemed far less important than pursuing the voices on the lake. The Orphist woman wasn't going anywhere, the witch decided, and she crept warily back toward the water line.

A mixture of laughter and crying was all she could interpret from the sounds, and the witch quickly deduced that the invisible scene adrift on the water was a reunion of mother and daughter.

She made it home.

The smile and twitch of pride in the witch came not from an admiration of her Source's individual effort, but from the blood that flowed in her veins, the blood that had fueled the remarkable accomplishment. Her own blood, the witch thought.

She waded slowly into the water until it reached her shins, careful to stay clear of the moon's glow. She now had another decision to make: should she swim to them? It seemed an absurd idea at first, considering all the advantages she now possessed—particularly that of knowing their current location, as well as where they lived—but time was against her. No doubt The System was en route already—the marksman neighbor having certainly made that call—and though the one officer, Officer Stenson, had been a puppet in Marcel's plan, as far as she knew, there was no influence on them otherwise.

The ability to swim the distance to the boat wouldn't pose the problem; it was the ability to do it quietly, she reckoned. The lake was deathly still, and even with the occasional jumping frog or fish periodically rippling the surface, she didn't see how she wouldn't be noticed before getting even halfway to them. The witch considered her choices again, and as she stood on the lake bank, she heard the voices become clearer. The tones were hushed and deep, but they were steadily approaching. She wouldn't need to swim to them, they were coming to her!

The witch ducked back in the thicket of trees where she had taken cover from the never-approaching neighbor. She narrowed her eyes and covered her head as far as possible with her cloak. Without a light source, she knew she was invisible from the bank.

The woman saw first the arrowhead shape of the canoe's bow, followed instantly by the silhouetted shapes of her prey. She held her breath, exhaling only slightly during the rattle of the boat as the two women parked it on the gravel shore. She extended her fingers, brushing the back of her saber-like nails against the trunk of one of the small trees in the clump. It was the preparatory move of an animal, instinctive and lethal. She stood slowly from her crouch and opened her mouth wide, touching the tip of her tongue to one of her incisors, relishing the bite of the blade-like point.

The two Morgan women—mother and daughter—started up the slope to the house, apprehensive and focused in their movements. The witch stayed still as stone as they passed her, no small restraint given she could have touched Gretel—killed her, easily—without even having to extend her arm fully. But that wasn't the perfect moment. She couldn't risk letting the older one get away. Not again.

The witch ducked a branch and stepped out from the thicket, assassin-like, placing her first foot firmly on the path before bringing the second foot out beside it. She stood pleased for just a moment, smiling at the seemingly endless talents the potion now endowed her with, watching the women obliviously make their way up the path. They never sensed her as she appeared behind them, closing in with claws extended.

She'd made the decision to kill the older one—Anika—and to keep the girl for further blending. She was strong now, but there was simply too much to risk trying to capture and hold two prisoners, particularly since she didn't yet know where she'd be living past today. So, yes, she'd kill the mother, and once she'd found a new location—a new lair—and had blended the new potion, she'd come back for the boy. She couldn't let that much power go free.

Her clarity about the future was suddenly staggering, with thoughts and strategies now flooding her mind, giving her confidence and energy. Her mind felt *organized*, without disease or ambiguity.

The witch drew her arm back as if to throw a punch, but instead of forming her hand into a fist, she kept it open with her palm down and fingers stretched, the tips of her nails pointed directly at the base of Anika's skull. The women had walked about ten yards from the witch when she began her advancement. She took two long strides at first and then skipped into some form of a human gallop.

Five yards away. Two. Her grin was wide with teeth shining.

And then the madness in her face changed at the sound of screams.

They had come from the women—both of them—and their shrieks had been bloodcurdling, as if the witch had suddenly materialized in front of them. But she hadn't, and they hadn't turned to see her; they had, in fact, made no sudden turns or suspicious pauses at all. Why the sudden terror?

And then she saw it—the figure—emerging from between the two Morgan women, crashing toward her like a giant warped arrow. Stunned, the witch opened her mouth to scream but the figure slammed into the bottom of her chin before a sound could escape. There was a sickening sound of cracking bone from the back of the witch's jaw, and the bottom row of her teeth exploded in every direction, including down her throat.

The Orphist!

CHAPTER THIRTY-THREE

"Gretel go!"

In the moonlight, Gretel could see Odalinde at the edge of the lake, her face coated in what appeared to be a mixture of blood and mud. Her eyes were open, but they were weary and fading.

"Odalinde? Odalinde! What's happening?"

"Go!" Odalinde repeated, this time with a wet cough culminating the statement.

"Let's go, Gretel," Anika said, beckoning her daughter up the hill.

"No!" Odalinde shouted, pulling herself to her knees. "Not that way. You'll be trapped." She caught her breath. "The canoe. Take it and go back to the Klahrs. Your father's dead."

"What about Mr. Klahr?" Gretel asked.

"He's gone."

"What?" Gretel cried.

"No, I mean...I mean he left. He's okay. There's no time Gretel. Go back!"

Gretel and her mother stood paralyzed, not sure whether to disobey the woman's instructions—who, after all, may have just sustained a violent head injury—or to trust her and go.

"She's still here, Gretel. She'll have you trapped up there. Go back. You have to get back to the Klahrs!" Odalinde looked to the ground, composing herself, and then continued in an even tone. "Go back, call The System, and get ready with every gun the Klahrs have."

Gretel suddenly considered the witch—whom she'd forgotten temporarily—scanning the area immediately in front of her and down by the lake. But darkness blanketed most of the area and she saw no one.

And then it came to her: the witch had been behind them. Hunting them. Ready to kill them both. And Odalinde had saved them.

Gretel grabbed her mother's hand and they descended the path together, back toward the lake from where they'd just come, to the spot where Odalinde lay.

"Fine," Anika said, kneeling beside Odalinde, "but you're coming with us.

"I can't," Odalinde said.

Her exhaustion was palpable, and Gretel could see by the wounds on the side of her head that she was badly injured.

"You can and you will," Anika replied, "My daughter came back for you, risked her life for you, so you're coming."

"Anika," Odalinde whispered, the faint trace of a smile forming on her face.

Anika grabbed the woman under her armpit and lifted. "It's nice to meet you. It looks like you've been through a lot. But still, I think you'll find my story trumps yours. And I'll never live with myself if I don't discover whether or not you agree."

Gretel had always marveled at this ability of her mother's. She'd seen her do this trick with her father a thousand times, expressing things in such a way as to create the impression that any option other than the one she proposed was nothing short of absurd.

Odalinde was wobbly as she stood, and her eyes looked like they were fading into unconsciousness; but somehow she made it to her feet, and Anika held her steady as they shuffled toward the canoe where Gretel waited alertly, oar in hand and ready to push off.

"She's coming," Odalinde whispered, her words coming out dreamy and delirious.

"It's okay," Anika replied, "It's going to be..."

But Anika Morgan never had the chance to finish her underscore of assurance. Before her muscles could react, before she could offer any semblance of protection, the witch had ripped Odalinde from her, yanking her by the hair. She held her still for just a beat, elevated, resting against her torso, before inserting her top row of fangs into the side of Odalinde's neck. The image was nauseating, something from a nightmare, and made all the more grotesque by the witch's twisted jaw and missing row of bottom teeth.

The witch tossed Odalinde's corpse to the ground and stood glaring at Anika and Gretel, who were now screaming in horror by the canoe. There was no hesitation from the witch this time, and she lurched furiously toward Anika, focused only on the final slaughter of her once-captive Source.

The opportunity flashed in a blink, but Gretel saw it, clearly, and speared it like a fish. The witch's single-mindedness toward her mother had given Gretel a moment of advantage, and, almost automatic in her motion, she swung the oar forward, rotating her hips and torso, creating drag with the weapon, and clipped the hag's head just above the temple. Two inches lower and the witch would have been dead, Gretel lamented, but she'd stunned her badly, and the witch collapsed to the ground like a satchel of wet clay.

Wasting not another second, Gretel pounced into the canoe and anchored the oars in place. "Mother, let's go!" she shouted, and before her mother's second foot was off the muddy bank, Gretel was launched and rowing.

Positioned facing the bank as the canoe pulled away, Gretel stared in disbelief at the wreckage in front of her, assessing the danger which—unbelievably—was already recovering from the blow. Gretel's breathing had been heavy and rasping from exhaustion and trauma, but was now escalating to panic at what she was witnessing. The witch was on her feet—already!—standing tall over Odalinde's body with her arms high above her head. She was pulling and struggling, reaching for the sky, and Gretel quickly calculated the woman was disrobing, a suspicion that was confirmed when the witch's ample cloak fluttered through the moonbeam into the clump of trees. But she didn't appear to be stopping with the cloak, and continued to strip down to her underclothing, and possibly beyond. She was coming after them.

Gretel had launched the canoe in the direction of the Klahrs and had no plans to deviate from the course, frantic now to get across to the orchard and up to the house where she could warn the others and help fortify the grounds.

"She's coming, Gretel. She's coming after us." Her mother had been watching the scene on the bank as well, and now turned her head back toward the front of the boat and Gretel, aware of the direction they were headed. "We can't lead her to the Klahrs, Gret. Not to Hansel. Not to those people."

"What?" Gretel continued in her current direction, not properly inferring her mother's words.

"Rifle Field, Gretel, head down the lake to Rifle Field." Anika's words were restrained but tense, carefully intoned to elicit obedience. "She'll follow us, Gretel, away from your brother. I need you to do this."

"But Rifle Field! We'll be trapped!"

"It's the only place close enough. And if you can get us there—get us there fast—I have a plan."

Gretel recognized the insistence in her mother's voice, and, with a grunt of reluctance, deftly turned the canoe south toward Rifle Field and began carving the oars into the water with the possessed repetition of a galley slave, guiding them and turning them over as hard and fast as she'd ever done before. The canoe glided easily, rapidly, as though it were motor-powered or thrust by a blast of wind. Her mother was right—she was strong. And she was going to get them to their new destination.

Her mother had again turned away, looking to the bank where the witch had been standing only seconds before. "I can't see her anymore, Gretel. I think she's in."

Gretel thought so too. In the dark, however, the bank had drifted too far away to see much, so she couldn't be sure the witch had taken to the water. But Gretel, and apparently her mother, had sensed it. Surely they couldn't be caught with the boat travelling at this speed, though, Gretel thought—particularly by a woman who was severely wounded. But...the woman had flown. Flown!

Gretel could see the first signs of the clearing to Rifle Field, and effortlessly decelerated the canoe and steered it toward the bank, guiding it slowly toward shore.

"I can't believe I'm back here again," Anika said flatly as she hopped from the stern seat into the shallow water at the shoreline, rushing to where she'd left her clothes.

"I never stopped believing you'd be back," Gretel replied. She was winded, and the words came out rushed and emotionless, but as she looked over to see her mother dressing, she realized what she meant. "Wait. You mean here? At Rifle Field? You were here? Why?"

"Let's go, Gretel, I promise you'll know everything later. Right now, we have to dig."

CHAPTER THIRTY-FOUR

Anika threaded her arms through the sleeves of her shirt and pushed her head through the neck hole; how thankful she was now that she had left her clothes and shoes behind, dry on the bank. She looked over at her daughter, who seemed to have already created a gap beneath the fence large enough for both of them to squeeze through and was continuing to dig with abandon.

Anika would never be able to explain what had inspired her to toss the shovel from the cannery window, only that it seemed the prudent thing to do at the time. Perhaps it had to do with the instincts that apparently ran in her family, a result of her mother's unique gift—a gift that had been revealed to Anika only hours ago—that had been genetically passed on to Anika, ever-ready to manifest itself in certain life-threatening situations to pull her to safety. She suspected this was the reason for her decision, but couldn't honestly commit to it. Maybe her instincts had just sharpened over the last several months and were much more dependable now. Or maybe she was just lucky. Sometimes your decisions were spot on, she thought, and other times (trudging through the woods after a car accident, for example) they weren't.

"Are we good, Gret?" Anika asked.

"I think so," Gretel replied. "I know *I* can fit."

Anika gave her daughter a cold stare. "Well, thanks a lot for that!"

Gretel let out a quiet burst of laughter. "I hardly mean it like that," she said. And then, "Do you think she's still coming?"

"I don't know, honey, but let's leave the canoe on the bank. I want her to know we're here."

Gretel walked back to her mother at the shoreline and, as the two women stepped toward the boat, they were halted by the twisted face of the tortuous witch rising from the lake.

Her face was gruesome, bloodied from head to chin, her mouth deformed and vacant, with a demented grinning overbite. In the dark of night, with her hair and body dripping with water, she looked like a corpse that had crawled from a tomb buried long ago at the bottom of the lake.

Anika stood palsied by the emerging face, stunned at the transformation it had undergone. Everything back on the bank had happened so quickly—the attack and Gretel's heroics—that nothing had registered in Anika's mind. But it was obvious now what was happening—even with all that destruction to the woman's face—Anika understood clearly what she was seeing. The torture. The blood. All of the extractions and the rank pies, all of the forced, unnatural rest and nursing, it had all been for this. This metamorphosis. This conversion of the hideous beast from the woods of the Northlands into a younger, more maniacal version of itself. A stronger version of itself.

"Now Gretel! Follow me now!"

Anika broke from her paralysis and sprinted to the fence and the awaiting burrow beneath it, with Gretel following obediently, barely a step back from her heels. She ushered her daughter through first, and Gretel slithered under the fence as nimbly as a human could. Anika was on the ground following before her daughter's feet had cleared the hole, sneaking peeks behind her, expecting the monster to grab her at any moment.

But the woman didn't pursue them, and Anika and Gretel made it through, quickly heading to the front side of the cannery. Anika opened the door and shuffled Gretel through, narrowly squeezing in herself before slamming the door behind them. Anika briefly considered that perhaps the warehouse would have been the better option, but the hill leading up to it was steep, and she didn't trust her legs at this point. And there were tools in the cannery. Weapons.

When Anika had been inside the cannery earlier—escaping the very grounds on which she now sought sanctuary—there had still been a hint of daylight by which to navigate. But it was nearly pitch black inside the building now, with only the radiance of the moon through the second-level window to see by.

Ideally, Anika would have blocked the door with a table or piece of large machinery, but she recalled the emptiness of the cannery floor and decided there was nothing accessible to serve that purpose, and there was no time to explore. Besides, Anika thought, the door swung out—not in—and any blockade would be easily conquered.

Anika grabbed her daughter's hand and, extending her other arm, felt the space immediately in front of her for any looming obstacles. The path to the stairs had been clear previously, she was relatively confident on that count, but she could little afford to be hobbled by a stray iron post or corroded hole in the floor. She and Gretel had to get to the second level.

"Where is she? Why isn't she following us?" Gretel asked, her tone hopeful, suggesting that perhaps the woman hadn't seen the hole they'd created, or perhaps hadn't been able to fit.

Or maybe she decided the effort was too taxing after all. Or, with God's Grace, had finally succumbed to her injuries. That was the one they needed. But Anika knew better; she'd seen the glee and determination on the woman's face. She was wounded, but she'd never stop chasing them. Any of them.

"She is, Gretel. But maybe she suspects a trap."

Anika stepped forward and felt the toe of her shoe against the side of the bottom step. "We're going upstairs, Gretel. There's no railing, so be careful."

With the moonlight shining through to the landing at the top of the stairs, the ascent got progressively easier as they reached the top, and Anika quickly looked around for the hammer she'd used earlier to clear out the window.

"Is there one?" Gretel asked.

"One what?" Anika replied, focusing on the floor, squinting her eyes in adjustment to the shadows on the floor.

"A trap? You said, 'Maybe she suspects a trap.' Is there a trap?"

"No. Not really. Not one that I've planned anyway. But if she suspects one, that's good. It will give us time to think of one." Anika realized this logic was somewhat specious, but the alternative—having the witch bounding up the stairs to maul them—was certainly worse.

Anika was on her knees now, feeling the dusty wood of the floor in search of the hammer. It had been here! She'd dropped it right here!

"Gretel," she whispered, "there's a hammer up here. On the floor somewhere. It should be here by the window. Help me find it."

A crackling sound on the ground below froze Anika, and she could hear Gretel's breathing stop midway through her exhalation. It could have been just an animal—a raccoon likely—Anika thought, and on any other night it would have been. She considered for a moment that maybe Gretel had been right: maybe the blow from the oar had been more severe than realized, and it was only the witch's adrenaline that had seen her through the lake. Maybe she'd staggered out of the water toward them in a last desperate attempt at murder until her body simply refused to go any further.

Maybe, Anika thought, but she was alive. And as long as she was alive, she'd be coming.

Every atom in Anika's body wanted to crawl to the window and peek out, just to get a glimpse of the ground below, to see if the woman was there, waiting for them, starving them out perhaps. But she knew if the witch was there—recovered and virile—that to give away their position at this point was suicidal; the witch knew they were inside the cannery, but not where inside. Anika and Gretel had to hold that advantage, no matter how slight.

"She's down there, Mother," Anika said, her voice so tempered that 'mother' came out as "other."

"I know."

"What are we going to do?"

"We'll hide here for now." Anika hadn't prepared for this recess. She'd figured that after they ran for the cannery the witch would have been a step behind them and that all of it—one way or the other—would be over by now. But that hadn't happened, and now she needed a real plan. "We'll move away from the window for now, out of the light, against the wall."

"And then what?" Gretel asked.

"I don't know, Gretel!" Anika immediately regretted her whispered bark, but let the effect of it stand. "Just move to the wall."

Anika scooted to the side wall of the cannery and frowned at Gretel, who had decided to move away from her to the opposite wall. Not really a good time for brooding, Anika thought, but she's just a child. And God only knew what she'd been through. A tear formed in Anika's eyes and her mind raced to red over the struggle that wouldn't be rewarded. The reward she deserved! Her life! Her children!

Anika quickly erased the tear, flicking it away in a redirection of anger. No. No. No. She wouldn't let her mind straggle off in a countenance of the inequities of life. Not now, and not ever again. There was simply no gain in it. There were gains from love—and sometimes from fight—but never from blame. Never from self-pity. Those were the things that bred regret. Those were the things that dissolved power.

"Mother." It was Gretel from the opposite wall, whispering only as loud as necessary to be heard.

"I love you, Gretel," Anika replied.

"I love you too, Mother. I can't wait until Hansel sees you."

This time Anika let the tear fall, and she wanted to run to Gretel, to spend her last seconds on earth—if that what was meant to be—in the arms of her daughter.

"And Mother," Gretel continued.

"Yes, angel?"

"I found the hammer."

CHAPTER THIRTY-FIVE

The witch staggered to the dry ground of the clearing and collapsed, gasping for air. She was thankful the women had run off—had they stood and fought, she may not have had the strength to defeat them both. She was desperately tired, and her injuries were not insignificant.

But this challenge was a mere formality, a honing of her abilities, a further test of her dedication to Life. Rest was all she needed to continue. Rest and more potion.

The old woman lay flat on her back now, breathing heavily through her damaged jaws. She could feel the effects of the magic broth trying to restore her once again, as it had earlier in the cabin after she'd been brutally attacked and left to die. But already she sensed the potency diminishing. In her bones and muscles she still felt young and strong, but she wasn't healing the same.

She needed more. She needed everything blended properly this time. And her earlier plans to kill the older one, her original Source, had to be recalibrated. She would need all of them. All of the Aulwurms. The girl and the woman she would get now, and later, when she'd regained control of the situation, the boy.

She watched her prey squeeze beneath the wire barrier, scattering like so many vermin she'd hunted in her day. Her rest would be short-lived it seemed, and the witch felt a pang of panic as she watched the women disappear into the darkness on the opposite side of the fence. She was confident she could scale the fence, or even fit beneath it, but such efforts would take their toll, and leave her vulnerable in whatever conflict eventually awaited her.

Still, she had to move.

She climbed back to her feet and stepped slowly to the fence, peering through into the blackness. She took a step back and scanned the metal barrier top to bottom, calculating what efforts would be needed to lift herself over the barbed wire. Certainly burrowing under would be far easier, but there would be several seconds of defenselessness, and it wasn't impossible that the women were waiting with a raised axe just on the other side.

But the witch was anemic, and even the idea of taking flight exhausted her. She couldn't wait to recover, and she couldn't risk a failed attempt that would leave her caught in the barbs. The hole at the bottom of the fence seemed like the only decision.

She kneeled back to the soft ground, preparing to follow the path the women had taken only minutes before, and froze at soft muffled sounds coming from the huge rusted building in front of her. There was silence for a few beats, and then the sounds again, coming from within. At first the woman assumed it was rats or bats, but then, magically, the faint hiss of whispers drifted down from the window above. The witch's smile grew wide with joy, and she had to cover her half-mouth like a schoolgirl to keep from chuckling.

She lay back down, this time at the foot of the fence just in front of the tunnel, and closed her eyes, listening to the sweet sounds above her, waiting for her power to return.

CHAPTER THIRTY-SIX

"How long are we going to stay here?" Gretel asked.

It was the first words either woman had spoken in at least ten minutes, both Gretel and Anika seeming to understand that silence was safer. But Gretel was growing restless, and with every minute that passed, more wary of the situation. This plan of her mother's to hide and fortify seemed as good as any before, but now it felt wrong, like it was working against them. Like they were trapped.

"It hasn't been that long, Gretel. It just feels that way," Anika replied.

Gretel could hear the doubt in her mother's voice and capitalized on it.

"We can't just sit here, Mother. Maybe she's gone by now. She doesn't know we came in here, right? How could she? Maybe she went off into the woods somewhere looking for us, and now's the time we should be leaving."

This didn't feel right to Gretel either—she suspected the witch was still near—but she wanted to move, be proactive. Sitting and waiting, as a rule, always seemed to Gretel like the wrong course of action.

"And if she's down there, waiting for us, what then?"

Gretel paused a moment and said, "Then we'll fight her...and kill her."

Gretel's words lingered for several beats, and then she saw the figure of her mother creep into view and head toward the window. She had her head bowed well below the height of the sill, like a bank robber dodging pistol fire with the local sheriff in some old movie.

"I'm going to take a look," Anika whispered, "but just understand, if she sees me, you'll get your wish. There will be a fight. So keep the hammer ready."

Gretel held the hammer up, and then, not sure whether she or the hammer was visible to her mother from where she sat, replied, "I've got it."

Gretel watched the back of her mother's head rise slowly up to the opening of the window, turning first in the direction of Rifle Field, and then rotating back in the direction of their property down the lake. She then stood up further to get a view of the ground directly below, and instantly collapsed back to the floor and turned toward Gretel, wide-eyed and stunned.

Assuming her mother had seen the witch walking below, Gretel stayed quiet, and simply turned her palms up and matched her mother's expression.

"She's down there. Outside the fence near the hole." Anika was barely auditory, doing little more than mouthing the words. "I think she might be dead."

Gretel looked toward the window. "Let me see."

Anika nodded, indicating she wanted Gretel's assessment about whether she also believed the witch dead.

Gretel walked on her knees over to the window and looked out, scanning the ground below, waiting for her eyes to adjust to the dark. The night was still clear and the moon offered plenty of light past the fence. But Gretel didn't see anyone. She scanned the grounds for a few seconds more and then turned back to her mother. "I don't see her. You said by the fence, right?"

"Yes, right next to the hole. Let me see."

Gretel backed off and allowed her mother to move in again.

Anika peered once again out the window. "I don't understand. She was..."

A hoarse, high-pitched cry shattered the quiet of the night and rang through the cannery like the bellow of a bull elephant. Anika, screaming in disbelief, lurched in terror away from the window—so far, in fact, that had she backed up even another foot, Gretel could see she would have gone tumbling down the open stairway.

A dark, amorphous blotch now filled the space of the window, blocking the full light of the moon, allowing only small strands of silver rays around its perimeter. It was the witch, and she was perched like a giant spider in the window, gripping the top corners of the frame with her long fingers. Her feet were wedged in the bottom corners. Gretel thought she looked like an enormous, disfigured bat.

"That's impossible!" Anika screamed. "How?"

"You, my sweet Source," the witch replied, "You are 'How.'" Her words were breathy and, with her mouth and neck mangled, nearly unintelligible.

Gretel watched the woman in the window silently, unable to look away from her destroyed face.

The witch stepped down from the sill and stood tall, dropping the hood of her cloak, never taking her eyes off Anika. Gretel noticed instantly the woman had not even glanced in her direction, and had instead stayed locked on her mother during the entire exchange. As Gretel had suspected earlier with her mother, it was possible the witch couldn't see her in the shadows.

"You've given me so much trouble, Anika Morgan, more trouble than I ever would have believed you capable of. But you've also given me so much life. And you will continue giving. You and your family." Blood and mucous dropped from the woman's lips, occasionally bringing with it a stray tooth or shards of bone.

Gretel's hatred was searing as she knelt, frozen in self-preservation, listening to the mutilated woman threaten her mother. This horrible, deranged creature—miscreation—who'd fragmented her life, first by stealing her mother, and then by killing her father. And Odalinde, whom Gretel had hated for so long, yet in less than a day had grown to care deeply for. Perhaps one day she'd understand Odalinde's tough love approach—and in some ways she supposed she did already—but there was no doubt now in Gretel's mind that she was there to protect them. To save them.

And now here this freak of life was again, threatening more torture and destruction, wielding the genius of Gretel's own descendants, shamelessly, to destroy everyone she loved, as if everyone's life belonged to the old witch and was lived for her pleasure alone. Gretel's own life. And Hansel's. And what of the Klahrs? And Petr? Certainly she wouldn't stop until they were dead too.

"I'll kill myself first," Anika shot back, "or, even better, I'll kill you."

The witch chuckled. "That opportunity has passed young pigeon, and it shall not come again." The witch took a step forward. "And though it is often thought so, killing one's self is not as easy as one might think. Besides, I know of your will, and the love you hold for your progeny. You, I know, would use any breath of hope—however vaingloriously—to keep me from them.'

Gretel placed her fingertips on the floor and began to gently push herself up to a standing position. She held her breath as she rose, thankful for the silence in her young bones and muscles. But the floorboards of the cannery were not so young, and as Gretel stood, the old wood detonated in a barrage of creaks and pops. The witch pivoted in the direction of the sound, but as she stopped to stare, her gaze was askew, off to the right slightly, in the direction of the window, hoping perhaps the light would drift over the source of the noise. Gretel knew, with certainty now, she was all but invisible.

"Ah, there you are. Gretel, yes? The very special Gretel. Your grandfather—and your father more recently—have told me of your talents, talents which they tell me you have not even begun to explore yourself. You are young now, with no one to show you. But I will. I will show you. I will bring these talents from within you. Why don't you come where I can see you better."

"I'll go with you," Anika blurted. "I'll go with you now." She hurried to her feet, nearly tripping over them and down the stairwell, and then lingered at the top of the opening, as if ready to follow the witch to whatever fate she had in store. "If you leave her alone, I'll go with you. I'll go with you and you can do what you will to me."

The witch looked over her shoulder at Anika and chuckled again, this time with more confidence. "You *will* go with me," she said, and spun her head back in the direction of Gretel, this time lining her gaze up almost correctly, but not quite. "And so will she." The words were bitter and hostile this time, her patience with coaxing and civility clearly at an end. "And once you're both secure—confined—I'll be back for the boy. Hansel, yes? I believe your brother's name is Hansel."

Hearing the monster speak her brother's name—threatening him—was the last evil Gretel could endure, and before she could consider the consequences of failure—consequences not only for herself, but for everyone still alive that she loved—she gripped the hammer, claw-end forward, and erupted from the shadows on the second floor of the cannery.

The sound of fear in the witch's scream, and the look of surprise and defeat in her eyes, fueled Gretel to the point of possession, and were the final sparks of power Gretel needed to bring the wide metal spikes of the hammer down and into the middle of the witch's forehead.

"No...no!" the witch begged uselessly, the words sounding gurgled and infantile, her hands flailing in the direction of the hammer, grasping at the iron lodged above her eyebrow but not quite able to touch it.

Gretel held the handle of the hammer tightly and pulled the woman close to her, staring at her coldly as she extracted the claw from the woman's head, causing a bloodfall across the witch's eyes and cheeks. And then, with more leverage and fury than before, Gretel brought the hammer down once again, this time to the top of the old woman's head.

The witch's eyes and mouth grew grotesquely wide, mummified in a silent scream, the blood and damage to her face now leaving her all but unrecognizable as human. Her body was still for a beat, and then began to convulse, wobbling ninety degrees at a time until the dying woman was facing forward and staggering drunkenly toward the stairs, the hammer jutting from her head like a deformed horn.

Anika took one step to the side as the old woman stumbled past her. The witch paused a moment, looking blankly at the women, and then, involuntarily, her foot drifted to the empty space of the stairwell. She collapsed like a stone to the ground floor of the cannery, hitting only the bottom step as she fell, her body ending face down in a crumpled mass, the hammer still jutting from her scalp.

Anika would later recall that the sound of the woman hitting the floor reminded her of a pie hitting a concrete wall.

CHAPTER THIRTY-SEVEN

Petr and Gretel descended the porch steps jointly carrying the last piece of major luggage: a large, antique trunk—the piratey kind, enveloped by bulleted leather banding and secured with brass lockplates. Gretel always imagined her mother had seen it fall from an old circus train one day and had decided to keep it for herself, perhaps to use one day when she, herself, ran off to join the circus. It was one of the first items Gretel had looked for the day after her mother went missing and was disappointed to find it.

The teenagers heaved the trunk onto the tailgate of the truck and pushed it cozy with the rest of the things. Anika stood in the bed of the pickup, arranging space for the small items that still remained.

"Is there anything else, Mrs. Morgan?" Petr asked. His voice was timid and whispery.

"No Petr," Anika replied without looking up, her tone with the boy curt and dry. "Perhaps Gretel has something."

Gretel had witnessed—without interfering—similar interactions between her mother and Petr over the last three weeks, and felt sympathy for both of them. But mostly she felt for Petr, who craved her mother's acceptance and seemed to be adjusting pretty well to his new life with the Klahrs.

He was certainly adjusting better to his new life than her mother was to her old one.

With Hansel, her mother had recalibrated fine, and had returned to being as sweet as she ever was to the boy. Perhaps she crossed the threshold into overbearing on occasion, but Gretel assumed such behavior was perfectly normal. With Gretel, she was also still loving, except that Gretel now detected more of a demureness from her mother, a newfound reverence toward her daughter that contained a dusting of dread. Awe was the word, Gretel guessed. Her mother was in awe of her.

But with everybody else her mother had been cold. Even to the Klahrs, whom she'd lathered with thanks and blessings for days afterward, there was an uncomfortable distance—a mistrust that only the saintly Klahrs could and did understand. And with Petr the feelings seemed to be especially true, though for Gretel the reasons why were no great mystery. So, as difficult as it was to witness, Gretel didn't intervene during these implied slights or moments of aloofness, and instead allowed her mother the room to recover. There was trauma to be worked through, and who could blame her for not being chipper and friendly after only a few weeks?

Petr lingered by the truck looking down at his shoes, which surprised Gretel since normally he took any opportunity her mother gave him to scurry out of the kill zone of awkwardness. But today he stood pat.

"I'm sorry," Petr said, his voice solid, though tears had begun to plop down to the gravel below. "I know you're angry at me. For what my father did to you. I never knew anything." He paused, "And that's not who I am."

The sentences came out quickly and evenly, as if he'd rehearsed them a hundred times; but there was emotion in every word, and on the last sentence Petr's voice cracked, and he turned from the truck and broke into a trot toward the house.

"Petr!"

Anika's voice stunned the boy, who was nearly past the porch and on the path down to the lake. He stopped immediately and stood tall, though he didn't turn to look at her.

Gretel moved aside as her mother stepped over the trunk to the tailgate and down to the driveway before running to where Petr stood, turning him toward her and pulling him in close.

The boy collapsed in Anika's arms, sobbing like an infant. And for the first time in Gretel's life, she heard her mother cry.

An hour later the truck was loaded with everything that would be travelling with the Morgan family—whatever remained now would simply remain. Gretel's mother mildly alluded to 'coming for it another day,' but Gretel doubted that day would ever arrive.

Gretel said her goodbyes to Petr—whom she imagined would live in her story as her first love, though love wasn't quite what it was. But it was something. Something to grow and learn from. And she would see him again. About that she was as certain as the sunset.

"We have to stop at the Klahrs, Mother," Gretel reminded, "don't forget."

"I want you to give them this." Gretel's mother handed her daughter a note. "It has all the information about where we're going. Once they have it, Gretel, they'll be the only ones—other than the three of us—who know where we are. I want you to tell them that."

"Where *are* we going?" Hansel asked, a pitch of pleasure and adventure in his voice. If his mother had said to the other side of the moon, Gretel knew Hansel would have been okay with that answer. She was home. They were together. That's all he cared about. He had it right.

"Pretty far, sweetheart," his mother replied, "pretty far."

Gretel had asked the question the night before and, essentially, had gotten the same answer, with the additional provocation of 'We're going to get some answers.'

But Gretel had already begun getting answers.

She opened Odalinde's copy of *Orphism* at the bookmarked page and began reading. Not much had made sense when she started a few days ago, even with the translation, and she had gotten only ten or twelve pages in.

But it was beginning to come together.

Dear Reader,

Thank you for reading GRETEL. I hope you enjoyed it.

The story continues with Marlene's Revenge, which has a jaw-dropping, chilling twist that will leave you wanting more.

In Marlene's Revenge, the witch has returned and no one is safe.

Almost a year has passed since Anika and Gretel's horrifying night in an abandoned cannery in the Back Country, and the subsequent beginning of their quest to the Old Country for answers to the mysteries of Orphism. But rumors are reaching the far shore that the evil Witch of the North, presumed dead since that night of terror, is alive and strong. And hunting again. But this time no one is safe. Everyone Gretel loves is in danger, and she must summon a new level of power and conviction to end her family's nightmare forever.

Order your copy of Marlene's Revenge today.

And please leave a review for Gretel. It doesn't have to be long. A simple, "I liked it!" is enough. That is, if you enjoyed Gretel, which I hope you did!

OTHER BOOKS BY CHRISTOPHER COLEMAN
THE GRETEL SERIES
Marlene's Revenge (Gretel Book Two)
Hansel (Gretel Book Three)
Anika Rising (Gretel Book Four)
The Crippling (Gretel Book Five)

THE THEY CAME WITH THE SNOW SERIES
They Came with the Snow (They Came with the Snow
Book One)
The Melting (They Came with the Snow Book Two)

THE SIGHTING SERIES
The Sighting (The Sighting Book One)
The Origin (The Sighting Book Two)

CHRISTOPHERCOLEMANAUTHOR.COM